Forever
Safe

Books by Jody Hedlund

Beacons of Hope ⬱ Book Four

Forever
Safe

JODY HEDLUND

 NORTHERN LIGHTS PRESS

Forever Safe
Northern Lights Press
© 2016 Copyright Jody Hedlund
Print Edition

www.jodyhedlund.com

ISBN: 978-0-692-69115-1
Library of Congress Control Number: 2016906755

Scripture quotations are taken from the King James Version of the Bible.

This is a work of historical reconstruction; the appearances of certain historical figures are accordingly inevitable. All other characters are products of the author's imagination. Any resemblance to actual events or locales or persons, living or dead, is entirely coincidental.

Cover Design by Lynnette Bonner of Indie Cover Design
www.indiecoverdesign.com

To all of the friends who were involved
in the creation of this book in one form or another

Your help was invaluable and your friendship is precious.
My deepest thanks for both.

Chapter 1

MAY, 1876
NEW YORK CITY

"*I* still can't believe that in less than six weeks I'll become Mrs. Nathaniel Winthrop III." Victoria Cole exhaled a blissful sigh and lifted her face to the glorious spring sunshine as she rounded a bend on the park pathway. The bright rays warmed the cherry blossoms overhead so that the sweet scent mingled with that of the tulips and forsythia to create a fragrant potpourri.

"You'll finally be in Mrs. Astor's elite circle," Theresa said with a tad of jealousy shading her voice.

With arms looped together, they'd already strolled most of the paths within Gramercy Park. Now their steps slowed and Victoria patted her friend's arm in sympathy. She and Theresa had been dreaming for years about making Mrs. Astor's official list. Victoria's own father had come close. At last, Victoria's marriage to Nathaniel Winthrop would secure her a place in the coveted upper echelons of New York society.

"I daresay, you'll join me very soon," Victoria said, smiling at her friend. "Especially since Philip Smith has asked to call on you."

"He has such a plain last name."

"Theresa Smith." Victoria tried the combination. "It isn't as fancy as Theresa Fontaine, but you can't keep your maiden name forever."

Theresa pursed her lips into an exaggerated pout. "If only he didn't look like a shaggy sheepdog."

Victoria bit back a laugh. "That's unkind to say."

"It's true and you know it."

"Perhaps you can suggest that he shave his eyebrows." Victoria earned a tiny smile from her friend. "At the very least, you won't have to worry about maintaining eye contact since he won't be able to see you from underneath the bushy mounds."

Theresa nudged Victoria with her shoulder. "Fiddlesticks. You're much too silly."

"That's why you love me." Victoria nudged her friend back, grateful for Theresa's undying friendship. Though they shared many of the same friends, aspirations, and tastes, Theresa was about as different in personality and appearance from Victoria as any one person could be. Unlike Victoria, who had fair hair and light brown eyes, Theresa had raven black hair and eyes as dark and bold as coffee. While Victoria considered herself an easy-going, positive person, Theresa was decidedly more pragmatic and realistic.

For a moment, they walked in silence. Victoria relished the vibrant green leaves of the artfully shaped trees and shrubs. Gramercy Park was always such a peaceful and pretty place in the spring. Besides the twittering of a family of birds somewhere in the meticulously groomed garden, their footsteps along with her bodyguard's were the only other sounds. Thankfully today, in the safe confines of the park, Arch was giving her some leeway. The giant of a man followed a discreet distance behind them.

The private Manhattan park was completely fenced in and closed to the public. In fact, only the residents who lived in the buildings surrounding the sprawling stretch of greenery had keys to the gate that led inside the wrought iron. Even so, Arch always insisted on accompanying her.

"Come on." She tugged Theresa toward the entrance. "I know you're anxious to see the new corsets I bought yesterday, the ones decorated with orange blossoms."

"Yes, I'm just dying to see them," Theresa said in her usual flat, sarcastic voice.

"You'll love them."

"Probably not as much as Nathaniel will."

"Theresa!" Victoria nearly tripped at her friend's bold insinuation. The corsets were for her trousseau, which was steadily growing with each passing day of shopping and fittings for the wedding and honeymoon.

Her saucy friend lifted her gloved hand to her mouth and pretended remorse. But her eyes were mirthless. "Oh, that's right. We mustn't speak of what happens after the wedding. It's supposed to be a big secret for all of us debutantes."

Victoria glanced over her shoulder toward Arch and prayed he hadn't heard a word Theresa had spoken. Even though her loyal bodyguard was bald beneath his hat and old enough to be her father, he had excellent hearing. Rarely did anything escape his attention. He was tall and burly and wore an attitude that said, "If you bother me, I'll crush you like a bug."

Her father had hired Arch after a frightening incident four years ago when she'd returned home from a trip to Michigan. An erstwhile enemy of her father's, Big Al, had gone to jail many years previously for attempting to have her father murdered. Once he was released from prison, he'd sought revenge against her father. As part of his scheming, Big Al had decided to target Victoria, kidnap her, and demand a ransom. Fortunately, he'd been captured while stalking their home and had been locked back in prison.

During the past four years that Arch had been her bodyguard, there had been several threatening letters and an incident at the opera when an employee from one of her father's competitors had grabbed her as she'd been exiting her carriage. But overall Victoria felt silly for having a bodyguard.

She knew her father had just been worried that even though Big Al was in prison, he might try to have some of his men strike again. And she knew that because her father was one of the wealthiest men in New York City, there were plenty who would stop at nothing to see him come to ruin. Even so, Victoria had long since concluded she didn't need Arch.

As much as she would miss her dear bodyguard, she had decided that once she was married, she'd convince Nathaniel to free her from the overprotective watchfulness. After all, he was amenable to whatever she wanted. He made it his number one occupation to give her everything her heart desired. That was only one of numerous reasons she loved him.

"Let's go." Victoria smiled again and counted her blessings, of which she had many, particularly a mother and father who adored her, a fiancé who loved her beyond reason, and faithful friends, like Theresa, who endured all her whims. "I'm sure Mother will have tea waiting for us."

Theresa picked up her pace. "And hopefully those

delectable lemon tarts she had last time."

They came to the gate, stood back, and waited as Arch inserted the family park key and unlocked it. He swung open the gate and glanced both ways down the street before waving them through.

Theresa started forward but stopped abruptly. "Oh dear." She held out her hands. "I've lost one of my gloves."

Sure enough, only one of Theresa's hands was covered in a lacy white glove that rose to the sleeve ruffles of her peach-colored polonaise of silk taffeta. The matching skirt was trimmed with layers of bustles in the back, much the same way Victoria's was. However, Victoria's gowns were all designed in Paris, a fact Theresa never failed to lament when reflecting on her imitation creations.

"I'll walk back and retrieve it," Theresa said, giving Victoria a push through the gate. "You go ahead." Without waiting for Victoria's acquiescence, Theresa bustled away.

"Are you sure you don't want help looking for it?"

"No. I remember exactly where I took off my gloves." Theresa's skirt swished in her haste. "I insist you go on without me."

"Very well. I'll wait for you outside."

Theresa lifted her hand in a half-wave to acknowledge Victoria's comment but didn't slow her pace. Victoria ambled out of the park past the tall black fence with posts that were spiked on the top like spears to keep out intruders. Her stately home stood directly across the street. The five stories of brownstone ended in a fashionable black slate mansard roof with ornate iron cresting.

She flounced her full skirt of sapphire faille and twisted to shake out the pleated train that lay on the ground like organ pipes. All of a sudden, Arch yelled and shoved her so hard that she would have fallen, except that the narrow fence bars caught her.

The metal was bruising, even through the layers of her garments. Her Belgian straw bonnet trimmed with ivory ribbons and sapphire feathers tipped over her eyes. For a moment all she could hear was scuffling and shouts behind her.

Then Arch grabbed her arm and dragged her forward without giving her the chance to right her hat. She blew at the feathers hanging in front of her face and attempted to keep up with him even though he was half-carrying her like a parcel under his arm.

"What's happening, Arch?" she asked.

But the burly man couldn't hear her over the instructions he was roaring at the footman of their Irving place mansion across the street. "Send for the police!" He sounded strangely winded and weak. "The attacker's getting away!"

"Attacker?" Victoria strained to see behind her, but once again the feathers and ribbons on her hat blocked her view. "Who was it?"

Arch stumbled across the street to the short flight of scrubbed stone steps at the front of the Cole home, with her in tow. Victoria was surprised when Arch's grip around her slackened and he deposited her none-too-gently on the landing in front of the footman. Her bodyguard was usually so much more careful with her.

"Take her in!" Arch bellowed breathlessly. "Now!"

The footman and several other servants who'd appeared in the doorway scrambled to obey the giant bodyguard. Within moments, Victoria found herself inside the front hallway. Her father was in the process of descending the curving marble staircase, and he, too, was calling out orders.

Servants rushed around her in chaos. When the sea of bodies separated, she caught a glimpse of Arch still on the front stoop. He'd fallen to his knees and was staring blankly ahead.

"Arch?" She elbowed her way toward him. But before she could reach him, he fell face down and hit the floor with a painful-sounding thwack. With his body sprawled across the threshold, several servants dropped to their knees next to him. Deep crimson began to form a puddle on the floor underneath him.

"Send someone for the doctor!" the footman yelled. "He's been stabbed."

"Stabbed?" Victoria dropped to her knees next to her bodyguard. Her pulse raced erratically as she took in his silent, unmoving frame. "Will he be all right?"

The footman and another manservant gently rolled Arch to his back, exposing the wide circle of blood near his waist. The blood had turned the wool of his dark blue coat almost black.

The footman lifted Arch's coat and then rapidly lowered it while sucking in a hissing breath. "The wound is deep."

"And he's already lost a lot of blood," said the other servant, with a glance outside.

Only then did Victoria see the blood on the front steps, trailing across the road from where Theresa stood, a lone figure in the open gate of the park.

Victoria stared at the blood and tried to make sense of what had happened. Arch had been stabbed and bleeding. Had he carried her to safety anyway?

She pressed a hand against his cheek expecting warmth but was met cold pallor instead. "He isn't—" she started in a shaking voice. "He isn't dead, is he?"

The footman turned and shouted at another servant in the

hallway. "Hurry!"

Victoria sat back on her heels, suddenly dizzy.

"Someone take Victoria away," her father said, kneeling on the other side of Arch. "This is too much for her."

Gentle hands were upon her instantly, helping her to her feet and guiding her toward the stairway. She couldn't find her voice or the strength to protest.

All she could think about was the fact that Arch was dying. And she was to blame.

Chapter 2

Tom Cushman eyed the glass doors that led to the second story balcony of the Cole mansion. The elaborate iron railing surrounding the spacious outside sitting area provided at least a dozen holds for a grappling hook. An easy climb for an intruder. Only one lock on the double doors. A simple latch-style lock that even an idiot could pick.

The balcony and doors were safety hazards. If he took the job, they would have to go.

A servant's heels clicked against the wooden floor in the hallway, nearing the sitting area where he'd been ushered exactly six minutes ago. Lighter footsteps than before. A different servant this time. A female. One hundred twenty pounds. A bunion causing her to favor one side, which meant she was probably middle-aged.

He rose as the servant entered the room. Sure enough, she was a petite woman with her hair pulled back into a tight bun revealing wings of gray at her temples. She wore a long black dress with a starched white apron over the top. From the pristine condition, he guessed she was probably the house-keeper in charge of all the other maidservants.

"Mr. Cushman?" she asked. The hint of chamomile sur-rounding her and the grains of sugar on her fingertips told him she'd just poured tea for someone. "Mr. Cole is ready to see you."

Tom jerked on the wide lapels of his suit coat to straighten them and nodded at the woman. He followed her down the hallway decorated on either side with enormous paintings from a variety of famous European artists, Gainsborough and Blake among them. Open doorways on either side revealed a music room, a library, and another sitting room. They were all as elaborately furnished as any of the royal households he'd worked in during the past five years. The palatial size of the New York home, the classical columns and cornices, the lush carpets, the brightly papered walls, the ornamentally carved furniture. None of it made him even blink.

But with each step he took through the house, he spotted safety hazards—a loose window latch, a broken fireplace grate, a door without a lock, and many other small issues that could mean the difference between life and death.

When the housekeeper reached a carved walnut door and knocked, Tom quickly reviewed all he'd researched already about Henry Cole and Cole Enterprises. The multi-millionaire had inherited a fortune from his father. However, in recent years, not only had he improved upon his father's lumber and mining holdings in the Midwest, but after the War Between the States, he'd invested in the booming steel and railroad industries, along with silver mines in the West. He was making more money than he could possibly use in one lifetime.

Henry Cole owned the Gramercy mansion in New York City, a newly built estate on Prairie Avenue in Chicago, a summer home in Newport, and a recently purchased villa in Italy. He had several yachts, dozens of racehorses, and two private country farms. Each home was staffed with enough servants that the man could form a small army with all his employees.

The family wasn't of old money like the Astors, Forbes, or Winthrops. But Henry Cole's wealth had pushed him high on the list of most prominent men in the United States. He had a reputation for being innovative, aggressive, and intelligent. Tom had heard nothing but praise for Mr. Cole.

The housekeeper swung open the door to reveal a dark-paneled room with a large mahogany desk, floor to ceiling bookshelves, built-in wall cabinets, and an elegant sideboard. A man Tom guessed to be approximately forty-five years of age sat in one of the leather wing-backed chairs in front of an expansive picture window that overlooked Gramercy Park. He replaced a china cup onto a saucer on the low table in front of him and rose.

He was slim but solid. His light brown hair was smoothed back and his chiseled face clean shaven. He wore a fine suit that included a dark brown worsted coat with a fine braid binding the edges, a collarless waistcoat of fancy white quilting, and light brown striped trousers, all of which were perfectly tailored. Apparently Mr. Cole had just looked at his watch because the flap on his waistcoat pocket was half-tucked in and half-out, with the triple-strand gold fob stuffed too far inside.

"Sir," the housekeeper said, "Mr. Cushman is here to see you."

"Thank you, Mrs. Hatfield." Mr. Cole nodded at the petite woman as she took her leave, closing the door behind her. "Come in, Mr. Cushman and have a seat." He waved at the leather side chair next to his, all the while studying Tom, from his dark short-cropped hair down to his shiny black shoes.

With his usual long stride, Tom crossed the room and extended a hand. "Pleased to meet you, Mr. Cole."

"You're earlier than I expected." Mr. Cole gripped his hand in return. A firm handshake that spoke of confidence and authority. But there was also a softness to it that indicated the gentler side of the man that Arch had vouched for.

"I always say better early than late."

"I like that policy." Mr. Cole released his hand and lowered himself back into his chair. As he reached for his tea cup, Tom glimpsed the ink on the man's right thumb and the indentation on his middle finger where'd he recently held a pen. The man had evidently been writing a telegram, hence the sight of the telegram delivery boy that had been leaving the house when he'd arrived.

Tom sat on the edge of his chair, and immediately his mind went to work plotting escape routes from the room. Although he had no need for a backup plan, no charges under his protection at the moment, the habit was hard to break even when he was off duty.

Mr. Cole took a sip of tea and continued to study Tom over the cup's golden rim. His eyes reflected both frustration and fear. And Tom could guess why. The man desperately wanted to keep his family safe, but without a bodyguard, he felt vulnerable and afraid. Tom could respect him for his concern. He'd seen too many wealthy men who didn't care. Who weren't faithful. Who treated their mistresses better than their wives.

From his research, Tom had learned that Henry Cole was extremely devoted to his wife, Isabelle. But sadly, she was blind. She'd inherited a disease that had caused her to lose her sight when she was a young woman. Not only did she need constant assistance, but she also apparently needed protection. A man of Mr. Cole's high profile and exorbitant wealth had made plenty of enemies over the years.

Mr. Cole had a daughter too. As Tom had scoured the old newspaper articles and gossip columns about her, he'd only shaken his head at the girl's frivolities. A column from a month ago had indicated that Victoria Cole was planning a late June wedding in Newport to the oldest Winthrop son. The wedding was expected to be one of the most lavish parties of the summer season. If she made it to the altar. Which Tom doubted she would, if her past antics were any indication.

"I have to be honest, Mr. Cushman," Mr. Cole said. "I wasn't expecting someone as young and handsome as you."

"Is that a problem?"

"It could be." Mr. Cole's expression was troubled. "Arch's description of you led me to believe you were older and scarred."

Tom had thirty wounds and scars of various shapes and sizes from his days as a Jessie Scout during the war. But he couldn't think why that would matter.

"You're clearly fit but much too good-looking for the job." Mr. Cole sat back as though baffled by the problem—a problem Tom didn't understand. As an unmarried man he'd made it his policy only to guard older women who were already married or widowed. Of course that didn't necessarily stop complications. But if Mr. Cole thought his wife might be attracted to him, then he was forgetting one critically important point. His wife was blind. She wouldn't see him. Ever.

Even so, if Mr. Cole didn't approve, it was no loss to him. After all, he'd only agreed to the interview with Mr. Cole because of Arch. His friend and fellow scout had sent him a telegram after his attack and begged him to apply for the temporary position. Since Tom was between jobs, he'd already considered returning to America because it had been so long since he'd seen his family. When he'd discovered that Arch was in the hospital, he'd left Europe immediately.

The first place he'd gone after docking in New York City was to visit Arch. His friend had lain on his bed at Presbyterian Hospital, pale, limp, and weak. When he'd pleaded again with Tom to take his place as a bodyguard for the "lady of the house," as he'd lovingly referred to Mrs. Cole, Tom hadn't been able to say no. Arch had been like a father to him during the war, had taken him under his wing, and had saved his life more than once during their dangerous scouting missions. He owed it to his friend to take the job. It was the least he could do.

Even though Tom had planned to spend a little time with his family out at Race Point Lighthouse on Cape Cod, he'd wanted to do Arch this favor. Wanted to keep the Coles from giving Arch's job to someone else so Arch could come back after he recovered from his wound.

"Arch had nothing but positive things to say about you," Mr. Cole continued. "Truth be told, after the way he went on about your bravery and experience, I half expected a demi-god to come walking through the door."

"Arch is a good friend. No doubt he exaggerated my skills."

"I thought so too. But I received a telegram from Arch-duchess Gisela. And she confirmed everything Arch said and more."

Tom nodded. So that's what Mr. Cole had been doing. Checking up on him with his previous employer. Likely after getting the notice from the Archduchess, Mr. Cole had written a thank you in reply and sent it with the telegram boy.

"It would appear that you're the best of the best," Mr. Cole said.

"I may not *be* the best. But I certainly *do* my best."

"Your list of past work references is quite impressive. Not only Archduchess Gisela, but also Princess Anna of Budapest and the Dowager Countess Elise. Why would you settle for a position with my family when you could have your pick of European royalty?"

"Arch asked me to do it." Plain and simple. Tom didn't like being in the States. There were too many ghosts that haunted him here. He was better off staying away and keeping busy in places where he didn't have to think about all that had happened. Already only three days after docking, he was ready to go back.

Mr. Cole studied Tom again through narrowed eyes.

"It doesn't look like I'm the kind of man you're looking for." Tom started to rise. "I'm sorry for wasting your time, Mr. Cole."

"You're not wasting my time, son." Mr. Cole motioned for him to sit back down.

Tom hesitated.

"I trust Arch more than anyone else, except my wife of course. If Arch recommended you in spite of knowing my concerns about having young bodyguards, then I suspect he had a very good reason."

"I understand the delicate nature of such a position." Tom sat back down in the leather chair. Guarding a woman meant he'd be in close proximity to her most of the time. He'd also be alone with her frequently. It was unavoidable, since he would be her constant shadow. But that was the point. He was a shadow, in the background, and hardly noticed. "I do my best to be unobtrusive while maintaining safety."

"I'm sure you can understand my concerns," Mr. Cole replied. "By hiring a bodyguard, I don't want to substitute one dangerous situation for another."

"I understand completely, sir." Even though Tom had a personal policy not to fraternize with the people he worked for, that didn't mean the women around him hadn't wanted more from him. He'd had to spurn advances on occasion. In fact, he'd had liaisons handed to him on a silver platter. Not from any of the women he'd guarded, but from their friends or younger relatives. He could have had his pick of sweethearts wherever he'd served. But he'd never given in to the temptation. And he didn't plan to start now. "I guarantee the utmost professionalism at all times."

Light footsteps in the room above alerted him to the presence of at least two females. The direction of their steps told him the ladies were moving across the room, exiting, and now walking down the hallway toward the stairs. Likely Victoria and one of her friends. The footsteps were spry—almost playful.

Mr. Cole pursed his lips and stared at Tom for an endless moment. Tom looked right back. Unflinching. He had nothing to hide. He was as good as his word. Mr. Cole didn't have to worry about him.

"I'm willing to try the arrangement for a month," Mr. Cole finally said. "Hopefully by that point, Arch will be fully recovered and ready to return."

"He's tough. I'm sure he will be." At least that's what Tom was counting on.

"Very well, Mr. Cushman." Mr. Cole stood and held out his hand. "You're hired. And rest assured, I'll pay you a fair wage."

Tom rose and shook Mr. Cole's hand. Even though a

month seemed too long, he'd do anything for Arch. "Thank you, sir. When would you like me to start?"

"Is today too soon?" Mr. Cole asked. "With the upcoming wedding, she has so many appointments, things to do, and places to go. And quite frankly, with the perpetrator still on the loose, I'm petrified to let her out of the house."

The two pairs of footsteps coming down the hallway were identical to those Tom had heard overhead moments ago. Victoria and her friend were approaching the office. He suspected she was coming to ask her father for money and the use of the carriage.

A soft knock was followed by the door opening a crack. "Father?" came the voice of a young woman.

Through the two-inch space, Tom noted a pretty face with high cheekbones, an elegant nose, pert lips, and luminous honey-colored eyes. He'd assumed she'd captured the attention of her various suitors because she was the heiress of a massive fortune. But she had more going for her than just her wealth. Maybe she was the "darling catch" of society that the newspapers had claimed she was. The only trouble was, she seemed to have trouble staying *caught*.

Her gaze snagged on him and her eyes widened. "I'm sorry, Father. I didn't know you were with someone. I'll come back."

"No, Victoria," Mr. Cole said quickly. "As a matter of fact, I was just going to ring a servant to retrieve you."

The door opened further, revealing that Victoria was attired in the latest fashion, a striped purple, form-fitting dress that showcased the figure so many women aspired to. Her tiny waist was likely enhanced by a tight-fitting corset as was true of most wealthy women he'd known. But it was also clear she didn't need the enhancement. She was naturally curved and slender in all the right places.

Her blonde hair was piled stylishly on her crown, but long ringlets hung down the back of her head. From the silk gloves in one hand and elaborately decorated bonnet in the other, he knew he'd called the situation right. She wanted to go out.

"Come in, Victoria," Mr. Cole said, his features softening as he gazed at his daughter.

She returned her father's smile, which only made her face all the more beautiful and vibrant. As she stepped into the room, Tom took in the young woman behind her, plainer and dour-faced but pretty nonetheless.

With the upcoming nuptials, he suspected that Victoria Cole and her friend were busy young ladies. He was surprised Mr. Cole would hire a bodyguard for his wife and not his daughter.

"Theresa and I were hoping to look at the samples of Brussels lace that I might use for my wedding veil. I'd really like to make the selection myself this time."

Tom inwardly smiled at his correct assessment of her desire to go out and spend her father's money. He was still as sharp as always.

Mr. Cole took his daughter's hand in his, which gave Tom a glimpse of Victoria's engagement ring—an enormous sapphire set into a circle of diamonds. Mr. Cole kissed Victoria's hand gently. "Of course you may go."

Her lips stalled around her next plea. She was clearly unprepared for her father's easy acquiescence.

"First, I want to introduce you to Mr. Cushman." Mr. Cole said.

Tom stepped forward. "Pleased to meet you, Miss Cole."

Her attention shifted to him, and she assessed him without any real interest but nodded politely.

"Mr. Cushman has agreed to work for us."

"Please. Call me Tom."

Mr. Cole nodded. "*Tom* is a personal friend of Archibald's and will be taking his place until he's recovered."

Victoria's attention flew back to him, and this time she assessed him much more carefully, so carefully, in fact, that Tom held himself rigid in his effort to keep from squirming.

After several long moments, she met his gaze directly, unabashedly. With the flecks of gold and brown, her eyes were striking. And suddenly Tom's instincts kicked into action. Something wasn't right.

"Promise me that you'll cooperate with Tom at all times." Mr. Cole squeezed Victoria's hand, which he'd yet to relinquish.

Alarm bells went off in Tom's head and clanged a deafening warning. He'd made a mistake. A rare mistake, but one nevertheless. Somehow he'd misinterpreted all the signals and information regarding the job. Because he knew with certainty now that Mr. Cole hadn't hired him to be the bodyguard for his blind wife. No. He'd hired him to play nursemaid to his social darling daughter.

Tom almost released a groan but he held it in. Only moments ago, he'd been smugly congratulating himself on his mental prowess. When in reality he was an idiot for not having put all the clues together sooner.

He had the overwhelming urge to bolt from the room and run. Run down the steps and out of the Cole mansion as fast as his feet could carry him. At the very least, he should explain to Mr. Cole that he couldn't take the job after all. He would simply explain his policy of guarding only older women and blame the misunderstanding on Arch...

His mental tirade came to an abrupt halt. Arch had

purposefully misled him. There was no other explanation for the mix-up. Arch knew his objection to taking on children and young unmarried women. Not only were there too many needless entanglements, but he didn't want to be a babysitter, especially to a spoiled rich girl.

Victoria hadn't taken her eyes from his. The amusement dancing in hers said she sensed his inner struggle, recognized her influence over him, and enjoyed her effect on men.

"Don't worry, Father," Victoria said with a growing smile. "I promise I'll *cooperate* with my new bodyguard."

Her emphasis on the word *cooperate* baited Tom. It was a challenge if he'd ever heard one. Victoria Cole was daring him to try to keep her out of trouble. She didn't think he was old enough or experienced enough to handle it.

Little did she know him. He'd show her exactly what he was made of and why he was in such demand. Even if the assignment was nothing more than a glorified nursemaid job, he'd prove to her that he was one of the best bodyguards out there. If she thought to use her charm to get him to do whatever she wanted, she was in for a big surprise. She'd learn soon enough that her pretty face wouldn't affect him. Not in the least.

Chapter 3

The landau pulled to a stop in front of Goodson's Bakery. Victoria reached for the door handle, but a strong arm shot out and blocked her.

She gave an exasperated sigh. "Must we go through this again?"

"Yes. Every stop." Her new bodyguard's voice was as steely as his muscles, which she couldn't help noticing were incredibly thick beneath his suit coat. He wasn't big boned like Arch, who certainly had been strong. Instead Mr. Cushman had a different kind of strength and sharpness that was nearly overpowering at times. Like now.

To say that he was handsome was an understatement. Theresa had summed it up well earlier when she'd mumbled under her breath, "He's gorgeous." His dark clipped hair, deep murky blue eyes, and chiseled features would have been enough. But there was something about the slant of his eyebrows that gave him a sad, wounded appeal and beckoned a woman to wipe her fingers across his forehead to soothe away his aches.

Except that now, Victoria had no notion to soothe him. Instead she wanted to box his ears. He hadn't allowed her to get out at Theresa's house when they'd driven her home. Theresa's father, Mr. Fontaine, was the only frightening one in the family, with his volatile temper and cold silences. But Victoria had learned to ignore him over the years. Certainly she had nothing to worry about while visiting with the Fontaines.

Victoria sat back against the plush black velvet seat while Mr. Cushman surveyed the street up and down several times through the cloudy coach window. Then he opened the door and scanned the surrounding area.

"Don't be a goose. It's perfectly safe," she said. "I've come here every day this week and nothing has happened."

"Then after today, you won't be coming back."

"Of course I will. This is my favorite bakery."

"Send one of your servants in your stead."

She crossed her arms with a huff and scowled at his broad back. Not only was he quite possibly the most handsome man she'd met, but he was also the most arrogant. "You're my bodyguard. Not my father or my jailor."

Without responding, he stepped outside and tugged on the lapels of his coat while he straightened to his full height. He scanned the bakery and the nearby storefronts, their awnings, the windows on the upper levels of each tall building, even the flat roofs.

She moved to the edge of the seat, anxious to be out of the carriage and draw in a fresh breath.

As though he had eyes on the back of his head, he stuck a hand toward her to prevent her descent.

"Mr. Cushman," she said in her iciest tone, "I really must

insist—"

"If someone is stalking you, he'll make it his business to know all the places you frequent."

Mr. Cushman's logic made such perfect sense that for a moment she was speechless. He was absolutely correct. The man who'd tried to attack her last week could possibly be among the people milling about the street. Maybe he was even now waiting to spring out at her as she made her way from the carriage to the front door of the bakery.

Mr. Cushman glanced at her over his shoulder. His eyes were somber and his square jaw set with determination. "I'm sending the coachman inside for you."

She managed a nod despite the vision that filled her mind of Arch lying in the doorway in a puddle of blood. Without the quick arrival of the doctor, Arch would have died.

"What do you need?" Mr. Cushman asked.

"The baker will have my order ready."

He nodded curtly before closing the door. She heard him issue brief instructions to the coachman and felt the rocking of the landau as Davis descended.

Although she'd complained about Mr. Cushman's insistence on dropping Theresa off at her home early, she could see the wisdom in it now. She was putting her friend in danger every time they were together. The next time someone attacked her, what if they got Theresa instead? Or her mother? Or her father? The thought made her shudder. She didn't want to be the cause of anyone else getting hurt. Arch was already one person too many.

All week she'd tried to make sense of what had happened. Her father and Arch were convinced that someone had purposefully attacked Arch in order to kidnap her. But if that was true, then why now? Was Big Al attempting to garner revenge upon her father again?

By the time the coachman returned and Mr. Cushman opened the door, her thoughts had tangled into an anxious knot. The coachman's arms were laden with several bundles wrapped in brown paper, which he proceeded to dump on the seat opposite her, giving Mr. Cushman little choice but to sit beside her.

As he lowered himself, Victoria scooted over as much as possible, but still the weight of his presence was even more overwhelming with him next to her.

"Three dozen sweet rolls?" he asked once the landau began rolling forward.

"No. They're raisin muffins. And I ordered two dozen."

"That's what the coachmen said too. But you're both wrong."

There he went again with his arrogance. "I think I know what I've ordered. Especially since I've asked for the same thing each day."

Before she could blink, Mr. Cushman was holding a knife and slitting the twine that tied the bundle together. He peeled back the brown paper to reveal creamy white rolls coated with cinnamon and sugar.

"Sweet rolls," she said, not sure whether to be more astonished by the change in her order or Mr. Cushman's accuracy in knowing what was beneath the paper.

"Three dozen," he said with confidence.

This time she hesitated in contradicting him. Instead she studied each of the packages more carefully.

"Actually, to be exact," he said, "there are thirty-seven sweet rolls."

The smooth wrap hid most of the contours of the contents. "How do you know?"

"The packages are identical except the one on the left. It has seven instead of six."

"Open it and let's see if you're right."

He slit the string and the paper, and she quickly counted them. There *were* seven.

She smiled in fascination. "How did you know they were sweet rolls instead of muffins?"

"The smell of cinnamon."

She shifted to study him. He wasn't smiling, but his features had softened a little. "Muffins have cinnamon in them too."

"It's not as strong. Besides, the rolls also have the scent of yeast."

She breathed in the aroma and tried to separate the ingredients the way he had, but they were so faint she couldn't distinguish any difference. She could only stare at him, her curiosity growing with each passing moment. Who was this man? What was his story? Why was he a bodyguard?

Before she could formulate a question, he spoke. "You're not going into the hospital."

She had to fight to keep her mouth from falling open. "How do you know that was my next stop? In addition to your skills at sorting out aromas and counting, can you read minds?"

"I heard you tell your friend earlier."

She faltered, her next witty response dying before she could formulate it. Yes, now that she thought about it, she had mentioned to Theresa that she was planning to stop by the hospital to visit Arch.

"You can't go in," Mr. Cushman said again, peering out the window at the tall brick buildings they were passing.

From the familiar landmarks, they were getting close to their destination. "I deserve to have my way this time, since

I've obeyed every one of your orders so far this afternoon."

"Every?"

"Well maybe not every. But almost all—"

"It doesn't matter. This is a very public place. You're not going in. Besides, unmarried females aren't allowed on the men's wing."

She wanted to respect his efforts to keep her and those around her safe, but he was much too bossy. "Mr. Cushman, I'd like you to know that I'm walking into the hospital, whether you like it or not. No one made a fuss about me visiting with Arch any other day, and I doubt they will start now." Especially because her father had donated large sums of money to help in the construction of the newest wing of the hospital.

"The coachman can deliver the sweet rolls to all the men on Arch's floor."

Her response sputtered out. How had he known that she'd been bringing baked goods to everyone and not just to Arch? She supposed he was taking a wild guess since she had so many rolls. Even so…

"I know you'll miss seeing Arch." His brows angled down into that sad slant, and his eyes took on a puppy-dog look. "But he'll understand. He'd want you safe."

For a moment, his gaze was irresistible. Gone was the tough dictator and cocky boss. Instead, a handsome man with devastating eyes was staring at her. The urge to please him rose strong and swift, along with the desire to do what she could to bring a smile to his face.

The landau came to a gradual stop in the carriage-port in front of the main doors of the hospital. Ahead a tall spire with a cross on the top towered above the chapel, which formed part of the front of the complex.

She wouldn't suffer if she took a break from visiting Arch today, would she? After all, even though Arch had been glad to see her, he'd warned against coming too often.

She bit her bottom lip. "You may be right…"

He turned to the door, but not before she caught sight of his lips quirked in the beginning of a self-satisfied smile.

Ah, so he was playing with her emotions to get his way.

She sat back against the cushioned seat with new admiration for his skill level. When she'd first met him in her father's office, she'd thought she'd be able to easily sway him. She'd suspected that he'd be attracted to her to some degree and have a hard time telling her no. After all, she rarely had trouble getting men to do whatever she wanted. They were usually eager to please.

But Mr. Cushman had proven much harder to influence than she'd anticipated. The fact that she was both pretty and rich didn't seem to matter to him in the least. He hadn't been awed, tongue-tied, or seeking her approval. Instead, he'd been distant, brusque, and all business-like. Until now…

Apparently, if his forceful tactics didn't work to persuade her to heed his commands, then he had a backup plan that involved using his charm—if it could even be labeled as such. What he didn't realize was that she was equally skilled in the art of manipulation when she wanted to get her way.

As he began to open the door, she quickly laid a hand on his arm. At her touch, he froze.

"I'm sure I'll have nothing to worry about," she said in a low voice, "since I'll have someone as big and strong as you right there to keep me safe."

His attention shifted to her hand.

"Unless of course, you don't think you're up for the task."

His gaze lifted to meet hers again. She was ready with her

trademark heart-melting smile and finished off the effect by batting her long eyelashes. She waited for him to blush, go wide-eyed, or even fumble to respond. But he wrapped his other hand over hers and extricated her fingers one at a time. He lifted her hand and gently replaced it in her lap. He patted it as though she were a little child and then opened the door.

She didn't give herself the chance to be frustrated over her inability to allure him. Instead, she brushed past him confident-ly and forcefully. Without waiting for the coachman's assistance, she descended from the carriage. Unfortunately, her legs tangled in her skirt, and she would have fallen, except that somehow Mr. Cushman was already by her side taking her arm and steadying her.

"You can't stop me from seeing Arch." She yanked free and started toward the door. She expected him to grab her arm, spin her around, and force her back inside the landau.

Instead he fell into step next to her. "You're forgetting something."

"No, I'm not."

"If you say so." He swung wide the hospital door and waved her through with a flourish. An antiseptic scent mixed with the sourness of vinegar greeted them. "I'm sure you'll find someone else to eat the sweet rolls."

She stopped and silently berated herself for her slow wit-tedness. She was certainly not making a good impression on her new bodyguard—not that she was trying. But she hadn't planned on making an utter fool of herself.

With an air of what she hoped was casualness, she glanced back at her coachman. "Davis, would you be so kind as to carry up the sweet rolls?" She didn't wait for his response but continued on her way.

Thankfully Mr. Cushman didn't smirk, although

technically he had every right to do so. From his tense, stiff posture and the way he was scanning the front desk and waiting rooms, she guessed he was too busy protecting her to poke fun at her.

Since he didn't make any further issue of her visiting Arch, she decided she wouldn't make any issue when he stopped her at each new stair landing, door, and hallway. At the pace they went, she was pretty sure it would take them several days to reach the third floor, where Arch had his bed in one of the public wards.

But when she finally stood at his bedside with his hand in hers and his adoring eyes staring up at her, she knew it was all worth it. She kissed his cheek, rubbed his bald head affection-ately, and then held tightly to his hand as she relayed to him all the day's events.

"So you see," she said, smiling down at his pale face, "Mr. Cushman has saved me from death at least a thousand times today. If not for his extraordinary vigilance and his Goliath-like strength, I'd most definitely be dead."

Arch shared her smile and glanced at Mr. Cushman, who stood across the room near the door with his thick arms crossed, his expression stoic, and his eyes seeming to see everything all at once. The rows of beds on either side of the long room, most of which were full. The doorways on both ends. The tall windows letting in the late afternoon sunshine. The one or two nurses who came and went in their spotless uniforms.

"He's a good boy, Victoria. Be patient with him while he adjusts to his new job."

"His new *temporary* job," she reminded Arch. "He's only staying until you're able to return, which hopefully will be very soon."

Arch shifted, and his face contorted before he gave a low moan.

She squeezed his hand and waited for the wave of pain to pass. When his breathing grew more rapid and his eyes closed, she glanced around frantically. "Where's the doctor? I have a patient here who needs the doctor."

At her declaration, Mr. Cushman stalked across the room, past the other beds, until he stood on the other side of Arch opposite her. "Arch?" Genuine worry laced his voice. "Tell me what's wrong? Where are you feeling pain?"

After today, she wouldn't have guessed that anything bothered Mr. Cushman. His emotions and his body were both like granite. But apparently he had a weak spot for Arch, and she liked him for it.

"I don't need a doctor," Arch said between gritted teeth. "I'll be fine in a minute."

Arch fumbled for Tom's hand. When he was finally holding each of their hands, his eyes flew open, first resting on Mr. Cushman and then on her. "This is good." He smiled, pressing their hands together. "Now I'm feeling better again."

"Are you sure?" She tried to ignore Mr. Cushman's fingers against hers, but Arch squeezed them closer.

"Why don't you make your deliveries to the others and visit with them," Arch suggested, blessedly releasing her hand. "And give me a minute to talk with Tommy boy."

"Tommy boy?" She quirked a brow at Mr. Cushman and waited for him to quip back.

He didn't take the bait but instead pressed his lips together grimly. He was much too serious and no fun. She sighed and retrieved one of the packages from the bedstead where her coachman had placed them. As she delivered the sweet rolls and chatted with the other patients, she could feel Mr.

Cushman's intense attention upon her. Even though Arch had always watched her vigilantly too, this was somehow different. Mr. Cushman was different. But she couldn't put her finger on exactly how.

Maybe she was more aware of his scrutiny because he was so good-looking. Or maybe he was just too close in age to her suitors, to Nathaniel, and to other men who'd admired her so that it was difficult to distinguish his attention from theirs. Whatever the case, every once in a while when she looked up and saw his eyes upon her, the skin at the back of her neck prickled with strange pleasure.

Once when she glanced his way, he and Arch seemed to be arguing about something. From the firmness of Mr. Cushman's mouth, she could sense that he was angry. Her father had mentioned Mr. Cushman was a personal friend of Arch's, but how? Arch was old enough to be Mr. Cushman's father.

Perhaps that was it. Arch had once told her that he and his wife had never been able to have children. After his wife had passed away, he'd had nothing holding him back from going into service as a professional bodyguard. Maybe without children or family, Mr. Cushman was like a son to him.

"You tricked me," she heard Mr. Cushman say under his breath as she began to cross the room to retrieve another package of sweet rolls.

Arch smiled sheepishly. "I knew it was the only way I could get you to take the job. I couldn't trust Victoria with anyone else but you."

"I'm not a nursemaid."

Victoria stopped at Mr. Cushman's declaration, and indignation shot through her. Did he think of her as a child?

Arch started to speak but stopped abruptly and put a hand to the swaths of bandages covering his side.

"Say no more," Mr. Cushman said, worry lines forming at the corners of his eyes. "You know I'll do anything for you."

"I'm fine," Arch reassured. "And you'll be fine too. At the end of this assignment with Victoria, I have a feeling you'll be grateful to me for getting you the job, instead of angry. I'm sure you'll end up being as fond of her as I am, if not more."

"I doubt it."

Even though Mr. Cushman's tone was low, she heard it clear enough, and it pricked her heart.

At that moment, he glanced at her again and caught her listening to his conversation with Arch. His jaw flexed, but his gaze was unrelenting and unapologetic.

She couldn't remember the last time anyone had disliked her or hadn't wanted to be with her. Normally everyone was vying for her attention.

She sniffed and lifted her chin. It didn't matter one tiny pin drop if he liked her. He was only a paid servant and a temporary one at that. She couldn't let him bother her. If he didn't like her, then she'd show him that she didn't care, that she didn't like him either. After all, she'd already learned that he was arrogant, boring, and unsociable—quite unlikable traits.

Even though she normally treated all her maids and household staff with the utmost consideration and kindness, as her mother had taught her, she'd watched the calloused and cold way some of her friends handled their servants, as though they were invisible and unimportant. She could do that to Mr. Cushman, keep him at a distance, refuse to form any bonds the way she had with Arch.

She only had to put up with him for the next month, and then she would never have to see him again.

Chapter 4

$\mathcal{T}$om stood near the door of the tiny shop, feet apart and arms crossed. He hadn't moved for the past thirty minutes, not even an inch. He didn't want Victoria to know how uncomfortable he was. She'd peeked at him in order to gauge his reaction to the various items that Madame Bisseau had tailored. But he'd schooled his face in a mask of passivity that he'd perfected. In fact, from the blush staining Victoria's cheeks, it was clear she was more embarrassed by the sight of lacy corsets and drawers and chemises than he was. After all, he'd been exposed to frilly undergarments during his previous assignments.

Even so, he'd still had the urge to fidget like a naive school boy who was seeing such private garments for the first time. He'd nearly sputtered an oath of protest when the silver-haired French seamstress had brought out a silky, floor length nightgown. It had been pure white with a fashionable bustle on the back, along with a train.

But more than that, the gown had been thin. He'd had to

recite the Lord's Prayer twenty-two times since seeing that night dress in order to fight away images of Victoria wearing it.

After that, he'd also prayed more fervently that God would deliver him from this job. He hadn't had any major problems over the past two weeks as Victoria Cole's bodyguard. No further attacks. Except for a threatening letter Mr. Cole had received yesterday, there hadn't been even a hint of a problem.

He hadn't experienced any emotional entanglements with Victoria either. He'd kept his word to Henry Cole that he would treat his daughter with the utmost professionalism. He'd purposefully put a wedge between them the first day on the job. He'd seen the hurt in her eyes that evening at the hospital when he'd made sure she overheard his conversation with Arch. He'd regretted that he'd had to pain her, but it was for her own benefit.

She was naturally affectionate, even if she was slightly spoiled and strong-willed at times. He'd been around enough rich women to know Victoria Cole hadn't let her beauty and wealth make her prideful. She had a freshness and innocence that was refreshing. She seemed to see the positive in every situation.

But that was the problem. She was too trusting, too sweet. She'd formed a deep attachment with Arch. And she also had friendly relationships with all the household servants. In fact, she treated them more like family than paid help. With her kind and generous spirit, he'd quickly surmised that she would grow attached to him too.

Sure, she was engaged and would be married in sixteen days. Nevertheless, he'd deemed it necessary to keep high walls between himself and Victoria. The best way to build a barricade was to hurt someone. Then the person usually erected a wall fast and furiously, just as Victoria had done.

Although truthfully, her wall was flimsy. She'd had a hard time maintaining her "I'm the master and you're my servant" charade.

"I honestly don't think you'll need to pack anything else beside that nightgown," Theresa said. She was sitting on the settee next to Victoria and had been a constant companion during the shopping expeditions.

"Of course I'll need more than the nightgown. I'm planning to do a great deal of sightseeing and shopping in all of the places I missed last time I was in Italy."

"With that nightgown, I'm sure Nathaniel will be doing lots of sightseeing too," Theresa said with a wicked glimmer.

Victoria gasped and slapped playfully at Theresa's arm. "Hush!" Even though Victoria was smiling, from the way her eyes widened and her pupils dilated, Tom could tell she was mortified by her friend's comment.

Tom had to admit, the comment unnerved him too. Not because he didn't like the thought of Nathaniel looking at Victoria. No, on the few occasions Victoria had spent time with Nathaniel, Tom had liked the guy. He was genuine and decent. Frivolous. Flighty. Spoiled. But honest. And after he married Victoria, he'd have every right to feast upon her beauty. In that nightgown.

Okay. Maybe he was unnerved a little by the thought of another man looking at Victoria. He supposed his overprotective nature was coming out more than usual because she was so young.

Whatever the case, the real reason he was uncomfortable was because he wasn't accustomed to the brashness some American women from the high society displayed. Most of the European royalty he accompanied were proper and polite, at least in public.

Madame Bisseau's frown indicated that she hadn't found Theresa's comment amusing either. The French woman finished folding the silk nightgown and gently placed it with several other items in a flat box.

Through the front shop window, Tom caught sight of Nathaniel climbing down from a bright yellow phaeton. It was new. From the condition of the tires, Tom could tell that it had only been driven a couple of times.

Nathaniel was impeccably attired, as usual. He wore a light gray pin-striped suit accented with a bow tie and top hat. He cut a dashing figure in his finely tailored outfit, and he had a carefree, fun-loving look about him, especially with his wind-tossed sandy brown hair.

Nathaniel inspected the side of his phaeton, took out a handkerchief, and polished a spot. He nodded and smiled to three young ladies who flirted with him as they walked past. But his attention on them was only fleeting. Tom couldn't fault Nathaniel for his devotion to Victoria. Even when other women vied for him, he had eyes only for his bride-to-be.

As Nathaniel proceeded toward Madame Bisseau's salon and opened the door, Tom surveyed outside the store to make sure nothing had changed since they'd arrived and that no one was lurking nearby. No strange carriages. No lingering passers-by. No oddities.

He stepped back inside just as Victoria stood and smiled at Nathaniel. She held out her hands to him in a welcoming gesture. Although her eyes lit up at the sight of him, there was something missing from her expression. Tom couldn't name what it was, but he'd noticed her reaction to Nathaniel before.

And he'd noted Theresa's too. Victoria's friend was in love with the man. Although she kept her feelings hidden from Victoria, she couldn't hide them from Tom. He'd noticed the sideway glances filled with longing, the rapt attention whenever Nathaniel spoke, the extra long laughter at Nathaniel's jokes that weren't funny.

At least Theresa had the decency to make the best of the situation. Tom could tell she was sharp. She'd apparently realized early enough that Nathaniel was thoroughly enamored with Victoria. Half the time he was so busy fawning over Victoria that he forgot Theresa was even there. Victoria was kind enough to draw her friend in and keep her from being left out.

"Are you ready for our lunch at Delmonico's, darling?" Nathaniel had taken off his hat and was raking his fingers through his hair and tossing the wayward strands back.

"I'm very ready." Victoria cast a sideways glance at the box Madame Bisseau was now tying closed with a silk ribbon. Her eyes rounded with embarrassment, and she quickly grabbed Nathaniel's hand and began to propel him toward the door.

"You'll be the first to ride in my new phaeton," Nathaniel said with a grin.

"She can't ride in a phaeton," Tom said.

Nathaniel halted abruptly, which in turn forced Victoria to stop. The excitement that had been playing across his features dropped into disappointment.

"With the open top, it's too dangerous." Tom offered the explanation before anyone could protest. The anonymous letter Mr. Cole had received yesterday might not mean anything. It had implied vague threats to the Cole family if Mr. Cole didn't back out of a particular railroad deal he was negotiating. Even if the threats were empty and had no connection to Arch's attack, Tom was trained to stay on high alert regardless.

"Delmonico's isn't that far away." Victoria proceeded to

tug Nathaniel toward the door. "I daresay a little ride won't compromise my safety."

"Maybe a *little ride* in Central Park after lunch." Tom had learned to always be strict first. If he said "no" right away, then his charge was usually more open to his subsequent suggestion.

Victoria paused as though considering what she believed to be his compromise but was actually his plan all along. "Very well." She sniffed in her attempt to be arrogant toward him. "But I shall take the ride with Nathaniel alone."

He'd suspected as much. "We'll see how busy the park is."

She hesitated, nodded curtly, and turned to Theresa, who was trailing after the couple. "Theresa, will you ride with Nathaniel to Delmonico's? I hate for him to be alone with his fun new toy."

Nathaniel smiled down at Victoria. "You're so sweet, darling. But I'll be all right."

"I don't mind," Theresa said. She stepped forward and slipped her arm through Nathaniel's boldly. "We can't let you have all the pleasure to yourself. You need to share some with the rest of us."

Nathaniel's eyes took on an excited glimmer again, but he attempted to dampen his enthusiasm as he looked at Victoria. "If you're sure you don't mind?"

"Of course not. I want you to have fun."

Nathaniel grinned, showing off his carefree charm, which Tom guessed appealed to young women. "Are you ready for the ride of your life?" Nathaniel said to Theresa.

Her eyes reflected eagerness. But Tom gave her credit for responding sarcastically and hiding her enthusiasm. "Just try not to kill me."

It was Victoria's turn now to trail behind the couple. As

Nathaniel joked with Theresa, Victoria beamed at the two. Apparently Victoria didn't think she had anything to worry about between her fiancé and her best friend. Tom hoped she was right.

A few minutes later, Tom was settled across from Victoria in the carriage. They followed the phaeton where Nathaniel and Theresa perched on the high open bench and were laughing and talking. Victoria hadn't seemed to notice that Theresa's arm was still linked with Nathaniel's. Or if she did, she wasn't bothered by it.

As a matter of fact, Victoria wasn't bothered by too much when it came to Nathaniel. She had none of the passionate emotions one would expect from a woman on the cusp of her wedding.

The crazy spinning in his mind came to standstill. "You don't love him."

"What?" Victoria's eyes jerked to his. She appeared startled, much like a cornered doe.

"You'll run away and leave him standing at the altar just like you did your last fiancé."

The golden brown flickered with confusion. "How do you know about that?"

"Who doesn't? Both of your previous broken engagements made the newspaper. Jacob Anthony Ratcliff in December of '73 after your debutante party. And Samuel Hildebrandt in '74."

She didn't contradict him. In fact, her expression told him she was indeed guilty.

"At least with Jacob you had the decency to break it off well before the wedding day. But poor Samuel."

She started to speak but clamped her lips closed.

"Don't you think you owe it to Nathaniel to end your

relationship before it's too late?" Especially, to avoid complications. Samuel, fiancé number two, had stalked Victoria for months after the called-off wedding until she'd gone to Europe. Even if Samuel wasn't stalking her anymore, the ex-fiancé had been at two parties that she had attended. And it was clear the man was still in love with her.

"You have no idea what you're talking about," she finally said. "Please refrain from saying anything else."

"So you're planning to go through with a loveless marriage?"

"Of course I am."

He quirked his brow. He'd caught her.

She rolled her eyes. "I'm going through with the marriage. What I meant to say is that it's not loveless."

"Then you love him?"

She started to nod.

"Be honest."

"I feel a great deal of affection for Nathaniel," she said slowly, as though weighing each word. "He's good and sweet and generous."

"So is my mother, but I'm not marrying her."

"He loves me," she rushed, her voice rising a notch to make her point.

"And my mother loves me."

She released an exasperated breath, forming her lips into a pout that he'd found strangely pretty the past couple of weeks. "I'm marrying him. He's everything I've ever wanted in a man. And that's that."

"Or maybe he's everything your father ever wanted."

The carriage bumped over a rut jostling her. But she rapidly regained her composure and lifted her chin. "I chose Nathaniel. My father had nothing to do with it."

Tom shrugged. Let her think what she wanted. He knew, however, that Mr. Cole wasn't the type of man to play roulette with his daughter's choice of a marriage partner. Tom had no doubt Henry Cole had been intimately involved in each of the negotiations long before Victoria had accepted the proposals.

"Maybe you've been picking the wrong kind of men."

"And I suppose you're the expert on the type of man I need?"

"Maybe."

"There you go being arrogant again and thinking you know everything about everyone."

He bit back a smile. He was enjoying this spar with her far too much. These were the kinds of heart-to-heart conversations he was supposed to avoid if he wanted the wall to stay up between them, though. He crossed his arms and settled into the thick seat cushion. A few more minutes wouldn't hurt, would it? The clatter of the horse hoofs on the cobblestone and the rattle of a nearby omnibus drifted in through the half-open window, bringing with it the waft of the delicacies served in the exotic restaurants they were passing.

He lobbed out his answer and waited for her to explode. "I know more than you think."

She sat forward and fisted her hands in her lap as though to keep from reaching out and slapping him. "You might be smart about a lot of things. But you certainly don't have me all figured out, even if you think you do."

"You're afraid of getting married."

"That's not true."

"I can see the fear in your eyes."

Her long lashes fell down and veiled her soul, but not before he'd glimpsed the truth.

He was right. He'd seen fear in her eyes from time to time.

And he realized now that the fear wasn't related to the attack. He should have guessed it had to do with her upcoming marriage. The signs had all been there—running away from two other fiancés, her shallow relationship with Nathaniel, a lack of enthusiasm.

Sure, she spent most her time planning for the wedding and honeymoon. And the last few days she'd been busy packing for the move to Newport. But all of it was a convenient distraction. A way to keep busy. So she didn't have to think about the real issue. She was afraid of getting married.

But why? What drove her fear?

It wasn't his place to ask. In fact, the entire conversation was out of place. But now that he'd started it, he needed to finish. "You should tell him," he said, trying to gentle his tone.

Her lashes swept up, revealing her eyes again. This time they were luminous, the golden flecks mesmerizing, the vulnerability magnetic. "Tell him what?"

"That you're afraid." Tom held her gaze, hoping to infuse her with the courage she would need to face the task. "He's a decent guy. He'll understand."

The carriage was slowing, and the surroundings told him they were nearing Delmonico's.

"If you admit your fear to yourself and to him, then maybe this time you can face it instead of running away." Even as he spoke the words to *her*, they hit *him* in the gut. He could dole out advice. But he wasn't great at following it. He'd been running away from his past for ten years.

The rolling wheels jolted to a halt. Outside the carriage, Nathaniel's voice was followed by Theresa's laughter. The heart-to-heart moment with Victoria was over. But neither of them moved to open the door.

Finally, she surprised him by doing the last thing he

expected. She reached across the carriage and took his hand into hers, folding her silky gloved fingers around his. She smiled up at him with the same kind of sweetness he'd seen her dole out to Theresa and Nathaniel and her parents. "Thank you, Mr. Cushman. Maybe I've misjudged you. Maybe you're a nicer man than you've led me to believe."

He shook his head. "No, I'm still the mean guy."

Her smile widened. "I don't believe you."

"Just wait. You'll hate me again soon enough."

She released his hand and reached for the door. "You might act tough. But you can't fool me any longer. Underneath you're a big softy just like Arch."

"Definitely not a softy."

She winked. "I promise I won't give away your secret."

He was tempted to chuckle but held it back. Instead, he opened the door and poked his head out. He was back on duty. He'd do best to remember to stay that way, to keep the walls up, no matter how easy it would be to tear them down.

Chapter 5

The bowls of fresh cut delphiniums on each of the elaborately set tables matched the color of the evening sky overhead. The scent of roasting scallops and lobster and oysters made Victoria's mouth water in anticipation of the feast to come.

She loved Newport in the summer. She always had, even as a little girl when she'd built sandcastles, waded in the cold saltwater in her bare feet, and collected shells. Even now, as an adult, she enjoyed the months spent in the little seaside town visiting with friends, sailing aboard yachts, and having dinner parties on the beach.

"Your mother always does a beautiful job with her parties." She allowed her shoulder to brush against Nathaniel's arm.

"I told her to make this extra special for you," he replied.

Guests mingled among the tables and along the shore of the private beach that belonged to the Winthrops. Their summer cottage sat back a fair distance from the water's edge.

Nicknamed *The Arbor*, the Italianate-style villa was three stories high and built of stately granite. A manicured garden with a center fountain graced the back of the house and provided a scenic ocean overlook. From the sandy shoreline, the house and garden were picturesque, perhaps even lovelier than the Cole cottage down the beach.

Victoria waved at Theresa, who was walking next to Phillip Smith. Although she was nodding at something he was saying, she was staring at Victoria and Nathaniel. Without waving in return, Theresa flipped her attention to Phillip and spoke to him as though he were the only one on the beach and the man just for her. Victoria could only pray he was.

She inhaled a deep, contented breath. The sea air was warm but pleasant, not yet containing the humidity that would come later in the summer. "Your mother is wonderful."

"That's because she adores you just as much as I do."

She smiled up at Nathaniel. "I'm not sure anyone can adore me quite as much as you."

"You're right." He tucked her hand more securely in the crook of his arm. He needn't worry. She wasn't going anywhere. Even though the tide was rising and the waves were sliding further up the wet sand toward them, she wasn't ready to end their stroll and rejoin the others.

He leaned into her. "Have I told you yet tonight how much I love you?" His tone was low and intimate. It should have filled her with wonder and excitement. Instead, unwelcome trepidation crept into her stomach and nibbled at the lining.

After Mr. Cushman had told her she was afraid of getting married, she'd wanted to deny it. But she'd finally grudgingly admitted to herself that perhaps he was partly right. So she'd done as he'd suggested and had told Nathaniel she was having a few wedding jitters. Of course, Nathaniel had soothed her and told her that every bride-to-be was nervous, that it was perfectly normal, and that everything would work out just fine.

But she didn't know if he believed his own words any more than she had. Ever since they'd had the brief conversation a few days after they'd arrived in Newport, he'd doubled his attention and gifts. She had no doubt he'd already been thinking about her two foiled engagements. Now with her admission, he was probably praying he wouldn't be Victoria Cole's third failed attempt.

She was praying he wouldn't be either.

"I love you," he said again, tugging her to a stop. He pulled a velvet box out of his vest pocket and held it between them. "This is just a little something to show you how much you mean to me."

Out of the corner of her eye, she glimpsed Mr. Cushman standing in the shadows of one of the bathing machines that Mrs. Winthrop had provided for her guests. The roofed and walled wooden carts used by bathers to change into their swimwear were now pulled out of the water and rested in the thick sand. Even though Mr. Cushman had kept his distance, she knew he was well aware of every move she made. What would he think if she accepted another one of Nathaniel's gifts?

It shouldn't matter what her bodyguard thought. But after their discussion about Nathaniel, she'd realized that Mr. Cushman was not only exceptionally skilled at seeing exterior details, but he saw much deeper than that too. Despite the short time he'd been her bodyguard, he seemed to know her better than anyone else, including herself.

Her fingers brushed against the velvet. By taking the gift, would she only be fooling herself and Nathaniel into thinking that everything was satisfactory?

But it *was* satisfactory, wasn't it? She *did* love Nathaniel. And she *would* marry him next week. Maybe she'd had doubts with the other two engagements, but she was more mature now. She'd come to understand that she couldn't base a relationship on feelings alone because feelings of infatuation and adoration would come and go.

Instead, she'd realized that love was a choice she had to make, regardless of the feelings. She was choosing to love Nathaniel, be his helpmate, and encourage him as best she could. All the rest would fall into place eventually.

She took the box and gingerly opened it. Against the black velvet backdrop, a diamond bracelet glittered in the evening sunshine. She sucked in a breath. "Oh, Nathaniel, it's gorgeous."

"Not as gorgeous as you." He carefully lifted out the jewels. The diamonds were in the shape of dewdrops and wrapped all the way around either side to the clasp. "May I?" He motioned toward her wrist.

She offered her hand to him. As he gently draped the bracelet around her wrist, his fingers brushed her skin. Desire flamed to life in his eyes. She willed herself to feel the same attraction at the brief contact, but instead her stomach growled, reminding her how hungry she was.

Nathaniel closed the clasp and reluctantly released her wrist.

She held it up, letting the sunlight reflect against the brilliant prisms. "Thank you, Nathaniel. I'll treasure it always."

Before she could protest or stop him, he reached for her hand again, brought it to his lips, and pressed a kiss against her fingertips. His mustache tickled her skin and made her want to giggle. But from the serious longing that tightened Nathaniel's face, she guessed she'd only hurt him if she showed her mirth.

He straightened and released her hand, and she said the words he liked to hear from her. "I love you."

At his ensuing grin, she knew she'd done the right thing. She'd made him happy.

"I see how you're able to keep Victoria's affection," came a nearby voice.

She and Nathaniel turned to find Samuel Hildebrandt ambling with a friend. Her former fiancé's eyes were hidden beneath the shadows cast by the brim of his silk top hat. But Victoria was sure they were shooting bullets.

She squirmed uncomfortably, her shoes sinking deeper into the sand. As Nathaniel's third cousin, Samuel's presence at family parties was inevitable from time to time. Nevertheless, things were always awkward between them, and she did her best to prevent confrontations.

"Maybe if I'd bought Victoria's love," Samuel said, "then I'd be married to her by now."

Nathaniel let go of her, puffed out his chest, and took a step toward Samuel. "That's an insult to Victoria. You know as well as I do that she has enough money of her own and doesn't need me to buy her love."

Victoria caught sight of Mr. Cushman pushing away from the bathing machine. She motioned to him not to worry about her, hoping he'd realize that she was perfectly fine. Samuel might resent their breakup, but he was the last person who would ever hurt her.

"Then admit it," Samuel said, stepping away from his companion and starting toward Nathaniel. "You stole her away from me."

"Maybe you never had her to begin with," Nathaniel responded.

"Maybe you don't either."

Nathaniel and Samuel were now face to face. Nathaniel's neck was turning red, a sure sign he was getting worked up. Usually he was a calm, level-headed man who didn't let much bother him. But clearly, Samuel was goading him. "I think you need to concede defeat," Nathaniel said, "and let go of Victoria once and for all."

Anger etched lines into the faces of both men. She hastened after Nathaniel and reached for his arm to pull him back, to keep him out of harm's way. Just as she caught hold of him, Samuel rushed into Nathaniel, wrapped his arms around his waist, and tried to tackle him. But instead of dragging Nathaniel down, Samuel only managed to propel him toward the water, pushing Victoria helplessly with him.

Amidst the wrestling, she found herself tangled in the train on her skirt. Before she could catch her balance, she fell backward and landed with a splash in the surging tide. A wave crashed around her, drenching her and leaving her gasping from the chill of the water.

She didn't have time to react when a second wave hit her. The water had hardly pulled away before Mr. Cushman was there. As if she weighed nothing more than a sand dollar, he scooped her into his arms. His blue eyes were darker than she'd ever seen them—almost black. His forehead was creased, and his brows were furrowed into that irresistible slant.

"Are you hurt?" he asked.

She coughed past the slight bit of water she'd swallowed. "I'm perfectly alright."

He hefted her higher against his chest and then waded out of the tide. The other party guests had stopped what they were doing and were now gathering in clusters to watch the spectacle. Samuel and Nathaniel had pulled away from each other and were staring at her, their expressions filled with both surprise and chagrin.

Nathaniel was the first to react. "I'm so sorry, darling." He rushed toward her and reached out to take her from Mr. Cushman. But Mr. Cushman leveled a glare at Nathaniel that made him freeze. He dropped his hands and stepped aside, having been thoroughly reprimanded by just one look. Mr. Cushman turned the same glare upon Samuel, but he only jutted his chin out and glowered back.

"What happened?" Nathaniel asked, but without making another move toward her. Blood dribbled from his nose and his hair was mussed. He'd been so focused fighting Samuel that he hadn't realized she'd been swept aside and dumped into the ocean. She couldn't blame him for her predicament. Besides, she wasn't in the least injured. Just startled. And wet.

"I'm fine," she reassured him. But she made no move to free herself from Mr. Cushman's hold.

"Please forgive me, darling," Nathaniel said again earnestly. "I was entirely too careless."

"Yes, you were," Mr. Cushman agreed as he started up the sloping beach toward the house.

"You may take her inside to one of the guest rooms," Nathaniel said.

Mr. Cushman didn't respond. He tromped through the sand as steadily as if he were on solid ground. She rested her head against his shoulder, knowing she should tell him that she could walk. Instead she relished the feeling of safety, something she hadn't experienced in a long time.

Through the thin wet layers of her garments, she felt the solidness of his chest and the muscles in his arm. She'd never been held by a man before. All her interactions with Nathaniel and past suitors had been chaste—holding the crook of an arm, a brief kiss to her hand, a simple pat on the shoulder. Samuel had kissed her once, on her cheek, but only quickly. It had really been more of a peck.

Now, in Mr. Cushman's arms, she was keenly aware that not only was he her bodyguard, but he was also a very attractive man. His strong chin brushed against her hair, the hard thud of his heartbeat resounded between them, the heat of his body enveloped hers. Even though she was wet and chilled, strange warmth spread through her stomach.

She was just embarrassed at her awkward predicament, she told herself. That was all. She would have felt the same way had Nathaniel been holding her.

Once Mr. Cushman reached the manicured grass of the garden, he veered in the direction of the carriage house.

"We're not leaving the party yet," she said.

"I'm taking you home."

She ought to protest. The Winthrops had servants who could divest her of her wet garments and help her dry off. She could send home for another fresh gown. Maybe the maids would have trouble re-fashioning her hair into dangling ringlets, but they could figure out something presentable.

But for a reason she couldn't explain, she didn't complain. When Mr. Cushman settled her onto the carriage bench, covered her with a wool blanket, and commanded the coachman to leave with all haste, she was surprised by the sense of relief that overcame her.

Within minutes, the carriage arrived at the Cole's beach cottage. She was disappointed when Mr. Cushman didn't pick her up again. Instead, he handed her over to the care of her servants, who ushered her to her dressing room and set to work, releasing her from her constrictive garments and tight corset.

An hour later she was in her boudoir, dry and warm and sitting in a lounge chair in front of a fire. She held a cup of tea between both hands and sipped the liquid slowly. The light chintz curtains had already been pulled even though darkness had not yet settled. The room was bathed in the soft glow of firelight and wall sconces, revealing the elegant striped wallpaper of alternating light and dark greens, the white wainscoting and cornice, and the large green rug that covered the hard wood floor. She'd had the small sitting room off the bedchamber redecorated several years ago by one of New York's top designers to reflect her growing maturity as a woman. Now it was one of her favorite places.

"You're sure you're warm?" her mother asked from her spot on the settee. Isabelle Cole was attired in an elegant wine-colored evening gown and matching ribbon tied around her slender neck. Her dark hair was fashioned into a high knot on top of her head. Her features were pale but flawless.

Her father always said Mother was as beautiful now as the day she'd pulled him from the sea after his steamer had wrecked in a storm.

He wasn't exaggerating. Her mother was beautiful. But she rarely left home. Even tonight, although Mrs. Winthrop had invited her to the beach party too, she'd only gone for a short while to put in an appearance before having father bring her back home.

She always had one excuse or another for why she didn't want to go out in public. But Victoria knew the real reason. Her mother didn't want to face the whispers and gawking. At parties, dinners, the opera, and other events, she had to accept the fact that she was blind and that people noticed it. Here in the confines of home, Mother could pretend she wasn't different. Here she expected everyone to ignore her sightlessness and treat her like anyone else.

Victoria had always indulged her mother. And at times, she even forgot that her mother was blind.

"It wouldn't do for you to take a chill so close to your wedding," Mother said.

"Don't worry." Victoria took another sip of the black tea that contained a hint of honey and lemon. "It was just a tiny tumble in the water. That's all."

Her mother seemed to peer directly at the diamond bracelet that Nathaniel had given her, which was now sitting on the end table next to Victoria's chair. Victoria held her breath and waited for her mother to comment about it. Even if Mother couldn't see it, she'd probably touched it when she'd come in to hug Victoria. Not only did her perceptive mother know it was there, but she probably realized why Nathaniel had given it to her.

"Nathaniel's a wonderful man," Mother said earnestly.

"Yes, I agree."

Her mother's sightless gaze moved to Victoria's face. For a moment, her mother seemed to be straining to see Victoria's features. Her golden eyes had a desperate hunger in them that Victoria had rarely seen.

Victoria held her breath, wishing that for just one brief instant her mother could see her. But the intense gaze lasted only a moment longer before her mother schooled herself back into her usual calm and dignified expression.

"Promise me that if you have any problems or concerns, you'll talk to me?" Mother asked.

"There aren't any problems, Mother," Victoria assured. "Nathaniel and I are getting along perfectly."

Her mother nodded, looked as if she wanted to say more, but then closed her mouth. She slid to the edge of the settee and rubbed her hand over the damask. "You brought the cross again."

Victoria glanced across the room to the bureau at the two dark pieces of driftwood that were fashioned into a cross. She wasn't sure why she felt the need to bring the rough-hewn cross with her everywhere she went, but ever since she'd been given the cross several years ago, she'd gotten into the habit of bringing it along on her trips.

During the life of the cross, it had become known as the cross of hope. Victoria didn't feel particularly in need of hope. Her life was wonderful. She had everything she ever wanted. Yet, she clung to the cross of hope anyway.

"Do you think I should stop bringing it with me?" Victoria asked.

"Not at all," her mother replied hastily. "I'm just glad it comforts you."

"Maybe I should give it away to someone who needs it more than I do?"

"I think you'll know when you're ready to let go of it." Her mother rose, kissed her gently on her forehead, and left the room.

In the quiet of the boudoir, with only the crackling of the fire for company, Victoria stared at the amber liquid in her cup. All she could see were her mother's amber eyes, hungrily scanning her face, trying desperately to see features that she never had seen and never would.

How must her mother feel? Victoria sloshed the tea around the porcelain and felt a painful heat slosh in her heart. Not only was her mother denied the pleasure of seeing her child, but she hadn't been able to look at her husband for years either.

Victoria didn't realize she'd been swirling the tea too high and fast until some splashed over the rim. She tried to ignore her shaking fingers as she replaced the cup on the saucer, but she couldn't ignore the emotions spilling into her chest— emotions she didn't want to feel, thoughts she didn't want to think, the very real possibility that she could turn into her mother some day.

A rap on the door was Mr. Cushman's signature call. She welcomed the distraction from very dangerous thoughts and feelings—thoughts and feelings that were better left locked away in a deep, dark chest at the bottom of the sea.

The door opened and Mr. Cushman walked into the sitting room, as composed and tough-looking as always. In one quick glance, he took in all the details of her appearance, her long damp hair, and the fluffy blanket draped around her, concealing all but the hem of her silk robe and her slippers.

"How are you doing?" Mr. Cushman asked, although she wasn't sure why he bothered to ask since he'd likely surmised exactly how she was doing even better than she had herself.

"I'm well enough to go back to the party." She wasn't sure why she felt as though she must challenge him, except that she didn't want him to think she was afraid of returning. Because she wasn't.

He peeked out the window through a slit in the curtain before facing her. "We want you to stay away from Samuel."

"We?"

"Your father and I."

She picked up her teacup, took another sip. "You don't think Samuel is behind Arch's attack, do you?"

"I doubt it."

"Then why are you worried? Samuel might be upset at Nathaniel, but he surely won't attempt to harm me."

"He may try to undermine the wedding plans."

"Do you honestly think Samuel would try to prevent me

from marrying Nathaniel?"

"Maybe."

She was ashamed to admit the thought didn't bother her. She lowered her eyes so that Mr. Cushman couldn't read her thoughts and confront her again. Her sights landed upon the side table and the diamond bracelet. She wished she'd thought to put it away before Mr. Cushman came into the room.

"Nathaniel is desperate to keep you." Mr. Cushman followed her gaze, and his meaning was all too obvious.

She gave a short laugh. "He's a generous man. And he gives me presents almost every time we're together."

"Because he's afraid he'll lose you."

"Because he's sweet." She hated that Mr. Cushman's conclusions too closely mirrored her own, but she wouldn't admit it to him.

Mr. Cushman shook his head. "He's dense if he thinks he can win you through gifts."

"Apparently among all of your other skills, you're also the expert on how to woo a woman?"

His upper lip twitched with the beginning of a smile. "Only for a select few women."

His words jarred her and reminded her that she wasn't the first woman he'd protected, nor would she be the last. In fact, the final time they'd visited Arch before leaving New York, Mr. Cushman had indicated that he'd only stay until she left on her wedding trip. After that Arch would have to take over again, or they'd have to find someone else. Mr. Cushman had made it abundantly clear that he was there only temporarily and that he was past ready to move on.

She was ready too. After the wedding she wouldn't need a bodyguard any more. Not with Nathaniel by her side day and night watching over her. Nevertheless, she still couldn't stop from wondering what types of women Mr. Cushman had protected in the past and how she compared to them.

"So..." She toyed with the diamond bracelet, waiting for him to settle his attention on her fully before sweeping up her lashes and gazing at him with what she hoped was her most beguiling expression. "What number am I in the list of women you've guarded?"

"Four." His placid expression didn't waver. She should have known by now that Mr. Cushman was immune to womanly charms. She had no doubt he'd rebuffed many women over the years and had plenty of practice withstanding an extraordinary amount of flirting and eyelash-batting.

"And how do I compare to the other three?"

"I don't make a practice of comparing."

"Am I prettier?"

He didn't respond.

She smiled. "I'll take your silence as a yes."

"I'm not surprised you would."

"Oh, so you think I'm conceited?"

"Most rich people are."

"That must mean you're very wealthy," she said beginning to feel testy toward him. "Because you're extremely conceited."

At that, he laughed. Not a mocking laugh like she was accustomed to among her circles. But a genuinely amused laugh. She couldn't deny that she liked the sound. Really liked it. She smiled at him, took another drink of her tea, and wondered if she could figure out a way to make him laugh more often.

Before she could try, a knock sounded on the door.

Mr. Cushman's humor immediately dissipated, and his stoicism was back in place. "It's Nathaniel."

"How do you know?" She'd learned not to doubt him. He was almost always right. Even so, she liked to hear how he came to his conclusions, the details he noticed that she missed.

"He's the only one around here who owns a Stanhope gig."

"And how do you know he's driving his gig?"

"The vehicle I heard had one horse and two wheels."

She smiled.

"Did I pass your test?" His brows were raised, revealing a glimmer of the previous humor.

"Yes, you passed with a perfect score."

Mr. Cushman started toward the door. "I don't want him to stay long."

"And why's that? What harm will come of him staying for a while?"

"You're in your bathrobe." He didn't look at her. "I'd suggest covering yourself back up."

She glanced down to see that her blanket had slipped off her shoulders, revealing the silky white bathrobe that was cooler for the summer, but certainly also less modest. Heat infused her cheeks at the realization that Mr. Cushman had seen her immodesty and hadn't been the least flustered by it. She readjusted the blanket around her shoulders and clutched it tightly in front so that her bathrobe was concealed again.

Her damp hair hung over her shoulders in long waves, completely unseemly for an unmarried young woman. She quickly swept it back into a knot, her fingers fumbling in her haste.

"Ready?" he asked, his back still facing her.

She nodded but realized he didn't have eyes in the back of his head, even though at times he acted as if he did. "I'm ready."

He opened the door, and Nathaniel stepped in carrying an enormous bouquet of yellow roses. He apologized again profusely, fussed over her, and attempted to amuse her with anecdotes from the dinner party she'd missed.

But all the while they conversed, her attention drifted to Mr. Cushman standing just outside the open door, his spine as stiff as always. She didn't know why she was more aware of his presence now than any other time. But for some reason, she was having a difficult time making small talk with Nathaniel without wondering what Mr. Cushman was thinking about their conversation.

Finally, after another awkward lull with Nathaniel, Mr. Cushman stepped into the room. "Victoria needs to rest."

"I guess that's my cue to leave." Nathaniel rose out of his chair across from Victoria's. His face reflected disappointment.

"Thank you for coming. And for the flowers." She meant it. "You're always so thoughtful."

"I can't wait until I can spoil you every minute of every day," he said.

She laughed lightly. "I think you're already quite accomplished at that." She peeked at Mr. Cushman, expecting him to roll his eyes. But he remained impassive.

Nathaniel looked at Mr. Cushman too, then at Victoria, and back at Mr. Cushman. Nathaniel's forehead was creased as though he were trying to understand the unspoken communication. She wanted to tell him there wasn't any—at least not on Mr. Cushman's end.

But before she could say anything, Nathaniel bent over and gently cupped her cheek. She was too startled by the contact and nearness to speak. He dragged in a breath and then dropped his mouth to hers. He pressed a kiss against her lips. The touch was warm and tender and was over before she could think about responding, although she wasn't sure how she ought to go about kissing a man back. As Nathaniel pulled away, she could only stare at him with a mingling of wonder and embarrassment.

He straightened and glanced everywhere around the room except at her. Silence stretched between them. Finally, he cleared his throat. "Goodnight, Victoria." He spun on his heel and walked briskly from the room, but not before tossing Mr. Cushman a look that seemed to say, "She's mine."

Once Nathaniel's footsteps in the hallway faded, she sat back in her chair and exhaled a breath. For a long moment she didn't move, and neither did Mr. Cushman. She knew she shouldn't care what he thought about Nathaniel's kiss, but she did. When she chanced a glance at him, he raised his brows at her, giving her a glimpse at the mirth lighting his eyes.

Did he think her moment of passion with Nathaniel was funny? Her ire rose swiftly and pushed her to her feet. "I fail to see the humor in this situation."

His lips quirked into one of his rare grins.

She clenched her fists and stomped across the room. "It's not funny. Stop laughing at me."

"I'm not laughing." Even though he rapidly smoothed away his grin, his eyes still flickered with amusement.

She stopped in front of him, every nerve in her body sizzling. "How dare you poke fun at my first kiss." She was half-tempted to reach out and slap his face.

"*That* was your first kiss?"

At the disbelief on his face, embarrassment returned in a rush, and she wished she could take back the words. Instead, she straightened and tried to bring some dignity back to the moment—one she hoped to cherish for the rest of her life. "It was a nice kiss."

"Nice?" His tone was disparaging and only irked her all the more.

"As a matter of fact, it was *very* nice."

"Kisses aren't meant to be *nice.*" His tone dropped, as did his gaze—to her lips. For only the flicker of an instant. But it was long enough to send heat spilling through her middle in a way she'd never experienced before.

When his gaze returned to hers, the dangerous slant of his eyebrows told her that his kisses would be far from chaste and proper. The glance was all it took to make her draw in a quick, dizzying breath. If he could elicit this kind of response by simply looking at her lips, what would it be like to kiss him? The mere thought made her tremble.

As if sensing her reaction, one side of his mouth cocked up again.

"Ooh," she said in exasperation, unable to stop herself from pushing his chest.

He captured her wrists in one hand and easily pinned her. The diamonds surrounding the sapphire on her engagement ring sparkled, as if reminding her to move away from him. She ignored the ring and the faint voice of reason murmuring in the back of her head.

"I guess you think you're the expert on kissing," she said hotly, "just as you're the expert on everything else."

"I guess so."

"Have you asked all the young ladies you've kissed for their opinions?"

"I don't need to ask." His response came in a whisper that did funny things to her stomach. His attention once again shifted to her lips, and this time it stayed there.

"Maybe you should." She couldn't keep from studying his lips in return. They were firm and determined, and she knew without a doubt his kiss would be nothing like Nathaniel's. Suddenly she wanted Mr. Cushman to kiss her. The desire for it rose strongly, unlike anything she'd felt for her other beaus. As if drawn by a will she hadn't known she had, she swayed against him so that his face was only inches from hers, so close that she could feel the warmth of his breath.

His grip on her wrists tightened and his breath quickened. He hesitated and then dipped his head closer. He was going to kiss her. She felt his desire for it in every taut muscle of his body.

She closed her eyes and waited in exquisite anticipation for his not-so-nice kiss. Her middle was flipping wildly, anticipating the first crushing touch—for she knew it would be hard and demanding. A man like Mr. Cushman was incapable of anything less.

For a torturous moment he didn't move.

She cracked open one eye only to find that he was studying her again with humor flickering in his expression.

"I don't need your opinion," he stated, releasing her wrists and propelling her back several paces.

She stared mutely, uncomprehending.

"I won't kiss you, Victoria." His voice was all steel. Gone was any trace of longing, almost as if she'd dreamt it in the first place. Maybe she had.

"You might enjoy trifling with other people's emotions," he continued, "but I don't."

Trifle with emotions? Was that what he thought she was doing? Before she could think coherently enough to offer a response, he dealt another low blow.

"You're practically married. You shouldn't want to kiss me anyway."

Mortification came crashing through her with the power of a hurricane gale. "Who said I wanted to kiss you?"

She retreated a step, anxious to put as much distance between herself and Mr. Cushman as possible. In her haste, she tripped over the blanket that had come loose and fallen to the floor behind her. Only his steady hold on her arm kept her from sprawling like an utter fool.

Hurriedly, she righted herself and jerked away from him, all the while giving him a withering glare and praying he wouldn't see her embarrassment. After all, she'd practically thrown herself on him and had all but begged for a kiss.

"You're just my bodyguard." She said the first thing that came to her mind. "Of course I have no thought of kissing you. Why would I?" She inwardly winced at the hurtfulness of her words, but she was desperate to scramble out of the awful hole she'd fallen into.

"Good." He pulled himself to his full height. His features were hard and businesslike.

"Maybe you're the one with the problem of self-control. Not me."

He didn't deny her accusation, and she took a small measure of satisfaction in it.

"In fact"—she couldn't stop herself—"maybe if you're having trouble controlling your desires around women, you should consider whether you're in the right profession."

He pressed his lips together, clearly wanting to say something in his defense but denying himself.

She bent down and retrieved her blanket, trying to hide her trembling fingers. She wrapped the soft cover around her shoulders, and then, without another word, she crossed the sitting room into her bedchamber and closed the door.

Only then did she crumple into a heap on the floor. A sob burned in her throat. "Oh, God." She cupped a hand over her mouth. "What have I done?"

Chapter 6

$\mathcal{T}$om checked the new carriage for the eighth time, noting the solidness of the wheels, the fact that every bolt was tight, the interior free of any hazardous objects. The coachman waited on his seat, attired in the new white suit the Cole's had purchased for him. The horses had been brushed earlier so their white coats glimmered in the morning sunlight and matched the white of the carriage.

"Five minutes until departure," Tom said. If Victoria didn't make an appearance in the next two minutes, he'd have to go back in and retrieve her.

Davis gave a shaky laugh and repositioned his white top hat. "I feel like I'm driving a princess today."

A princess indeed. Tom ducked his head underneath the carriage and pretended to examine the axle. Victoria had looked every inch the princess when he'd peeked inside a few minutes ago. In fact, she'd looked so beautiful, she'd stolen his breath away. He hadn't been able to look her in the eyes for fear she'd see the truth there. The truth he'd been trying hard all week to hide behind brusqueness.

The truth was he'd wanted to kiss her that evening in her sitting room. His gut had twisted when he'd had to stand back and watch Nathaniel kiss her. And after Nathaniel had left, he hadn't been able to resist belittling the kiss. He shouldn't have. He was ashamed of himself for doing it. But at the time, a strange need had prodded him, until he teased Victoria right into his arms.

He withdrew his head from underneath the carriage, but not far enough. He bumped it against the edge, and pain pierced his skull.

Served him right. He deserved to be strung up from a tree. Shot through the heart. Tarred and feathered. And then dropped into the ocean with stones tied to his ankles.

He'd almost kissed Victoria Cole. He'd been a second away from it. Mere inches from her lips.

Only the sight of her trusting expression had stopped him. She'd trusted him over the past month to protect her, including from himself. If he'd kissed her, he would have destroyed that trust. As it was, he'd destroyed every ounce of goodwill and friendship he'd formed with her. She loathed him now. Had hardly spoken to him the rest of the week. And for good reason.

He'd been almost cruel to her. He'd had to. In order to hastily rebuild the walls between them. Sure enough, he'd only had to be an idiot for a minute before she'd erected the barricade as fast and as high as she possibly could.

Why had he allowed the carefully constructed barrier to come down between them in the first place? How had it happened?

He pressed a hand against the sore spot at the back of his head. But the pain there couldn't compare to the pain in his heart. And the regrets. He'd started off his job as Victoria's bodyguard determined to maintain the proper boundaries. But somehow, somewhere he'd slipped up.

"That's why I only take jobs for older married women," he muttered. His instincts had told him to flee when he'd first discovered he'd been hired to protect a pretty young lady like Victoria. But he'd ignored them, had believed he'd had enough inner strength.

But apparently he'd been too proud of his abilities. Didn't the Bible say, "Pride goeth before destruction, and a haughty spirit before a fall"?

Well, he'd fallen alright. In a big way.

He'd learned his limitations. No more younger women. Only old ladies from now on.

The morning after the incident, he'd gone to Mr. Cole and given his resignation, effective immediately. Mr. Cole had narrowed his eyes and asked him why. Tom hadn't been able to give him the real explanation. He wouldn't think about bringing even a hint of a blemish to Victoria's reputation. So he'd told Mr. Cole his family needed him.

It hadn't exactly been a lie. He'd received the telegram from his sister last week letting him know she and her husband had left Race Point Lighthouse because Greg had developed consumption and was too sick to work. They'd had to leave Mom and Dad alone, and they'd asked him to fill in until an assistant keeper could be found.

Of course, he'd had no intention of going out to the lighthouse and being the assistant. But he'd telegrammed Ruth and told her not to worry. He'd find someone to help Mom and Dad. He'd had inquiries out all week.

After the explanation, Mr. Cole had been understanding of his resignation. But he'd pleaded with Tom to stay until

Victoria's wedding. "Victoria needs you," Mr. Cole had said. "You know I won't be able to find someone else on this short of notice. And you and I both know she's in danger. It's not a matter of *if* the attacker will strike again. It's a matter of *when.*"

Victoria needs you.

Mr. Cole was right. If someone was intent on sabotaging the wedding, they would strike again. So he'd told Mr. Cole that he'd see Victoria safely to the *Independence* in New York Harbor the day after her wedding, and then he'd be done.

The door opened and several maids clustered together, one holding Victoria's arm, another arranging her veil, and still a third carrying the long train. Victoria stood at the threshold, and Tom made the mistake of looking at her.

Again, as before, his breath snagged in his chest. There were no words to describe the vision she made in the layers of silk and tulle. All he knew was that he'd never seen anyone or anything more beautiful. The dress fit her to perfection. Her hair was piled in cascading ringlets. And a strand of pearls circled her neck accentuating the creamy smoothness of her skin.

She took several steps outside, moving into the sunshine. But at the sight of the carriage, she halted abruptly and recoiled.

"Did you forget something?" the servant holding her arm asked.

"Yes, I..." Victoria's eyes had a wildness that reminded him of a soldier facing the point of a bayonet. Her gaze darted back to the house as if she were planning to bolt back inside and lock the door behind her. Was she having doubts about the wedding?

For a second, Tom was tempted to let her run, let her flee to her room, lock the door, and jilt another groom. That would be just fine, because as far as he was concerned, Nathaniel wasn't right for her. He was too doting, too sweet, too easy on her. She needed someone who would stand up to her, challenge her, and make her a better person.

She took another step backward, causing the maid holding the train to stumble and nearly fall.

Yes, she should have figured out months ago that she needed someone different, someone stronger.

Her gaze darted around with growing panic, her expression stricken. From the stiffening of her arms and firm set of her chin, he could sense she was about to turn around and run. And all he could feel was relief.

But just as soon as the unexpected emotion wafted through him, a bolt of guilt punched him in the gut. He had no right whatsoever to find any satisfaction in her insecurities. If he was half a man, he needed to go to her, soothe her nerves, and ease her fears.

She pivoted so that she was fully facing the front of the Cole beach house. Even though Victoria referred to their Newport home as a cottage, the three-storied stone mansion resembled a castle with its tall front turret and long windows and crenellations.

"Wait!" He bounded toward her. She hesitated, which allowed him to catch up with her and block her path so she couldn't retreat. He waited for her to push him aside and stride around him with anger flashing in her eyes—anger that had been there often this past week.

But instead, her eyes were wide and frightened.

"Victoria," he began, not knowing quite what to say, except that he had to reassure her somehow.

She waited as though everything hinged upon what he had to say. He could tell her to walk away, that Nathaniel wasn't right for her, and she'd do it. But deep down, he knew that he couldn't be the one to dissuade her.

"You'll be all right," he started again. Before he realized what he was doing, he reached for her arm and gripped it firmly, hoping to give her some of his strength. She glanced at his hold and he quickly released her. He had no right to touch her. He simply needed to encourage her. "You can do this. You're strong enough."

She searched his face, all of her doubts out in the open for everyone to see. Fortunately, only her three maids and coachman were witnesses of this moment of insecurity. From the anxiety wreathed on the faces of the servants, Tom had no doubt they were well aware of Victoria's wedding day history and were afraid she was about to repeat it.

"Nathaniel is a good man, Victoria. And he loves you."

She nodded, but the movement lacked conviction.

"He'll take care of you. And give you the kind of life you deserve."

She stared at him a moment longer before the stiffness began to ease from her shoulders, and she released a long breath.

"You can do this," he said again holding out his elbow.

She gave him a wobbly smile and hooked her hand around his arm.

"Ready?" he asked.

"Okay."

Delicately, as though she were made of fine lace, he escorted her down the front walkway to the waiting carriage. He swung open the door and started to help her inside when she paused. "Thank you."

He nodded and attempted to keep his expression from reflecting the swell of melancholy that was rising within him.

She climbed inside and sat on the bright red velvet cushion. He stepped aside to allow her maids to situate her train and the folds of her skirt. The carriage gave a sudden lurch that sent two of the maids toppling to the ground.

Tom assessed the teams. Nothing seemed amiss. Before he could move, the carriage began to roll forward.

"Hey!" Tom called. "We're not ready."

Davis didn't turn. Instead he slashed the reins and urged the horses to move faster.

The maid still inside with Victoria gave a cry as she fell back against the opposite seat. The carriage door was unlatched and swung open and closed.

"Davis!" Tom yelled again. "Give us another minute."

At the sight of the coachman, Tom's pulse careened. The man driving the carriage wasn't Davis. Although he wore a white suit and top hat identical to Davis's, the man's shoulders were thinner and his wrists showed beyond the coat sleeves, unlike Davis, whose suit had been tailored and fit to perfection. Beneath the hat, this man's hair was an inch longer and a shade lighter.

"Stop!" Tom called, but the horses were already galloping forward and picking up speed. Without waiting to make sense of the situation, Tom sprinted after the carriage. He couldn't let anything happen to Victoria. He had to stop the imposter before he got away.

Tom forced his legs to move faster, but the gap between himself and the carriage widened. The driver glanced briefly over his shoulder, giving Tom a glimpse of hard-set features, a thin nose, gaunt cheeks, and a long forehead. He didn't recognize the man from any of the places he'd been with Victoria over the past month. But from Arch's sketchy description of the man who'd attacked him, Tom had a feeling they were one and the same.

The man slashed at the horses with more force, but with a corner up ahead, he'd have to slow the carriage or risk toppling it. Tom glanced around for residents or servants who might be able to help him, but unfortunately, the large estates with sprawling yards were deserted. Everyone was already at the church awaiting Victoria's arrival.

He sucked in a deep breath and ran harder. His heart rammed against his ribcage in tempo with his hard slapping footsteps. Without slowing his chase, he dislodged the small pistol he wore strapped beneath his vest. He didn't want to shoot. But he would if he had to.

As the carriage neared the corner, Tom eyed the terrain at the bend—two willow trees, one long hitching post, and four boulders. If the carriage turned over and Victoria or her servant fell out, they could easily hit one of the barriers. And at that speed, the blow could be deadly.

Victoria needed to close the door.

As if she'd heard him, she grabbed the swinging door and poked her head out.

"Close it!" he shouted.

She leaned out further, her veil flapping in the wind. The carriage hit a bump, causing her to lose her balance. If not for the maid grabbing Victoria's arm, she would have fallen out.

The corner was fast approaching, and the driver showed no signs of slowing down. Panic spurted through Tom. "Get back inside, Victoria! Now!"

Hanging on with one hand, she lifted her other into the air.

Tom squinted. She was holding something. Was it her shoe? Before Tom could shout further instructions, she flung the item, which was indeed one of her wedding slippers. She missed the driver by a league. In fact, she couldn't have been further away from him than if she'd purposefully thrown the shoe the opposite direction.

"Get in and close the door!" he yelled again, irritated at her for her dangerous stunt. She was already in enough danger without dangling halfway out of the carriage.

Once again, rather than listening to him, she leaned out and lifted her arm in readiness to throw. She flung her other shoe toward the driver. And this time, much to Tom's surprise, the pointed slipper hit the man in the back. The impact startled the driver so that he jumped and knocked his hat loose. He fumbled after his falling hat, but in the process, he leaned too far to the left and jerked the horses that direction. The movement propelled Victoria back inside the carriage and thankfully slammed the door closed behind her.

Instead of careening dangerously around the corner, the horses continued straight, running off the road and narrowly missing one of the willows. Swerving between two of the boulders and continuing across a lawn straight through a flower bed, the driver yelled curses at the team as he attempted to bring them back under control. The grass and dirt did their job to slow down the carriage, but the frightened horses were no longer responding to the driver's frantic efforts to direct them back onto the road. They rumbled past a stately home and clattered down a small hill that led to the beach, picking up speed in the process.

As soon as the wheels hit the sand, the vehicle slammed to a halt. At the unexpected force, the driver flew off and landed on his back near the horses, which were straining to move forward and kicking up sand. But the carriage was stuck and wouldn't budge.

Tom raced to catch up, but he was already spent and his lungs burned from the effort of running. He watched in frustration as the driver scrambled to his feet and started to sprint away. Thankfully, the man's feet sank into the sand, slowing his progress. Even so, by the time Tom neared the edge of the beach, the driver had already reached the neighbor's yard and was disappearing around the side of the house. Tom hesitated for only a moment before deciding to follow the driver. If he lost the man, he'd have no way of getting valuable information that could tell him who was behind the attacks, and why.

Out of the corner of his eye, he saw the carriage door open and Victoria fall out onto the sand. She had her hand cupped over her mouth and nose, but blood dribbled between her fingers and streaked the front of her wedding dress.

At the sight of her blood, Tom's own blood ran cold.

Immediately, he spun around. His feet couldn't carry him fast enough through the sand. When he reached her side, he dropped to his knees. "Victoria." His breath was ragged, and he could hardly speak past his air-starved lungs. "Where are you hurt?"

From the amount of blood, he guessed she'd hit her nose. She wasn't favoring any limbs, which hopefully meant she'd hadn't broken a bone.

He jerked his shirt out of his trousers and ripped off a swath of linen. Then he moved Victoria's hand out of the way, used the fabric to stanch the flow, and pinched her nose closed.

She winced.

"Sorry," he said.

"It doesn't hurt too much." Her voice was nasally.

But his apology went deeper than the nose bleed, especially as the reality of what had happened began to sink in. Victoria had almost been abducted. And it was his fault.

"This shouldn't have happened." In the hot sand with the

sun beating down on him, sweat trickled down his back.

"I fell against the opposite seat," she said.

The maid hadn't fared as well. She was sitting in the doorway. From the way she cradled her arm, Tom suspected she had a fracture.

He could only shake his head in frustration. "I should have noticed that man wasn't Davis."

Victoria pushed Tom's hand away from her nose and took the ripped piece of his shirt from him. "He looked exactly like Davis. None of us noticed."

"I should have. That's my job." How had he missed it? His powers of observation were usually so keen. What had caused him to make such a terrible mistake?

She dabbed at the blood still flowing from her nose. "Don't blame yourself. At least I'm free. And you scared him away."

He'd been captivated by Victoria when she'd come out of the front door, and he hadn't been paying attention to the carriage or Davis at that point. He'd been admiring her instead. Then she'd started to run away, and he'd been distracted while trying to calm her down.

Inwardly, he groaned. He'd let his personal feelings and interactions affect his ability to do a thorough job for his client. Just as he had the night he'd almost kissed her. This time his ineptness had been disastrous. Victoria could have been taken away to only God knows where and held for ransom. Or worse.

"Let's look on the bright side." Victoria smiled tremulously. "I'm perfectly fine, and once my bleeding stops, we can make it to the church without being overly late."

He raised a brow. He hadn't expected her to want to continue on her way to the wedding so soon. He figured he'd have to send a messenger ahead and let everyone know about the delay and, more specifically, inform Mr. Cole about what had happened. "Your maid needs medical attention first."

"Yes, of course." Victoria gave the woman an apologetic smile.

"And I'll need to find someone to help me pull the carriage back to the road."

Victoria nodded. "Very true."

"While I do that, you can clean up and put on a different dress."

A frown creased her forehead. "A different dress? That's absolutely unthinkable." She glanced down to the white satin that had pooled around her. Then she uttered a cry as she took in the blood that streaked through the tiny pearls sewn into the bodice. Against the unblemished white, the red stains were vibrant. There was too much blood to hide with quick cosmetics. In fact, she was covered with so much blood, it looked as though she'd just come off a battlefield. He'd seen enough during the war to know.

"My dress is ruined," she wailed, spreading out the material even as more blood dripped from her nose onto the skirt. She buried her face in her hands as though she couldn't bear to see the dress a moment longer. "And now my wedding is ruined too."

"It doesn't have to be."

"It is," she said into her hands. "It's utterly and completely ruined."

"We can postpone—"

"I thought this time with Nathaniel, I could do it. I really did," came her teary voice. "But I should known it wouldn't work. I should have known I'd end up doing something to ruin it." Her sobs were muffled but heart-wrenching.

Tom sat back on his heels and wiped the perspiration off his forehead. He was accustomed to crying women. He'd been around theatrics and tantrums and drama as long as he'd been a bodyguard. But this was different. She wasn't putting on a show or attempting to manipulate him. Her pain was genuine and went deep.

He watched her, unsure what to do. She didn't need his platitudes or promises. And she didn't need to hear all his doubts, especially that he hadn't thought Nathaniel was right for her in the first place.

All he could think to do was lay his hand on her back. At his touch, she leaned into him and pressed her forehead against his chest. Her body shook with sobs. He knew he should set her away from him or, at the very least, help her stand and walk back to the grassy embankment. But with the warmth of her body so near, with her tears soaking into his shirt... He hesitated for only a moment before pulling her close and wrapping his arms around her.

She melded against him, and he held her, knowing he shouldn't. But he was helpless to do anything else.

Chapter 7

$\mathcal{V}$ictoria leaned against the closed door of her father's study. She shouldn't be eavesdropping, but after saying goodbye to Nathaniel, she hadn't been able to ignore her father and Mr. Cushman's voices deep in conversation, discussing all that had happened earlier in the day.

Mr. Cushman had been relaying details about the investigations he'd done that afternoon. He'd attempted to follow the perpetrator's trail, had gone into town and asked around, had visited all the haunts where a criminal might hole up. He'd even questioned Davis several times. But the coachman hadn't seen the attacker who'd knocked him out before climbing up and taking his place. Mr. Cushman had found Davis hidden under a hedge, unconscious and bleeding from a head wound.

Now her father and Mr. Cushman were talking about a letter that had been placed on the front step of the house only an hour ago. She trembled at the thought that the kidnapper was still on the loose and might try to come after her again.

"Do you think the letter and this morning's attack are

related?" her father asked.

"Yes." Mr. Cushman's voice was low and earnest. Victoria could picture him sitting in a chair across the desk from her father, his shoulders straight and stiff, the muscles in his jaw flexing, and his brows slanted in frustration. "Which means we can't have the wedding tomorrow."

Victoria had been so convinced earlier that she ruined everything again. That perhaps she was the one sabotaging her attempts at getting married. That her fears were rising up and causing all the problems.

When Nathaniel had reassured her that none of day's events were her fault, she'd wanted so badly to believe him. He'd promised her that any dress she chose for the wedding would be sufficient, that he didn't care what she wore. And he'd very gently and sweetly convinced her to reschedule the wedding for tomorrow.

The tables and chairs and decorations for the wedding breakfast were all still set up on the spacious veranda at the back of the house. The guests were still in town. Mother had insisted that the flowers could be put in water and preserved.

Even now her mother was down in the kitchen speaking with the cook about what could be salvaged from the food they'd prepared for today and what would need to be remade. Already, her mother had hired several more cooks who were willing to work through the night to prepare another lavish feast for the wedding guests.

"We have to postpone," Mr. Cushman insisted.

"But if I hire a few extra guards, plan a different route—"

"It would still be too dangerous."

When her father didn't contradict Mr. Cushman, Victoria guessed the threat that the letter contained must be serious.

Mr. Cushman lowered his voice so that Victoria had to

press her ear against the keyhole to hear him. "I suggest putting Victoria into hiding."

Her father didn't respond. She guessed he was sitting back in his leather desk chair, his hands pressed together at his chin, and pondering Mr. Cushman's advice thoughtfully. Finally, her father spoke in the same low tone as Mr. Cushman. "For how long?"

"A month should be enough to find the attacker."

"And how do you propose to do that?"

"Arch has offered to search for him. If he can't track him down, we'll bait him." The words were spoken so softly she almost didn't hear him. She didn't understand exactly what Mr. Cushman intended, but the deadliness of his tone made her shiver.

Again, her father was silent in contemplation. "Do you have any suggestions for a safe hiding place? One of my horse farms? Perhaps my home in Chicago? Or do you think Europe would be best?"

"None of those. It can't be any place connected with you."

What if she didn't want to go into hiding? Did either of them consider that? Surely they were exaggerating the seriousness of the situation.

But even as she attempted to stay positive, the memories of the dangerous ride down Ocean Drive came crowding back. The terrifying moment of not knowing who had captured her, where he was taking her, or what he would do to her. The terrible feeling of helplessness. One look into the maid's frightened eyes had spurred Victoria to try to do something to save them while she still could. Of course, Mr. Cushman had scolded her severely for leaning out the carriage and throwing her shoes, but he had reluctantly admitted that the distraction had likely saved them.

"I have a place I can take her," Mr. Cushman said. "Where no one will find her until I'm ready for them to."

"What do you have in mind?"

The voices faded to whispers for several moments, and she sighed in frustration.

"And you'll be chaperoned?" her father's question was barely audible, but his concern was loud enough.

"Yes..." Mr. Cushman hesitated. "But Victoria will have to pose as my wife."

The suggestion was so unexpected that Victoria sucked in a breath.

"No," her father replied. "That's taking things too far."

"An unmarried man and woman traveling together would stand out. We'd be much easier to trail for anyone who might search."

That made sense. If he acted as her bodyguard, his usual protective demeanor and habits would likely draw too much attention to them. But if they were disguised as a married couple. . .

Warmth coiled in her belly at the thought. Rationally, she knew that he wouldn't have suggested it if there were any other feasible plan. Even so, the idea of spending a month with Mr. Cushman pretending to be his wife sounded deliciously appealing.

Another silence stretched in her father's office, during which her mind spun with all the possibilities, particularly the thought of Mr. Cushman doting on her and calling her sweetheart and spending time with her, not in the background as her bodyguard. But always next to her side. As her husband.

"No," her father said again. "I don't want to put her reputation at risk. I have nothing against you, mind you. You're a fine young man. But if anyone discovered the plan, they could spread rumors, and then she'd ruin her chances with Nathaniel."

"He loves her enough to go along with it."

"Maybe. But I don't think she'd be willing to go to such extreme measures."

"Let's ask her."

"Very well," her father responded.

"You can come in, Victoria," Mr. Cushman said.

Victoria jumped. How had he known she was standing outside the door listening? She put her hand to the knob and opened the door a crack.

Her father glanced up in surprise. "Have you been listening to our conversation?"

"I'm sorry, Father." She slipped through the door and closed it behind her. "I shouldn't have. But when I heard you talking about me..."

The familiar scent of leather and chamomile enveloped her as she stepped into the dark paneled room that served as her father's office when he was in Newport. It was smaller than his other offices but had an enormous picture window that gave him a spectacular view of the ocean. The sun was beginning to set and had left the sky streaked with clouds of pink and purple over the calm water. A few distant sailboats and yachts were taking advantage of the calm summer evening. Even a coal barge hauled by tugs passed in the distance. A gentle breeze was blowing through the open window, bringing the sound of the constantly lapping waves.

Her father and Mr. Cushman both stood while she crossed the room and positioned herself in the chair next to Mr. Cushman's. When the men had reseated themselves, she folded her hands in her lap and tried to control the unexpected tremor in her fingers.

"Would you be so kind as to inform me of the newest threat contained in the letter?" She looked pointedly at the sheet that lay on the desk in front of Father. She caught a glimpse of the scrawled handwriting before he grabbed the paper and folded it.

Father shook his head. "I don't want to worry you."

"It's another kidnapping threat," Mr. Cushman replied. Father scowled at Mr. Cushman, but he continued, unperturbed. "Victoria needs to know the truth about the danger she's in. The more she knows, the better she'll cooperate."

In the fading evening light, Father's handsome face contained a haggardness that Victoria hadn't seen there before. He studied Mr. Cushman through narrowed eyes for a moment before nodding. "Very well, Mr. Cushman. Go ahead."

Mr. Cushman met her gaze, and the seriousness within his dark eyes reminded her once again of the gravity of her predicament. "We believe the note is written by the man who attempted to kidnap you today. He says he'll get you the next time. And that if anyone tries to come after you, he'll hurt you."

Her ready response died on her lips. *Next time?* Was her attacker already planning another abduction? "Do you think he'll try to kidnap me again tomorrow?"

"Yes."

She appreciated that Mr. Cushman was always straightforward, never mincing words. But every once in a while, she wished he'd soften the blow. She swallowed the lump of fear forming in her throat. "If we know someone is lying in wait, then we can hire more guards."

"It's not worth the risk."

Her father nodded in agreement. "Once I inform Nathaniel of this newest threat, he'll gladly postpone the wedding. And in the meantime, Mr. Cushman thinks you need to go into hiding."

"Yes, I heard," she said. "We're to pretend to be married."

"You don't have to do it, Victoria," her father interjected, "if you don't want to."

She tried to gauge Mr. Cushman's feelings regarding the plan. Did he want to pose as her husband? Did he find the idea as secretly thrilling as she did?

His expression was impassive, as usual.

Her father gave a tired sigh and sat back in his chair. "We will attempt to minimize any repercussions that might come from such an arrangement, but you should know there is some risk of soiling your reputation."

Heat stole into Victoria's cheeks, and she glanced at her tightly folded hands. "I understand, Father."

"Nothing will change in our working relationship," Mr. Cushman cut in. "I'll maintain strict and appropriate boundaries at all times."

"If nothing changes," she countered, "then no one will believe we're married."

Mr. Cushman hesitated only a moment before nodding in agreement. "Very well. We'll pretend in public, but resume our regular interactions in private. I'll still be your bodyguard and you my client."

Her father nodded his approval.

"Then we shall be actors?" Victoria liked the thought. She'd always imagined it would be fun to be in a play. She was sure she could do justice to her role.

"Yes."

"Where will we go?"

"I'm not telling anyone except your father. It'll be safer that way." He looked at Father, who nodded his acquiescence.

Maybe their destination would be somewhere new and exciting, like Philadelphia. She'd heard the shops there were quaint and the gardens spectacular this time of year. Perhaps they could go to the theater together. She'd take some other name like Marie or Meredith. Marie Cushman. She rolled that name around her mind and then tried Meredith Cushman. Which one sounded better?

"You can tell me where we'll stay," Victoria insisted. "I promise I won't say anything."

"So you're willing to go into hiding?" Father asked.

She nodded. "Do I need to wear a disguise? Dye my hair? Buy new clothes?"

"No," Mr. Cushman said. "We can't draw any undue attention."

"And when shall we leave?"

"We'll sneak out early in the morning, before light."

The plan was getting more exciting by the minute. She smiled and moved to the edge of her chair. "That means I need to get busy packing my trunks."

"One bag." The steel in Mr. Cushman's voice stopped her. "With only your plainest, most serviceable clothes."

She started to protest, but the silent plea on Father's face stopped her. He was asking her to trust Mr. Cushman and listen to him. "Very well." She could always purchase new garments and accessories once they reached their destination. That would be much more fun anyway.

Perhaps he was taking her to Boston. She'd heard there were several excellent French seamstresses there. She'd thoroughly enjoy having some new designs.

She rose to leave. She had a lot to do if she was to be ready by the early morning.

"You'll need to act normal and go to bed," Mr. Cushman

instructed. "Don't tell anyone about our plans. Not even your mother."

She stopped mid-stride.

"I'll inform her in the morning," Father reassured.

"But I'd like to say goodbye."

"You can't this time." Mr. Cushman was rising from his chair.

"She'll understand," Father said. "And so will Nathaniel."

Nathaniel. In the flurry of the new plans, she was ashamed to admit she hadn't thought of attempting to say goodbye to him. She hadn't considered how he might feel, not knowing her location or how she was faring.

The slight quirk of Mr. Cushman's eyebrow told her he'd guessed her oversight.

She lifted her chin in defiance. "I really must say something to Nathaniel."

"No." Mr. Cushman's tone was stubborn. "Not a word."

"That's not fair to him."

"Your father can explain everything."

"He deserves to hear it from me." She pressed her hands into her hips. "At the very least, I will write him a note telling him goodbye."

"A short note. But without any hint of our plans."

"Very well." She sniffed and crossed the room to the door.

"Your acting career starts now," Mr. Cushman said. "Pretend you're still upset about the delayed wedding."

She stiffened at his subtle insinuation. "I won't have to pretend. I am upset."

When he didn't say anything else, she made a grand exit, closing the door heavily behind her. Fuming, she stomped down the hallway.

That man was so irritating at times.

She'd prove to him she could handle anything that came her way during the next month. She'd also show him she loved Nathaniel. In spite of all of the obstacles, she still planned to marry him. Eventually. Didn't she?

Chapter 8

At four o-clock in the morning, Victoria was wide awake. The truth was, she'd been awake all night and hadn't even tried to sleep. The chilled air coming off Newport Bay caused her to shiver beneath her silk shawl. Or perhaps it was the excitement of her impending adventure.

The sky was still black with night. A few lingering stars and a half moon provided some light as she walked ahead of Mr. Cushman down the gangplank to *Lady Caroline*, a luxury steamboat her father often chartered. It was the only vessel lit up among the many others docked at the private marina.

The lap of the waves and their footsteps echoing against the wooden planks seemed especially loud at the early hour. But it wouldn't be long before the air would be alive with the sounds of area fishermen readying their sloops and heading out to catch the mackerel, butterfish, and even squid that she loved to eat every summer. The lobster fishermen would be rowing out too, in their dories, manning their boats and setting their traps.

Mr. Cushman still hadn't informed her of their final destination, even though she'd interrogated him on the short ride
over. All she knew was that her father was waiting to say goodbye at the steamer.

As she stepped on board, Mr. Cushman reached for her
arm and steadied her. He didn't speak but guided her with the
pressure of his hand toward the lounge. Thick tapestries hung
in the windows, but a sliver of light emanated from a gap
where one of the curtains had been pulled slightly aside.

The gentle sway of the boat and the rumble of the steam
engine below her feet only added to her sense of adventure.
Even though she was running away under dire and dangerous
circumstances, and even though she knew she should be sad
that she was leaving Nathaniel behind, she felt strangely free.
She breathed in deeply of the damp sea air and relished its
coolness against her cheeks.

Mr. Cushman rapped twice on the lounge door and it
swung open immediately to reveal her father. He pulled her
into the elegantly furnished room, and Mr. Cushman quickly
shut the door behind them. She was surprised to see they
weren't alone. Her father's longtime friend Judge Baker was
sitting at a glossy oak table and rose at the sight of her.
Although he was older than her father, with silver hair and a
short clipped beard and mustache, he was every bit as
distinguished.

"There's been a slight change of plans," her father said
exchanging a glance with Mr. Cushman. "Would you like to
tell her or shall I?"

"Go ahead, sir." Mr. Cushman had placed their bags on the
floor near the door and now stood stiffly surveying each
window and door.

Her father cleared his throat. "We feel it's in everyone's

best interest if you and Mr. Cushman actually get married instead of merely pretending."

"What?" Her knees nearly buckled at the news. She fumbled for a chair, but Mr. Cushman beat her to it. He pulled one out and helped her sit. The chandelier above the table swayed, making her feel even more off-kilter.

"I know it's rather strange and sudden," her father said, "but we've talked this through for the past few hours and have decided that the disguise will work best if you're married rather than pretending."

"But what about our futures? Nathaniel—"

"The marriage will be in-name only," Mr. Cushman explained and her father quickly nodded. "At the end of the month of hiding, we'll get an annulment."

"Judge Baker has drawn up the terms," her father interjected. "Mr. Cushman has already signed a legal and binding agreement that stipulates he'll walk away from you without a making a single claim to your fortune, either now or in the future. And if he does so, he'll be subject to prosecution."

She glanced from one man to the next until her gaze came to rest on Mr. Cushman's grave face. "I don't understand why it's necessary to get married when our acting married would suffice."

Her father spoke before Mr. Cushman could. "The marriage certificate will allow Mr. Cushman to stay with you wherever you go, especially if anyone should question your liaison."

"But who would question it?" she persisted. She wasn't opposed to the idea of marrying him for a month. Not really. Not if they would get an annulment at the end and no one would ever be wiser to their ruse. Even so, she didn't understand the proposal, or the fact that her father was so willing to go along with it considering all the implications a temporary marriage could have if anyone ever found out.

Weary lines had formed at the corners of her father's eyes, and the angular lines in his aristocratic face were hardened with frustration. "Whoever is making these attempts on your life will be looking for a wealthy, single woman. Not someone who's married. So if getting married temporarily will help save your life, then I'll consider anything to protect you, Victoria."

But wasn't marriage sacred? How could she enter it lightly, even for her protection?

"Where we're going," Mr. Cushman added, "we have to be married or I could get myself and others into a great deal of trouble."

"Then let's find a different place to hide," she suggested.

"We've considered every feasible option." Her father sighed as though in defeat. "And Mr. Cushman's hiding place is the best and safest of them all."

She was quiet for a moment, her mind racing with a thousand thoughts. She trusted her father's judgment. He'd clearly agonized over how to keep her safe. If he thought a temporary marriage was the best plan, then she had to accept it. She reached out for her father's hands and squeezed them.

Her father pressed a kiss against her fingers. "You're the most precious gift your mother and I have. We don't want to lose you."

She smiled tenderly at him. "You know I'll do whatever you and Mr. Cushman believe is in my best interest."

Before she knew what was happening, Judge Baker had pushed a piece of paper and pen in front of her. She signed her name where he indicated. Then he passed the paper to Mr. Cushman who did the same. The judge pronounced them man and wife, and they were done. The whole affair took less than a minute, and she felt completely unchanged as though it had never happened.

Her father and the judge didn't linger. Her father shook Mr. Cushman's hand. "Take good care of her," he said gravely. "If you break your promise to keep everything professional and proper, you'll wish you'd never met me."

"You have nothing to worry about, sir. She's absolutely safe with me."

Her father wrapped her into an embrace. "Be a good girl for Mr. Cushman."

She mimicked Mr. Cushman's confident assurance. "You have nothing to worry about."

"I mean it, Victoria. Promise you'll behave, stay out of trouble, and not do anything that might compromise your reputation."

She kissed his cheek. "I promise."

By the time the sun had risen, Victoria and Mr. Cushman were well on their way into Buzzard's Bay.

The boat was deserted except for the captain in the pilot house and a couple of crew members below in the boiler room. "I figured it out. We're going to Boston," she told Mr. Cushman as she reclined on one of the cushioned deck chairs in the shade.

He leaned against the rail watching the paddle wheel rhythmically spraying water and didn't reply except to turn his attention upon her.

"Shall I call you by your given name now that you're my husband?" She batted her eyelashes at him in an attempt to lighten the mood.

He didn't blink an eye.

"Since you're so enthusiastic about it," she said, "then I shall take that as my sign to do as I please."

"I think you would do as you please whether I'm enthusiastic or not."

She smiled.

His hand was stuffed into his trouser pocket and from the movement, she could tell he was twisting something around and around. She'd never seen him nervous before and the thought that he might be even slightly worried about their travels today made her sit up.

"We'll be safe, won't we?" She hated that her voice caught.

He nodded. "Your father paid the pilot and crew handsomely to stay silent." His features were more somber than she'd ever seen them.

"Then what's bothering you?" she asked.

He removed his hand from his pocket, crossed to her, and held something out. As she took it, she realized it was a simple gold ring with a tiny engraving of roses at the front. "You'll need a wedding band," he said. Without waiting for her to slip it on, he returned to stand at the rail once again, his back and shoulders stiff as he peered out over the water.

She knew she shouldn't be hurt by his abruptness, that their marriage was in-name only and would be over in a month. Even so, she couldn't hold at bay the doubts that came creeping back in. What if God didn't want them to play at an institution meant to be revered? Was Tom having doubts too?

When they docked in Bourne, they boarded a stagecoach. She'd expected the coach to take them north along the coastal road to Boston and was surprised when, after only an hour or so, they stopped in the small town of Sandwich.

They purchased tickets and headed up the gangplank of another steamer, this one a far cry from the private luxurious boat they'd ridden on that morning. Not only was it small, but the white paint that hadn't yet peeled away was a dirty, smoky gray. The deck was warped in places and some of the rail slats had fallen away. She was taken aback further when Tom led her down the steps to the boiler deck filled with children running around, babies fussing, and parents attempting to manage the unruliness. She started to protest and insist that Tom take her upstairs to nicer accommodations, but he ushered her to an empty spot, claiming that the crowded area was the best place to hide.

Before she could argue with him further, an older couple took the bench across from where she sat. The man unrolled a newspaper from under his arm and began reading. not seeming to notice her and Tom in the least. However, his dour wife, attired in all black, apparently decided that she and Tom were to be her entertainment for the afternoon. The woman stared openly as Victoria instructed Tom to fetch her shawl from her bag. When Victoria proceeded to ask him to close one of the windows because of the draft, the older woman pursed her lips as if she didn't believe in men doting on women.

"He's such a good husband, isn't he?" Victoria held up the wedding ring Tom had given her on the *Lady Caroline*. "We just got married."

The woman's brow quirked skeptically. "Is that so? I would have guessed he was your manservant."

"Oh no," Victoria said quickly. She obviously wasn't playing her role believably enough. Although Tom had doted on her, he'd been much too silent and aloof, always on duty, noticing everyone and every detail. Even now, he was standing next to their bags, his feet braced and his arms crossed. Indeed, he looked more like her hired help than her husband.

Victoria stretched to reach his hand. "Come sit down and relax, dearest." At first he began to pull away, but she tightened her grip on his fingers and forced a smile. "This woman doesn't believe you're my husband," she said under her breath. "We certainly can't have her thinking that, can we?"

Tom glanced at the woman, who was now looking at him cynically. Her hair was pulled back into a tight bun and her lips pinched tightly, making her look like a severe school teacher who would rap their knuckles for the slightest infraction. He hesitated only a moment longer before sitting on the bench next to Victoria. Even then, he kept a proper distance between them and relinquished her hand.

Victoria had to refrain from elbowing him. She wasn't an actress by any means, but she'd been to enough theatrical productions over the years that she wasn't completely ignorant. If they were going to convince anyone they'd just been married and were on their wedding trip, she would have to do the work herself.

She scooted closer to Tom and reached for his hand again. This time she laced her fingers through his. "Don't mind him," she said to the older woman. "My devoted husband is prone to sea sickness. As a matter of fact, his stomach is always queasy whenever we go sailing. The last time we were on my father's yacht, he had a little accident. He ate too much shrimp and decided to put it all back into the sea. If you know what I mean."

The woman's eyes widened, and this time she coolly assessed Victoria, staring at her hat, which was rather plain with only a few ribbons and flowers, and trailing down her serviceable traveling outfit. When Tom had come for her earlier that morning, he'd told her the gown was too fancy for the trip but hadn't made her change, since they'd been in such a hurry. She'd tried to explain that the lavender outfit was one of her oldest from last summer season. She was rather appalled to be wearing it and had only managed to don it by reminding herself that it was merely a disguise. Not one of her acquaintances would ever suspect that she would wear something so outmoded, and now Victoria prayed this older woman didn't know enough about fashion to tell she was a fraud.

Tom squirmed against her hand, but she grasped it more firmly. "Yes, my darling has such a weak stomach. He can't stand the smell of poached eggs. He goes green in the face every time our cook makes them."

Tom suddenly jumped to his feet and tugged her up after him. He plastered on a false smile for the older woman. "Will you excuse us for a minute?" Without waiting for the woman to respond, Tom propelled Victoria toward the nearby window that he'd closed for her. Once they were a safe distance away from the couple, he hissed through his fake smile. "What do you think you're doing?"

She smiled too brightly in return and whispered back. "I'm trying to pretend we're married. Which is more than you're doing."

"Sailing? Yacht? Shrimp? Cook?" His eyes flashed with anger. "You might as well just tell her your father is the wealthiest man on the East coast."

Her retort died. She supposed she had given too much away. "You're right. I need to act poor."

Tom's smile grew more forced. "Just sit quietly."

"She's growing suspicious." Victoria chanced a sideways glance at the woman, who was still staring at them. "She doesn't think we're married. She thinks you're my hired help."

He raised his brow. "I *am* the hired help."

"But we still need to act our roles around other people."

"Then let's be a couple who's been married for a while and

doesn't like each other anymore."

"You did hear me tell her that we just got married, didn't you?"

The strong lines in his jaw flexed, and he took a deep breath. Then before she knew what was happening, he pulled her into an embrace. Not just any embrace, but a full body hug, his arms wrapping around her and pressing her against his long torso.

"What are you doing?" She pushed away, but he held her tight.

"Acting," he whispered. "Now hug me back."

She didn't waste any time arguing, not that she particularly wanted to. She slipped her arms around him and rested her head against his chest. For a man of his power and strength, he exuded a tenderness that was unexpected. Yesterday she'd been too frightened and upset to consider exactly how it felt to be in his arms. But today she was all too aware of his presence, his nearness, the pressure of his body against hers.

His hands were on her lower back. She was conscious of each finger touching her, as well as the hard contours of his back beneath her hands. The steady rhythm of his heartbeat echoed against her ear, and she caught the faint scent of bay rum from his aftershave lotion.

He moved his hands to her hips and shifted her away enough so that he could look into her face. Something in his eyes sparked a fire in her belly, and again she was sensitive to his fingers, almost as if they were brushing her bare skin instead of layers of skirt. Then he laid on her a grin so devastating that her body began to melt and her knees weakened, swaying her toward him.

Speechless, she allowed him to lead her back to the bench, where he sat next to her and draped his arm across her shoulders.

The older woman hadn't taken her sights from them during the entire exchange, and now she watched, her eyes growing rounder by the second.

Under normal circumstances, Victoria might have smiled in amusement. But with Tom's arm brushing the back of her neck, she couldn't think of anything else, especially when his fingertips skimmed her shoulder. She wasn't sure if he'd done it on purpose or not, but the touch sent tingles down her arm.

He leaned into her and, in the process, tipped her hat up. Before she could react, he angled his head and brought his mouth near her ear. His breath was warm and caressed her neck so exquisitely she bit her lip to keep from gasping. When his lips pressed against the hollow part of her ear, she couldn't prevent a soft cry of pleasure from escaping.

He pulled back and straightened in his seat.

Embarrassment coursed through her at her reaction to him.

He glanced at the older woman, whose mouth now hung open. "Lover's quarrel. But we've made up."

Then he smiled so innocently and beautifully that the woman's pale face began to color under his charm. She closed her mouth and fumbled at the clasp of the bag sitting at her feet. She dug inside and retrieved two knitting needles attached to a skein of black yarn. She plopped it onto her lap and began to knit with rapid clicks.

Victoria couldn't move, could hardly breathe.

When Tom leaned into her ear again, her lungs constricted in anticipation of his touch. The tip of his nose brushed a curl dangling by her cheek and his lips grazed her ear, sending a tremor through her. "Is my acting good enough now?" His whisper was barely audible.

She could only nod, afraid her voice might come out too squeaky or breathless. He was a *very* good actor. For a brief moment she half-wished he wasn't pretending, that he really meant every touch and caress. But as soon as the wish came, she was mortified with herself for so easily forgetting about Nathaniel.

Nathaniel. By now Father would have delivered her letter. The one she'd written last night after she'd sent her maids away. What had started as a simple goodbye had turned into so much more. Even now, she cringed at all she'd written and prayed she hadn't made a huge mistake. She'd told Nathaniel she needed to break off their engagement, at least for the duration of their separation. She'd assured him she loved him, but that she needed time apart to test whether she was really ready for marriage. Quite honestly, she didn't know if the month of separation would be long enough to determine her feelings.

In the meantime, she wasn't being fair to ask him to wait for her, and she'd given him the freedom to move on, if that's what he wanted to do. She supposed now that she was legally married to Tom, breaking off the engagement was the right thing, at least temporarily. After all, who'd ever heard of an engaged married woman?

Even though she'd broken her engagement, she hadn't planned on forgetting about Nathaniel. Especially so easily.

She squirmed on the bench, but that only made her aware of Tom's thigh pressed against hers. While he sat so nonchalant and seemingly unaffected by her nearness, she wasn't sure how she could endure the rest of the steamer ride in such close proximity to him.

At a popping on the deck overhead, the muscles in his arm rippled against her shoulder. He glanced toward the stairway that led to the upper deck. The seriousness in his eyes told her that he was worried about her safety.

He stretched his arms casually above his head and then stood. "I need fresh air."

She nodded, still too flustered to speak.

He took a step away but stopped and brushed her shoulder as though he had every right to caress her whenever he wanted. "Stay here."

She nodded again.

He disappeared up the stairs, and after he was gone, she felt strangely alone. She hadn't been without him at her side in public for the last month. He'd never been more than several feet away. If a man had dared to abduct her with her bodyguard standing beside her carriage door, what might someone attempt with him well out of sight?

Her attention shifted to a man in a shabby suit several benches away. He'd pulled out a pocket watch and was staring at it with tired, glassy eyes. Then her gaze darted to one of the other men, who was lying down on his bench, his hat covering his face, his chest rising and falling with slumber.

Her mind told her that Tom wouldn't have left her alone if he hadn't already assessed every person in the room and deemed her safe. He'd probably guessed each person's occupation, place of residence, and reason for traveling. If anyone had been the least threat, he wouldn't have budged from her side. Even so, she shivered, in spite of the warmth of the room.

He returned a few minutes later, making his way through the crowded deck toward her, dodging children and carpetbags. When he lowered himself onto the bench, she was more relieved than she wanted to admit. Even though he didn't say anything, she could see from his expression that whatever had happened didn't involve her, that she was safe.

Although he took the spot next to her, he didn't touch her again. She couldn't deny she was disappointed. She'd rather liked the playacting. But she also realized how easily his merest touch affected her and that she'd need to be careful not to take things too far. Beside she'd promised Father that she'd do her best to behave. After all, she wanted to be able to walk away from this situation after a month with a clean conscience. And of course, Tom had promised her father that he'd keep their relationship professional. No matter what they did when they were acting, they had to remain faithful to their promises.

When the steamer finally docked and they disembarked, Victoria came to an abrupt halt halfway down the gangplank as she took in the little town before her. It contained none of the factories, big businesses, and bustling seaport trade of a large city. "This isn't Boston."

"You're stopping traffic." Tom took her elbow and guided her the rest of the way down.

Numerous long piers lined the waterfront along with all varieties of sailboats and sloops, some with sails raised and others empty and deserted. In addition to the piers, wharves and fish houses were built out over the water and were filled with rack after rack of fish laid out in the glaring summer sun.

As a gust of wind blew against her, so did the overpowering odor of the fish. She pressed a handkerchief against her nose to keep from gagging. "What are they doing with all the fish?"

"Salting and drying it." Tom tugged her along the pier toward the sandy beach. "The salted cod used to be sent to sugar plantations in the West Indies as the basic food supply for slaves there. Even after slavery was abolished, it's still remained the primary occupation and source of income here."

"Where exactly is *here*?"

"At the top of Cape Cod in Provincetown."

"Provincetown?" Beyond the busy waterfront, the town was quaint and pretty in a smallish sort of way. A tall steeple of a church rose above the roofs of plain clapboard homes, most painted white. Still others were constructed of the typical cedar, which was more resistant to the weathering and rot that came from being located on the sea.

A main road led away from the waterfront and wound through what appeared to be a downtown area with a few stores but certainly not a busy metropolitan full of shops, taverns, and people.

It reminded her of some of the Midwestern towns she'd stayed in when she'd gone with her father to visit his mining and lumber holdings in Michigan. Although she'd enjoyed being with her father and exploring a new region of the country, she'd been grateful when her father had shortened their itinerary because he'd missed seeing Mother. The small towns just hadn't appealed to her.

"We can't possibly stay here," she said.

"We're not."

"Well, that's a relief."

Tom guided her out of the flow of others disembarking around them. Once they were on the beach, he put their bags down and studied the piers to the east as though he were looking for someone.

The summer sun was unrelenting, and the treeless beach didn't provide a spot of shade. The heat from the sand soaked through the thin leather of her shoes and through the layers of her bodice. Her parasol and fan were both in the bag. And her stomach was beginning to rumble after having gone without a meal since the simple breakfast she'd had on the *Lady Caroline*.

She glanced again toward the town, hoping to spot a restaurant or some place they could go to get out of the sun. "Since we're here, we may as well explore the town," she said, trying to remain optimistic while fanning her face with her lacy handkerchief.

"There's no time." Tom waved at a stooped shouldered man who was in the process of rolling up a fishing net. "Wait here."

Without waiting for her to respond, he strode down the beach. She couldn't stop herself from admiring his long, purposeful stride and the muscular build of his body that his suit didn't hide. When he stopped to talk to the fisherman and motioned back at her, she quickly looked away, hoping he hadn't caught her ogling. Instead, she feigned interest in several fishermen in another boat shoveling piles of silvery fish into crates, although the very sight made her stomach churn.

Thankfully, Tom didn't speak to the old man long before turning and trotting back to her. "We're all set." Beads of perspiration had formed on his forehead beneath the rim of his hat. Evidently, he was hot, too.

"Let's go get something to drink," she urged. "Perhaps a cold glass of lemonade? Wouldn't that be lovely?"

He was already picking up the bags, but he paused and regarded her, his brows slanted in empathy over his lusciously dark eyes. "I'm sorry, Victoria. It's best if we keep to ourselves. The more people who meet you, the more suspicion we'll attract."

"But we're not staying here."

"It's close enough." He started back to the stooped shouldered fisherman.

But she didn't move. She had the sinking feeling he wasn't planning to take her to Boston or Philadelphia or any other big city where she could amuse herself with new activities and events. In fact, she had the horrible suspicion he wasn't taking her anywhere near civilization.

"Tell me where we're going first," she said.

His steps halted. His muscles visibly tightened, and then he turned, his expression rigid and ready to do battle. "We're going with a friend in the cutter."

"Where is he taking us?"

"Somewhere you'll be safe."

"I've willingly gone along with your plans all day. But I'm not taking another step until you tell me exactly where we're going."

Tom glanced at the group of fishermen in the nearby boat. They leaned on their shovels watching her interact with Tom and were silent except for the creaking of their dock line and the slapping of the waves against the hull.

With his jaw rippling—likely from the effort it cost him to stay silent—he crossed the distance back to her. "You're causing a scene." He spoke through gritted teeth. "Just come with me."

"No." She attempted a stomp of her foot, but the effect was lost in the sand. "I should be consulted on the final travel arrangements."

He clamped his lips together, a motion that said quite loudly that he wouldn't divulge anything.

"I'd much prefer to be somewhere more metropolitan and exciting than a small town in the middle of a sandy desert." She waved around at the sandy cliffs and dunes that rolled endlessly down the coastline. "Even if it happens to be a friend's lovely cottage or resort, I'm not a country girl."

"You'll adjust," he whispered with a nod at the fishermen who were still staring.

She knew she needed to stop drawing attention to herself, but the cockiness of Tom's attitude irked her. "You can't take me somewhere I don't want to go."

"Don't make me pick you up and carry you."

"You wouldn't dare."

"Try me." The hard set of his features told her he would indeed, and that if she didn't want to be totally humiliated in front of everyone, she'd have to get in the waiting boat, whether he answered her questions or not. She had no choice but to go along with him for the time being. But that didn't mean she couldn't make arrangements to leave once she got there.

With a sniff, she started down the beach, holding her chin as high as she could and hoping to maintain some of her dignity, even though she was tired and hot and frustrated. When she reached the boat, she was momentarily taken aback by the small size of the old, rusty vessel.

"Jimmy," Tom said behind her. He'd raised his voice as if his friend were hard of hearing. "This is my wife."

Wife. The word startled her. If she hadn't been fuming, she might have liked the way it sounded.

The old fisherman smiled, revealing a mouth devoid of most of his front teeth. His leathery face crinkled like a well-worn pair of gloves. But his eyes were kind. "Very pleased to see Tommy finally has a bride. And a fine one at that."

"Thank you," she replied, giving him a friendly smile. After all, it wasn't his fault she was in this predicament.

Tom placed their bags in the boat and then reached out to assist her. But she ignored him and climbed down by herself, which was no easy feat, considering the fact that her feet tangled in her train, causing her to plop ungracefully onto the middle bench. She straightened her skirt around her, pretending that she made an everyday occurrence of flopping into boats all the while praying that neither of the men had noticed. When she peeked up from under the wide brim of her hat, unfortunately both were watching her. They exchanged a look before Tom nodded at the stern. "I'll row in the back."

"You're coming back?" Jimmy asked.

"No," Tom spoke louder and emphasized each word. "I'll row in the stern."

Jimmy waved a hand. "Naw. No need to row. She's ready to sail."

Tom climbed in and helped Jimmy with the rigging. Once the foresail filled with wind and they were underway, Tom clambered over the coils and bags and sat on the bench next to her.

She ignored him and focused on the endless blue of the bay that spread out on one side of the cutter and the sand cliffs and heathlands that made up the coast on the other. It was pretty in a wild, untamed way, but suddenly she was too tired to care. After having been up all night and now having traveled all day, she was exhausted, especially with the sun baking her.

"We're going to stay with my parents," he said. The wind and the spray of the waves captured his words, and she wasn't sure if she'd heard him correctly.

"Your parents?" She swiveled to face him.

He was staring off into the distance at a point of curving land. "My dad is the head keeper at Race Point Lighthouse."

All of her protest from earlier dissipated. For a reason she couldn't explain, the idea that he was taking her to his home seemed so sweet and personal and trusting. "I didn't know your father was a light keeper," was all she could think to say.

"I grew up living in lighthouses."

The revelation made her realize how little she knew about

him. She was ashamed to admit most of their conversations and interactions had revolved around her life. She supposed she'd been so consumed with her wedding plans that she hadn't thought about much else. Plus, he'd always kept himself aloof, had clearly been dedicated to doing his job with the utmost professionalism. But now . . . Well, maybe she'd have more opportunities to get to know him better.

"So you must be glad to be going home." She brushed a loose strand of hair out of her eyes. The breeze had picked up in intensity and had thankfully grown cooler. The sails flapped overhead, and although Jimmy was steering them further out into the bay, the coast was still well within sight.

"My mom and dad are great people."

He'd avoided her question. "But you don't like Race Point?"

At her persistence he looked at her. "Every time I visit, I like it well enough."

"Then you've never lived there yourself?"

"No. Dad's only been there since '70. I haven't lived at home since before heading off to war in '63."

She did a quick mental calculation and realized that if he were in his late twenties as she suspected, then he'd only been a boy when he'd left, probably no older than fifteen or sixteen. What had he done in the war at that age? Certainly he hadn't fought, had he?

Before she could pry further, he spoke. "I've taken the post as assistant keeper at Race Point."

Oh. Now his plans began to make sense. "So we're hiding there under disguise as the assistant keeper and his wife?"

Tom nodded. "My sister Ruth and her husband were helping. Greg was the assistant. But I got a telegram that he had to leave. His consumption has worsened."

"I'm very sorry."

"He's getting treatment. But he probably won't be able to go back. The climate's too damp."

"So you're taking over?"

"Temporarily. Which is why we had to make things legal."

"And why is that?"

"If the inspector visited and discovered that we weren't legally married, I'd put my father's career in jeopardy."

He'd mentioned the inspector earlier, and now she finally understood. Her mother, having grown up in lighthouses, had told Victoria about the surprise visits inspectors often made to ensure that a lighthouse was operating smoothly and in top-notch condition.

A wave swelled against the bow, and the boat rose and fell with a splash. She clutched at the bench to keep from toppling forward. A cool mist fell like rain droplets upon her, salty but refreshing.

So he was taking her to live in a lighthouse. She mulled over the thought for a moment, tasting it much like the sea spray—unexpected but not entirely unwelcome.

"My mother lived in lighthouses, too," she said. "Her father was a retired sea-captain turned lighthouse keeper."

"Yes. Your grandfather was well respected."

She wasn't surprised Tom already knew that information about her since he seemed to know everything else. "I always enjoyed visiting him, although it wasn't often." He'd passed away three years ago, and she'd never expected that she'd ever visit a lighthouse again.

"Then you'll resign yourself to hiding at Race Point?" he asked.

"It's not my preference, but I shall try."

"Good."

It would certainly be a world apart from Boston or Philadelphia. But she could survive a month there, couldn't she? She loved seeing the inner workings of the lantern and the view from the top of the tower. Although she wouldn't have nearly as much to do, the lighthouse would hopefully be stocked with books, so she would get plenty of reading time. Surely there would be cards for games. Maybe she could practice her sketching. She'd had lessons several years ago and had found that she was actually quite good at it, a talent she must have inherited from her mother, who'd filled sketch books before she'd gone blind. And if she grew too bored or restless, perhaps she could convince Tom to take her to Boston for a few days. Surely he'd be willing to do that.

As Jimmy sailed around the bend of Provincetown Harbor, the wind and the waves increased in intensity. The cutter rose on the swell of another large wave lifting her from the bench and threatening to wrestle her hat from her head in spite of the pins. Tom slipped his arm around her middle and held her firmly against his side. Once again she was conscious of the pressure of his body against hers, the hold of his fingers on her arm.

The roar of the wind and the crash of the waves made any further talking difficult. She was content to rest against him, knowing she was secure, even though the waves seemed to engulf the little boat.

When a distant tower began to come into sight, Tom's arm around her began to relax. The conical tower was made of brick and painted white with a wide black lantern room at the top. It wasn't as tall as the last lighthouse her grandfather had operated, but she could see that it was a solid structure over forty feet tall. It sat well away from the shore amidst low growing shrubs that apparently were able to thrive in the arid soil.

Next to the lighthouse, but not connected, stood a large keeper's house, likely roomy enough for two families, the keeper's and his assistant's. The red shingles on the roof contrasted the white of the house, making for a bright spot of color amidst the endless waves of wind-sculpted sand dunes. Two other small structures sat nearby, and Victoria guessed one to be the oil house and the other a fog signal house.

"Remember," Tom said as the boat drew nearer the shore. "We need to act like we have a real marriage."

She pulled back slightly to see his face. "Will we really be able to convince your parents?"

He was staring straight ahead, his expression rigid. "We have to try."

"Don't you think they'll see through our charade?"

"Not if we're good actors."

"We're bound to slip up from time to time," she said. "I think we'd be better off admitting the truth to them."

"If they discover the true nature of our relationship, they won't let us stay together."

At his insinuation, she fidgeted with her skirt.

"They're God-fearing people," he continued. "They have strong ideas about what marriage should be like. If they learn I'm only married to you temporarily as part of my job, they wouldn't consider the union valid. They'd insist that I find another place to live."

"Where would you go?"

"There's nowhere else. And even if there were, it's my job to watch over you."

"True." He was still first and foremost her bodyguard.

"Besides," he said, "it's safer if everyone believes we're happily married. Then we won't have any accidental slipups."

She hesitated. It was one thing to act in front of people they would never see again, like the older couple on the steamship. But his parents? She didn't have a good feeling about deceiving them. But what else could they do? "Very well. If you really think we should."

He nodded as if the matter were settled. "We need to get our back ground information straight."

As Jimmy guided the boat toward a nearby pier, Tom rapidly outlined the story of how they'd met and gotten married. He'd been introduced to her in Europe when she'd been visiting. They'd carried on a correspondence over the past year. When he'd returned last month, they'd gotten engaged. They'd had a simple, small wedding. Now they planned to help at the lighthouse until Tom got a more permanent job.

As the fabrication deepened, so did Victoria's discomfort. She didn't like the idea of lying, but if Tom thought it would keep her safe, how could she argue?

The door of the keeper's house opened and a man exited. He tugged his hat down further on his head and started down a path through the sand dunes that led to the waterfront.

"If they ask about my parents," she asked her nerves fraying, "what should I tell them?"

"Fortunately, my parents won't know anything about your father or any other millionaires. I'd be surprised if out here they even know who's president."

"So I can be free to share about my past with them?"

"Within reason." His gaze was sweeping over the lighthouse, the keeper's dwelling, and the surrounding grounds, seeing and assessing everything. "As hard as it will be, try not to mention Nathaniel, especially the fact that you're engaged."

He was goading her, reminding her of her flimsy

connection with Nathaniel. Rather than defending herself, she responded vaguely and succinctly. "I won't, since I'm not." As the words sank in, his gaze swung to hers, and his eyes widened. "I broke it off last night in the letter I sent Nathaniel. It wasn't fair to keep him waiting this month."

"So you only broke it off for the month?"

"For now. That gives me time to discover my true feelings, doesn't it?"

"Maybe."

Before she could read his expression and judge his reaction, he stood. Jimmy was steering the boat alongside the pier, and Tom stretched to help. Within minutes, the boat was secured opposite another cutter and Tom was helping her onto the pier surrounded on both sides by a narrow beach. Scalloped seashells poked through the sand. In some places slimy seagrass had washed up on shore and dozens of gulls now poked among the stringy masses searching for their next meal.

"Tom?" The man who'd come out of the house was striding through the sand with the same ease as Tom.

Tom lifted a hand in greeting. "Hi, Dad."

The man picked up his pace. Beneath the brim of his black bowler hat, Victoria could see that his face was tanned and leathery from days out in the sun. It was clear Tom had inherited his striking features from his father. Even with a scruffy beard and side whiskers, Tom's dad had a handsome face with the same dark blue eyes. He was smiling in genuine delight at the sight of his son.

"You said you'd visit, but we weren't sure when," Tom's dad said as his boots clomped against the wooden planks of the pier.

"I wasn't sure either." Tom stuck out a hand in greeting, but Mr. Cushman ignored his son's hand and instead grabbed him into a hug, slapping his back and then squeezing him tight.

"It's good to see you." Mr. Cushman pulled back, and his face practically beamed. "Two years is too long."

Tom hadn't seen his parents in two years? Victoria almost choked. Why had he chosen to visit so infrequently? She studied Mr. Cushman again, noting his waders, his brown trousers, and coat just a shade darker. Both were worn and faded, unlike Tom's clothes, which were always clean and pressed and like new. She'd never once noticed Tom being anything other than perfectly groomed, which she supposed was one of the reasons he was good at his job. He looked professional and dignified enough to fit into a wealthy crowd.

"It's good to see you too, Dad." Tom straightened his suit coat lapels before holding an arm out to her. For an instant she caught a glimpse of vulnerability in his eyes, something of the child he might have once been, a child who'd wanted desperately to please his parents but had been unsure how. With a sudden desire to make him proud, she took his arm and moved to his side.

As she did so, Mr. Cushman's brow rose.

"I'd like to introduce you to, Victoria." Tom's bicep flexed beneath her hand. "My wife."

First astonishment and then wonder flashed across Mr. Cushman's face. "Your wife? Well, I'll be..." He took a closer look at Victoria, starting at her hat, which was surely in disarray by now from the wind during the boat ride, and then taking in her travel garments. She wished she'd had time to change into something clean and new and pretty.

Nevertheless, she offered him a smile. "I'm pleased to meet you, Mr. Cushman."

As though remembering his manners, he smiled in return. "Call me James. I'm pleased to meet you too, Victoria. You'll have to excuse me. I'd lost hope that Tom would ever consider getting married. So to have him show up here with a bride... Well, it goes without saying that I'm more than a little shocked."

Victoria tucked away that new nugget about Tom to quiz him on later. For now, she had the urge to convince Tom's dad that she was worthy of his son, that Tom's wait had been worth it. "I guess Tom just hadn't met the right woman until he met me. I came along and swept him off his feet." She curled her fingers more intimately around his arm and attempted her most flirtatious look. "Didn't I, darling?"

From the glint in his eyes, she thought he might contradict her, but his words came out smoothly. "Yes. Completely."

"I'm happy for you both," James said with a grin. "So very happy." With that, he reached for Victoria and drew her into a hug. She hugged him back, relishing his easy acceptance. His beard was scratchy against her temple and had the spicy hint of tobacco. He was about the same height as Tom but decidedly not as muscular. When he turned to hug Tom again, Tom accepted the congratulations, although not quite as enthusiastically as she had.

"Your mother will be thrilled," James said, patting Tom on the shoulder. "You'll make her the happiest lady in Massachusetts."

At the thought of deceiving Mrs. Cushman, guilt swooped in and poked Victoria like a seagull pricking its prey. If the marriage would make Tom's mom that happy, then she would be devastated when she learned of the annulment. From the flicker of a shadow on Tom's face, Victoria guessed he was feeling the same guilt.

James didn't neglect to greet Jimmy or invite him to stay for dinner, which the old man agreed to do just as soon as he secured his sails. He refused Tom's offer of help and shooed them away. As they made their way up the beach to the keeper's house, Victoria caught sight of a piping plover resting in the dune. The sandy-colored shorebird blended in so well, that Victoria might have missed it except for the black ring around its neck and black band across its forehead.

Tom steadied her with a slight touch to her elbow as they followed James. The man more than made up for Tom's lack of conversation with a steady stream of news about Greg and Ruth and all that had led up to Tom's brother-in-law having to finally give up the assistant keeper's position.

When they reached the house, Victoria admired the hydrangea bushes that had been planted across the front. The white flowerheads were in full bloom and clustered into big puffy balls. After crossing a simple porch, they entered through the door into a wide hallway. She followed Tom and James into a front room with a window that overlooked the ocean. Ruffled white curtains were pulled back with ties on either side, and the walls were painted white, giving the place a clean, airy feel. Several beautiful paintings hung around the room, paintings of lighthouses and the sea.

Near the window at a round pedestal table sat a thin, petite woman. Her legs and lap were covered with a crocheted blanket, in spite of the warmth of the day. Her brown hair was graying, but her face was delicate and pretty. A well-worn Bible lay open on the table in front of her. At the sight of Tom, she gave a cry of delight and held out her arms. "Tom! You're home!"

He cut directly across the sparsely furnished room to her, bent, and wrapped his arms around her. "Hi, Mom."

Mrs. Cushman held onto him as though she never planned to let go. Victoria smiled at the tender reunion. Out of the corner of her vision, she caught James wiping at his eyes, clearly moved by his wife's happiness.

Finally, Mrs. Cushman released Tom, but not before kissing him on the cheek. "You look taller."

Tom grinned. "You say that every time you see me."

James walked to his wife's side, and, much to Victoria's surprise, he stooped down and kissed her. Not a quick peck. Not a chaste brush of lips. But a full-mouthed kiss that was long enough for Victoria to look away in embarrassment. She happened to glance at Tom at the same moment he peeked at her. He lifted his shoulders as if to tell her this was normal.

James pulled away and pressed a kiss upon the top of his wife's head before straightening. "Tom has some good news."

Mrs. Cushman's cheeks had turned a deeper shade of pink that made her look younger and in love. Her eyes sparkled as she looked at her son in anticipation.

Tom cleared his throat and then held out a hand toward Victoria. She took that as her sign to cross toward him. As his fingers closed around hers, she felt the tiniest of tremors. He was nervous.

She squeezed his hand to reassure him, although again she had a twinge of remorse for allowing his mother's hopes to rise high, knowing they would crush them at the end of the month.

"Mom." Tom's grip tightened. "This is my wife, Victoria."

Mrs. Cushman's mouth opened and then closed. She stared first at Victoria and then Tom, her expression frozen with disbelief.

"That's right, Zelma." James's wide smile filled his face. "Our Tom finally got married."

"Married?" She said the word as if it were an impossibility.

"Yes, just recently," Tom said quickly as if he needed to reassure himself as much as his mom.

Mrs. Cushman turned her bright eyes upon Victoria, eyes that seemed to peer straight into Victoria's soul.

Victoria held her breath, wondering if Tom's mom could see her for the fraud that she was. But the woman only smiled at her gently. "Victoria." The one word was laced with welcome and acceptance, and Victoria knew immediately that she'd love Zelma. She held out her hand and Victoria took it.

Zelma, like her husband before her, drew Victoria into a hug and held her tightly. "You're most welcome here, Victoria," Zelma said. When Victoria straightened, she decided that she was going to enjoy her stay at Race Point much more than she'd thought possible.

"You're very kind," Victoria said, and then she embarrassed herself by yawning. She managed to cover it, but not quickly enough.

"Your wife is tired," James said to Tom, almost with a note of accusation in his voice.

"We've had a long night and day of travel," he replied.

"Why don't you take Victoria upstairs?" his mother said. "She can refresh herself and rest before dinner."

Victoria realized she was so weary she could hardly stand. Somehow she managed to excuse herself from Tom's parents and follow him up a stairway. Another long hallway ran through the length of the second floor, with two bedrooms on either side. She supposed two were for the keeper and two for his assistant. The room Tom led her to was at the front of the house facing the ocean and had a large double bed, a tall chest of drawers, and a sofa in front of the window.

The walls were painted a light shade of blue. White ruffled curtains like those in the big sitting room downstairs hung at the windows, and a matching white bedspread covered the bed. A couple of paintings graced the walls, and, like the others she'd seen, these were of the sea. Although the room was small and rather plain, it was pretty and clean. She could survive a month in it, couldn't she?

Tom issued her several instructions, but she was too tired to pay attention. After he left and closed the door behind him, she sat on the edge of the bed, worked off her shoes, and rolled down her stockings, letting them fall in balls on the floor. She wiggled her cramped toes and realized that sand was gritted between each one. She searched the wall for a pull cord, a way to call one of the servants to bring her a basin of water for washing, but as she stretched, she fell back onto the mattress.

The breeze blowing through the open window tousled the loose tendrils of her hair and cooled her cheeks. She closed her eyes, telling herself that she would rest for just a moment, that she had nothing to worry about here at Race Point, that she was finally completely safe. But as her eyelashes hit her cheeks, her thoughts returned to Tom and their marriage. And she couldn't keep from thinking that perhaps her heart was in the greatest danger of all.

Chapter 9

$\mathcal{T}$om knelt on the floor of the lantern room and scrutinized the bridge, to which the chain was attached. He tightened the small screw that held the upper end of the chain until it wouldn't budge. Then he slipped the small weights in the plunger through the opening at the top plate. "That ought to do it."

His dad squatted beside him and peered into the pedestal. He held up an oil light to shine on the various gears and weights that made the fourth order Fresnel lens operate. He squinted at the plunger that Tom had just replaced before sitting back on his heels. "Well, let's turn her on and see how she does."

Tom stood and wiped the grease from his hands as he studied the beehive-shaped lens with its heavy glass prisms mounted into bronze frames and bolted together. The lens itself was in perfect condition. Dad had kept it shining like a diamond. But without Greg's mechanical help, some of the inner workings were beginning to give Dad grief.

The fuel supply was already refilled and the wick trimmed. His dad raised the damper-tube and lifted the chimney-holder to the surface of the burner the way Tom had seen him do thousands of times during his childhood. Next his dad touched the flame to the wick and then adjusted the chimney and the damper-tube to prevent any smoke. He kept the flame low at first to heat the chimney slowly. He'd gradually raise the wick until the flame was at its best, but he usually waited about thirty minutes before doing so.

The beam rotated all the way around, which distinguished Race Point from other lighthouses on the Cape. Tom counted the seconds it took for the beam to rotate, flashing white every ten seconds, and calculated the distance it would reach to passing ships. He guessed sixteen nautical miles. The view from the lantern room, as always, was breathtaking, especially with the setting sun casting its glow on Cape Cod Bay to the west.

Tom breathed the cool sea air coming in through the half-galley door. He might fight ghosts from the past whenever he was around his family, but he couldn't deny that he always loved being up in the tower.

His dad laid a hand on his back. "It's wonderful to have you here, son."

Tom nodded. He loved his parents. But being with them reminded him that he'd killed their firstborn son. Maybe he hadn't plunged the knife into Ike's heart. But he'd been the cause. Even more than his regrets over Ike's death, he couldn't bear to witness what his foolishness had cost his mom. It was too awful to see, and every time he came home, there was no escaping the pain.

"Thanks for coming to visit. I know it's not easy." His dad's voice was gentle.

"It's good to see you and Mom." They never made him feel guilty about Ike. But how could they not blame him?

"How long will you be able to stay?"

Tom had always cut his visits short in the past which had always disappointed his parents even though they didn't say so. At least this time he would please them. "I'm your new assistant."

His dad's expression went from guarded to wide-eyed in an instant. "My assistant?"

"For the short term."

"Assistant?" His dad repeated as though he hadn't heard Tom right.

"Yes."

A grin split his dad's weathered face. "How did this come about? And why didn't the inspector send me a telegram?"

Tom had made the arrangements last evening with the inspector via several telegrams. The inspector had been glad to fill the position with a qualified man. But of course, Tom couldn't tell his father the truth about why he was really there. "I agreed to fill in until the inspector could find someone permanent."

His dad studied his face. Could the wise man sense more to the story than Tom was admitting? "That's fine. Very fine. I'll take you as long as you're available."

"I didn't want you to be alone."

"We've managed. Your mother never complains. Even though I'm not the greatest cook in the world."

"You made a good meal tonight."

His dad chuckled. "I didn't burn it."

Tom couldn't fault his dad for much, if anything. He'd been a good father and was an excellent husband. He hadn't deserved so much tragedy.

They fell silent and stared out the window at the fading orange glow on the horizon. The distant crash of the waves reached out to soothe Tom and the guilt over his deception with Victoria that had been nagging him since he'd hugged his mom.

"Victoria is beautiful," his dad said quietly.

"Yes, she is," Tom admitted, although it wasn't hard to do. He thought back to the picture of her asleep on the bed when he'd gone in to let her know dinner was ready. He'd tried to wake her, but she'd rolled away from him, deep in slumber.

"I always knew that when you got married, you'd attract a pretty woman."

Was Victoria attracted to him? He didn't think so. She might flirt with him once in a while. But that's the way she was with men. "Guess I take after you. You always said Mom was the prettiest girl you ever met."

"That's true. She still is the prettiest girl I ever laid eyes on."

Tom nodded. His dad had always spoken of his mom with the highest praise. In fact, Tom couldn't remember ever hearing his dad speak a negative word about her.

"Victoria seems like a nice girl," his dad pressed.

"She's very sweet." Again the admission was easy. Victoria might be spoiled and self-centered. But she had a good heart.

"I pray that God will bless you with the kind of marriage that your mother and I have."

Even if his relationship with Victoria had been genuine, he didn't see how it would be possible to have the kind of marriage his parents had. He'd seen few like theirs. But he said the words he knew his dad expected. "Thanks, Dad. I hope so too."

He sensed that his dad wanted to say more, but after a

moment he moved toward the hatch and the ladder protruding from it. "Speaking of your mother, I need to go check on her and carry her up to bed."

Tom's gut twisted at the thought of his dad caring for his mother day after day, especially over the past week without any help or relief from Ruth or Greg. He wished there was more he could do. Perhaps he'd check into hiring a nurse to live with them. For now, while he was there, he'd do all he could.

He took one last look up and down the coast, assured himself that no one was in sight, and followed after his dad. "I'll help you."

Against his dad's protest that he could do it himself, Tom carried his mom up to his parents' bedroom, which was directly across from Victoria's. He helped to situate his mom on the edge of the bed and tried not to notice how much thinner and frailer she was compared to the last time he'd seen her. After kissing her goodnight, he offered to watch the lantern so that his dad could have a night off. But his dad insisted that Tom get a good night's sleep.

Tom crossed the hallway and peeked in on Victoria. Seeing that she was still asleep, he closed the door and backed away. The room he'd given her had belonged to Greg and Ruth. The smaller room at the rear of the house had belonged to their two young children. He could sleep in one of the beds in there. Maybe he could even push the beds together to be able to stretch out more comfortably.

He hesitated.

"Is something wrong?" The question startled him, and he spun to see his mom and dad, both sitting on the edge of their bed, watching him. Dad had his arm around Mom, and she'd leaned her head on his shoulder.

Inwardly, Tom chastised himself for his sloppiness. He should have closed their door on the way out. Even then, he should have made a show of going into Victoria's room like any eager new husband would. He didn't want them suspecting anything was wrong this early in the month.

Instead, he smiled. "Nothing's wrong. I wasn't sure if I should disturb Victoria. She's sleeping so soundly."

"I'm sure she won't mind a little disturbing from you." His dad winked.

The implication brought forth a bucket full of images, especially ones from earlier in the day when he'd embraced Victoria on the steamship and all of her soft curves had pressed against him. When he'd nuzzled her ear, he'd caught the fragrance of hydrangeas and tasted the delectable smoothness of her skin. He may have started off acting, but his body's reaction had put him in a dangerous state of mind. He'd needed to cool off, and so he'd gone above deck for a few minutes.

"Go on in," his mom said with a knowing smile. "I'm sure she'll be glad to have you nearby."

If Victoria awoke and found him sleeping in the same room, she certainly wouldn't be glad. She'd be livid. But what choice did he have now?

"You're right." He smiled again, hoping the smile didn't look as stiff as it felt. "Goodnight."

"Goodnight," his mom replied cheerfully.

"Don't stay up all night." His dad winked again. "After all, I'm planning to put you to work tomorrow."

Tom had never blushed before in his life, but at his father's brashness, his face was on fire. He couldn't seem to find the doorknob and enter the room fast enough. When he was inside, he leaned back against the door and exhaled. Then he couldn't help grinning at the absurdity of his predicament and his parents' comments.

He'd grown up watching his parents kiss and show unabashed affection for one another and had thought that was the way every married couple acted. But now that he was older and more worldly-wise, he realized they had a rare treasure to still love one another so passionately after more than thirty years of marriage.

He never planned on getting married—at least in the true sense. Marriage was out of the question with the kind of life he led as a bodyguard. Even now, he wondered if he'd made a mistake in having this temporary marriage with Victoria. It was just that yesterday, after the kidnapping attempt, he'd panicked. He'd decided that the only place she'd truly be safe was here, at Race Point.

Situated at the northernmost tip of Cape Cod, the lighthouse was completely isolated. Hiking overland from Provincetown was possible. But through the sand and dunes, it wasn't an easy trek. And if someone came by boat, Tom would be able to see them coming long before they arrived at the doorstep. Besides, no one but Victoria's father knew exactly where they were. In fact, Tom hadn't even given the lighthouse inspector Victoria's name and had only referred to her as Mrs. Cushman.

Henry Cole had been reluctant to the marriage part of the plan. He'd likely had concerns about Tom attempting to make claims on Victoria's inheritance or going public with the marriage and ruining his daughter's chances of a future match. But Tom had reassured Mr. Cole that even though the marriage certificate would make their stay at Race Point legal, the document was only a piece of paper and no one else would ever have to know about the arrangement. He'd promised Mr.

Cole the same thing he'd promised him when he started the job, that he'd treat Victoria with the utmost professionalism at all times. Then once the assailant was captured, he'd leave for Europe and wouldn't speak of the temporary marriage ever again. Mr. Cole hadn't needed to make him sign a legal document relinquishing rights to Victoria's fortune and outlining the terms of the separation. Tom wouldn't have ever even dreamed of trying to gain anything from the marriage. But he'd gone along with Mr. Cole's stipulations anyway.

Tom pushed away from the door and crossed to the window. He closed it halfway against the cool night air and then stared outside at the lighthouse beam rotating over the water.

Yes, yesterday the plan had seemed solid. But now, with his parents sitting in a room six feet away and their faces filled with so much hope, he doubted himself. He hadn't anticipated their enthusiasm. What would he tell them at the end of the month?

More importantly, how would he endure the month sharing a bedroom with Victoria?

He glanced at her outline on the bed. The cover he'd draped over her earlier had fallen off her legs. In the faint light coming in through the window, he glimpsed her feet poking out from the tangle of her skirt.

Tentatively, he made his way to the bed. He lifted the blanket back over her feet but couldn't stop from noticing the lovely curve of her ankles. He took in her sleeping form and then rested his attention on her face, the high cheekbones, delicate nose, and dainty chin. Her long lashes fanned against her unblemished skin. And when she gave a soft sigh, his pulse jolted with the memory of her tiny moan of pleasure when he'd breathed into her ear on the steamship. He'd enjoyed that sound way too much and was ashamed to admit he wouldn't mind hearing it again.

"No," he whispered, giving himself a mental shake. He'd given his word to Mr. Cole that he'd respect Victoria. Even though they would have to appear to be a happily married couple for the next month, he'd steel himself for what he must do. As Victoria said, they were acting. He'd just have to make sure that he *only* acted and nothing else.

Chapter 10

The angry grumbling in Victoria's stomach woke her. She opened her eyes, and the first thing she saw was a spider crawling across a cracked ceiling.

With a start, she sat up. Where was she?

At the sight of the light blue walls and lacy curtains, the memories from yesterday came rushing back. She was at Race Point Lighthouse in a quaint keeper's house with Tom's parents. She smiled at the memory of their hugs and sweet welcome. She hadn't spent much time with them, but she'd immediately sensed their warmth and kindness.

With a lazy yawn, she stood and stretched. Her corset pinched her ribs, reminding her that she'd slept with it on. She patted her head and realized that she'd also slept with her hair coiled into the same knot her maids had arranged for her wedding. Large swaths had fallen out and now hung in disarray.

She must have been exhausted from the day's travel to sleep in her clothes all night. But it didn't matter. She'd start the day with a bath and perhaps have the maid wash her hair. It certainly was dusty after all the traveling.

Scratching her head and extracting a loose pin, she crossed to the window. She pulled back the curtain to see that the sun was already high in the sky. From the way the light shimmered above the ocean, she could tell that the day would be a warm one.

She would have to don one of her light cotton garments.

With a sinking heart, she spun to find her lone bag sitting on a cedar chest in the corner. She'd only packed two additional dresses—one traveling suit and one everyday dress. She'd assumed she'd have access to a seamstress and be able to enhance her wardrobe with pretty new outfits and accessories.

But now… What would she do?

She lowered herself to the sofa. Its braided edge was frayed and the blue faded to almost white. She nibbled her lip and stared at her bag. The tip of her wooden driftwood cross poked out, her cross of hope, reminding her to have hope and to find the best in every situation, which she clearly needed to do now.

Perhaps she could send Tom over to Provincetown to locate a seamstress there. Even better, he could telegram one of the well-known seamstresses in Boston and have her visit the lighthouse and create her wardrobe.

In the meantime, she'd have to get by with the two dresses she'd packed. Certainly she could survive a few days. After all, she wouldn't have to worry about any of her friends seeing her.

Her stomach rumbled loudly, and she pressed her fist against her middle to dull the ache. First, however, she needed food. As she searched the room looking for some way to call the maid, it dawned on her that there might not be a maid.

This was a small house and wouldn't require the number of staff that one of her father's homes needed. The Cushmans probably had a single housekeeper who attended to all of the duties.

Victoria sighed. She supposed she would have to get dressed on her own. She'd had to do so in the past when she'd taken the trip to the Midwest with her father. She hadn't relished the experience. But she could do it if she had to.

For several minutes she worked at extricating herself from her dirty traveling gown. When she was down to her corset, she rubbed at the chafed skin on her stomach where the whale bones had dug into her. She wanted to loosen the tight-fitting stays, but she couldn't reach her arms around the back far enough to find the laces. The more she reached, the more the whale bones poked into her.

Finally, with a sigh, she gave up. She'd have to find the housekeeper later and ask her to come up and assist her. For now, she was stuck.

By the time Victoria finished putting on a fresh gown and buttoning and lacing all of the layers, she was over-heated with the effort. She was appalled at how wrinkled the garment was and decided that the housekeeper would have to iron it, perhaps while she was having her bath.

The open window allowed in a breeze, but it was clearly growing warmer and more uncomfortable in the upstairs room. She was too hungry and hot to take the time to do her hair properly. So instead of styling it in the usual coil with ringlets, she settled for brushing out the tangles and pulling it back into a simple knot.

When she finally felt attired sufficiently to leave her room, she made her way downstairs, which was unusually quiet. She peeked into the room at the back of the house and discovered a tidy kitchen with a cast iron stove in one corner, a work table at the center, and a wash basin against another wall. But the housekeeper wasn't in sight, and neither was any food.

Across the hallway from the kitchen was a dining room with a long table that looked like it could seat two families. A vase at the center of the table was filled with a strange collection of dried flowers and grass. A sideboard sat along the far wall decorated with an assortment of tableware, including a white pitcher, oval platter, and a coffee creamer and sugar bowl.

Her mouth watered at the prospect of freshly brewed coffee. Although she hadn't seen a coffee pot in the kitchen, surely the housekeeper wouldn't mind making her a cup.

If she could locate the housekeeper.

She headed down the hallway toward the front of the house and the entryway. When she reached the sitting room, she poked her head in hesitantly.

"Good morning," came a motherly voice. Zelma sat in the same spot at the pedestal table where Victoria had seen her yesterday. Again, her Bible was open on the table in front of her. She smiled up at Victoria and motioned to the chair across from hers. "Come in. I've been waiting to see you this morning. You were sure tired when you got here last night. I hope you slept well."

"I didn't wake up once," Victoria replied, returning the smile and lowering herself across from Zelma. "I didn't sleep at all the night before, and so I guess I really needed the rest."

Zelma's smile widened. "Ah, the life of newlyweds."

At Zelma's conclusion for the cause of her sleepless night, Victoria felt herself flush from her neck to her cheeks. She was too utterly embarrassed to make a sound, much less speak.

Zelma laughed, and the sound was like the tinkling of

silver bells. Victoria couldn't help noticing, as she had last night, that Zelma was lovely. She had very few wrinkles in her creamy complexion. Her eyes were especially pretty and had a youthfulness about them that made Zelma seem too young to have a son Tom's age.

"I'm sorry, dear," Zelma said, reaching across the Bible and capturing Victoria's hand. "I shouldn't tease. Not everyone is quite as open as we are in our appreciation of married life."

Victoria looked at the hand holding hers, the delicate fingers that had veins showing through the thin layers of skin. "I'm still adjusting to being married," Victoria said shyly.

"Did you have time for a wedding trip?" Zelma asked.

Victoria shook her head. "No. Tom was anxious to get here." If she'd married Nathaniel, she already would have been sailing to Europe, likely relaxing in one of the luxury suites on the *Independence*. She'd been looking forward to returning to Europe, had planned what she'd wear and what she'd see down to the last detail. Even if she and Nathaniel ended up getting married later in the summer, she doubted they would be able to make the trip that late in the year.

"Don't worry." Zelma patted Victoria's hand. "I can see that you're disappointed, but I'm sure I can persuade James to give Tom a few days off so the two of you can have some time alone right here."

Oh, my. Once again Victoria flushed. She couldn't even begin to imagine how she and Tom would handle that type of situation under his parents' noses.

"I've embarrassed you again." Zelma gave another light laugh. "Forgive me, dear. I'll try to be more tactful."

Victoria was thankful when Zelma changed the conversation to her daughter Ruth, son-in-law Greg, and their two children. She spoke about how much she missed them and was praying fervently for Greg's health. Then she talked for a little while about the grandchildren, and it was clear that Zelma loved her family dearly.

Finally Victoria's aching stomach prodded her up from the table. "Where might I find your housekeeper?"

Zelma peered up at her with uncomprehending eyes. "Housekeeper?"

"Your hired help?"

"We don't have any hired help, dear. Ruth took care of everything, and my grandchildren worked hard too."

No housekeeper or hired help? Victoria stood unmoving, and her mind spun as she tried to grasp the situation. Without help, how were they surviving? Without help, how would *she* last an entire month?

After a moment, Victoria smiled. She had the perfect solution. Maybe God had brought her here to this forsaken place to solve the problem by hiring someone for them. "Do you know where Tom is this morning?"

"He's outside making repairs on the lighthouse." Zelma reached for the teacup near her and took a sip. "He's been hard at work for a couple of hours, and I'm sure he's ready for a break so that he can spend time with his bride."

Victoria started toward the door with a lightness in her step. "I'll be back in a few minutes."

"Take all the time you need, dear," Zelma called after her.

Victoria let herself out and crossed the porch into the bright morning sunshine. She hesitated on the front step as the heat of the sun touched her face. She ought to go back for her hat or parasol. She'd religiously kept her skin lily white, and she certainly didn't want that to change here. But at the sight of Tom on a ladder working on the lighthouse tower that sat a short distance away, she started down a well-worn sandy path toward him.

The wind coming off the ocean was refreshing. The never-ending lap of the waves against the nearby shore reminded her of her family's cottage in Newport, except that the waves seemed louder here and more constant. Several sandpipers with their skinny legs and long thin beaks waded in the wet sand. In the distance, she caught sight of the sails of fishing boats along with a steamer, its puff of smoke the only cloud in the clear blue sky.

When she reached the broad white tower, she stopped at the base, shielded her eyes with her hand to block out the sun, and looked up at Tom, waiting for him to see her. He was perched at the top of his ladder, a bucket in one hand and a tool of some kind in the other. She hesitated in calling out because she didn't want to startle him and risk him falling.

After a long minute, with the dampness of perspiration already forming between her shoulder blades, she wondered if she should wait until he was done to discuss the matter. She started to turn away.

"You're finally awake." He spoke without glancing at her.

She should have known he'd notice her standing there. In fact, he'd probably seen her coming the second she stepped out of the house. "Yes, I've been awake for a little while now."

"Fifty-five minutes."

He'd been keeping track? She knew better than to question him. Instead, she watched him work. He dipped his tool into the bucket, removed it, revealing a gray glob on the end, and then smeared the paste on a crack in the bricks. He wasn't wearing his usual dark suit, but was instead attired in a pair of faded blue trousers and a white linen shirt that was rolled up at the sleeves. His arms were just as thick and muscular as they'd felt through his coat. She supposed he couldn't very well wear a suit every minute of the day while he was at the lighthouse, and she had to admit, that even in the plain clothes he was still striking.

"I know you didn't come out just to stare at me." He scraped his tool along the crack, smoothing the gray paste.

"I'm not staring." But that's exactly what she'd been doing. "I came to discuss an urgent matter with you."

"Urgent?" His tone was skeptical.

"Very. I wouldn't bother you otherwise."

He smoothed the tool over the bricks for another moment before finally putting it back in the bucket and starting down the ladder. When his feet were back on the ground, he pulled a handkerchief out of his pocket and wiped the moisture from his brow. "What's wrong?"

She gave him what she hoped was her most enticing smile. "I'd like to hire a housekeeper for your parents."

"No."

She'd been prepared for his negativity and had a ready answer, her perfect solution. "I'm prepared to pay the entire cost. It would be my way of saying thank you to your parents for letting us stay with them this month."

"No." He leaned down and picked up a leather canteen leaning against the tower.

"Your mother said Ruth took care of everything, and now that she's gone there's no one to do the work."

"There's someone now." Tom unscrewed the cap.

"There is?" The news took her by surprise. Maybe Tom had already anticipated her needs and made the arrangements. "Who?"

"You." He lifted the canteen to his lips.

"Me?" She laughed. "I'm not trained to be a housekeeper. I'd much prefer to hire someone who knows what they're doing and can give us the assistance we require."

He guzzled water from his canteen, his Adam's apple rising and falling. His neck and chin had a slight layer of dark scruff, which was out of character since he was normally so cleanly shaven.

"Besides, if I don't hire someone, then your mother may think I expect her to wait upon me, and that would be awkward, don't you think?"

Tom wiped the back of his hand across his mouth, and his eyes turned dark, almost dangerous. "My mom won't be waiting on you, Victoria. Not now. And not ever."

His voice contained a bite that she'd never heard there before, and it gave her pause. Before she could think of a suitable response, he spoke again in the same low tone.

"Apparently, you've been too preoccupied to notice that she doesn't have any feet."

His words seemed to reach out and slap her across the cheeks and she stumbled back a pace. "I didn't know... I've only seen her twice and both times she was sitting at the table. I didn't look..."

"That's my point. You need to get better at looking at the needs of others instead of focusing so much on yourself." Tom screwed the lid back on the canteen with jerking, almost angry movements.

Victoria swallowed a sudden rise of bile, not sure why she was suddenly sick to her stomach. Perhaps from Tom's accusations? Or the fact that his mother had no feet?

He turned and started up the ladder without a backward glance.

Her heart pattered with the sudden need to prove herself to him. "Since your mother is impaired, isn't that all the more reason to hire a housekeeper? Just think of how much help it would be to her."

"To you," he said. "You want the help for *you*."

She couldn't deny him, and somehow that made her feel even worse. "I'll admit, a bath would be delightful."

Tom swiped off his hat and jammed his fingers into his damp hair. He looked as though he wanted to say more. But then he slapped his hat back on and put a hand on the next rung. "You're not hiring anyone, Victoria. It would jeopardize your safety."

With that, he started back up the ladder.

She watched with growing helplessness. Who would iron her dress? Who would help her with her bath? And who would find her something to eat?

"I'm hungry. Could you at least bring me breakfast?"

Tom climbed higher. "You'll find food in the pantry."

"Pantry?" She'd never been in a pantry. She wouldn't know where to find it, and even if she did, she wouldn't know what to do with any of the supplies.

He stopped near the top and looked down at her. "My dad hasn't slept more than a couple hours straight for the past two weeks. Today he is. Do you want to know why?"

She thought she knew. But before she could answer, he continued.

"Because I'm here to help him. And you're here to help Mom."

How could she possibly help Zelma? She'd never waited on anyone before. "I won't know how to do anything—"

"You're smart. You'll learn fast." With that, he dug his tool back into his pail and began to work again.

She wasn't sure she wanted to learn. But she couldn't sway Tom. Once his mind was made up, he was too stubborn.

She sighed and mopped a sleeve across her damp brow.

For now, she'd have to resign herself to being without a housekeeper, even though she didn't have any idea how she'd manage for herself, much less be of any use to Zelma. But she could try, couldn't she? At the very least, in the short term, she could ask Zelma if she needed anything.

Then later, when Tom was done with his work, she'd corner him again and ask him to reconsider. He'd have to go into town to locate a seamstress. What harm would come from hiring a maid too? He owed her that much, especially since she'd already acquiesced to his plan and come out to the middle of nowhere. Since she'd compromised, he should too.

When she returned to the front sitting room, she was tempted to peer under the table at Zelma's legs. But hadn't her own mother's condition taught her something? Her mother didn't want other people to gawk or treat her differently because of her blindness. She wanted people to treat her like they would anyone else. Surely Zelma wanted the same.

"I have to admit, I've never been in a kitchen, except in passing," Victoria said, as she stood next to the table wondering how to go about satisfying the ache in her stomach.

"If you're used to having a housekeeper, then your family must be well-to-do," Zelma said, eyes still warm and welcoming.

"Yes, my father has profited with his lumber and mining holdings," Victoria replied, wondering how much Tom would allow her to share. Probably less was better at this point.

"Well, I'm not surprised Tom caught your eye. I always figured that, with his handsome features, he'd draw attention from some of the rich ladies he associated with."

Victoria had no doubt Zelma was right and that Tom had gotten plenty of attention wherever he'd worked, but at the moment she was too hungry to think about it. "So, as you can probably guess," Victoria said, "I'm fairly useless when it comes to household tasks."

"Not useless, dear." Zelma lifted the blanket covering her lap and pushed her chair away from the table. "Just not instructed."

Once Zelma was removed from the barrier the table had provided, Victoria noticed the large wheels on the sides of the chair and a small one in the back. Apparently the chair was portable.

"I've always believed that anyone with a willing attitude can learn anything new." Zelma gripped the two wheels in front and strained against them, causing the chair to roll backward even more. "Especially if they have a patient instructor."

With the blanket pulled up almost to her knees, two uneven stumps were visible beneath Zelma's skirt. Victoria could only imagine the many things Zelma had to learn to do without having her feet, just as her mother had to learn to do things differently after she'd lost her sight. If Zelma and her mother could overcome obstacles and adjust to challenges, certainly she could too.

"I've had to learn a lot of patience over the years," Zelma said following Victoria's gaze to her missing limbs. "So if you need a patient instructor, I'm more than happy to be one for you."

Victoria nodded. "Thank you, Zelma."

"You can call me Mom if you want to."

Victoria knew she should decline, that to call Zelma *Mom* would only take the deceit about the true nature of their marriage relationship to new level. But the hope in Zelma's eyes was too hard to resist. "Thank you. Mom."

With that, Zelma smiled. "Now, why don't you get behind

me, dear, and help wheel me into the kitchen. We'll start with learning how to make coffee. How does that sound?"

Victoria rounded the back of the chair. "That sounds perfect."

Chapter 11

*T*om picked at the charred cod, searching for any edible pieces. He moved his knife to the fried potatoes, and was met with the same problem. The food Victoria had prepared wasn't worth feeding to the sharks.

Across the dining room table, his dad was shoveling bite after bite into his mouth without a break, as if the meal was fit for a king. His dad paused with the fork halfway between his plate and mouth. He pointed his forkful of food at Tom's plate, and his eyes held a rebuke. Tom could almost hear his dad's voice—*Every good husband eats the food his wife puts in front of him gratefully and without complaint.*

"I like the seasoning on the beans," Dad said to Victoria, his mouth half full. He looked pointedly at Tom again.

And a good husband always finds something positive to say to his wife, even when there doesn't seem to be anything. Tom had grown up with his dad's nuggets of wisdom and had seen him practice everything he preached. But he'd never had the opportunity to test any of the advice himself. Until now.

Next to him, Victoria sat in her chair stiffly. Strands of her hair were plastered to her forehead, and her face was flushed—likely from the heat of working in the kitchen on an already sweltering day. Although the interior of the house was cooler than outside, it was still uncomfortably hot with the humidity that had rolled in.

She'd only taken five tiny bites from her own plate. And she'd nearly choked on two of them. If Victoria couldn't eat the meal, surely Dad didn't expect him to attempt it, much less compliment her.

But Dad continued to eat, and Mom did likewise, albeit much more carefully and slowly. Another glare from Dad told him that yes, indeed, he was expected to follow Dad's example. Tom hesitated and then dug his fork into the potatoes. Before he could talk himself out of it, he gulped a mouthful and swallowed.

Not bad, if he didn't let the food settle in his mouth.

He picked up another spoonful, shoveled it in, and forced it down quickly. Now he understood why his dad was eating so fast. So that he didn't have to taste it. Maybe there was hope after all.

After the third mouthful, his dad cocked his head toward Victoria. The look told Tom it was time to pay the compliment.

When she'd suggested hiring a housekeeper, he'd been so irritated by her helplessness and the way it reminded him of his mother, that he'd worked right through lunch without a break. As the day had passed, his irritation had spent itself in the heat and the hard work of repairing the tower. He'd been left with a dull ache in his chest, knowing that Victoria wasn't to blame for her desire to have a maid. That kind of lifestyle was all she'd ever known, and he couldn't expect her to want anything different. Besides, she'd return to her opulent way of living after a month. In fact, the hard labor was a change for him as well. He was accustomed to a life of ease now too.

The real truth was that he was angry at himself. It was his fault Mom needed the help in the first place. If he hadn't failed in his scouting duties that fateful day in '64, she wouldn't have had to trek through the wintery weather to rescue him and Ike from the Confederates. She would have stayed home, safe and dry.

Now, seeing her only made him loathe himself all over again.

His dad paused in his eating and stared at Tom. Waiting.

Tom swallowed another burnt bite and cleared his throat. None of this was Victoria's fault. In fact, he gave her credit for spending the afternoon in the kitchen and attempting a meal. At least she'd made an effort to help, even if the results were awful. He could compliment her for that, couldn't he?

"I can tell you worked hard today, Victoria," he said.

At his quiet statement, a sob broke from her lips. She cupped her hand quickly over her mouth and scooted back from the table. She rose to her feet, her eyes brimming with unshed tears.

Startled, Tom pushed back too. Before he could stand, she rushed across the room, and he stared at her retreating back in confusion. She ran out of the dining room to the stairway. Then she clomped up all twenty steps, ran down the hallway, entered their bedroom, and slammed the door.

So much for paying her compliment.

Her footsteps crossed the bedroom, and from the squeak of the bedsprings, he guessed she'd lain down.

Maybe she was just tired.

He sighed and began to scoot his chair back, only to stop at the ominous silence in the room. He glanced across the table to find that both Mom and Dad were staring at him. Reproach was written all over their faces.

"What?" he asked.

"*You worked hard?*" Dad said in a low voice. "That's the best you could come up with?"

"Well, she did."

"You couldn't find something praiseworthy about the meal?"

Tom glanced at the blackened fish and the mushy burnt potatoes. "No."

"Then you didn't dig deep enough." Dad tossed his napkin onto the table and pushed away, his eyes full of fire.

Mom laid a steadying hand on Dad's arm. "It's my fault everything burned. I got so busy instructing her on how to make a pie that I forgot to have her flip the fish and potatoes."

He dreaded to see the pie, but instead of making another remark that would anger Dad, he kept silent.

Dad was quiet for a moment too, as though trying to rein in his anger. Finally, he spoke. "The key to a good marriage is to do all you can to uplift your wife and treasure her—even in her worst moments."

Tom wanted to blurt out that it wouldn't matter if he had a good marriage to Victoria, because it would end in a month anyway. But he nodded respectfully. "You're right."

"You should go up and apologize to her," Mom said gently.

Apologize for a compliment? Tom started to protest.

"Your mom's right," Dad said. "She usually is."

Mom smiled and leaned toward him, lifting her face for a kiss. He eagerly obliged, kissing her with the same fervor he always had.

Tom shifted in his chair and examined the painting on the

wall above the sideboard, even though he knew it more intimately than anyone.

"There," Dad said, finally breaking the kiss. "You go on up, apologize, and earn yourself a kiss just like that."

Mom's cheeks were a rosy pink and love radiated from her eyes.

Tom rose to his feet and began to gather the dishes.

"Shoo." His dad waved him away. "Go to her right away. The longer you wait, the madder she'll get."

Victoria wouldn't be mad at him for his attempt to compliment her, would she? She was usually so strong, so sure of herself, so in control. Even when her carriage had been hijacked on her wedding day, she hadn't cowered. She'd thrown her shoe at the driver.

"She won't be angry at me," Tom said. "But I'll go up and make sure she's okay."

His parents nodded their approval, and he made his way up to their room. He paused for a total of five seconds before taking a deep breath and opening the door.

He stepped inside and was greeted with a scream and a flying shoe. He sidestepped, and the shoe hit the wall behind him.

Victoria was sitting on the bed with her bodice off, revealing her corset, which covered her waist and bust but left the upper edge of her soft flesh exposed, along with her shoulders, neck, and arms.

Tears streaked her face and mortification had widened her eyes. "Get out!" she shouted and scrambled to pull the coverlet off the bed. She yanked it over her shoulders, attempting to cover herself, but not before he caught sight of at least half a dozen red welts forming under her arms, where apparently the corset had chafed her skin.

"I just came to check on you—"

"I don't need you to check on me." A strand of hair had fallen across her face, sticking in the sweat and tears. Heedless, she wrapped the blanket around her tighter, even though the air in the upstairs room was stifling. "Just get out."

Perspiration was forming on his back standing there doing nothing. "I wanted to apologize—"

Her other shoe went whizzing past his head and smacked the wall. "I don't want your apology. I just want you to leave." In spite of the tears, her eyes flashed with anger. She started to reach for a hairbrush on the bedstead. He wasn't sure if she was intending to throw that at him too. He didn't wait to find out but backed out and closed the door.

She apparently needed some time to herself. Or maybe she was upset at him for refusing to hire a housekeeper.

He shook his head, retreated downstairs, and slipped out the back door in an effort to avoid another encounter with his parents. No doubt they'd heard Victoria scream at him and order him from the room. And no doubt they blamed him for her bad mood and would tell him to go back to her.

But they didn't understand that Victoria was pampered and that he had no need to apologize for telling her *no* about the housekeeper. It was for her own protection. Besides, it wouldn't hurt her to start doing some things for herself. And he certainly wasn't being overly demanding by asking her to help, Mom. Was he?

He made his way to the shed that held the fog horn. Dad had mentioned that it wasn't working properly. Now was apparently a good time to tinker on the amplifier. But as he hunkered down and worked, he couldn't concentrate. He kept seeing the tears streaking Victoria's cheeks, kept hearing that sob after his comment at dinner, kept feeling the anguish in her voice.

Finally, after hitting his thumb for the fourth time, he stood, wiped his hands, and started back to the house. When he entered, Dad was in the process of situating Mom in the sitting room. At the sight of him, they both grew quiet.

Tom sighed. "Yes. I'm going back up."

Dad smiled. "That's my boy."

"You won't regret it," Mom added.

Tom wasn't so sure about that. Nevertheless, he knew he wouldn't have peace until he made peace with her.

"The Bible says not to let the sun go down on your anger," Dad said. "I've applied that to our marriage, and it's helped us work through plenty of problems and disappointments."

"You've had problems?"

At the surprise in his tone, Mom laughed. "Of course we have. We're both sinners, aren't we?"

"I never noticed anything wrong."

Mom reached for Dad's hand and looked up at him with respect. "That's because your dad insisted on working through any issues before we climbed into bed."

Tom glanced overhead to Victoria's room, which was silent. Maybe she'd already fallen asleep. Or what if she was awake and threw the brush at him?

"You can do it," Dad said, as if sensing his hesitancy.

"Your dad always figured out a way to soften my heart." Mom giggled. "Remember the time when I was upset about having to move again, and you went out and dug up all my tulip bulbs so that I could take them with us?"

Dad nodded.

"Or that especially hot summer after Ruth was born when I was grouchy all the time. You made me my own private tidal pool where I could cool off whenever the house got too hot."

Tom remembered those times too. Dad could have reacted in anger and frustration to Mom's moods and the difficulties. But instead, Dad had gone to extraordinary efforts to show his love. He'd nurtured and tended her like a gardener his flowers. As a result of his faithful efforts, his marriage now flourished so beautifully.

Even if Tom's marriage to Victoria was short-lived, he could still follow Dad's example, couldn't he? He could do something for her tonight. To soften her heart. Considering all the changes she'd had in the past two days, she'd done well. And perhaps he had been a little hard on her.

"Where do you keep the bathing tub?" he asked.

Dad grinned. "Do you want the one big enough for two?"

Heat hit Tom square in the face, and he ducked his head. "The regular one will work fine." His voice came out squeaky, and he quickly cleared his throat.

Dad chuckled.

"It's in the pantry," Mom said. "And you go ahead and get some of the lilac soap from my room. She'll like that."

"Make sure to offer to scrub her back." Dad's voice was light and teasing.

"I always like when your father brushes my hair," Mom offered.

Tom wanted to plug his ears and start humming. He didn't need to know any more details about his parents' love life than he already did. So he hustled away before his parents could say anything else to embarrass him.

He warmed up some water to add to the cold well water so that the temperature was perfect for cooling her, but not cold enough that she wouldn't enjoy it. He sloshed pails of water up and down the stairs filling the large tub in the hallway so he could surprise her. As he worked, he tried not to think of his parents' comments about scrubbing Victoria's back or brushing her hair and what that actually might be like.

He had no claim to such intimacy, even if his parents believed he did. Whatever the case, the bath was for her. He didn't expect anything in return.

When he finally dumped the last pail, he was sweating rivulets from his exertion. And the heat of the second floor only made him hotter. He caught his breath before listening at the door. She was so quiet he might have thought she'd somehow runaway, except that the octagonal shaped doorknob was in the same upright position he'd left it.

He knocked softly. "Victoria, I'm coming in." He listened again, and when she didn't protest, he opened the door a crack and peeked in.

She'd sprawled out on her stomach across the bed, still clad in her corset and skirt. From the gentle rise and fall of her torso, he guessed she was asleep. Even from the doorway, he could make out more of the bright red marks where the whalebones in her corset had rubbed her skin raw. From the way the laces were tangled and knotted, it was clear she'd been attempting to free herself from her corset.

He let himself in and hefted the tub to the middle of the room before closing the door. She would be mad at him again for coming in when she was undressed, but what else could he do? His stomach twisted at the thought of his parents listening to every step and noise they made. This pretend marriage was going to take a lot more acting than he'd anticipated.

With a sigh, he splashed some of the tepid bath water onto his face and then wiped himself dry with his sleeve. He arranged a clean towel and the lilac soap next to the tub, and then stood back and fidgeted with his shirt collar.

He couldn't leave. His parents would scold him and order

him back to the room. But there was no way Victoria would bathe with him present—not that he wanted her to. Far from it. She'd already tried to kill him for barging in while she was in a state of undress. She'd never willingly shed more in front of him.

He searched the room for a place he could get out of her way. But then an idea began to formulate. Maybe he didn't have to leave the room or hide after all.

For several minutes he worked at his plan, trying to be as quiet as possible. When he had everything ready, he stood back with satisfaction.

He glanced again at Victoria still asleep and frowned at the corset and the way that it was pinching her flesh. With only a moment's more hesitation, he crossed to the bed. She was lying on her stomach, with half of her face against the bed and the other half exposed. Her long lashes rested against splotchy cheeks, still damp with tears. Her hair had come completely loose and fell in tangled waves over her back.

She was beautiful, even when she was wilted and hot and asleep.

Should he leave and come back later? Or should he wake her and let her know about the bath. He lowered himself to the edge of the bed next to her.

She didn't move.

He lifted a hand above her hair and again hesitated. He needed to be careful. There were boundaries he couldn't—wouldn't—cross. But at this moment, with the evidence of her tears and heartache still so fresh, he let his fingers dip into her hair, into the golden silk. The softness was exquisite against his fingertips, and he combed into her hair deeper, sweeping it off her back, away from her over-heated skin.

At his movement, she stirred.

He combed another wave off her back, and this time his fingers grazed against her smooth flesh, which was a mistake. Once his senses registered the satiny texture of her skin, he had to run his fingers over it again, the spot between her shoulder blades.

She sucked in a quick breath, and her eyes flew open. He expected her to sit up, push him away, and tell him to get out. But instead, she lay motionless, not breathing at all, as though waiting. Waiting for him to touch her again?

He moved his fingers higher toward the base of her neck and then very slowly and softly swept aside more hair, letting his fingers linger against her neck.

Her eyes closed, and she began to breathe again, her chest rising and falling with a rapid succession that sent a strange ripple into his gut. With her hair combed away, he didn't stop himself from looking at her delicate shoulder blades and backbone so perfect.

Stop looking, an inner voice warned. And definitely don't touch her, it yelled louder. But in the process of lifting his hand, he let his fingers trail against one of her shoulders. At his touch, she released a soft kitten-like noise, which melted his insides faster than honey in the hot sun. Suddenly, all he could think about was flipping her over and kissing her.

He moved his hand to her waist, telling himself that he wouldn't kiss her, that he was only going to help her sit up for her bath. But as he began to roll her, she cried out, this time in pain. At the sight of the corset digging into her tender flesh, he bit back a frustrated oath and gently released her onto her stomach.

"Why haven't you taken off your corset?" he asked, trying to keep his voice gentle.

She laughed almost bitterly. "Because I'm useless. I can't

do anything for myself."

He studied the strings and understanding dawned. "You're not useless." He extricated the small knife he kept hidden against his calf beneath his sock. "The strings are just knotted too tightly."

"In all my efforts to untie them, I think I only made it worse."

He lifted his knife, and she gasped and started to squirm. "Hold still, Victoria. I won't hurt you."

She stopped moving. Once again she held her breath.

He carefully wedged the blade into the crossed strings at the bottom. She had to be very uncomfortable and in pain to obey him so readily, especially knowing that he was about to rip open her corset and expose her even more.

Slowly, he worked the sharp knife up through the laces until the last one at the top snapped. The corset fell away, revealing red, irritated skin and three places where her flesh had been rubbed raw.

She remained motionless except that she started to breathe again. "Thank you," she said, her face buried against the covers.

"I'm sorry I didn't realize your predicament sooner."

"It's not your fault."

Maybe not. But he was still angry with himself that she'd suffered. Before he thought to stop himself, he touched a red spot on her back.

She stiffened, and he immediately pulled away and reached for a discarded sheet at the end of the bed. "Here." He covered her back before he did something really foolish.

She grasped the edges of the sheet and tucked it around her front, shielding herself before sitting up and tossing the corset aside. She folded her knees under her and secured the sheet modestly around her body. Her hair spilled down her shoulders, and she looked at him with her clear guileless eyes.

He found himself sinking into her, needing her, wanting to do anything to make her happy. Was this some kind of spell she was capable of casting? Was that why she had so many men vying for her and falling in love with her? He'd always thought Nathaniel was a weak man for giving Victoria everything she wanted. But maybe he'd experienced this same need too.

Tom rose from the bed before he lost complete control of himself. "I prepared a bath for you."

"You did?" Her voice filled with surprise, as if she hadn't expected his help with anything.

He walked over to the makeshift tent he'd formed, and he pulled back the blanket to reveal the tub.

She gave a delighted squeal and scrambled off the bed. With an eager smile, she scooped up her discarded clothing and skipped toward the bath. She ducked under the tent and dipped a hand into the water before coming back out. Her smile moved to her eyes, chasing away all of the sorrow he'd seen there only moments ago.

"It's my apology," he said.

"Apology for what?" She cocked her head just slightly.

He didn't know exactly what he'd done to offend her today. Likely quite a bit. So he decided he'd better just take Dad's approach and humble himself. "Sometimes I'm an insensitive idiot."

The words were magic. Her smile widened and genuine warmth radiated from her eyes. He had the feeling that if they'd been married, he might have benefitted from the tub built for two. Just the thought made him look away, lest she see something in his eyes that didn't belong there.

"I know you'd prefer that I leave while you bathe"—he lowered his voice—"but my parents are watching every move we make."

"They sure are."

He nodded toward the sofa in front of the window. "I'll wait there."

She hesitated.

"I promise I'll keep my eyes on the window the whole time."

"Okay."

He spun away from her, needing to prove to himself that he was as strong as always. As he sauntered toward the window, he could feel her watching him. He tried to appear nonchalant, even though every nerve in his body was attuned to her.

When he finally plopped down and rested his head on one end of the sofa and crossed his feet on the other, he could hear her move into the tent. It took only a minute before the soft splash of water told him she was lowering first one foot and then the other into the tub. He closed his eyes to block out the image of her submerging in the water. But at her low moan of pleasure, sparks shot through his veins, heating his blood.

With each splash of water and her soft sounds of content-ment, his muscles coiled tighter until he wasn't sure he could bear another minute. Finally, when she stood in the tub, he gritted his teeth and jumped up from the sofa. He stuffed his hands into his pockets and stared unseeingly out the open window. He was hot and uncomfortable and desperately needed to escape from her presence. He'd never endured such torture in his life and prayed he'd never have to again.

"Do you want to take a bath now?" she asked, and from the exertion in her tone, he guessed she was rubbing herself dry with the towel he'd laid out for her.

He opened his mouth to speak, but his throat was burning.

"It really cooled me off," she said.

"I'll be okay," he managed. Heaven help him. The only way he would cool off was by diving head first into high tide.

She was silent for a moment before resuming her dressing, this time minus the blasted corset, which she'd left in a discarded heap on the bed. When she finished, he heard her lift the blanket and step out of the tent. He tried to compose himself, tried to put on his most stoic expression, tried to hide the strange way she was making him feel.

Her footsteps crossed the room and stopped behind him. He knew he should turn and smile and pretend that everything was normal. But he needed another minute before he could face her.

She waited a few seconds before tentatively touching his arm. "Tom?" The uncertainty in her voice told him that she was confused by his aloofness. If he wasn't careful, he'd end up hurting her feelings again, and he didn't want to do that simply because he was a weak man who couldn't contain his desire for her.

He gave himself a mental shake and decided he'd have to act around her too now. He'd have to pretend that he wasn't attracted to her, that nothing was different than before. He took a deep breath and turned.

Her hair hung in wet strands, and her bodice stuck to her skin where she'd neglected to completely dry herself. But she was still utterly breathtaking, especially when she offered him a smile. "You should take a dip."

"I'm fine." He tried to smile and prayed it didn't come out a grimace.

She studied his face for a moment before her gaze shifted

to his chest. Her lashes fell shyly against her flushed cheeks.

Had she seen the desire in his expression? It was likely written all over his face. He shifted, intending to put more distance between them, but before he could move, she leaned into him and slipped her arms around his waist. Then she buried her face into his chest and hugged him.

For an instant, the move took him by surprise. He stood frozen.

"Thank you," she whispered.

In response, he slid his arms around her and hugged her back, relishing the way she fit so perfectly against him. The lingering scent of lilac soap surrounded her, and her damp hair brushed his chin.

"You were very sweet to prepare me a bath," she said.

He let himself stroke her wet hair.

At his touch, she snuggled against him, and he had to close his eyes to think rationally. "And thanks for treating me normally today. Everyone has always handled me like I'm a breakable piece of crystal. No one's ever been as honest with me as you are."

"And that's good?"

He could feel her lips curve into a smile. "Yes. You challenge me to be a better person. And no else does that, except maybe my mother."

"So what are you saying?" He tried to infuse humor into his tone. "I'm too soft and womanly?"

She laughed lightly and tightened her arms around his waist. "Maybe."

He pulled back in mock horror.

She laughed again, louder. He loved the sound of it.

"So, with the bath, do you think we've convinced your parents that we're—" She blushed.

"Hopefully." He could just imagine both of them sitting downstairs listening to the sounds coming from the bedroom and exchanging smug smiles. "But I should warn you, I have to sleep in here too."

Her eyes widened, and her lips formed around words of protest.

He quickly silenced her with a finger against her lips. "I slept on the floor by the window last night."

She glanced from the bed to the floor and back and then visibly swallowed. She wasn't frightened was she? Surely she knew him well enough by now to realize she had nothing to worry about.

He lowered himself to the sofa and patted the spot next to him. "We might as well get settled. They won't expect us to come out for a while."

Again, Victoria blushed. But she quickly complied and sat down on the opposite end of the sofa. When she finally chanced a glance at him and nibbled her lip, he had the urge to close the gap between them and pull her back into his arms. But the inner conscience he'd worked so hard to cultivate reminded him of his promise to Mr. Cole. He chastised himself for his wayward desires and prayed he'd have the strength to survive the next few weeks without going mad.

He leaned back casually. "So try to tell me something about you that I don't already know."

Chapter 12

$\mathcal{V}$ictoria placed a fork next to the last plate and then stood back and admired her table-setting efforts.

"It looks lovely," Zelma said from her spot at the dining room table, where Victoria had already positioned her in the moveable chair.

The white hydrangeas Victoria had clipped from the front bushes decorated the center of the table. And the flaky golden biscuits she'd baked earlier in the afternoon were arranged in a tower, with raspberries placed strategically around the outer rim of the platter. She'd folded each of the napkins into a fan shape and garnished each plate with a cup of raspberry cream pudding that Zelma had shown her how to make just that morning.

"You're such a quick learner." Zelma gave her a proud smile.

"You're just a good teacher." Victoria brushed her hands against the bright orange-checkered apron that had apparently once belonged to Zelma. It was hideous, but after practically ruining two of her three outfits cooking during the past several days, Victoria had put aside her vanity in order to save her last remaining skirt from stains.

She'd tracked down Tom in the fog house after lunch and had told him that she needed to hire a seamstress to come out to the house and make her new clothes. But the conversation had gone the same way it had when she'd approached him about hiring a housekeeper. She'd ended up stomping away and threatening to leave with Jimmy in his cutter the next time the elderly fisherman delivered provisions. Since Jimmy had just come that morning with a supply of fresh produce, she didn't know when he'd come again.

After letting her anger cool the rest of the afternoon, she'd decided she wouldn't carry through on her threat. Nevertheless, she was still vexed at Tom for denying her again—even if she had told him earlier in the week that she'd appreciated his honesty. This time, she wasn't acting selfishly. She really did need more garments, especially since she hadn't liked learning to wash clothes nearly as much as she was enjoying cooking. She didn't want to repeat the laundering process again for the rest of the month if it could be helped. Her hands still hadn't recovered from the harsh soap.

"You've learned to cook well in such a short time," Zelma said as she stirred the creamy peas and potatoes. "I certainly didn't do so well my first week of marriage."

"I'm sure your first meal was better than mine." Victoria smiled at the remembrance of the burned food she'd served and how Tom had tried so hard to eat it to please her. Then, even though everything had all been her fault, he'd still tried to console her, had even prepared her a private bath. He'd been so tender and sweet. And afterward, they'd talked on the sofa until he'd finally left to carry his mom up to bed.

Victoria couldn't deny that their evening talks on the bedroom sofa were the highlight of her day. Tom was a good listener and always seemed genuinely interested in anything she shared. She'd also gotten him to open up and talk more about his past, his childhood, living at various lighthouses, and his work as a bodyguard in Europe. One night she'd asked him about his time in the war, but he'd immediately closed up and hadn't spoken about himself again all night. Other than that, she'd learned more about him in the past week than she had the previous month.

She exhaled a long breath as she rearranged the biscuits and centered the top one on the pinnacle of the tower. They had been getting along so well. Maybe she shouldn't have brought up the idea of hiring a seamstress after all.

"It's all right, dear," Zelma said gently. "It's normal to have disagreements."

Victoria straightened in surprise, ready to issue a word of denial. How had Zelma known about her spat with Tom?

Zelma continued before she could speak. "You're two different people, from different backgrounds, with unique personalities and quirks. So of course you'll both have to adjust. In fact, those early years of marriage are all about working through differences and learning to compromise."

"Yes." Victoria sighed. "I think we're as different as land and water."

"James and I were very different too."

"You were? But you seem so good together, so much in harmony." *And so passionate*, but Victoria bit back the too-intimate words.

"It's taken years and lots of hard work to develop that kind of unity." Zelma gave the peas and potatoes one last stir before tucking the spoon deep into the bowl and pushing it toward the middle of the table. "I've come to believe one of the reasons God designed marriage was to help us grow in holiness and character. We get to practice on a daily basis being humble, kind, sacrificial, self-controlled, and so much more."

Victoria had never before heard anyone talk that way about marriage. "I guess I'd always believed that some couples made a perfect match and others didn't."

Zelma laughed. "That's only a myth. The reality is that no couple starts out the perfect match. They have to work for that. Maybe some more than others. What I've learned is that the more I work on growing as a person, the more my marriage grows."

Victoria picked up one of the napkins and tucked the folds tighter into the fan shape. She'd never really thought about the need to grow in holiness. No, she knew she wasn't perfect, that she was a sinner. That's why she needed a Savior. But she'd always assumed that overall she was living a godly life.

But here, away from the comforts of home, away from everything she'd ever known, and in the context of being married, she was getting a glimpse of some of her weaknesses.

"In our marriages," Zelma continued, "we can let the difficulties drive us apart or drive us to our knees."

The clomping on the steps cut off their conversation. The men were coming down—James from his day of sleeping and Tom from changing his work clothes. The two had come up with a rotation. James took the night shift in the tower. And Tom did all of the cleaning and repair work that needed to be done during the day. Victoria had overheard James insisting on the schedule so that Tom could spend his nights with his new bride. Of course, Tom had protested, his voice tinged with embarrassment. But James hadn't listened to any other plan.

Victoria hurried to untie the ugly apron and hide it in a

drawer in the sideboard.

"I thought I smelled something delicious," James said, walking into the dining room first, his dark hair freshly groomed and his face relaxed from his hours of slumber. He smiled at Zelma and bent to kiss her on the top of her head.

"Victoria made fried chicken tonight," Zelma responded.

As Tom entered the room, Victoria busied herself taking the lid off the platter of chicken. She retrieved a long serving fork and placed it next to the chicken pieces, which were golden with batter and spices. She tried not to notice Tom, but his presence in a room was difficult to miss—the heat of his body, his darkening skin after a week in the sun, the fresh bay-rum scent from his soap. And his eyes, so dark and brooding, so beckoning. Always making her want to go to him and smooth away the lines in his forehead.

"The meal looks pretty," Tom said, pulling out her chair and helping her get situated before taking his seat next to her. Although he was never as gushing as his dad, she appreciated Tom's compliments every night. In fact, during the afternoons when she was planning and making the meals, she couldn't deny that she was doing it for him, to earn his praise and to make him happy.

"Thank you." She offered him a smile, but his smile in return was forced. Clearly, he was still upset at her for asking to hire a seamstress. From the unyielding dark blue of his eyes, she knew he wasn't planning on giving in to her need.

Her smile faded, replaced rapidly by irritation. He couldn't expect her to wear only three outfits all month, especially now that two were nearly ruined. She'd already given in to his plans and wishes enough. It was his turn to compromise.

Across the table, James glanced between them, as though sensing their coldness to one another, but Victoria bowed her head in preparation for the blessing that James spoke before every meal. Out of the corner of her eye, she saw Tom do likewise.

"Before we pray, I'm in need of a kiss from my wife," James said, turning to Zelma. "I haven't had one since this morning, and I'm hungrier for a kiss than for food."

Zelma's tinkling laugh of delight was cut short by James's crushing kiss. Victoria had finally begun to grow accustomed to their displays of affection. But as this kiss continued and turned more passionate, Victoria fidgeted in her chair and stared at the dish of raspberry cream pudding on her plate, her face growing hotter with each passing second. She was embarrassed by the strange warmth that blossomed in her middle, a warmth that made her wonder what that kind of kiss would feel like.

Next to her, Tom shifted, and she could sense his discomfort. "Excuse me, Mom, Dad," he finally said. "Dinner is getting cold."

James broke away, grinning from ear to ear, and Zelma was breathless and flushed. "Now, that's what I call a kiss," James said.

"I should say so," Zelma responded with a shaky voice.

James looked at Tom and narrowed his eyes. "Your turn."

Tom's brows rose as fast as sparrow wings. "My turn?"

"Yeah, let's see if you can top that."

"No."

"That's because you can't." James glared at Tom, daring and rebuking him at the same time.

"I know how to kiss." Tom's voice was low.

"I doubt it." James took Zelma's hand. She started to say something, but at a squeeze of his fingers she closed her mouth. "I haven't seen you kiss your wife all week. No wonder she's mad at you."

"Maybe we're more private than you."

"Or maybe you need to take a few lessons from me."

"I told you, I can."

"Then prove it." The two were deadlocked in a stare.

The entire exchange took Victoria by surprise. But she was even more surprised when Tom reached for her, turned her just slightly, and then slipped his hand up behind her neck. He leaned in and hesitated only a moment before dropping his sights to her lips.

Her heart did a wild flip at the realization that he was going to kiss her. She couldn't deny that she'd wondered what it might be like, especially after that time he'd held her during the steamboat ride. But he'd kept himself at a proper distance from her, even though they were legally married and sharing a room. She may have been concerned about the propriety of the situation the first night after she'd learned that he had to sleep in the same bedroom, but he'd behaved like a perfect gentleman all week. He'd kept to his spot on the sofa and his bed on the floor, had allowed her all the privacy she needed when dressing, and hadn't initiated any physical contact. In fact, she'd been the one to hug him the night of the bath.

Now, with his warm fingers against the back of her neck, capturing and positioning her, she held her breath in anticipation. His gaze briefly met hers, seeking her approval. She didn't want to say no, even though a part of her told her she should. The truth was she'd been waiting for him to kiss her.

He must have read her acquiescence because he licked his bottom lip and focused on her mouth again. His fingers on her neck guided her at the same moment that he bent and angled his mouth to fit against hers.

When his lips touched hers, he was tentative. But the

warmth and damp pressure sent a heady rush through her. Behind the tender, sweet kiss she sensed a restrained passion and strength that made her tremble.

Before she could move to open her lips and kiss him back, he broke away and released his hold on her neck. His dark eyes glowed with something she didn't understand, but that made her heart beat faster. Without giving her time to explore the swell of new feelings, he swiveled to face his dad. "Did I pass your test?"

His dad snorted. "Absolutely not. No wonder she's kicked you out of the bed and you're having to sleep on the floor."

They knew? Victoria's heart lurched, and she was sure her face revealed her mortification. She was thankful for once that Tom was schooled in hiding his emotions, that his expression remained unchanged at his father's revelation.

"What happens in our marriage isn't your concern," Tom said in a steely voice.

"Kiss her like you mean it." His dad's voice was equally steely, and Victoria realized where Tom got his stubbornness.

"I already did."

Once again they locked glares, neither willing to back down. And once more Zelma started to speak, but James patted her arm, and she remained quiet.

Victoria tensed. Should she intervene and put an end to the stand-off? She had the feeling Tom wouldn't kiss her again, that he was too noble to push himself on her, even to prove himself to his dad. Maybe if she let Tom know he could kiss her again...that she wouldn't mind. Because she wouldn't, would she? She could allow another kiss for his sake.

Underneath the table, she slid her hand over to his, which was fisted tightly. The muscles in his arm were taut. She ran her fingers over his wrist and tugged him in her direction. His gaze snapped to hers, and his brows rose, revealing the tumult rolling in the dark depths of his eyes.

She tugged him again and leaned in. She wanted to say, "Just kiss me." But she wasn't that bold. Instead, she prayed he could read the message in her tentative smile.

Before she could catch her breath, he moved so swiftly and strongly she felt as if he'd knocked her completely off her feet. He captured her face between both large hands and brought his lips down against hers. This time, his kiss was powerful, his mouth open and demanding.

His lips unlocked her own passion, unleashed something she'd never known was inside her. As his hands moved from her face to her hair and then down her back, she was helpless to do anything but wrap her arms around him in return. All the while, his mouth never wavered from hers. His lips pressed harder until her body was on fire with a need for him she didn't understand.

"Oh." She couldn't contain the soft gasp against his hungry lips. The gasp brought his hands back up to her hair, to her neck, as if he couldn't get enough of her. Each brush of his fingers was invitation to kiss him more deeply, to take him in, to love him.

Love him?

Her kiss stilled for a moment. But it was apparently long enough for him to sense her hesitancy. He wrenched his mouth from hers and pulled back a fraction so that his labored breaths bathed her mouth.

"Now that was a kiss worthy of the Cushman name," James said, grinning.

Zelma was beaming.

Suddenly Victoria was more mortified than she'd ever been in her life. She'd just kissed their son, and not a chaste little kiss. But a passionate long kiss that had involved lots of touching and even her gasp.

She couldn't look either of them in the eyes. She doubted she'd ever be able to again. Or look Tom in the eyes. What must he think of her now after she'd thrown herself into his arms?

"Let's say the blessing," James said, "and eat before the food gets cold."

"Good idea, dear," Zelma said.

Tom slowly released his grip on her. His breathing was still ragged, and he seemed almost reluctant to pull away.

"Of course, we can always put yours in the warming oven for later." James waggled his eyebrows at Tom.

Tom sat back in his chair, unable to hide a ripple of embarrassment that crossed his face. "No, Dad. We'll eat now."

Somehow Victoria made it through the meal. She wasn't sure how she managed to speak coherently. Or how she managed to swallow any of the food. She certainly didn't taste a single thing. All she could think about was the fact that Tom was only inches away. She could feel the heat from his leg when it brushed against hers under the table. And when he reached for a second biscuit and his arm touched her, she almost gasped again.

She was relieved when dinner was finally over. As she rose to begin clearing the table, James waved her away.

"Go on," Zelma said. "We'll clean up. You two go spend some time together."

James chuckled. "Yeah, go burn off that heat."

Victoria froze, her hand on the plate in front of her. Was the heat that noticeable? A flush crept up her neck, and she had the sudden urge to flee and hide until she could cool down and think more rationally.

166

Tom touched her arm, and she jumped. "Come on," he said, holding out a hand.

He wasn't planning to lead her upstairs to the bedroom, was he? For more of that kind of kissing? Her pulse jumped from both nervousness and desire.

"Let's go for a walk." His eyes were a warm blue that held only tenderness. No anger. No aloofness. No shame. No regret.

"That sounds nice." She took his hand, and when his fingers closed around hers, she couldn't help thinking of those same fingers touching her back, neck, and waist. She'd liked it. Very much.

And she liked the gentle pressure of his hand against hers as he led her out the house and down to the path to the beach. The horizon was clear, not a boat in sight. The summer evening was still warm from the day, but the brilliance of the sun was beginning to fade, promising a cooler night. When they reached the shore, he kicked off his boots and pulled off his socks before rolling up his trousers.

She laughed at the sight of his bare ankles and calves. "You look like a sandpiper."

He grinned and nodded to the mound of sand behind her. "Sit down."

She complied and was unprepared when he kneeled in front of her and took one of her feet into his lap. "What are you doing?"

He didn't answer but instead began to unlace her shoe. Once it was off, he tossed it next to his in the sand. He didn't look at her as he found the garter at her calf. As he untied the lace and made contact with her leg, she sucked in a breath. He focused on the stocking and quickly rolled it down over her toes. She was afraid of her reaction should he touch her bare foot. Thankfully, he only placed her foot into the sand and began the work of unlacing her other shoe and removing the garter.

Even though his touch had been brief with each foot, the fire within her blood had come blazing back. When he finally glanced at her from where he knelt in front of her, she could see a fire smoldering in his eyes too.

What was happening between them? What had those innocent kisses ignited?

Certainly she'd never had any feelings close to this with Nathaniel or any of her other suitors. She'd never been kissed the way Tom had kissed her. He'd been right. His kiss hadn't been *nice*. It had been powerful and beautiful and earth-shattering.

A shadow fell across his face. "Listen, Victoria—"

"Don't apologize for kissing me," she said almost vehemently. "I don't want to hear it."

He ducked his head, and she longed to dig her fingers into his hair. "But I shouldn't have—"

"I don't regret a single second of it."

He kept his head bent. "I should regret it," he whispered hoarsely. "But I don't."

She smiled at his confession. "Good."

"But I can't do it again." Meeting her gaze, his expression was tortured and earnest all at once.

"Can't kiss me again?"

"Not ever again."

He was right, even if she was secretly disappointed at the thought of never having the chance to experience another one of his kisses.

"I promised your dad that he had nothing to worry about with our marriage arrangement, that you'd be safe with me."

She nodded. Even without Tom's promise to her dad, she'd made a promise to Nathaniel to think about their relationship. She certainly wasn't respecting him if she was already kissing another man.

"So if we can't ever kiss again, then can we at least be friends?" she asked.

"Perhaps if we're friendlier toward each other around my parents, they won't pressure us so much."

"Oh, my." She squirmed just thinking about all their comments and kissing. "I daresay, they are determined to make us a good married couple, aren't they?"

"Very."

"At least they care about us. If we were a real married couple, their advice and help would be a blessing."

Tom shook his head. "I don't know how Ruth and Greg handled their meddling."

"I think their so-called meddling is cute."

"It's frustrating." Tom glanced back to the house and tower not far down the beach from where he'd led her. Against the backdrop of sand and sea in the fading evening, the lighthouse was picturesque.

In hindsight, she could see the wisdom of hiding at Race Point. She'd never guessed that she could live without all the comforts of home. But she'd already survived one week, and she could admit she liked being at the lighthouse better than she'd imagined.

"Your dad's very hard to resist."

"That's an understatement."

"Now I know where you get your powers of persuasion."

Tom smiled and stood, brushing the sand from his trousers. He reached for her hand and helped her to her feet. "Then let me persuade you to wade with me in the low tide."

She took his hand and allowed him to assist her to her feet. As they started forward, the sand squished between her toes, still warm from baking in the sun all day. She expected him to release her and resume a respectable distance, but he kept hold of her. He even placed a kiss on her temple.

A tremor of delight coursed through her, and she brushed her arm against his. "I thought you weren't going to kiss me ever again."

"That wasn't a kiss," he said softly. "You should know that now."

Her insides fluttered. Oh yes. She knew what a real kiss was like now.

"Besides, Mom and Dad are watching us from the window."

"Oh, so you're putting on a show for them?" She started to pull away, not sure why the playacting should bother her now after all the acting they'd already done. But somehow his words stung.

His grip tightened preventing her escape. "Their prying gives me an excuse."

"An excuse?"

"To hold you."

This was one time she liked his blunt honesty, and in response she rested her head against his shoulder.

"As a friend, of course," he added with a mirthful emphasis on the word *friend*.

"Then I won't object. As a friend."

The sand became wet and cold as they walked out where normally the waves and water crashed. But with low tide, the beach was exposed, leaving small translucent jellyfish and tiny crabs out in the open for the seagulls swirling overhead.

She hadn't walked on a beach barefoot since she was a little girl. Now, next to Tom with the damp sand beneath her feet, the sea breeze caressing her face, and the softening glow of the sun painting a masterpiece over the water, she couldn't imagine any other place she'd rather be.

When they reached the ocean's edge, they stopped and let cold but gentle waves lap their toes. They stood silently, and when she glanced at Tom, she could see deep satisfaction in his features, a peace there she'd never noticed before.

"You love the ocean," she stated softly.

"I always have." The wistfulness in his tone twisted her heart. She couldn't stop herself from pulling her hand from his and sliding it around his waist instead. When he did likewise, so that she was tucked against his side in the crook of his arm, she realized she was exactly where she wanted to be. She didn't miss the parties or the shops or the theater or the yacht races. She didn't miss her home or her maids or even her friends.

She'd never been more content than at that moment. Only one thing could have made it better, and that was another kiss.

"We could give your parents something more to see." She tried to keep her voice light and teasing, even though deep down the craving for another kiss was growing. "That is, if you think they need a little more convincing that we're a happily married couple."

"We've moved out too far to give them a show."

"Shall we move back within their sights?" The tide was turning, and the waves were getting higher, splashing the hem of her skirt even though she had it bunched with one hand.

Except for the tightening of his arm against hers, he didn't move. He seemed to wage an inner debate before letting go of her. "As long as the show doesn't involve kissing." His voice was stern.

She smiled and gave him a playful shove before moving away from him. "Of course it won't."

"All right."

"Then let's go." She started running back the way they'd come. "I'll race you."

"You'd never be able to outrun me."

She hiked up her skirt and ran faster. The hard-packed wet sand was much easier to traverse than the loose grains. "I doubt you can catch me." She smiled at him over her shoulder.

He hadn't moved, and he watched her almost lazily, his lips curving up into a devastating, lop-sided grin. "I'm giving you a head start."

"I don't need it." She was nearing the sand dune and their shoes, and the dry sand was beginning to slow her down. She stumbled along, laughing and breathless.

"I'm starting." And with that, he jolted forward at a sprint.

She shrieked at his speed and tried to increase her pace. But now that she was in dry sand, her feet sank and she could hardly move.

"You better pick up the pace," he called.

She only laughed and tried to push herself the last dozen paces. But her feet felt as though she'd strapped stones to them. Before she could beat him to the place where they'd left their shoes, he reached her and grabbed her waist to stop her. Under his momentum, they both tumbled forward. He somehow managed to wrap her in his arms and twist around so that she found herself landing on top of him. As his back hit the sand and she crushed him under her weight, he grunted and closed his eyes.

She sucked in a rapid breath of concern and quickly rolled next to him. "Are you okay?"

He didn't respond.

She lifted a hand to his cheek. The thin layer of stubble was rough against her fingers like the grains of sand. "Tom?"

He remained motionless.

She'd hurt him. Or maybe he'd hit his head in the fall. "Oh no," she whispered starting to rise.

But at that moment, his arms snaked around her, preventing her from moving. His eyes popped open, and he grinned. "I caught you."

Her body sagged against him with relief. "No. I think I made it."

He glanced at their shoes two feet away. "You missed."

"I'm close enough."

"Not quite."

She reached out an arm in an attempt to snag one of the shoes, but he pulled her back so that she couldn't reach her prize. She was suddenly conscious of his nearness, of the solidness of his body next to hers, and the fact that his face was only inches away. The rapid intakes of his breath made her all too keenly aware of the closeness of his mouth.

It would be all too easy to bend in and let him kiss her again. Much too easy.

As if thinking the same, he gave a soft groan and released her. He scrambled back and then sat up, holding his face in his hands. "I'm sorry, Victoria. I need to be stronger and more careful around you. I can't—won't—break my word to your father."

"I promised my father to be careful too. But we're not doing anything wrong."

"Victoria." He lifted his face and met her gaze, revealing his inner turmoil. "Try to understand."

She did. This something between them was definitely real, something they could no longer ignore. But he was a man of honor in every way. And she loved that about him. He'd given her father his word to remain professional as her bodyguard. If he allowed himself to become involved with her in a deeper relationship, then he was betraying himself. He would be going against his principles. And she didn't want to be the cause of that. He'd only loathe himself and perhaps, eventually, loathe her as well.

She didn't want to hurt him. She truly wanted what was best for him. But she wasn't sure she was strong enough to let him go. Not when she was falling in love with him.

Chapter 13

$\mathcal{T}$om tucked the thin blanket around his mom's waist. "Can I do anything else for you?" He couldn't look at the end of the bed, at the flat spot under the covers where her feet should have been. The only way he was surviving was by keeping busy all day and spending his evenings with Victoria so that he minimized the amount of time he was with Mom.

She waved him away from the bed. "No. I'm just fine. You go on and be with Victoria. I can tell you're ready to wrap her in your arms."

"Mom," he whispered, glancing out his parents' room to the closed door across the hallway. Victoria would be sitting on the sofa like she usually was, ready and eager to talk to him. The first night he hadn't been sure what they'd find to discuss. But after spending every night for the past week talking with her, now he wasn't sure how he could go without their conversations.

"Don't be embarrassed, dear." With a satisfied smile, Mom leaned back against the mound of pillows at the headboard. A book rested on the nightstand next to an oil lamp that was turned low. He knew she'd read for a while before going to sleep. Even now she was a light sleeper—always had been. She likely heard every move they made. "It's perfectly normal to desire your wife. Especially one as sweet and beautiful as Victoria."

Sweet and beautiful. Yes, she was. And desire her? Yes, he did. Too much. Way too much. His blood spurted at the barest remembrance of sharing those forbidden kisses earlier in the evening. Since coming back from their walk on the beach, he'd beaten himself up a dozen times for kissing her.

He couldn't let it happen again. However, he was beginning to realize that by coming to Race Point to hide, he'd created a situation that was too tempting. He'd overestimated his ability to keep Victoria at arm's length. With the combination of his parents' pressure and his own attraction to her, he seemed to be fighting a losing battle. If he couldn't keep things under better control, he would need to cut short the month.

As much as he wanted to deny his attraction to her, he couldn't fool himself any longer. His feelings for her were different than any other woman he'd worked to protect. And it wasn't just because she was younger than the others. There was something special about her, a vibrancy, spunk, and spirit that he liked. He was hard on her at times, but she didn't whimper or cower. She may not have liked all the decisions that he'd made recently, but she didn't wallow in despair or hold onto grudges. She adapted and made the best of her circumstances. Through it all, she remained poised and lovely.

He couldn't deny that he enjoyed spending time with her, not only conversing in the evenings, but also at meals and, tonight, walking along the beach. She was talkative and lively and fun to be with. Like when she'd challenged him to a race.

She'd been adorable, smiling at him over her shoulder like she had. At that moment, she could have asked him for the world, and he would have given it to her. It was a good thing she hadn't known his thoughts.

"I'm glad that you made up to each other." Mom picked up her book from the night table. "I could tell you were having a good time together on the beach."

"You and Dad are nosy."

Mom laughed. "What do you expect? We're just excited for you."

He wanted to tell her that they needed to stop butting into his relationship with Victoria. They were making his job a hundred times harder.

Mom reached for his hand and patted it. "You'll have to excuse our exuberance. The son who told us he'd never get married is madly in love with his bride."

Madly in love? He almost choked at the declaration. Mom was reading much more into their relationship than was there. Wasn't she?

"At least you worked through your little spat," she continued. "Your dad always said that a couple can never stay angry for long when they're kissing."

Tom supposed he'd have to be careful not to show any irritation toward Victoria for the duration of their visit, especially around Dad, or he'd make them kiss again. The problem was, Victoria was bound to get mad at him again if he didn't find a way for her to have more clothes.

"She's upset that I won't agree to hire a seamstress." Once the admission was out, Tom wasn't sure if he should have said anything.

Mom looked up at him thoughtfully. "Ruth left behind several dresses that no longer fit after birthing her children.

They would be too big for Victoria, but I'd be happy to help her take them in."

He doubted Victoria would accept hand-me-downs from his sister. But it was better than exposing her to one more person who might recognize her or her family name.

For a moment, the breeze coming in the open window rattled the string of shells mom had hung from the curtain rod. The sound took him back to his childhood, to the memories of walking along the beach with her, collecting shells of all shapes and sizes, seeing the beauty in every detail, even in the tiniest horseshoe crab. That life now seemed like it belonged to a different person altogether.

"You know, I've never stopped praying for you since Ike died," Mom said as though she could sense his reflective mood.

Her words made him stiffen. Didn't she remember he didn't like talking about anything that had happened in the past? He'd left home plenty of times during previous visits at the slightest mention of Ike.

"I've prayed for you every day," she said, her smile waning and tears pooling in her eyes.

"I know, and I appreciate it." No matter where he'd gone in the world, he'd always known that somewhere Mom was lifting him up to God. It was something he hadn't been able to do for himself since the day he'd recovered consciousness and saw the stumps at the ends of her legs where her feet had been amputated.

"God is finally answering my prayers." Mom's voice wobbled. "With Victoria."

Tom didn't have the heart to tell her she was wrong. Victoria wasn't God's answer, not by any stretch of the imagination. He simply squeezed her arm and said goodnight.

Thankfully, she didn't say anything more.

He followed his mom's instructions on where to locate Ruth's old clothes in the attic. After rummaging around, he found them in a crate and made his way back down the ladder. Before entering the bedroom, he drew in a fortifying breath. He needed to be at his strongest, because just the thought of being near Victoria again was enough to send his pulse sluicing like river water through a paddle wheel.

As he entered and latched the door behind him, he clutched the knob, praying that might anchor him and keep him from crossing to her and sweeping her into his arms.

At the sight of him, she rose from the sofa and offered him a welcoming smile. She'd lit a lantern, which cast a soft glow over the dark room. A breeze blew in through the open window, tousling the curtains and dispersing the heat that remained from the day. Her cross lay on the couch next to where she'd been sitting. It was a rugged, unpolished cross, not something he'd expect a wealthy woman like Victoria to carry around with her. But she was obviously attached to it and usually left it on the bedside table.

"I missed you," she said. In the lantern light, her brown eyes were large and her golden hair was glossy. With the wind swirling the long locks around her shoulders and over her arms, she was breathtaking.

He gripped the doorknob harder. "You've only been in here for forty-three minutes."

"Are you sure it's not more like forty-four?" Her voice was serious, but her eyes teased him. "Whatever the case, it's been too long."

He'd felt the same way. But he couldn't say so. If he encouraged Victoria's feelings for him any more than he already had, he'd only end up hurting her at the end of the month when he left for another position in Europe. He didn't want to cause her any heartache.

Maybe it was better to argue with her and make her mad at him. Then he wouldn't have to worry about all of these feelings. And he knew just what would stir up strife. The subject of the seamstress. "Mom said you could remake Ruth's old dresses." He reached for the few outfits he'd tucked under his arm and held them out to her.

He was surprised when she crossed to him and took them without arguing. She unfolded each one and laid them on the end of the unmade bed before standing back and studying them. "Even if the style is rather plain, at least the colors are bright and pretty."

"You would look pretty in anything." Once the words were out, he wanted to bash himself over the head. He was turning into Nathaniel. Flattering and fawning over her. And the thought scared him.

She smiled and gathered the dresses together before depositing them haphazardly on a wooden chair. Then she sat down on the end of the bed and patted the spot beside her. "Come on. Sit down so we can talk." She whispered, as they'd gotten in the habit of doing so that his mom wouldn't be able to hear every conversation they had.

He didn't dare let go of the door. "Victoria." His voice came out a growl.

"What?" Her elegant brows rose in innocence. "Your parents know you've been sleeping on the floor. So I thought we'd better move our talks to the bed."

"That's not a good idea."

"But then they'll stop thinking we're mad at each other."

Apparently he had to spell this out for her. "I'm not a monk. If I sit on the bed, I won't have talking on my mind."

"Oh." A hue of becoming pink colored her cheeks. She

twirled the wedding band on her finger. "Then what do you suggest we do?"

He glanced to the open window. The steady crash of the waves beckoned him to take a night swim. He needed to cool off and start thinking levelly again. "We have to remember that this isn't real, Victoria," he said in a hoarse whisper. "It's my job."

Her fingers lingered on her wedding band, tracing the rose pattern. "What if it doesn't have to be your job anymore? What if we made it real?"

The hopeful way she looked at him, as if she might really care for him, as if she truly wanted to be with him sent a tremor through his body.

He'd never considered getting into a serious relationship. He'd always figured that if he hadn't been able to keep his brother or Mom safe, then he didn't deserve to have a wife or family because there was the chance that he wouldn't be able to keep them safe either. He'd always believed he was better off spending his life alone, making amends by protecting strangers the way he should have protected the ones he loved.

But what if he'd been wrong? What if he could move on? After all, he was much older and wiser than he'd been during the war.

Even so, he was ludicrous to consider her proposal. They couldn't have a relationship. They were worlds apart, she from the upper echelon of society and he from a simple working class family. She was atrociously rich. He had nothing, not even a home. She was accustomed to a life of opulence and pleasure. He was content with simplicity.

Then there was the tiny factor that her father would never approve. Henry Cole wanted a son-in-law with old money, like Nathaniel Winthrop III. Not a poor light keeper's son.

The hope in Victoria's eyes was too much. He hated to disappoint her, but he couldn't change who he was. There was no getting around the fact that he wasn't the right man for her. He expelled a frustrated breath and walked to the window. He stuffed his hands in his pockets and stared out at the beam of moonlight making a path across the water.

After a moment, the squeak of the bed told him she'd risen. She padded across the room, and her soft footsteps stopped behind him.

"Tom," she said. "I know you're probably thinking of all the reasons why we shouldn't have a relationship." She touched his back lightly, but it was enough to burn through his shirt and heat his skin.

"Like the fact that you're still Nathaniel's?"

"I broke off the engagement. You know that."

"But he still thinks you're his. He's waiting for you."

She slid her arms around his waist, leaned into him, and rested her face against his back. At the pressure, he closed his eyes and fought against the desire to hold her. "Being with you is so different," she whispered. "I never, ever felt this way about Nathaniel."

"What way?"

"Like I'm falling in love."

She was falling in love with him? Her words poured over him. Victoria Cole was falling in love with him? How was that possible? What did she see in him?

She rubbed his arms before finding his hands and lacing her fingers through his. For a long moment, he couldn't move. He simply wanted to stand there and imprint every detail of the moment into his memory. The warmth of her arms, the smoothness of her fingers, the pressure of her body.

"What do you feel for me?" she finally asked tentatively.

"I'm trying to sort it out." He didn't know how else to respond. He couldn't lie to her and tell her he felt nothing. But if he admitted the depth of his feelings, then he might possibly take them down a path he didn't want to traverse. He'd already compromised his work. This would make things even worse.

As if reading his mind, she spoke. "I know you gave my father your word that our arrangement would stay professional and you're a man who lives by his principles. I respect that about you. I don't want you to do anything that would make you loathe yourself."

The tension in his muscles eased, and he relaxed against her. This was one of the things he loved about her, that she was perceptive and unafraid of facing difficult issues.

"So that's why I think you should stop being my bodyguard. Then you're free. You wouldn't have to worry about me being your client and the implications from that."

He'd never stop worrying about her. Even if he wasn't her bodyguard. From the moment he'd almost lost her in the carriage-ride kidnapping, he hadn't been able to shake the terror of losing her. If he was honest with himself, he knew he never would have brought any other client home. He wouldn't have suffered through the experience of facing his haunted past for anyone else.

But he'd do anything for her.

And yet, could he do this? Give up his position as her bodyguard? He hesitated. "I promised your father—"

"All my father wants is for me to be happy. If I'm happy with you, he won't object. In fact, I think he'd give us his blessing." With that, she tightened her hold around him. His pulse picked up its pace at the thought of giving in to all the feelings that had been growing for Victoria since the first time he'd met her.

No, he told himself sternly. He couldn't give in to *all* of the longings. If he decided to explore a possible relationship, then he would start slowly and court her properly. It didn't matter that they were already married and had shared a few passionate moments together. She deserved more than stolen kisses. They needed time to get to know one another, to explore and test their feelings, and to determine if they were a good fit or not.

"Tom?" Her voice was hopeful.

He squeezed his eyes shut for a moment. He didn't want to let Mr. Cole down. But he had the feeling Victoria was right. Mr. Cole coveted his daughter's happiness. If this was what Victoria wanted, then surely it wouldn't hurt to take the next couple of weeks to discover if they really could have a future together.

"Okay."

She released her grip and spun him so that they were facing one another. Her features were lit with a delighted smile.

"But," he said quickly, "we have to do things right."

"Like how?"

"Like basing our relationship on friendship, not physical attraction."

Her smile widened. "I like the sound of that."

"Then if things don't work out, you're free to move on."

"They will work out." She lifted a hand to his cheek. "I won't want to move on."

A shiver of anticipation trailed up his spine, which he rapidly attempted to squelch. "I mean it, Victoria. We keep our hands off each other."

"But we're married." Her sights moved to his mouth and stayed there. The desire that blazed to life in her eyes was almost his undoing. He was sure she had no idea that her longing was so readable. If she knew, she'd be embarrassed.

He took a step away from her to keep himself from crushing her in his embrace. He was certain that if he started kissing her right now in their bedroom, he would have a difficult time stopping. "At the end of this month, if we know we belong together, then we'll have a proper wedding."

"Very well, Mr. Cushman," she said. "If I agree to your conditions, then you have to agree to one of mine."

She sauntered away, so saucy, so full of life that his chest ached just watching her. When she glanced at him coyly over her shoulder, he knew he wouldn't be able to resist her condition, not even if he tried.

"What?" he asked.

She kept walking until she reached the bed. "We can kiss every once in a while." As she spoke the words, a flush moved into her cheeks.

He was glad she was on the other side of the room. If she'd been anywhere near him, he would have shown her his answer.

He tried to find his voice to speak coherently. "Only once in a great while," he managed.

"Okay." She turned away from him, but not before he caught her smile.

With weak knees and his heart sputtering, he collapsed backward onto the sofa so that he was staring up at the ceiling. Then he allowed himself to smile too.

Chapter 14

$\mathcal{V}$ictoria peeked past the curtain of the studio window and finally saw Tom striding up the sandy path from the tower. His head was down against the wind that had begun to increase in ferocity as the afternoon passed. The clouds had been rolling in and growing darker by the hour.

Her heart pattered in anticipation of seeing him. With a smile, she let the curtain fall back into place.

"Tom must be coming for another break," Zelma said, wearing a happy smile of her own.

Victoria crossed toward the door of the closet-like side room that Zelma used as an art studio. "I'll go see if he'd like a glass of the lemonade I just squeezed."

"You do that dear. I'm sure he'd appreciate it." Zelma dipped her brush into the palette and focused on the canvas in front of her. "Although I'm fairly certain that's not what he's coming up to the house to get."

Victoria felt her cheeks heating, but she rushed into the kitchen to the pitcher and waiting glass. She poured one and garnished it with a slice of lemon on the rim.

Then she ran a hand over her outfit, smoothing away any wrinkles. She'd spent the past week remaking Ruth's skirts. With Zelma's help, she'd resized them and added ruffles around the bottoms and bustles to the backs, as best she could. And today she'd finally worn one. Even though the garment was better than it had been, she still felt strange and somewhat out of sorts in the plain clothes. But she had to admit, like with the cooking and baking, she'd enjoyed learning to sew much more than she'd thought she would.

She checked her reflection in the window and tucked a lose strand of hair back into the coil. After almost two weeks of having to do her own hair, she'd started experimenting with different styles and found several that were easy and rather becoming. She pinched her cheeks then hurried into the hallway and was waiting at the front door when Tom opened it.

A gust of wind blew in ahead of him and threatened to push her back with its strength. He wrestled the door closed and turned with expectation. When his gaze landed upon her, his eyes darkened and his brows slanted in that magnetic way that never failed to turn her limbs to liquid.

"Hi," she said, suddenly breathless. She held out the glass. "I thought you might like some lemonade."

He took it from her and drank several long gulps without shifting his attention from her, which only made her stomach turn to liquid too.

She loved when he took breaks from his work during the day. In addition to joining her and Zelma for lunch, he'd started taking a few minutes in the morning and afternoon to come back to the house. The reason for his visit was always different—to change his sweaty shirt, to get a snack or a drink, or to find a new pair of gloves. She wanted to believe those were all excuses, that he was really coming to see her. But she could never be certain. Either way, she was always impatient to see him and surprised by how much she longed to be with him when they were apart.

"How's your afternoon going?" she asked, admiring the way the muscles in his neck and jaw rippled as he finished the drink.

He set the empty glass onto the half-moon console table near the door. Then he reached for her, his strong hands sliding up her arms possessively before winding around her waist and pulling her against his chest.

"It's going better now," he whispered against her ear.

She sighed and closed her eyes, pure contentment and pleasure coursing through her. She wrapped her arms around him and relished his strength. This was where she wanted to be. In fact, she'd started living for these few short moments every morning and afternoon when he'd hold her, when she'd breathe him in and listen to his heart beat, when his heat and solidness surrounded her.

He'd hold her only for a few minutes, never long enough, before pressing his lips against her crown in a hard kiss that promised so much more and made her wish he'd kiss her lips that way. But he'd always pull back and set her away before she could work up the courage to lift her face and capture his lips with hers.

His grip around her was hard and unswerving. And his lips came against her hair too soon. She wanted to cling to him and make the moment last longer, but she knew he was trying to take things slow, and she wanted to respect his wishes.

His lips were warm and his breath heavy against her head. His fingers tightened for a moment, and then he set her away from him as he usually did. She smiled and tried to pretend for herself and for him that she didn't want more, that she was content with this tiny morsel of his affection.

He reached behind him for the doorknob. "I have to get back to work." But his gaze lingered on her face.

"Okay. I'll see you at dinner." If only his dad would make Tom kiss her again.

Tom turned away from her and began to open the door. Then he stopped. "Come with me to the tower." His voice was tight. "I want to show you something."

Her breath caught at the invitation. All week, she'd been able to tell he was making efforts not to be alone with her. Other than their late evening talks on the sofa, he'd kept their time together out in the open and had exerted extra caution because of the undeniable attraction between them.

"Sure." She tried to keep her tone normal. "I'll let your mom know where I'm going."

Of course Zelma waved her away with a smile and a knowing look. "Go have fun, dear. I'll be fine here with my painting."

As Victoria followed Tom down the trail to the tower, the sand swirled so that it was almost biting. The roaring of the wind and the crashing of the waves made talking impossible. When they stumbled into the tower and closed the door, the silence was eerie compared to the clamor outside. The wind howled under the doorjamb, but the only other sound was their heavy breathing.

She hadn't yet been inside the tower. But it was similar to the ones her grandfather had worked in. Painted white bricks lined the walls, and a narrow metal staircase spiraled up with a landing every so often. The first landing had a small window that afforded enough light to guide their way.

Tom started up the steps, his boots clanking against the iron. She followed after him, and the higher they rose, the more she could feel the power of the wind swaying the structure. It was sturdy enough to withstand a great deal of weathering and battering. Even so, she held onto the rail tightly as she ascended. When they reached the top, he climbed through the hatch first and then held out his hand and helped her up.

As she straightened, she glanced around with interest. The lantern in the middle was unlit, but the glass prisms of the Fresnel lens shone like polished crystal. The windows, too, were perfectly clear, without a handprint or speck of dirt. Even the metal floor was scrubbed clean.

Outside, the foaming ocean waves crashed on one side and the sandy hills with beach grass covered the other. The long grass was dry and yellowing from the hot summer and was bent nearly to the ground by the wind.

"I've always loved being up in a lighthouse tower," she said. "There aren't too many other places quite as beautiful."

He took in the landscape too, his features softening with satisfaction. Then he reached for a brass nautical spyglass on a tall table that sat next to the galley door. He lengthened the mechanism and peered through the glass at the narrowed end. He was quiet and intent for a moment before speaking. "They're still there."

He passed the spyglass to her, and she held it to her eye, pointing it in the same direction he'd looked just seconds ago. She held it steady, but all she saw were the daunting waves with their foamy caps.

"Here." He moved behind her so that his chest touched her back. He reached around and put his hand over hers on the spyglass. His fingers were both strong and gentle, and he tilted her to the north.

"Do you see anything now?" His voice rumbled near her ear. For a second she was too distracted by his nearness to pay attention to what she was viewing on the other end of the spyglass. She could only think about the contours of his chest pushed against her, his arm brushing hers, and his breath tickling her neck.

She tried to focus again. "What am I looking for?"

He took the spyglass from her, looked into it for a minute, and then carefully, without moving his aim, lowered it to her eye.

She attempted to be just as careful and focused as best she could. After a few seconds she saw a whale burst from the water and splash down on its back into the waves. "Oh, my!" Before she could say anything else, another whale, this one slightly smaller, arched out of the water and twisted, with its long flippers extended, exposing its white underside.

"Incredible," she whispered, awestruck.

"They're humpbacks." His voice was laced with awe too.

As she watched, one of the whales lifted its fluked tail out of the water and splashed it back down. "They're beautiful."

"Some say they're being hunted to the brink of extinction," he said.

She lost sight of the majestic creatures and handed the spyglass back. He didn't move but relaxed against her, putting the spyglass to his eye and watching the distance.

"Did you know they only eat in the summer?" he asked.

She settled back into his hold. "How can they survive the winter?"

"They feed off their stores of fat."

She couldn't see the whales anymore but was content to rest in his arms and listen to him talk about the whales, their feeding habits, migration patterns, and the singing done by male whales and the fact that the songs could last for ten to twenty minutes.

"Have you ever heard them sing?" she asked.

"Plenty of times."

"Then sing one of their songs for me."

"No."

"Oh, please." She craned her head and smiled up at him. "I'm curious to know what a whale song sounds like."

He took the spyglass away from his eye and cocked his brow. "Do I look like a whale?"

She pretended to study him. "Maybe a little."

The corners of his mouth twitched with the beginning of a smile. "In what way?"

"You're big and strong."

His grin broke free. "I'm still not singing."

"Please. Please. Please." She twisted so that she was facing him.

"Never."

"Then you'll force me to take drastic measures."

Again he lifted one of his brows, revealing the humor in his eyes. "I'd like to see what you think is drastic."

She smiled. Then before he could stop her, she tickled his stomach. He didn't budge. She tried his sides, but he stood unmoving, completely unaffected.

"You're not ticklish?" she asked.

"Not in the least."

"No fair." She pretended to pout. But before she could complete the face, his hands came up to her waist and his fingers found the sensitive area there. She jumped with a gasp.

"I see that you are." He tickled her again, his eyes alight with humor.

She couldn't contain her laughter. As he tickled, she wiggled and shrieked. Finally, breathless, she called, "Stop! I surrender. I won't ask you to sing the whale song."

His hands slid away from her sensitive sides and wrapped around her back. "Promise?"

"For today." She fell against him. "But I make no guarantees for the future."

He grinned down at her, and she couldn't keep from admiring the strong chiseled lines and the dark handsomeness of his features.

He languidly studied her face too, and as he did so, his mirth faded. He lifted a hand to her cheek, hesitated only a moment before grazing her skin and making her knees weak. For just an instant his eyes cleared, giving her a glimpse of his feelings for her—the intensity, the passion, and yes, even the love.

As the truth of how much he cared about her sank in, a tremble started in her stomach and rippled to her legs. It wasn't a tremble of joy. It was one of fear—the same kind of fear she'd felt on her wedding day when she'd been walking out to the carriage and the reality of getting married to Nathaniel had become entirely too imminent.

She turned back to the window, praying that Tom wouldn't see the fear that haunted her, the fear that she tried never to think about. She forced her mind away from it with practiced ease, pushing any unwelcome thoughts into a closet where they would be contained and chained and forgotten.

"Thanks for letting me see the world from up here." She peered out the window again.

He didn't move or say anything for a moment.

"The waves are so majestic and powerful," she continued. "And the ocean is so endless."

Still he was quiet.

"I don't think I'd ever tire of this view." She was rambling but she couldn't stop.

He touched her side. Then she felt his body with all its warmth and solidness move behind her. He wrapped his arms around her, pulling her back into his chest. She breathed out the tightness in her lungs and relaxed against him. For a minute, they stood wordlessly watching the ocean, the waves rising and falling, and the dark clouds on the horizon blowing across the sky.

When he brushed a strand of hair back from her neck, she released another sigh, this one of contentment. She'd silenced her fears, and now she basked in the satisfaction of being in his arms. He drew the rest of her hair behind her ear so that her neck and ear were laid bare.

He dipped down, his chin brushing her cheekbone, the scruffy stubble a strange but pleasant sensation. His arms tightened around her, and he lowered his head until his lips skimmed her ear. The touch was feathery light, sending tingles across her skin.

She crossed her arms over his and tilted her head to the side. It was an invitation to linger.

Accepting her offer, his lips dropped to the hollow of her ear. He pressed a kissed there, his breath echoing loudly. It stirred her belly into a swirling whirlpool. After a long tantalizing moment, his lips moved to her earlobe and then grazed her neck.

At the contact, she almost cried aloud. Even though she managed to bite back most of the cry, a small squeak slipped out.

The heat of his ragged breath and the moisture of his lips moved to the arch between her neck and shoulder. This time she couldn't hold back a gasp. Her small noises only seemed to inflame him. He released a soft moan before turning her and taking possession of her mouth. His lips settled over hers with the fervor she'd been dreaming about since his last kiss.

If she was honest with herself, she'd waited for this moment all week. She'd longed to be connected with him again in this way, to feel his passion, to know that she stirred him the same way he did her.

His kiss deepened, and she arched upward. His hands at her waist splayed as though he wanted all of her. She didn't know exactly what that meant, had only heard whispers from her friends, especially from Theresa, who had always been bolder than others.

Victoria's body seemed to turn to fire wherever he touched. And as his kiss raged, she didn't care if she was consumed. She wanted to go wherever the kiss meant to lead. And she could sense he wanted that too.

"I'm coming up!" James called from the stairwell.

Tom broke away and released her.

"Make sure you're decent," James called again, his voice echoing in the hollow passageway and clearly full of humor.

Tom ran one hand across his mouth and jaw and with the other tucked in his shirt, which had somehow come loose.

Had she pulled it out?

Her face burned at the thought, but she quickly wiped at her own face and hair and bodice, her fingers shaking too much to bring about any semblance of order.

"You ready?" James voice came from the landing just below the hatch.

Tom cleared his throat. "All set."

The ping of boots against the ladder was followed by James's head popping through the hatch. At the sight of them, he paused. His grin was wide and his eyes sparkled. "I'm sorry for disturbing you."

Tom's face was a shade darker than usual, and he combed his fingers through his hair. "We were just about done."

"I don't know about that, son." James chuckled. "From what I could see, it looked like you were just getting started."

Mortification washed over Victoria. Had James witnessed their moment of passion? She glanced back in the direction of the house and realized that if he'd been walking from the house to the tower, he would have had a clear view of the tower room. He would have seen them kissing like there was no tomorrow.

The muscles in Tom's jaw worked up and down, as if he too realized all his dad had witnessed.

James climbed the rest of the way up. Even though his eyes were warm with affection in addition to his humor, Victoria avoided his gaze. "Your mom told me not to disturb you. I tried to hold off as long as I could, but the storm is gaining momentum." He cocked his head to the window.

Sure enough, the dark clouds were drawing closer. They were heaped upon the horizon and stretching tall, exposing their angry underbellies. Lightning flashed deep within and seemed to incite the waves to join in the tumult.

"I wanted to let you finish," James said. "Your mom and I have lots of happy memories of our times together in light-house towers—"

"Dad." Tom cut James off with a pointed, slightly tortured look.

James laughed heartily before checking the wind direction and turning to adjust the vents. While his back was turned, Tom reached for her hand, his eyes radiating apology. Was he sorry for kissing her? Or sorry about his dad's interruption?

She hoped it was the later and smiled at him in reassurance. She squeezed his hand, hoping to send him the message that she wasn't in the least sorry for this, any more than she was for the last time they kissed.

"I need to get the lantern lit before it gets too dark," James said as he worked. "It's just a precaution."

"I'll help you," Tom offered.

"I'll be fine. You go finish your business with your wife somewhere else."

Even though James's bluntness was becoming more familiar, Victoria still heated at his insinuation. Tom shook his head, but a surge of wind rattled the tower windows with such force that the metal tube attached to the glass chimney of the lantern popped away from the wall and slammed against the window with such force that Victoria expected the glass to crack. Wind roared through the vent opening, and both Tom and James lunged to grab the dangling tube before it could do damage. For a moment they struggled to lift and position it back in place against the incoming gust.

As they worked and shouted instructions to each other, she realized her moment with Tom was over, especially when the wind broke the vent off again. This time it almost knocked into Tom.

"Go back to the house," he called to her. "It isn't safe up here now."

She nodded as the wind roared into the small room, swirling her skirt and hair and making conversation virtually impossible. She descended, and on her walk back to the house, she fought the swelling gusts and blowing sand.

All the while, she couldn't stop thinking about that kiss. How far would the kiss have led this time if James hadn't interrupted? Tom wanted to take things slowly. Wanted to focus on their friendship first. Wanted to take the rest of their month at Race Point to test their relationship. She wasn't helping matters by throwing herself in his arms every time she saw him.

She had the feeling that once again, he would be frustrated at himself for failing to keep the boundaries he'd established. He would beat himself up and perhaps even pull away from her. Surely she could be more careful and help him preserve his sense of integrity.

"Zelma?" she called once she'd entered and shaken the sand from her skirt.

"I'm still in here, dear." The sweet voice came from the art room.

"Can I get you anything?" Victoria asked as she made her way to the little room at the rear of the house.

"I'm perfectly fine," Zelma said. "James lit a lantern before he left."

Victoria stepped into the cozy room, the walls of which were covered in paintings from floor to ceiling. Zelma still sat in her chair in front of her easel with the lantern buzzing on the pedestal beside her. She had a blanket draped over her lap and a fresh cup of tea and biscuit.

"James is so sweet," Victoria said, thinking of all the ways he doted on Zelma.

"He's a very good man." Zelma concentrated on the canvas in front of her. "And Tom takes after him."

Yes, Tom was a good man. Victoria smiled thinking about his desire to show her the humpback whales and the fun that they'd had.

"I take it you had a lovely time?" Zelma dragged her attention away from the canvas to glance at Victoria with the kind of look that made Victoria pluck at the edge of her sleeve with renewed embarrassment. Zelma knew exactly what they'd been doing in the tower.

"Tom wanted to show me a couple of whales he'd spotted off the coast."

Zelma dipped her brush into first one color and then another, mixing them. "He's always loved sea life."

Victoria stepped behind Tom's mother and took in the nearly finished landscape, a beach at sunset with a young couple wading hand in hand in the low tide. It was beautiful. And strangely familiar.

"Yes, it's you and Tom," Zelma said with a smile. "Your young love is inspiring. I had to capture it."

Their love? She'd known she was falling in love. But she hadn't been sure about Tom. She thought she'd caught a glimpse of it in his eyes up in the tower. But what if she'd only imagined it?

"You're a talented artist," Victoria said, glancing at all of the other pictures around the room. "You must have a hundred pictures scattered throughout the house."

Zelma swirled a pinkish orange color in the sky. "I wish I could take credit for all of them. But many of them are Tom's."

"My Tom?"

Zelma laughed. "Yes. Your Tom. Is that so hard to believe?"

"Actually, it's impossible to believe." Victoria couldn't imagine Tom painting anything. He'd never even shown the remotest interest in art work, hadn't even glanced at the paintings on the walls of the keeper's house.

"He loved to paint as a child and a young man, before he left home." The paintbrush in Zelma's hand stilled, and sadness transformed her features. The wrinkles around her eyes seemed deeper and the grooves around her mouth more pronounced.

"He's never once mentioned it." Victoria studied the pictures, as if seeing them for the first time.

"The one of the Cape Henry on Chesapeake Bay there in the middle is his." Zelma pointed to a painting of an octagonal-shaped brick tower. "You can tell which are his by the tiny initials he put in the left corners."

Victoria crossed the room to inspect the painting more carefully. The detail was perfect, even down to the seagull circling in a blue sky dotted with realistic-looking clouds. Sure enough, a TC was painted in the corner.

"I'm shocked." Victoria traced the crude wooden frame that surrounded the painting. "I wonder why he's never told me?"

Zelma laid down her paintbrush and folded her hands in her lap. "I don't suppose he told you how I lost my feet either?"

A gust rattled the window, followed by a burst of heavy rain splattering against the glass. Outside the day had turned almost as dark as night, causing shadows to spread over the room.

Victoria tried to squelch a rising sense of unease at the realization that perhaps she didn't know Tom as well as she'd believed. "Tom hasn't spoken much of his past," she admitted.

Zelma sighed. "I figured as much."

"I didn't want to ask you about your feet," Victoria added quickly, "because I know how it makes my mother feel when people focus on her blindness."

"I didn't know your mother was blind," Zelma said gently.

Victoria nodded and turned back to Tom's painting. "She wasn't born blind. But once she became an adult, her eyesight gradually failed." Victoria didn't like to think about her mother's disease. In fact, she tried very hard not to dwell on it. If she ignored it, she could also ignore the haunting fact that her mother had inherited the disease from her mother. Victoria had never met her grandmother, but she'd learned from her father that her blind grandmother had fallen to her death from a lighthouse tower. Her mother never spoke of it. And no one in her family ever talked about the fact that the disease was passed from mother to daughter. It was almost as if in not speaking about it they could pretend the possibility didn't exist for Victoria.

"Mother doesn't want people to treat her like she's blind," Victoria said. "So we don't talk about it, and we act as though she isn't."

"I see." Zelma's comment was soft. She was quiet for a moment, and the steady pelting of rain on the window filled the room. "Come sit down, dear." Zelma reached for a wooden chair near hers. It scraped across the floor as she drew it nearer.

Victoria hesitated. She didn't want to talk about her mother's blindness perhaps any more than Tom wanted to talk about Zelma's feet. She supposed they were both alike in their avoidance. But Zelma patted the cushion on the chair, and the kindness in her face was too difficult to refuse.

Reluctantly, Victoria sat down, and she didn't resist when Zelma reached for her hands and clasped them in hers. "Don't worry, dear. I won't pressure you to talk about your mother's blindness until you're ready."

Victoria would never be ready, but she kept that to herself.

"However, I want you to know that I'm not ashamed or embarrassed to talk about my condition. I think it's better for us to be open and honest about everything rather than pretend nothing is wrong with me. Because the truth is, I don't have feet. I can't walk. And it doesn't help us to ignore my condition."

Victoria should have guessed that Zelma would be as frank about her lack of feet as she was about everything else. Even so, Victoria was surprised by the ease and openness with which Zelma discussed the matter.

"I lost my feet from severe frostbite," she continued, her gaze unflinching. "At the time, James was an assistant keeper at Cape Henry Lighthouse in Virginia. It was the winter of 1864. Tom and our older son, Ike, had both joined up with the Jessie Scouts."

"Arch, one of my bodyguards, was a Jessie Scout," Victoria started. But then she caught herself, unsure how much information Tom would want her to share.

Zelma's eyes widened, and she studied Victoria's face for so long that Victoria wondered if perhaps she'd said something entirely wrong. "Arch is a good friend of Tom's," Zelma finally said. "I've only met him once, when he came to visit Tom after the escape. But I liked him, even if he's part of the reason Tom chose to be a bodyguard."

Victoria inwardly cringed and prayed that Zelma wouldn't make any connections and figure out that Tom was actually her bodyguard. She attempted to steer the conversation to a different topic. "What do you mean 'after the escape'?"

"You do know that the Jessie Scouts were spies and involved in dangerous missions behind Confederate lines?"

Victoria shook her head. Arch had told her only the basics, probably a watered-down version fitting for a young lady. But Tom had never once spoken of his days as a Jessie Scout. She was embarrassed to admit that she'd never known he was one.

"I wasn't too keen on my boys being involved in such

duplicitous operations. But once Ike became a scout, we couldn't sway Tom. He always wanted to do everything his big brother did. He rode off one night to join up with Ike, and there was nothing we could do to stop him."

Zelma released a long heavy sigh. "Only the Lord knows what kind of trouble those two faced every day. I still can't bear to think on it. I prayed harder and more often in those two years than I ever have before or since." She paused and glanced down to her folded hands, as though she'd traveled back in time. She was quiet again, and the raging of the wind and rain echoed in the room.

"God answered my prayers," she finally said in a voice so low Victoria almost couldn't hear her. "His answer wasn't what I expected. It usually never is." She set her shoulders and continued in a stronger voice. "One of the other assistant keeper's sons was fighting for the Confederates and sent word that Ike and Tom had been captured and were sentenced to hang as spies."

Victoria's muscles tightened at the thought of Zelma's anguish at getting the news.

"James rode off immediately for Petersburg, where he thought they were being held. But not long after he left, the assistant keeper's son showed up in the middle of the night and told me Ike and Tom were being held less than two miles away. He put his own life at risk to tell me. I was grateful, but I had no idea what to do, especially without James."

Victoria squeezed Zelma's hand. "You don't need to tell me any more, if it's too painful."

"It's all right, dear." Zelma patted her hand. "I moved as fast I could in the dark of night. But the ground was marshy and wet. And it was January. By the time I reached the Confederate encampment, I'd lost feeling in my feet. I had to wait in the shadows for another hour before I discovered where the boys were being held. By that point, I could hardly walk. But God continued to provide the strength I needed. I was able to cut Tom's bindings loose. Unfortunately, the boys were both too weak to stand and make a run for it. So of course, Ike insisted that I take Tom. But Tom wouldn't have anything to do with the plan, wouldn't hear of leaving Ike behind..."

Victoria waited for Zelma to continue. But she didn't say anything more.

"What happened next?" Victoria finally asked, her pulse pumping hard at the image of the dark, cold night and both Zelma and her sons' lives in danger.

Zelma sighed. "I'll leave the rest of the escape details for Tom to share with you. I think those are his to tell when he's ready."

"Obviously you and Tom made it." Victoria wanted to know how, but she didn't push.

"At first we didn't think Tom would live," Zelma supplied. "But he eventually recovered physically, even if he never did make peace with what happened."

Perhaps that's why he hadn't told her about being a Jessie Scout. Maybe it brought up too many painful memories.

"As hard as the doctor tried to save me from losing my feet, they were too frost-bitten after being wet and cold for so many hours. He had to amputate them to save my life." Zelma smiled, and there wasn't a hint of anger or regret in her eyes. "God used my feet to save my son's life. It was worth the sacrifice. I would have given up my entire life for him if it had come down to it."

Heat pushed at the backs of Victoria's eyes, and emotion clogged her throat. "You're a remarkable woman, Zelma."

She shook her head. "I don't claim that it was easy learning to live without walking. It's forced me more than ever to rely upon the strength and joy of the Lord."

Victoria wished she could say that she'd be able to face future trials with as much courage as Zelma. But if she couldn't muster enough courage to face just the *thought* of a trial, how would she do when a real trial came?

"The Lord has brought me to a place of peace and acceptance over all that happened," Zelma continued. "But Tom isn't there yet."

"How do you know?"

"During the past ten years, his longest visit was only two days." Zelma's voice wobbled.

Victoria squeezed Zelma's hand, hoping to lend her a measure of comfort, although she wasn't sure there was any for a parent who'd experienced such heartache. "We've been here two weeks. So see, that must mean he's on the mend."

Zelma's eyes were glassy with unshed tears. "You're right. God's doing something in his life. And I believe He's using you to do it."

"Me?"

Zelma nodded. "With you at his side, Tom can no longer run away from his fears. He has to stay and face them."

Run away? From fears? Tom had once accused her of doing that very thing. Was he guilty of the same?

She stood, anxious to talk to him, to allow him to bare his soul to her. She'd wrap her arms around him and ensure him that she understood. Their time on the sofa that night couldn't come soon enough.

Chapter 15

$\mathscr{T}$he storm shook the keeper's house, and Victoria was afraid the shingles would tear away with each new strong gust. She huddled under the covers in the darkness, unable to sleep knowing that Tom was out there with his dad.

Since the storm had begun, Tom had only come back to the house once. He'd been drenched and windblown and had informed them that he and James would both be working the night shift for the duration of the storm. Victoria had sent a basket of food back to the tower with him. Then she'd provided a simple fare of bread and leftover stew for her and Zelma.

She'd washed the dinner dishes, tidied the house, and finally helped Zelma prepare for bed. Since Victoria wasn't strong enough to carry Zelma up the stairs to the bedroom, she'd made a bed on one of the settees in the sitting room for the sweet woman.

After lingering long enough to inspect all of the pictures on the first floor to find out which ones were Tom's, Victoria had ascended to her room. She'd prayed the storm would cease so that Tom could come in and they could have their regular talk, especially because, after Zelma's disclosure, she had so many questions she wanted to ask him. She was struck again by how little she actually knew about him and his past.

When the storm showed no signs of abating, she gave up hope of seeing him, donned her nightgown, and crawled under the covers.

After tossing and turning, she finally fell asleep only to be awakened some time later by the blare of the fog signal. The "beee-ooohhhhh" was like a low throaty groan amidst the angry rumble of thunder and testy whine of the wind. Occasional flashes of lightning revealed the low thick clouds that now hung heavy over the water and would make travel hazardous.

The fog signal tapered off, and she tried to make herself comfortable in the humidity of the damp night. She closed her eyes, but another long mournful groan of the fog signal startled her to full wakefulness. As she listened for several minutes she finally realized that the obnoxious horn wasn't stopping any time soon, that the noise blared about once a minute and likely would continue to do so for the rest of the night.

She sighed and stared up through the darkness at the ceiling. There was no way she'd be able to get any more sleep now. Should she just get up?

Before she could make up her mind, the door opened, and her breath caught with relief at the sight of Tom. He soundlessly closed the door behind him. Through the dark, she could see him began to unbutton his shirt. He shrugged out of first one suspender then the other so that they hung down his trousers. From the effort he made tugging out of his shirt sleeves, she guessed that his garments were wet from the rain. He tossed the shirt to the floor and reached for the clasp of his trousers.

"Tom," she said quickly, guessing he didn't realize she was awake, or else he wouldn't have undressed quite so openly.

His hands stilled.

"Is everything okay?" she said, shifting the covers away and sitting on the edge of the bed.

"You should be asleep," he whispered.

"The fog signal woke me."

"I'm sorry. Like most wickie kids, I learned to sleep through the noise. So I forgot it would bother you."

"I'm all right. Besides, I feel guilty sleeping when you're out working so hard." She stood and started to cross to him.

He didn't move.

"Was there any more damage to the tower?" She stopped close enough so that she caught the damp, sea-tossed scent that lingered on him.

"One of the windows leaked. But we have it temporarily patched until we can caulk it."

Back in New York she never would have guessed that Tom was so capable with tools and repair work. But here in his home environment, he'd been full of surprises. "I'm sure your dad really values all of your help."

"That's why this lighthouse needs an assistant keeper. It requires more maintenance, especially with the fog signal."

"So you're not off duty yet?"

"I came back for dry clothes. I'll be on working in the fog house until the fog lifts. The boiler needs a hefty amount of water and coal to keep going."

"Oh." Disappointment weighted that tiny word. She couldn't help it. She'd been looking forward to his return.

He was silent, and the air between them seemed hotter. A flash of lightning lit the room for a few seconds giving her a glimpse of the way that his damp undershirt clung to his chest, outlining every solid bulge of muscle.

"I had a lovely evening with your mom," she said trying to think of something else beside the fact that he was so near.

"Thanks for helping her."

"I love being able to do it." She'd never thought she'd ever say such words, not when she'd always had someone at her beckoning to respond to any need or whim. She'd never had to help herself, much less anyone else.

The foghorn intruded into the peace of room again. She wished she dared to reach out and squeeze his hand, to know he still cared, to know he'd been thinking about her the same way she had him.

"I missed you tonight," she said. "But I suppose I should let you finish changing out of your damp garments so you can return to your duties."

"Yes."

"Then good night," she said, forcing herself to do what was best for him. She took a step back.

His hand closed around her wrist, preventing her from leaving. "I missed you too." His voice was strained and filled with something she couldn't name.

Her pulse thrummed to life. For a long moment, he kept her at arm's length, as though waging an inner battle. Finally, he tugged her toward him so that she had no choice but to fall against his solid but damp torso.

Her breath caught as his arms slid behind her, pulling her flush and letting her feel every ridge and valley of his chest. His heartbeat was rapid and strong. Her thoughts returned to the passionate kiss he'd given her in the tower, and her blood flamed to life with the need for another.

His hand tightened at the small of her back, and the other rose into her long loose hair. "Victoria," he murmured, nuzzling the hair near her ear.

"Hmmm," she mumbled back, unable to think coherently.

"I lose all control when I'm with you." His hand dug deeply into her hair. "Before walking in, I told myself not to look at you in bed. I knew if I did, I wouldn't be able to resist my desire for you."

She smiled at his confession.

His fingers wound through her long strands, and his lips found her ear. The pressure was hot, his breath ragged, and when he whispered her name again she almost swooned. His lips lingered against her ear, his kiss growing more ardent.

"Help me, Victoria," he managed with a gasp.

For a second, she was tempted to ignore his plea and to instead kiss him back. All she had to do was guide his mouth to hers, and she would seal her relationship with him. If he kissed her here, now, in the dark of the bedroom, it would only lead to more. She sensed it in every one of his taut muscles.

But again, as before, she realized that he would only hate himself for going against his honor and principles. He wanted to do things the right way and had been trying so hard to respect her.

She could do the same for him, couldn't she? Besides, as much as she cared about him, perhaps they did need more time before they sealed their relationship with finality.

His chest heaved against hers, and his mouth lowered to her jaw line, his irresistibly delicious kisses moving closer to her lips.

She had to move away. Now. Before it was too late for her too.

Help me, Victoria. His plea echoed in her mind. If she truly loved him, she would help him as he'd pleaded with her to do.

With a deep breath, she pulled back and broke free of his arms. "Let's talk for a few minutes before you have to go back out." She was embarrassed by the breathy desire that laced each of her words.

He started to sway toward her, but she spun and forced herself to walk away from him to the sofa. Before lowering herself, she picked up the afghan he often used at night and draped it about her shoulders.

He didn't follow her but stood where she'd left him.

For a second, she wondered if she'd done the right thing by putting distance between them. Maybe he was mad. Maybe he wouldn't want her anymore. "I'm sorry," she started. "I was just trying to do what you asked..."

"Thank you." He wiped a hand across his eyes and took a backward step toward the door.

"No. Don't go yet." She didn't care that her words came out rather desperate. "Can't we talk for a few more minutes?"

"I'm not safe around you. Not here. With you in your nightgown."

She glanced down in the darkness at her simple summer gown, sleeveless and satiny, falling all the way to the floor. It was one among many that Madame Bisseau had made for her trousseau, a more modest one that she'd grabbed in her hasty packing the night she'd left Newport. She hadn't stopped to consider how such a gown might affect Tom.

She wrapped the afghan around her more securely. "There. Is that better?"

"No, the only thing that will make our situation better is if we end our stay."

"Our stay?"

"Here at Race Point." Resignation gave strength to his voice.

She shook her head. She wasn't ready to leave. She loved being here with him, having him all to herself. If they left, he'd return to his role as her silent protector. And she'd have to return to her life in Newport and try to make sense of everything, including what to do about Nathaniel. She wasn't ready to face any of that.

"Tomorrow I'm going to Provincetown and sending the first telegram."

She didn't understand what he meant by sending a telegram. But it didn't matter. She wanted to have their fairy tale just a little longer. "Please don't. I want to be with you here. Besides, you said we needed a month."

"I can hardly make it through one night." His tone was laced with frustration. "Much less finish the month."

She'd known he would be hard on himself for crossing his self-imposed boundaries. Even so, she was sorely disappointed to think of this special time with him coming to an end. "I don't want to lose you," she admitted.

He didn't reassure her, which only added to her anxiety.

"I thought we agreed that we would see where our relationship took us, that maybe we wouldn't need to put an end to it when our time here is over."

"Victoria." His tone turned soft and placating. And she didn't want that.

"There's still so much we don't know about each other, so much left to explore..." She sat forward on the sofa, wishing she could drag him over and force him to sit down with her. "Like the fact that I never knew you were a painter. And not just any painter, but a very talented one with such depth and realism in each picture." She waited for him to say something, anything. But he was silent. "Why didn't you tell me about that part of you?"

"It's not part of me anymore."

"Sure it is. That's who God made you to be."

"It was a childhood whim."

"Those aren't the works of a child."

"I don't paint anymore." His voice was flat.

"But—"

"Never again."

The tightness in his statement gave her pause, reminded her of his stubbornness. He wouldn't be swayed by her arguments. At least not right now.

"Very well, we won't talk about your paintings, but will you at least tell me more about your brother, Ike?"

"No!" The word was as frosty as the ocean in the winter.

"You didn't mention that you had a brother," she pressed. "How are we supposed to really get to know each other if we aren't honest and open about our pasts?"

"Maybe my present is all I have to offer."

"Your mom told me about how she lost her feet and how—"

"I don't want to talk about it," he said sharply in a tone he'd never used with her before.

"Please, Tom. Talk to me. How can we build a relationship if we keep our feelings hidden from each other?"

"Maybe we can't build a relationship." Again his tone was cold.

A warning in the back of her mind told her that she should stop the conversation, but she could feel him pushing her away, and she was suddenly desperate to cling to him. "Your mom told me you didn't want to leave Ike behind, but she wouldn't tell me anymore than that."

"She shouldn't have told you anything."

"She's accepted what happened and found joy in living."

"Joy in losing her son? Joy in losing her feet?" The anguish in his voice ripped at her. "You don't know anything about loss or hardship, Victoria. So don't preach to me."

She didn't realize her hands had begun to shake until she folded them in her lap. Her mind scrambled to find a response that wouldn't anger Tom even further. "I'm sorry. You're right. I don't know about hardship. But I'd like to help bear your burdens. If you'll let me."

He stalked to dresser and opened the drawer that contained his clothes. "I'm bearing my burdens just fine by myself."

"By running away from them?"

Through the darkness she could tell he was jerking out several items. "You would know, since you're the queen of running away."

The hard cutting edge in his words took her breath away. He spun away from the drawer without closing it, strode across the room, and exited without another word. She could only stare at the door and try to make sense of what had just happened between them.

She'd only wanted to talk to him, to make him change his mind about leaving Race Point. But she'd had to ruin it all by digging into his past pains too deeply, by pushing him to talk about things before he was ready. Her chest ached and her throat burned with the need to cry. But she swallowed hard, willing herself to remain calm.

She wouldn't let a little thing like an argument get in the way of something beautiful that was growing between them. Maybe she'd run from relationships in the past. But she wasn't running this time. Not now. Not ever again.

Chapter 16

"Five telegrams and one letter." From the center of his cutter, Jimmy held out the bundle to Tom. Even though the boat swayed with the force of the high waves, Jimmy didn't falter, as comfortable and stable in his cutter as on land.

From the dock, Tom took the stack of correspondence and sifted through them. One telegram each from Nathaniel, Henry Cole, Mrs. Cole, Victoria's friend Theresa, and even one from Mrs. Winthrop, Nathaniel's mother. The letter was from Arch.

"The big bald guy who wrote the letter said not to tell anyone except you that he's in Provincetown."

Tom nodded. Four days had passed since he'd sailed to Provincetown and posted the telegram. The slew of responses wasn't unexpected. Now that he'd made Victoria's hiding spot public, he figured he had one, maybe two days left before her perpetrator arrived. At least, he hoped the news of her location would bait the attacker to come and get her. And this time, he'd be ready, especially because Arch was helping him.

With Arch positioned in Provincetown, Tom hoped he'd have some advance warning if the man who'd attacked Arch and tried to kidnap Victoria made an appearance. Although communication between Race Point and Provincetown was slow, Arch had a horse ready to ride out to the lighthouse when needed. If Arch rode fast enough, he'd be able to arrive before an attacker could sail over.

Nathaniel's name on the top telegram seemed to reach up and slap Tom, and he quickly moved it to the bottom of the pile. For a brief instant, he thought about letting it drop into the water to be swept away by the waves.

But he straightened his back and glanced to the side of the house where Victoria was attempting to hang recently laundered clothes on the line. She had a pair of his father's trousers in her hand, dangling between her thumb and forefinger as though she couldn't bear to touch them. The garment dripped enough water to form a small stream. Hadn't she used the wringer to dislodge the excess water? If the sagging, dripping garments already pinned haphazardly to the line were any indication, she'd neglected that important part of the laundering process.

"Mighty fine woman there," Jimmy said, following Tom's gaze. A grin cracked his leathery face.

"That she is."

"Eh?" Jimmy cupped his ear and leaned toward Tom. "What did you say?"

Tom didn't have the heart to repeat himself, especially louder. In fact, he had to look away from Victoria before the pain in his chest overwhelmed him.

"A real beauty." Jimmy whistled softly between his missing front teeth. "You're a lucky one, Tommy."

Lucky? Not him. He was about as unlucky as any man could get. His conversation with her the night of the storm had been a wake-up call. Her words still blared in his mind just like the deep moan of the fog signal. *How are we supposed to really get to know each other if we aren't honest and open about our pasts?* If he couldn't be honest with her now, then they had no hope for a healthy long-term relationship.

He didn't deserve her, and he never would. He was a broken man with a broken past. He wasn't sure that he'd ever be able to forgive himself and move on. It was so much easier to keep running then to have to stop and face the pain. A woman like Victoria needed so much more than what he could give. She deserved to have a wonderful, open, and happy marriage like his parents.

The truth was, he was married to a woman he couldn't have. And not just any woman. No, he was married to the most beautiful, most gracious, most forgiving, most fascinating, most passionate, most—

He shook his head to cut off his litany.

Even though he'd pushed her away all week since the stormy encounter in the bedroom, she'd accepted and adjusted to the situation, just as she had to everything else. She'd even apologized for asking him about his past.

His dad had been angrier about how he was treating Victoria than she was. Dad had argued with him, told him to put aside his pride, and make things right with his bride. After the tenth nagging, Tom had been tempted to tell his dad the truth, that Victoria wasn't his, never had been, and never would be.

Jimmy began the process of unloading several other crates of food and supplies. Tom stuffed the telegrams into his coat pocket and helped Jimmy until the cutter was empty.

"Why don't you stay for dinner?" Tom suggested as he

wiped his sleeve across his damp forehead. Even though the day was hazy and the sun behind the clouds, the humidity made the air sticky and heavy.

"Stay and win her?" Jimmy's eyes widened, and he glanced again at Victoria, who had bent over to retrieve another sopping wet garment from the basket of laundry. Ruth's hand-me-down skirt pulled taut against Victoria, revealing a very womanly figure.

Tom quickly averted his gaze but couldn't stop the slow burn from fanning inside his gut. It was always there, always smoldering even though he'd done all he could that week to douse it. He had the feeling that after Victoria read all of the telegrams, she'd help him snuff it out once and for all.

Jimmy glanced away from Victoria. The confusion in his eyes would have been laughable, if Tom had been in a laughing mood. Which he wasn't. "Stay. For. Dinner," he repeated louder.

Jimmy's grin re-appeared. "Why didn't you say so? I can do that without worrying you'll break every bone in my body."

Tom carried the crates up to the house with Jimmy and then waved the old fisherman inside to visit with his mom. Tom couldn't put off this encounter with Victoria, one he'd been dreading since sending the telegrams that revealed her location to the world.

As he approached the laundry line, he heard her humming. At the sight of him, she paused in the process of lifting another wet piece of clothing and gave him a warm, welcoming smile. "I hope Jimmy is planning to stay. I have a pot of clam chowder on the stove."

For a second, he could almost believe she'd been born to this kind of life, that she could live in isolation indefinitely, cooking soup and hanging the laundry to dry, instead of relying upon a host of servants to do it for her. He tried to picture her as she'd been in New York when he'd first met her, in her lacy gowns, big flowery hats, fancy hairstyles, and dainty gloves and parasols. That was her world. And this would never be, no matter how comfortable she might appear at present.

He thrust the telegrams at her, knowing he had to get the inevitable over with. "These are for you."

With curiosity lighting her eyes, she started to reach for them. But at the sight of the large bold print "Western Union" filling the top half of the envelope and her name scrawled on the bottom, she jerked her hand away. "I don't want to see them."

"You can read them privately, or I'll read them to you aloud."

She spun back to the rope that served as a laundry line, and she lifted the wet garment she'd been holding and gave a sharp gasp. It was her nightgown. The same one that she'd been wearing when he'd nearly lost control of himself.

She rapidly bunched up the gown and dropped into the basket before stooping and retrieving another item. His shirt. The one that he'd shed that same night. She paused, and he caught a slight tremble in her fingers before she moved to pin the shirt to the line.

He released a slow exhale, trying not to think of her. Of them. Of the fire that so easily sparked whenever they were together.

"Who are the telegrams from?" she asked, focusing on her task and avoiding his gaze.

"Your parents. A friend. Nathaniel."

At the mention of Nathaniel, her hands stilled. "You told Nathaniel where I am?"

"Yes."

Her shoulders sagged like the wet laundry.

Was she disappointed that their time here was over? He knew he shouldn't feel any satisfaction that she'd rather be with him than Nathaniel, but he couldn't help it.

"I didn't think you wanted anyone to know where I was," she finally said.

"Read the telegram and you'll understand."

Finally, she turned back to him and reluctantly took the envelopes. She opened Nathaniel's telegram first. The typed print was longer than any telegram Tom had ever seen and had probably cost quite a bit to send. But then again, money wasn't an issue for a man like Nathaniel.

Color drained from Victoria's face as she read. When she came to the bottom of the note, she lifted her gaze to his. Her beautiful honey-brown eyes were wide with hurt. "Why does he think the wedding is happening again in two weeks?"

The look, the tone, the stance all begged him to deny what he'd done, or at the very least give her an explanation that would ease her pain. His chest tightened with the need to give in. He wanted to pull her into his arms and never let her go.

But he swallowed his emotions. He couldn't cave in to his selfish desires again. Victoria was better off with a man like Nathaniel, who could give her the kind of life she needed and understand the world she belonged to. Sure, she could adjust to living at Race Point for a few weeks. But she'd grow tired of it eventually and long for all she'd left behind, the glamour and shopping and maids. Tom would never be able to give her a life even close to that.

Besides, if he wanted to have a relationship with Victoria, he'd have to quit his bodyguarding. It was demanding work— the kind of job he wouldn't be able to easily leave behind every night to go home to a wife. And if he quit protecting people, what kind of employment would be available to him besides being a light keeper or assistant keeper? Such work would be filled with too many of the memories he wanted to leave in the past.

No, any chance of having a relationship with Victoria was over. He shouldn't have allowed himself to harbor any hope that they could have something in the first place. Now it was best not to prolong the separation.

"You're marrying Nathaniel in two weeks." He forced the words, even though his heart tore as he said them.

For a moment she seemed at a loss for a response. Then her brows furrowed and her eyes began to cloud with a coming storm. "Maybe you've ordered my life and told me what to do in everything else, but not in this. You can't choose whom I marry."

"It's already been arranged." He nodded at the other telegrams that she held. "That's why Nathaniel's mother sent you a message too. Mrs. Winthrop is helping with the planning."

"I called off my engagement with Nathaniel, and I have no intention of marrying him anymore." Her tone turned icy. "Not in two weeks, two months, or two years."

"You belong with him."

She pushed aside the wet garments that hung listlessly in the damp air and launched herself against him, wrapping her arms around him. "I belong to you, Tom." She laid her head against his chest. "I want you. Only you."

Heaven help him. He gritted his teeth and fisted his hands to keep from doing the thing he wanted to most—hold her close. Instead, he counted to five silently and then pried her loose. As he set her away, the chagrin in her expression was too difficult to witness.

He turned and started crossing to the house. He hated

himself for hurting her. But he had no other choice. "Once you're with Nathaniel again, you'll see that I'm right."

"You can push me away." Her skirt swished as she followed him. "But you can't push me back to Nathaniel."

He kept walking.

"Even if you throw away what we have, I won't marry him. I'll write to him today and tell him."

Her words stopped him. He spun and retraced his steps. "Don't you dare."

She straightened her shoulders and lifted her chin. "I'm sending a note back with Jimmy." With that she made to sweep around him toward the house.

He grabbed her arm. "You can't."

"I can do whatever I want." Her eyes flashed with all the pain and anger that he'd brought her. But as in the past, he knew making her angry at him was for the best. Then she'd go out of her way to avoid him, and that would make leaving her easier. Maybe.

Before leaving her, however, he had one more job to do. Find her attacker and make sure she was completely safe. During the past few weeks, Arch had been tracking leads. But unfortunately his friend had only run into dead ends.

So, during an exchange of telegrams last week, they'd decided to implement their backup plan regarding the perpetrator. They would disclose Victoria's location and hopefully lure the attacker out to the isolated Race Point Lighthouse.

"If you want me to find your attacker, then you can't cancel the wedding." He hadn't wanted to say it, to give her the more logical explanation for why he'd sent the telegram to Nathaniel.

She pressed her lips together in a line of determination that told him she wouldn't be satisfied until he explained himself.

"I do think you belong with Nathaniel," he started, and when she began to tug away from him, he rushed to finish. "But that's not the only reason I sent him the telegram."

She ceased struggling and gave him her full attention.

"I've come to the conclusion that the attacker was hired by someone who doesn't want you to get married."

"How can you be sure?"

"A dozen little clues." He'd been slowly putting all the pieces together. The attack on Arch had been planned by someone who knew Victoria's habits. If he'd wanted to kill her, then he wouldn't have simply attempted to stab her. No, the stabbing had been intended to wound her enough to postpone the wedding. When that hadn't happened and the Coles had hired him to be her new body guard, the perpetrator had to think of a different way to stop the wedding. Swapping drivers on the way to the ceremony had been so well-timed, perfected down to the last detail.

"Who wouldn't want me to get married?" she asked. He couldn't keep from noticing the redness of her hands, likely from the strong lye soap. The pungent odor was strong in the damp air. "That makes no sense."

"Maybe one of your father's competitors feels threatened by your marriage." He'd heard Victoria talk with Theresa on more than one occasion about how her marriage to Nathaniel Winthrop would move Victoria's family into Mrs. Astor's elite circle. Such a move would benefit Mr. Cole's business aspirations. A competitor would want to stop the advantage. And anyone who knew how much Mr. Cole loved his daughter would also be willing to capitalize on that affection. Continued threats would make Mr. Cole desperate enough to give in to any demands his enemies might make.

"Whatever the case," he continued, "the new wedding plans are already public. And so is your current location."

She glanced around the beach, the horizon, and then inland to the sand dunes, as if expecting to see an attacker. "So I'm no longer safe here?"

"If anyone comes, I'll see them. That's why I chose this place."

"What if someone tries to sneak out here at night under the cover of darkness?"

"Hopefully Dad would see them." And of course, Tom intended to stand guard. His plan wasn't foolproof, but it was still the best way of trapping and netting their culprit. He was counting on the imposter not knowing exactly how isolated the lighthouse was and believing it would be an easy place to capture Victoria. He was also hoping the attack would happen sooner rather than later.

"And have you told your parents?" She looked first at the upstairs window of the bedroom where Dad was sleeping and then toward the sitting room where Mom was chatting with Jimmy. "Do they know the truth now?"

"No. They don't need to know."

"You're planning to let them think you're still married to me indefinitely?"

"For a while." Once they captured the attacker, he'd return Victoria to Newport, get the annulment, and leave for Europe. Maybe he'd tell his parents about the annulment the next time he visited, explain that he and Victoria were just too different and that parting ways was the only option. In the meantime, he wouldn't say anything. He'd let his mom and dad stay blissfully ignorant as long as possible.

"I don't feel right about deceiving them any longer," she said. "Maybe we should tell them everything."

"No. Dad would kick me out." Or maybe kill him. Both of his parents loved Victoria without reservation. Yes, she was easy to love. But he had no doubt they'd accepted her because they wanted to support him. If they discovered the depth of his deception, they'd be deeply hurt.

Victoria was studying his face, likely reading his indecision. "We don't have to deceive them. We can stay together." Her eyes lit again and the frustrated lines in her face softened. Hope seemed to come so naturally to her. If only he could find hope as easily.

"Please, Tom." Her voice dropped to a whisper. "I love you."

Her words dried his throat and radiated down into his chest, lodging there painfully.

She reached for his hand and her fingers twined around his.

How could he let her go? He closed his eyes and forced back his own declaration of affection for her. He'd gone over this a hundred times in his mind. He was determined to relinquish her, and he had to stay resolute this time.

"I can't." He tugged his hand loose but felt as though he were leaving his heart within her grasp. Then he strode away. And he didn't look back, even though the empty, aching cavity in his chest begged him to.

Chapter 17

Victoria twisted the wooden cross in her chapped hands. The dark pieces of wreckage were smooth now with the passage of time. How many years had it been since her father had been shipwrecked and fashioned the cross? She guessed at least twenty.

Her father had given the cross to her mother. Eventually her mother had given away the cross too, with an accompanying letter that explained the story behind the cross and the hope found in God.

Over the years, the cross had apparently passed through many different hands, giving hope to all the lives it touched. Then finally, through circumstances that had surely been divinely ordained, Victoria had ended up with the cross during the summer she'd gone with her father to Michigan. A young school teacher by the name of Tessa Taylor had been living in Eagle Harbor, one of the mining towns her father owned. Her father had happened to see Tessa with the cross and had immediately recognized it as the same cross he'd made when he'd been stranded at Presque Isle Lighthouse in Michigan as a young unmarried man. Of course, Tessa had been delighted to return the cross to them, and Victoria had kept it close ever since.

Even though her mother's original letter had instructed the bearer of the cross to pass it along to someone who needed hope, Victoria hadn't wanted to part with the treasure. She'd felt as though the cross had come home, that it was hers to keep.

The breeze from the open bedroom window eased her discomfort from the heat just slightly, no more than the cross had eased the pain radiating in her chest.

She'd always believed the cross was supposed to bring her hope. Wasn't it? At least that's why her father had designed it all those years ago when he'd been stranded away from his family in the Michigan wilderness after a shipwreck had nearly killed him. It had been his reminder to hope and pray. Of course, all had ended well for her father. He'd met and fallen in love with Mother. They'd gotten married and were still happy together.

Ironically, Victoria had fallen in love and gotten married too, not quite in that order. But apparently she wasn't destined to have the same happy ending that her parents had found.

With a sigh, she bent down and tucked the cross back into her carpetbag, which she'd packed several days ago after Tom had rejected her love with a finality that had broken her heart. She supposed she'd been harboring hope until then. But when he'd told her that he couldn't love her in return and had walked away without a backward glance, he'd taken all her hope with him.

Before Jimmy had sailed away, she'd given him a telegram to deliver to the Western Union office in Provincetown, and ever since then she'd been waiting. Every day she had to stay was torture—being near Tom but knowing he didn't love her or want her as his wife.

She pulled back the curtain to her view of the tower, where he was sitting on his makeshift platform painting for the second day in a row. He'd been avoiding her every bit as much as she was him. He hadn't slept on the sofa, hadn't eaten meals with her, hadn't come to the house for breaks.

James was angry with Tom, and at least once a day she heard him encourage Tom to humble himself and work out his problems with his wife. But Tom remained as silent and unmoving with his dad as he was with her.

He was tense and on high alert, back to his bodyguard role. She suspected he wasn't getting much sleep. He was always up early in the morning, and she never heard him come in the house at night. Even though his words about expecting the attacker to arrive any day had scared her a little at first, she'd quickly shed her fear. If someone really decided to come all the way to Race Point to attack her, she had no doubt Tom would keep her safe.

When Tom waved to a rusty cutter docking on the waterfront, Victoria's heart gave a leap. Jimmy had come. Finally. And from the lack of usual supplies weighing down his boat, she knew that he'd come for her.

Even though her pulse pattered with both trepidation and anticipation, she quickly put into place the plan she'd been formulating since she'd sent the telegram. She'd already had her bags mostly packed, so it only took her a matter of seconds to finish stowing away the few toiletries she'd used that morning. As she made her way downstairs, she rehearsed what she would tell Zelma.

"I'm going to Provincetown today," she said after bending

down and kissing Zelma's head, as she'd grown accustomed to doing in the mornings. But this time she couldn't meet the perceptive woman's gaze. "I've arranged to visit with some of my friends there."

It wasn't exactly a lie. She *was* going to Provincetown and meeting with friends. But it was more than a simple visit.

"That sounds like fun, dear," Zelma said, resting her hand on the open Bible in front of her. Her cup of coffee sat next to the big book. "But surely you know by now that you're welcome to invite your friends to visit here. I'd love the chance to meet them."

"You're too kind." She couldn't keep from bending and drawing the dear woman into an embrace. Her hug probably lasted a smidgen too long, because when she finally stood and tried to keep her tears at bay, Zelma's brows came together.

"Why, Victoria, what's wrong?"

What wasn't wrong? She forced a smile and infused cheer into her voice. "I'll just miss you. That's all."

The crease between Zelma's brows didn't go away. If anything, the lines in Zelma's face deepened.

Victoria wanted to say that she loved her, for she truly had grown to love Tom's parents, even if they were a tad exuberant at times. But if she allowed herself to become even more emotional, she'd only raise Zelma's suspicions further. Besides, she had no time to waste. She had to reach the cutter before Tom could stop her.

When she chanced one more kiss upon Zelma's head, the woman reached for her hand and clasped it tightly. For a moment, Zelma looked as though she might say something more. But then she simply smiled, a little too sadly, and let go. "God be with you, dear."

As Victoria picked up her bag in the hallway and rushed

out the front door, guilt trailed her. She tried to shake it loose as she ran down the beach toward Jimmy, who'd just secured the boat. From the corner of her vision, she could see that Tom was lowering himself to the ground. She had no doubt he'd already figured out Jimmy hadn't come to deliver supplies.

"Victoria," Tom called. "Stop!"

Without acknowledging him, she continued down the sandy embankment until she reached the dock.

Jimmy welcomed her with a gap-toothed smile that crinkled his brittle face. "Mrs. Cushman, you're just the person I was hoping to see."

"Same with you."

Jimmy dug into his coat pocket and retrieved a folded sheet of paper. "A fancy young gentleman told me to give this to you. He paid me good money to make sure that I put it directly into your hands and none other. And he told me he'd pay me double to give you a ride into Provincetown today."

Victoria took the paper with shaking hands. She was glad Nathaniel had followed her instructions and hadn't insisted on coming to get her himself. She wasn't sure how she would have explained his presence to Zelma.

As it was, she had to convince Jimmy to leave right away without lingering for his usual meal. She glanced over her shoulder to see that Tom was almost to the ground. From the slant of his brows, she could see that he was frustrated.

"I'm ready to go." She tossed her bag into the boat and began to climb in.

"Whoa there." Jimmy caught her and eased her down. "What's your hurry?"

"It's such a lovely day for a ride."

Jimmy's weathered face wrinkled. "You're going to cry?"

She shook her head, even though he was close to the truth. She did feel like crying. "I'm fine. I'll just miss being here."

Jimmy's expression remained confused. "Kiss him here?"

"Kiss who?"

"Eh?" This time Jimmy put his hand to his ear, and she realized he hadn't understood a word she'd spoken.

"Victoria, don't leave," Tom called, sprinting toward the boat. He was attired in the work clothes that he'd worn since arriving to Race Point. Several buttons were undone on the shirt, and paint stains dotted his trousers.

She hadn't expected to be able to leave without Tom making an effort to stop her. But now that she was in the boat, the only way he could get her out was by bodily lifting her against her will. "I'm going and there's nothing you can do about it."

His boots clomped across the dock until he towered over her, his shadow dwarfing her.

"You asked Nathaniel to come get you. He's waiting in Provincetown. And is planning to take you home."

He was right. As usual. "Does it matter?" She arranged her skirt around her legs and refused to look up at him.

"Yes, it matters."

Her head snapped up, and she was embarrassed by her desire to hear him tell her that *she* mattered, that he didn't want her to go, that he didn't want to lose her. If he would but say the words she would stay. She would climb out and never leave him.

The muscles in his jaw flexed, and he rubbed a hand across his eyes, as though trying to block her out. "Victoria," he said in a soft agonized voice. "Don't do this. You're making things harder."

"How?"

"It's easier to watch for the attacker here."

Disappointment rushed through her. He hadn't changed his mind. He truly didn't want her to stay for himself.

"Jimmy," she called to the old fisherman who stood at the stern, his wide-eyed gaze flying back and forth between her and Tom. "I'm ready to go."

"I'm going with you," Tom stated. "But I need to change out of these old clothes first."

She shrugged. She'd suspected he wouldn't let her sail away unless he came along. Even if he didn't love her and didn't want her, he'd never shirk his responsibilities as long as he was her bodyguard.

Tom glanced at the house as though debating whether he should chance leaving her with Jimmy.

She released a humorless laugh. "You surely don't think Jimmy will hurt me."

"Of course not. But I'm worried that you'll sway him into starting off without me."

"If I do, you'll just chase me down."

"True."

"Then go change and say goodbye to your mom. I'll wait."

He was back in less than five minutes, wearing his dark navy trousers and matching suit coat over a white shirt. They were slightly wrinkled, and the day-old growth on his jaw and cheeks was out of place, but otherwise he looked sharp and gentlemanly and much too handsome.

He helped Jimmy prepare for their departure, and once they were underway, she was surprised when Tom took the seat next to her. With the sun shining down on them and the spray of salt water hitting the cutter, she was reminded of their ride out to Race Point, of the attraction that had already been building between them, of the promises and possibilities the month would bring.

If only she didn't feel as though she were returning as a failure, that somehow she'd ruined her marriage and wasn't enough for him.

He didn't say anything for most of the journey. Even though she was tempted to engage him in conversation, she refrained. She'd said all she had to say earlier in the week when he'd given her the telegrams. She'd poured out her heart in one last desperate attempt to win him. But he'd rejected her with a finality that told her he'd already made up his stubborn mind, that nothing she could say or do would sway him.

"I wish you would have waited," he said quietly as the cutter moved into the bay and the outline of Provincetown grew visible on the shore.

"I've waited long enough. If someone was really planning to attack me again, don't you think they would have found me by now?"

"Maybe."

"Maybe you're overly worried about this whole affair. Maybe bringing me all the way out here wasn't necessary. Maybe I would have been fine staying in Newport all along."

He didn't respond, except for the twitch of a muscle in his neck above the white collar that contrasted his sun-bronzed skin.

"It was a foolish plan. And I shouldn't have agreed to come." Her voice cracked, and she quickly bit her lip to hold back a swell of sorrow and heartache. She stared straight ahead and blinked back the wet heat that stung her eyes.

She was angry with herself for wishing he'd contradict her, wishing that he'd tell her the month had been the best in his life, even if their time together couldn't last. But he was silent again. He didn't speak until the shingles and clapboards of the Provincetown homes were visible and the calls of the fishermen along the seafront greeted them.

"I hate myself for hurting you," he said so softly she almost missed it above the slap of the waves.

When she tilted up her wide-brimmed hat to get a better view of his face, she glimpsed a haunted sadness in the depths of his eyes.

"I'm sorry, Victoria." The sincerity in his voice and expression was difficult to resist. She might be angry at herself for falling for him. But she couldn't stay mad at him. It wasn't his fault that she was leaving with a broken heart. He'd tried to maintain proper boundaries, hadn't wanted to cross them, had tried hard not to. But she hadn't heeded his warnings. She'd plunged forward like she usually did into relationships. Only this time she was the one leaving with the wounds instead of the other way around.

"I forgive you," she said, realizing she could do nothing less, especially since she'd done the hurting all too many times with her previous relationships.

Tom's brows rose, revealing his surprise at the ease of her forgiveness. "Thank you." His whisper still contained a note of sadness that plucked at her empathy. He was hard on himself. Too hard. She guessed that's why, even after all these years, he couldn't forgive himself for what had happened to Zelma. She guessed he blamed himself for the loss of her feet and maybe even blamed himself for Ike's death, although she didn't see how he could, not if they were prisoners of war. Not if Zelma had made the decision for herself to try to save her sons.

"When you see Nathaniel, you have to continue with the plans."

She shook her head. "I can't deceive him."

"Then wait to say anything until I can talk to him in private."

She wanted to refuse. She'd been a part of enough decep-tion during the past month, and it had only led to trouble. It was time to embrace honesty, even if it compromised her safety.

"I'll explain the plan to him," Tom continued, "but until then act like a bride-to-be."

"It's not fair to him if I—"

"He'll understand."

Nathaniel would do anything for her, even if it meant acting like they were getting married so that they could lure the nebulous attacker. Even so...

"Please."

Was the bossy, stubborn, determined Thomas Cushman actually asking her to do something politely instead of demanding as he usually did? "Could you say that again?"

His expression was earnest. "Please, Victoria..."

She put a hand to her head and pretended to faint. "Oh, my. I can't believe what I'm hearing."

His brow lifted.

She tossed back her head and feigned shock. "You said *please*."

A semblance of a grin quirked the corner of his mouth. "I'm capable of it on occasion."

She sat up and smiled. "Very well. Since you asked so nice-ly, I'll comply."

"Comply?" It was his turn to feign shock. He held a hand to his heart and leaned back.

"I'm capable of it on occasion," she retorted.

His grin broke free in all its breath-taking glory. And for just a moment, she felt as though they were on good terms again. But as the cutter brushed against the dock with a scrape, the bump jolted her back to reality, to the fact that she was going home.

Tom must have sensed it too, because his smile disappeared and his stoic bodyguard mask dropped into place.

As Jimmy secured the cutter, she twisted the simple wedding band beneath her glove, until finally she tugged off the tight satin and slipped the ring over her knuckle and into her palm. She stared at the ring, wrestling with the desire to keep Tom, to hold him tightly, and to make him love her in return. Somehow.

She could force his hand if she really wanted to. She was inventive enough to scheme and plot to get her way. But she didn't want a love that was coerced. She wanted him to give it to her freely. Since he obviously couldn't, she had to let him go.

"One last thing," she made herself say as Tom assisted her out. She placed her hand into his and pressed the ring into his palm.

His eyes widened. But once she was standing on the dock, he accepted the ring and stuffed it into his pocket without giving it a glance. The action had a finality to it that snagged her chest, made worse by the fact that he didn't seem to be affected by the show of severing their marriage.

In fact, as Tom led her away from the waterfront past the racks of drying cod, he was stiff and alert, not displaying the least bit of emotion. Even though she knew by now that his expressionless face meant he was doing his job, she wished he'd demonstrate a little bit of grief at their parting.

When they finally reached the hotel where Nathaniel was staying, she tried to resign herself to the fact once and for all that she and Tom were destined to go their separate ways. As they stepped inside, the mustiness of cigars permeated the stale interior. Except for the hotel proprietor behind a front counter, the small lobby was empty. This hotel wasn't nearly as fancy as those she was accustomed to staying in. Even though the striped print seat cushions of the arm chairs and settee were slightly frayed, the room was tidy. A bowl of seashells sat on a low coffee table. More seashells of all kinds and sizes lined the large picture window overlooking busy Main Street.

Tom stepped in behind her, and his attention moved from one window and door to the next, assessing every detail.

"Victoria, darling." Nathaniel's voice echoed in the stairwell. His patent leather shoes tapped a rapid rhythm as he descended. He wore a Newmarket black coat with a gardenia in the lapel buttonhole. His double-breasted waistcoat was of buff drill that coordinated with his gray checkered Angola trousers.

He crossed rapidly toward her and didn't give her the expected chaste kiss on her hand or even a slight kiss on the cheek. Instead, he pulled her into an almost desperate embrace.

"I've been so worried about you," he said against her ear.

"I'm sorry I worried you," she replied. "But I'm doing just fine. I promise."

He held her tightly for several long seconds. Behind her Tom cleared his throat, and she wriggled to free herself. Nathaniel released her but immediately reached for her hands. She was glad for the gloves hiding her chafed skin. Even so, her gloves were no longer the pristine white that they'd been when she'd left Newport.

His eyes sought hers, warm and tender as always. His mustache and hair were groomed with care, and he looked every bit the dashing gentleman who had captured her heart at the start of their relationship.

"How are my mother and father?" she asked.

"They send their love." Something reserved in Nathaniel's response told her that perhaps her father wasn't a proponent of her early return.

"And your parents?"

"Mother is excited to be planning the wedding again. And Father is, well..." His eyes reflected a pain she seldom saw there, usually only when he thought about his father. "He's busy," Nathaniel finished with a forced smile.

Everyone in New York society knew about Mr. Winthrop's moodiness and the fact that he disappeared for months at a time. No one knew where he went or what he did in his absences, and the one time she'd asked Nathaniel, he'd only shaken his head and said he was sworn to secrecy.

"Oh, darling, I've missed you so much," he said.

She squeezed his hands and struggled to find the right words to say in response. She couldn't very well tell him that she'd missed him too. The truth was that she'd hardly thought about him. So she settled for the next best answer, which was partly true. "I'm glad to see you again."

"You made me the happiest man in the world to get your first telegram telling me that you wanted to renew our engagement and go forward with the wedding."

Words of denial were on the tip of her tongue, but she could almost feel the tension radiating from Tom's body. When she glanced at him, his dark eyes were full of warning. And a plea to stick with the plan.

How could she deny him, especially after he'd asked her so sweetly? But at the same time, how could she move from one charade to the next?

Nathaniel was pulling something out of his coat pocket, and before she knew what he was doing, he was down on one knee in front of her, holding out her engagement ring, the enormous sapphire set into a circle of diamonds that she'd once thought was the most beautiful ring in the world. "Please, put this back on and promise you won't ever take it off."

Again she peeked at Tom. He didn't say anything. Something like uncertainty flashed across his features. Was he having second thoughts about pushing her together with Nathaniel, or was he simply feeling guilty for perpetuating a lie?

Nathaniel didn't wait for her answer and tugged off her glove.

She drew back. How could she do this? Especially with Tom standing behind her watching. "Nathaniel, I—"

He captured her hand and proceeded to slide the ring on.

She started to protest again, but her stilted words halted at the sight of a newcomer descending the stairs. With a soft exclamation of delight, she stepped around Nathaniel and rushed toward the young woman. "Theresa!" Before Theresa could descend the last step, Victoria was already drawing her friend into a hug.

Theresa gave a shaky laugh at Victoria's exuberance. "Oh, my. I guess it's good to see you too."

Victoria embraced her friend a moment longer before pulling back with a smile. "Look at you!" Victoria studied Theresa's two-toned sage green silk taffeta, which had a bodice that molded Theresa's slim body all the way to her waist. Her luscious dark hair was pulled up stylishly so that curls formed at both temples. "You look beautiful, and I'm very jealous of your gorgeous gown. Is it new?"

"Made in Paris." Theresa swished the skirt.

"I absolutely love it." Victoria stood back and nodded with appreciation at the fine workmanship.

"I told her the colors are perfect," Nathaniel added, moving to Victoria's side and tucking her hand into the crook of his arm. Although he seemed to be complimenting Theresa, he was staring at Victoria's face with unswerving adoration.

Theresa's smile which was directed at Nathaniel dimmed, and her attention dropped to Victoria's hand and the engagement ring that sat on her finger. It shone brighter than a first order Fresnel lens, the biggest and brightest lighthouse lantern. Theresa's eyes widened in surprise and her lips pursed, before she looked pointedly at Victoria's traveling suit, at the stains and less than stellar ironing job. Victoria had no doubt Theresa recognized the gown as one she'd worn last summer season.

"You look stunning yourself..." Theresa's voice contained the usual sarcasm. "I hope you're not attempting to start a new fashion with your freckled nose and..." Her friend's gaze strayed to Victoria's simple coif, the best she'd been able to do on her own without her maid. Theresa laughed but rapidly cupped her hand over her mouth.

Suddenly Victoria saw herself the way Theresa did, rumpled, dirty, and bedraggled. "I know I look rather ridiculous, but—"

"No, darling," Nathaniel said. "You look as beautiful as always. In fact, I was just thinking how a little color in your face suits you."

She smiled up at him, grateful for his kindness. She loved this quality of his, the ability to put people at ease, to find the good in strained situations. It's one of the many reasons she'd agreed to marry him, because ultimately Nathaniel Winthrop III was a worthy man. Among her circles of peers, she probably wouldn't find anyone else more sincere and kind-hearted than he.

"Thank you, Nathaniel." She patted his hand.

Out of the corner of her eye, she could see Tom standing

near the front door, with a view of both the street and the lobby. His thick arms were crossed, his feet braced, and his attention riveted to the street.

Was Tom having a difficult time watching her interact with Nathaniel? She hoped so.

"You're lovely all the time," Nathaniel assured her.

"And you're one of the sweetest men I know." She didn't want to hurt him again. She'd already done it once when she'd called off the wedding. How could she do it again? And did she really want to? After all, if she couldn't have Tom, then Nathaniel was a good option for her. She'd be happy with him. Maybe she wouldn't experience the same attraction or depth of passion or camaraderie she had with Tom, but Nathaniel was still a wonderful man. She couldn't go wrong with him, could she?

Victoria linked her arms through Theresa's and Nathaniel's. "It's so good to see you both again. You must tell me all that I've missed while I've been gone. Every detail."

She tugged them forward toward a small sitting area beyond the check-in counter. Nathaniel chuckled. "As anxious as I am to talk with you, there's a steamer leaving for Falmouth at noon. If we catch it, we may just make it back to Newport today and not have to stay another night."

"Another night?" Victoria asked. "How long have you been here?"

"We arrived yesterday." Theresa extricated herself from Victoria's hold and smoothed the lacy ruffles at the cuff of her three-quarter sleeve. "But both Nathaniel and I agree that one night is much too long in this provincial establishment." Theresa glanced around with a visible shudder. "It's positively barbaric."

Victoria pressed a finger to her lips and peeked at the

proprietor standing behind the counter. Even though he wore his spectacles at the end of his nose and appeared occupied with his ledgers, Victoria didn't want him to hear Theresa's complaints. The place might be antiquated, but it looked clean and well-kept. He was likely a hard-working man who could benefit from their gratitude.

Nathaniel took out his slim pocket watch and flipped open the shiny gold-plated case. "Darling, there's plenty of time for you to freshen up and change before we need to leave." Nathaniel closed his watch and tucked it back into his waist-coat. "If you'd like."

"Oh, please say yes to Nathaniel." Theresa once again eyed her gown. "I'd be entirely mortified to be seen with you wearing that thing."

Victoria felt her smile begin to slip away. She wasn't sur-prised by Theresa's attitude. She'd probably had the same views at one time. But perhaps living for several weeks without all of the luxuries she was accustomed to had started to change her perspective. Or perhaps she had forgotten how to shrug off Theresa's negativity.

"Of course, I'd be happy to freshen up," Victoria started. "But I'm afraid that I'm ill-prepared. I haven't anything else to wear."

"Your mother anticipated your needs and sent along two traveling suits." Theresa moved to the stairs. "They might be slightly wrinkled, but you can request that one of the hotel staff iron them for you."

Victoria released Nathaniel and followed Theresa. "Don't be a goose. I think I shall leave it wrinkled since I know how much you like it that way." She had a smile ready for a witty comeback from Theresa. But Theresa didn't turn to acknowledge her comment. If anything she stiffened and lifted her chin higher, as though Victoria didn't deserve a reply.

Victoria's steps faltered. Maybe Theresa was upset with her because she'd hidden so much from her this past month. She'd always confided in Theresa everything, good or bad. And she could only imagine how her friend must have felt when she'd received the news secondhand that Victoria had called off her engagement with Nathaniel and then gone into hiding.

"You may use my room, Victoria." Nathaniel's voice echoed from the bottom of the stairs. "I'm packed and have no need of it."

"Thank you," she called as she hurried up the stairwell after her friend. She'd tell Theresa the truth now about everything. Well, maybe not everything. She couldn't very well admit she'd been married to Tom for the past month and was in fact technically still his wife. Theresa wouldn't believe her.

"Theresa, wait." Her friend was already at the landing and the hallway that lead to the second floor rooms.

Maybe she couldn't tell Theresa about Tom, but she could start by apologizing that she'd had to exclude so much from her. Maybe she'd even ask Theresa for her opinion on whether to go through with the wedding with Nathaniel. After all, Theresa had been there during each of the other failed engagements. She'd always understood and had provided a listening ear.

Firm, rapid footsteps behind her were followed by a hand on her arm stopping her, a solid, warm touch she'd recognize anywhere.

"Don't say anything to Theresa," Tom whispered from the step below her.

She turned to find that the stair difference put her at eye level with him and that they were close. Too close. She only had to look at his chest to remember all the times that he'd held her and that she'd rested her cheek against him. If only she could throw herself into his arms again and stop time. Because she didn't want to re-enter her world, where young women were consumed with fancy clothes and pretty jewels and fashionable hair styles. Where she would be swept into an endless routine of dinner parties, balls, and operas. Where people were constantly scrutinizing and gossiping and trying to make themselves feel better by putting others down.

She hadn't known she was locked into that kind of dizzying lifestyle until she'd broken away from it, until she'd experienced a simpler existence with Tom at Race Point. Now, she was about to be thrust into it all over again.

"I know she's your friend," Tom said, backing down a step and putting distance between them. "But you need to wait." His coat stretched across his strong shoulders and hugged his biceps. Yes, she admired his physical strength, but she'd learned that he had an inner strength as well, one that gave her courage to do hard things. He pushed her to be stronger, to be better, to do more than she'd ever thought herself capable. He wasn't afraid to challenge or confront her. He saw her weaknesses and didn't excuse them. He'd seen her at her worst and had cared for her anyway.

"Tom," she whispered, not caring that her voice—and likely her face—contained all her longing.

His jaw clamped more firmly, and he stepped down another stair. His actions told her all she needed to know. He was sticking by his decision to relinquish her and their marriage. There was nothing she could do or say to sway him.

She sighed and resumed her walk up the steps, albeit much slower this time. "Okay. I won't share anything with Theresa."

Chapter 18

*T*om stood outside room B3. He'd investigated the bed chamber before allowing Victoria to enter. He'd made sure the room was empty, that the windows were properly locked, and that no one lurked on the balcony that wrapped around the second story of the hotel.

He hadn't liked the balcony, in spite of the fact that the door accessing it was at the end of the hallway. Even with only one entrance and exit onto the balcony, it would be all too easy for a perpetrator to climb onto it and attempt to break into Victoria's room.

Victoria's soft footsteps in the room told him that she was leaving the mirror, where she'd finished fastening the row of tiny buttons running up the front of the bodice. And now she was going back to the bed to retrieve her hat.

From the timing of her dressing routine, he guessed she hadn't put on a corset, although one had been among the articles of clothing her mother had sent with Theresa. Of course, she hadn't had any help to put it on. But he wanted to think she'd learned her lesson about wearing the useless thing. Tom almost smiled at the memory of cutting the laces on the one she'd been wearing when they'd first arrived at Race Point.

A squeak of floorboards drew his attention to Theresa's room across the hallway. After delivering the dresses to Victoria, Theresa had retreated with the flimsy reason that she needed to fix her hair.

He'd seen through Theresa's excuse. Her hair was already styled well enough. The truth was, she hadn't wanted to be with Victoria. The hurt in Victoria's eyes at Theresa's coldness was obvious, and Victoria's eagerness to repair her strained relationship with Theresa had also been obvious.

Tom had seen the tight pain on Theresa's face when Nathaniel had knelt in front of Victoria and slipped the engagement ring on her finger. Strangely, Tom had empathized with her pain. His lungs had burned with the need to tell Victoria to take it off. Even now, the simple wedding band she'd returned seared him every time he touched it in his pocket.

Theresa wasn't as proficient as he was at concealing emotions, but she'd managed to hide her pain before Victoria turned around. However, his glimpse of Theresa's anguish had told him she was still in love with Nathaniel. And Nathaniel was still unaware of Theresa's feelings and had eyes only for Victoria. Had Theresa hoped by having this short trip with Nathaniel, she could win his affection? Had she been working the whole month Victoria was gone to make Nathaniel notice her?

Tom's spine turned into a steel beam. Was Theresa the one sabotaging Victoria's wedding plans? His pulse picked up speed at the possibility, and he stared at her door, wishing he could see through it.

His mind scrambled to find any clues that might link the attacker to Theresa, but he came away with nothing. However, Theresa certainly had the financial means to hire someone. She had the motivation. And she'd never been a particularly warm friend. Nevertheless, Victoria had always seen the best in Theresa, as she was apt to do with most people. She'd accepted and loved her friend in spite of her shortcomings.

The realization sent a strange shimmer through Tom. Victoria was a special young woman to offer her friendship and love so freely, as she'd done to him, even after he'd pushed her away. He gave a frustrated shake of his head. He didn't need one more reason to care about Victoria. He already had plenty.

He fixed his attention on Theresa's door and attempted to gauge what she was doing on the other side. If she was the person behind all of the attacks on Victoria, then what might she be planning next?

He tried to put himself into her situation, to think as she might. What would make the most sense for a desperate, lovesick young woman? If she realized that all of her attempts to win Nathaniel had failed, if she realized that Nathaniel was still in love with and determined to marry Victoria, what would she do?

A thousand scenarios played through his mind, and none of them pleasant. Of course, he could also think of dozens of ways to stop Theresa, and none of those methods were pleasant either.

In reality, he had no proof yet that she was involved in the attacks. He might be misinterpreting his sudden suspicion and making more out of her behavior than was there. Another perpetrator could, even now, be lingering somewhere in Provincetown, hired by one of Henry Cole's competitors.

Tom needed to talk with Arch. Then he would have a better idea of the goings-on in and around Provincetown. He had no doubt Arch had learned of Nathaniel and Theresa's arrival and had likely watched them for a time. If Arch had noticed anything suspicious, he'd relay it all to Tom.

Yet something in Tom's gut told him he needed to talk to Theresa now. Just in case she was the one. Just in case she was planning something else. All he had to do was tell her the truth, that he'd sent the telegram to Nathaniel about re-scheduling the wedding, that Victoria didn't love Nathaniel any more, if she ever really had.

Such news would reassure Theresa and could keep her from doing anything to hurt Victoria. He started across the hallway toward Theresa's room, but as he reached the center of the hallway, her door swung open.

"I was just coming for you," Theresa said, pulling up one of her gloves. "I was hoping you might be willing to carry my luggage down to the lobby." She cocked her head toward the foot of the bed where she'd piled several bags and hatboxes.

Was she attempting to lure him away from Victoria's door? If he carried the items downstairs and left Victoria alone and unprotected, Theresa wouldn't have much time to do anything. But still, he couldn't take that risk.

"I'll carry your things," he said, crossing to her doorway, "but I'll need to wait to take them down until Victoria is ready."

She shrugged one of her petite shoulders.

He entered into her room and stepped to the end of her bed. His fingers closed around the handle of one of her valises. At the same time, he sensed the presence of another person behind the door, even before he caught sight in his peripheral vision.

He started to spin, and his hand flew to the knife case strapped under his suit coat. Before he could grasp the weapon, a blunt object slammed into his head. The force and the excruciating pain sent him to his knees. Blackness seeped into his conscience, but he fought against it. He needed to stay alert for Victoria's sake. If he didn't, Victoria would be next.

With a groan, he tried to push himself up. He managed to dislodge his knife. But he was too disoriented, too stunned by the blow to move as quickly as he needed. The object rammed into his skull again. This time the hit knocked him flat. His forehead slammed into the floor. And everything went black.

At the sound of scuffling in Theresa's room, Victoria paused in adjusting her bonnet of pale blue with a dark grey velvet trim. She listened for a moment, but at the ensuing silence, she looked back into the mirror.

After wearing Ruth's simple, loose dresses, this new form-fitting polonaise with its long bodice and narrow sleeves was constricting. She could hardly lift her arms. And the tightly tied-back skirt made walking difficult, especially with the pointed high-heeled shoes her mother had packed.

"How did I ever manage?" she said to herself, casting a glance at the corset on the bed. She hadn't attempted to put it on, hadn't even wanted to.

She ran her fingers along the row of buttons down her chest and the trimming of looped bows. The two shades of blue were pretty, and the garment accentuated her figure. If only she didn't feel so trapped in it.

With what was probably her hundredth sigh, she checked her hair again, repositioned her hat, and decided she couldn't stall any more. She had to return home. The longer she stayed, the harder it would be to let go of her feelings for Tom. And the longer she stayed, the more chances she had of making a fool of herself by begging him to love her back. Actually, she'd already made a fool of herself one too many times in her attempts to declare her love.

He didn't reciprocate. She needed to accept that. And the best way to do so was to go back to her old life.

She finished packing, set her shoulders, and marched to the door. "I'm ready to go," she said, swinging it open. She expected to see the back of Tom's suit coat pulled taut across the breadth of his shoulders. But strangely, he wasn't there. She peered up and down the hallway and didn't see him anywhere.

Where had he gone? He'd been so careful since setting foot in Provincetown. He hadn't wanted her to change in Nathaniel's room, hadn't wanted her to be alone, and had told her he would be waiting outside her door. So why did he leave?

She checked the stairway and then went back to the room and peeked past the curtains to the balcony. She didn't see him anywhere.

The door across the hallway opened. Theresa stepped out with her valises looped over her arms and closed the door behind her.

"Have you seen Tom?" Victoria asked.

"No. But I heard him tell Nathaniel that he was leaving."

"Leaving?"

Theresa nodded curtly before starting down the hallway. "He told Nathaniel that you were in good hands now and that you didn't need him."

Victoria frowned. She couldn't imagine Tom ever saying anything of the sort. "Are you sure?"

Theresa stopped so abruptly that both of her bags swung

forward without her. When she spun to face Victoria, her expression was calm, but she couldn't hide the irritated twitch in her cheek. "Are you calling me a liar?"

Victoria offered her friend a smile, although it felt wobbly, just like their friendship. "Tom's so careful about guarding me. I didn't think he'd leave yet."

"Maybe he has more important things to do than coddle you." Theresa started down the wooden stairs, her footsteps echoing sharply.

Victoria's shoulders deflated. Maybe Tom had decided that he'd rather not go back with her. Maybe he didn't want to face her father. Or maybe he didn't want to be her bodyguard anymore and just didn't know how to tell her.

She rushed after Theresa as fast as her constricting skirt would allow. She caught up with her in the hotel lobby. "You're acting a bit strange. Is anything the matter?"

"What makes you think something is the matter?" Theresa didn't slow her steps to wait for Victoria's answer, but instead exited the hotel, giving Victoria little choice but to follow after her.

"You're getting upset at everything I say."

Theresa halted in front of a waiting carriage. "Maybe you're just overly sensitive."

"You're angry with me, aren't you?"

Theresa didn't answer the question.

Victoria took her silence as an affirmative. "I knew it. You're upset that I left Newport without telling you where I was going into hiding."

"Your powers of perception truly astound me." The sarcasm in Theresa's voice was so caustic that it once again stung Victoria.

Victoria was at a loss for what to say to her friend.

Fortunately, a young boy approached the carriage carrying Victoria's luggage, and his presence and the commotion of loading their things covered the awkward moment. When the coachman finished strapping their bags, he opened the carriage door for them.

Victoria climbed inside, although she was sure she looked as stiff and encumbered as a wooden toy soldier. Sitting was even difficult. When she finally managed to get comfortable, she expected to find Theresa across from her, giving her another rebuking glare. Instead, Theresa stood outside whispering with the coachman. When she glanced up, she tugged her ear. "I've lost one of the diamond earrings that my grandmother gave me, and I need to go back up to my room and search for it."

Victoria tried to scoot forward. "I'll help you look."

Theresa waved her back. "You go ahead to the dock. Nathaniel will be expecting us. He's already there purchasing tickets for the steamer." Theresa had already started back to the hotel. "Tell him I'll be there shortly."

Victoria hesitated, but when the coachman closed the door, she reclined against the hard leather seat and tried to sort through all of the confusion that had moved in like a thick New England fog. What was wrong with Theresa? Where had her dear friend gone, and who was this snapping person who had taken her place? If Theresa was angry with her, then why had she come with Nathaniel in the first place? And why would Tom abandon her after his determination all along to protect her from her attacker?

She stared out the window as the carriage rolled along the Provincetown streets. Her thoughts traveled back to the picture of Zelma sitting at the table this morning with her Bible open in front of her. When Victoria had said goodbye, the dear woman had clung to her hand, almost as if she'd sensed Victoria wasn't coming back.

Victoria couldn't keep from smiling at the memory of the passionate kisses Zelma always had for her husband and the tenderness James always had in return. Zelma had patiently taught her a great deal over the past month. She'd been a kind instructor, never rushing her and always encouraging. Victoria would miss the cooking and sewing lessons, along with Zelma's sweet company.

Zelma was clearly a wise and godly woman. But she'd been wrong about one thing. She'd said that God was using Victoria to work in Tom's life, that with her at his side he wouldn't be able to run away from all his mistakes any longer.

Victoria hadn't seen how God had used her to work in Tom's life. Tom hadn't wanted to stick by her side. Even when they'd been together, he hadn't wanted to talk about anything from his past. He was still running from his mistakes.

"Oh, Tom." She sighed and closed her eyes against a sudden swell of tears. In comparison to what she felt for Tom, she wasn't sure she had truly loved any of her other suitors. Tom had been so unlike them. And it wasn't simply because he was a common man who didn't belong to the same social circles she did.

No, the differences went much deeper than money and prestige. Tom himself was different. He didn't coddle her—as Theresa had suggested. Unlike other men, he wasn't afraid to tell her no. He treated her like a person, not a wealthy heiress.

Of course, Nathaniel was different too, at least different from most New York society men. He was everything a woman like her could want—sincere, good-natured, and kind. She'd met too many rich men who could put on a congenial facade for a short time, but underneath they were full of their own self-importance and too enthralled with social-climbing to care about her. With her fortune, she was simply a means for them to accomplish more and look better.

Even though she ought to be happy with a man like Nathaniel, and even though she ought to rejoice in their future, she couldn't conjure any joy no matter how hard she tried. Instead, her thoughts returned to the time she'd spent with Tom at Race Point.

For a few moments, she allowed herself the secret pleasure of reliving those weeks. All of the laughter and talking. All of the quick, heated embraces. All of the brief contacts and the simmering glances. And the few kisses they'd shared. Her stomach did several flips at the memory of the last one in the lighthouse.

At the bump of the carriage wheels in a rut, her eyes flew open. She caught hold of the door handle to keep herself steady on the seat. As she peered out the window, she savored the landscape—the sandy hills and tufts of willowy beach grass growing in clumps here and there. It amazed her that anything green could grow in such a barren environment.

She shifted and glanced out the opposite window. Under the clear sky, the ocean had taken on the same shade of blue. Although they were driving a fair distance from the shore, she could vividly picture herself walking with Tom in the low tide at sunset.

"Victoria Cole," she scolded herself, "you stop all of your wallowing this instant." She would only make herself miserable if every time she looked at the ocean she remembered Tom.

Instead, she adjusted her hat and fortified herself for meeting Nathaniel. The drive had been rather long. And the cab was getting stuffy. She hadn't realized the dock was so far from the hotel.

Twisting as best her garments would allow, she glanced out the back window. She expected to see some evidence of Provincetown. When the glimpse showed her nothing but sand dunes, she sat forward with a start.

How far had they driven? She scooted across the seat from one window to the other, searching vainly for any sign of Provincetown or a steamer. Where were they?

Perhaps she'd misunderstood. Perhaps they were traveling to another location on the Cape. Maybe they weren't riding on a steamer after all but were taking a train.

Even as Victoria tried to make sense of where the carriage was going, Theresa's words came back to her, that Nathaniel was at the dock buying tickets. And when Nathaniel had mentioned they would ride on a steamer to Falmouth, he'd made it sound like they would leave from Provincetown.

A bubble of panic formed in Victoria's chest. What if the driver had mistaken her destination?

As much as she tried to convince herself that nothing was wrong, dread began to gnaw at her. She pulled the fan out of her pocket, flipped it open, and fanned herself. Yet the air seemed even staler than before, and the gentle breeze she created did nothing to ease the perspiration forming on her brow.

She needed to question the driver. He would set her mind at ease. He would assure her of the plans. If they were off course, she could direct him back. That was easy enough.

She tugged on the bell pull and waited for the driver to respond to her call. After several long moments, she pulled it again, this time harder. When nothing happened, she sucked in a deep breath, reached for the door handle, and rattled it. She pushed it harder, and it didn't give way.

"Stay calm, Victoria," she admonished herself as she slid across the seat to the other door. Her fingers closed around the latch, and she silently prayed. *Please let the door open.* She pressed harder, and...it didn't budge. She yanked on it again. Both doors were stuck. Or locked.

Had the driver purposefully locked her inside?

She probed at the edges of the window, looking for a way that she might be able to pry it open. Then she searched the rest of the carriage but couldn't discover any other way that she might exit.

With a frustrated cry, she pounded her fists against the glass. "Let me out this instant!" When the vehicle continued to roll down the rocky road without slowing, Victoria beat against the front of the carriage in hope that the driver would hear her and stop.

But no amount of noise made a difference. She banged one last time against the front panel before collapsing into the seat. She was breathing hard, and her hat had fallen off.

The driver was clearly ignoring her because there was no way he could miss all her racket. If only he would stop, she could get answers. But something in the pit of her stomach told her everything she needed to know.

Although normally optimistic, she had the feeling all the positive thinking in the world wouldn't get her out of her current predicament.

She'd been kidnapped. And this time Tom wouldn't be coming after her.

Chapter 19

*T*om gave another heave, but the chair scooted only a fraction. Although he had just two feet to go until he reached the door, the distance seemed a mile away. He heaved again and again, as he had been for the past thirty minutes since his captor had left the room.

His skull throbbed. The open wound at the back of his head stung. And dizzying blackness threatened him every time he moved. He'd awoken to find his hands tied to the spindles behind the chair, his feet bound to its legs, and his mouth gagged.

Of course, he hadn't moved right away, not even to open his eyes. He'd wanted to learn as much as he could about his situation before alerting anyone to his wakefulness. After several minutes of complete silence, he'd begun to believe he'd been abandoned. But then a slight shift in a nearby floorboard told him someone was standing at the window looking outside.

Only a minute later, faint footsteps in the stairwell and

hallway had told him Theresa was returning. She came in and spoke in hushed tones to a man she called Splash. Every word they'd spoken had frozen Tom's blood. An accomplice was in the process of driving Victoria away to "dispose" of her. After the deed was done, the man they referred to as Butch would return under cover of darkness and help Splash get rid of Tom.

In the meantime, Splash had been charged with watching Tom and making sure he didn't escape while Theresa boarded the steamer with Nathaniel. Tom had no doubt she'd come up with a plausible excuse for why Victoria had abandoned Nathaniel once again.

Tom had wanted to roar in protest. But he'd held himself motionless until well after Theresa had left. From the way Splash's stomach had growled, Tom had figured it was only a matter of time before the man decided to go get something to eat.

He'd been right. From the moment Splash had left the hotel, Tom had begun the trek across the room to the door. Now his time was running out. Splash would be back soon. Theresa had indicated in her hurried whisper that she wouldn't give the men their final payments until she knew for sure they'd rowed out to the middle of the bay and dropped him overboard too.

Too.

Every time he thought about the word, his panic mounted. What if at that very moment, Butch was in the process of forcing Victoria into a boat and rowing her out into the bay?

Tom propelled his body forward. He attempted to drag the chair further this time. It scraped noisily. But it only moved another inch. The panic pumping through every muscle wouldn't let him give up. He'd already crossed most of the distance from the side corner where he'd been shoved out of sight. Once he reached the door, he could bang it. Hopefully the noise would alert someone to his predicament.

Oh, God, his heart cried. *Help me so that I can help her.* Of course, God had no reason to listen to his pleas. He hadn't been on speaking terms with God for years. After what had happened with Ike and his mom, he figured God hadn't wanted to hear from him. Even if an all-loving God still loved him, he wasn't worthy of that love. Not after all the destruction he'd caused.

It hadn't mattered what his mom had told him, hadn't mattered that she didn't blame him or that she was supposedly at peace over all that had transpired. He held himself responsible and would until the day he died.

He didn't deserve God's grace for himself, but he wanted it for Victoria. "God," he silently pleaded again, "*get me out of here on time so that I can save her.*" He'd do anything for her, even beg and bargain with God.

He paused in his efforts and sucked in a breath. Fifteen inches left. At the pounding of shoes on the stairway at the end of the hall, he rocked harder. Only seconds left until Splash returned. Now he wouldn't be able to alert anyone for help. But at least he could block the door and prevent Splash from coming back inside and knocking him unconscious again. Or killing him.

Tom pushed forward. Urgency and frustration spurred him on. He had to buy himself more time to figure out another plan.

The footsteps started down the hallway.

He gave a final desperate lunge. But the chair began to tip. He had no way of stopping it or bracing himself for the impact. He twisted as much as he could, and his shoulder hit the door. The impact jarred his wounds. Blackness filled his vision. He blinked hard. He had to stay conscious for Victoria's sake.

He'd already failed her by letting down his guard with Theresa. He should have been more careful, should have been more alert, should have known this would happen.

"You can't know everything, Tommy." Ike's calm words rose into his conscience. *"You think you can figure out every detail. But some things are beyond our control."*

Ike had been shivering in the back of the Confederate wagon, wet and exposed to the wind and rain when he'd spoken those words. The piles of stinking Confederate corpses next to them had caused Tom to retch until his stomach ached and his throat was raw. But at least Ike hadn't been forced to walk.

Tom had ripped the cleanest part off his shirt and stuffed it into the gaping bullet hole in Ike's thigh. As the miles had drawn them closer to their trial and hanging, he'd doctored Ike's wound and told himself he'd find a way to protect his brother.

"You can't be perfect," Ike had said. *"No one is. That's why we need God."*

No matter how much Ike had reassured him, Tom blamed himself for what had happened. He should have seen the ambush, should have known they were walking into a trap. His keen senses had saved them from plenty of trouble on other missions. He'd always noticed the broken branches, the footprints in the wet grass, the faint sourness of sweat or horseflesh. How had he not heard, seen, or sensed the trap like he usually did? Even after all these years, he didn't understand how he'd missed the clues.

Tom leaned his head against the door and waited for the first shove against it.

He should have been able to protect Ike just like he should have been able to protect Victoria. How had he failed so miserably once again? The thought that Victoria might be hurting or suffering was driving him crazy. Every second apart from her was stirring him into a frenzy. If he could work his hands free from the bindings, he'd kill Splash when he walked through the door.

However, Splash apparently knew how to tie a knot that couldn't be loosened. Tom had tried every trick he'd ever learned, but the rope hadn't budged. The only thing left was to break one of his thumbs so that he'd have room to slip his hand free.

First he had to stop Splash from coming through the door. That would give Tom at best three minutes to break his thumb and free himself before Splash realized he could get into the room from the balcony.

Fighting to stay alert, Tom pressed the weight of his body against the door.

Victoria peered out the window. At the sight of several buildings, she realized they were nearing a town. A low-lying warehouse and two old abandoned homes sat near the shore. Further down the road was what appeared to be a thoroughfare that ran through a business district.

She sat up and pressed her hands to the glass. Once she was closer to civilization, she'd renew her efforts to gain attention. Surely some passerby would notice her frantic pounding and take mercy upon her. Or at the very least alert the authorities.

When the carriage made a sudden turn, Victoria let out a cry of frustration. "No!" As the carriage halted at the rear of the warehouse, she shouted even louder. "Help! Help! Someone, please!"

The wide double doors of the building were open,

revealing a dark interior. She couldn't see any movement either inside or out. With tall withered weeds growing around the perimeter and the rusted chain that hung from the door handle, the place looked deserted.

Her spirits sank. But as the carriage bent under the weight of the driver's descent, she came up with her next plan of action. Once the coachman opened the door, all she needed to do was explain her situation. She'd offer him a large reward if he returned her to Newport unharmed.

She braced herself for the door to open, but the driver disappeared into the warehouse. Something about his tall thin form and long arms reminded her of the driver who'd attempted to kidnap her on her wedding day. Was this the same man? And why hadn't she noticed his appearance when he'd loaded her bags?

A shudder formed in her tailbone and worked its way up her spine to the back of her neck. Tom had been right about everything. Now she was ashamed she'd ever thought he was overprotective. The threat had been real and serious, and she'd taken it much too lightly, hadn't wanted to believe that someone was really capable of hurting her.

Tom had been wise to insist on her waiting at Race Point after he'd disclosed her location. As it was, in Provincetown she'd been such easy prey, especially getting into the carriage. She was just glad that Theresa hadn't joined her. The lost earring had likely kept her friend from grave danger. If only Victoria had gone to help search for it.

Unless Theresa had known.

Something about Theresa's behavior and attitude didn't make the idea far-fetched.

The possibility was too horrible to entertain. Victoria cast it aside. Theresa was her best friend. They'd always done everything together. Theresa wouldn't have any reason to bring her harm.

A movement outside the opposite carriage window caught Victoria's attention. She slid over and peered out. Several dilapidated boats were tied to an old weathered dock and looked as if one angry storm could sweep them into the sea. She searched for any person she could call to rescue her. But the only sign of life was a single gull circling above the boats.

What if Theresa had lied about Tom?

The thought forced its way into her head unbidden. She didn't want to think the worst of Theresa, but she still couldn't comprehend the possibility that Tom would leave her, especially not if he suspected she was still in danger.

What if the driver had done something to Tom first? Maybe injured him? She swallowed hard, unwilling to consider the possibility that he'd been killed.

"Lord, please, no." The prayer squeaked out past her tight throat. She didn't want Tom to get hurt or even die on account of her. She didn't want him to be in the slightest danger at all. "God, please watch over him," she whispered. "Don't worry about me. Just keep him safe."

She realized with sudden clarity that she'd give her life for Tom. She'd sacrifice everything to keep him alive. She'd never felt that way for anyone else. In fact, she was quite sure she'd always just thought about herself, what she wanted and what was best for her. She'd lived selfishly without ever having to make any sacrifices that had mattered.

How many people had she hurt as a result of her selfishness? How many beaus? How many friends? Perhaps even Theresa?

"I'm so sorry," she whispered, more to God than to anyone in particular.

Clinging to Nathaniel was just one more selfish act. She didn't love him. And it wasn't fair to marry him for what he could do for her. He deserved so much more than that. He deserved a young lady who would passionately love him and appreciate all he had to offer.

She tugged off her left glove one finger at a time. When her hand was finally bare, she held it up. The large sapphire was beautiful, but it didn't belong to her. It belonged to some other woman who would be the kind of wife Nathaniel needed.

She removed the ring. Once she got out of her predicament, she would return it to Nathaniel the first opportunity she had. She'd tell him how sorry she was for hurting him, for leading him on. Even though she couldn't marry Tom, she wouldn't relegate Nathaniel to her second option. He deserved to be someone's first choice.

The carriage door jerked open, startling her. When a hand reached in and shoved a rag against her nose and mouth, she lashed out, clawed at his hands, and wrenched her body in an effort to free herself from his grasp. But the fumes overpowered and weakened her.

"Miss Fontaine didn't mention that you'd be such a fighter," came a male voice.

Miss Fontaine? As in Theresa Fontaine? Her best friend? The world began to turn fuzzy.

"Got to quiet you up," the man spoke again, although from a distance. "Or you'll alert the entire Cape of your whereabouts."

She attempted to push his hand away but this time only batted at air. The man must be mistaken about Theresa. He had to be. She tried to form a denial, but her tongue was too heavy to speak, even if she could have gotten the words past the rag.

She began to fall backward and couldn't stop herself. When she landed against the seat, Nathaniel's ring slipped from her hand. As much as she wanted to deny what was happening, she couldn't. Her heart told her the truth. Theresa had betrayed her.

Chapter 20

$\mathcal{T}$om leaned into the door with all his weight and silenced his heavy breathing.

The footsteps in the hallway picked up pace and veered directly toward his room. Suddenly, he realized they were different than Splash's, heavier and flatter.

"Arch?" he croaked past the gag.

"Tommy boy?"

Tom's chest loosened at the sound of his friend. He banged on the door in answer.

The doorknob rattled.

Tom released his pressure against the door. He wanted to instruct Arch to pick the lock, but the telltale clicks told him Arch was doing just that.

Within seconds, Arch had the door unlocked. He forced it open, pushing Tom back in the process. At the sight of the enormous man, Tom wanted to weep with relief.

Arch's eyes were narrowed and radiated worry. He wasted no time in slitting the binding in Tom's mouth. "Where's

Victoria?" he asked as he moved behind Tom to cut his hands loose.

"Being driven south of Provincetown." Even though Theresa and Splash hadn't exactly said so, Tom had surmised that south was the only direction the carriage could take her from the northernmost part of the Cape. Rather than being seen with Theresa, Tom guessed her accomplices had landed in North Truro, the next town to the south. He suspected that's where they would return to murder Victoria, a more secluded area where they would draw less suspicion.

"My horse is out front." Arch was none too gentle in his sawing, and the rope bit into Tom's flesh. But he didn't care. He just wanted to be free as fast as possible. He knew Arch sensed it.

The rope fell away from Tom's wrists, and he flexed his fingers as Arch moved to his left leg. "You go to the steamer. Tell Nathaniel everything and stop Theresa."

"Theresa's behind the attacks?"

"She wants Nathaniel for herself."

Arch nodded. "Her father is brutal. Pompous. Conniving. I wouldn't doubt he's pushed her into going after Nathaniel."

"She's brutal too."

With one leg loose and Arch working on the second, Tom heard footsteps on the stairway. He took the knife from Arch. "We have company."

Arch straightened.

"Hide behind the door," Tom whispered, cutting his leg loose and jumping to his feet. He fought back a wave of dizziness but positioned the knife behind his back. "I'll lure him toward me. You attack from behind."

The door swung wider. And Tom got his first look at Splash, a short man with bulky arms and bruised knuckles that told Tom he was a boxer. At the sight of Tom free of his bindings, Splash grinned, revealing several broken and missing teeth.

"I see you've been busy while I've been gone." Splash unsheathed his knife and pointed it in Tom's direction with a deftness that left Tom no doubt this man was good at what he was hired to do.

"Very busy." Tom stepped toward the window. Then he swung Arch's knife out front.

At the sight of the weapon, Splash's eyes widened. He didn't have time to react before Arch picked up the chair that Tom had abandoned. In one swift move, his friend smashed it against Splash's head.

The man crumpled to the floor, and his knife skittered toward Tom.

Tom scooped it up and tucked it into the sheath where his own knife had been before Splash had disarmed him. Then he started toward the door. Without slowing his stride, he passed Arch's knife back to him.

"Are you sure you don't want me to come with you?" Arch asked as he rolled Splash over and began to bind his hands. "Your head wound looks serious."

"I'll be fine," he called over his shoulder.

"Spoken like a man in love," Arch said, the hint of smile in his voice.

Tom didn't reply. He sprinted down the hall, took the steps three at a time, and thundered across the lobby heedless of the stares he was drawing. Once outside, he found Arch's horse loosely tethered to the hitching post.

It wasn't until he was galloping at top speed out of Provincetown that Arch's words began to bounce around his head. *A man in love.*

Tom hadn't wanted to admit to himself the depth of his feelings for Victoria. He'd tried so hard to deny them. But the rampaging of his heartbeat and the throbbing of anxiety wouldn't let him ignore how he felt any longer.

He loved her with all of his body, soul, and strength. He didn't care that they were from different worlds. He didn't care that theirs was a love that wasn't meant to be. If he reached her in time, he wouldn't waste another second in telling her the truth. He wanted to be with her. Forever.

Victoria awoke to the swaying of a boat, sunshine pouring over her and blinding her. For several long moments, her groggy mind refused to focus. The squawk of a seagull beckoned to her, but she relaxed to the gentle back and forth movement and the caress of the sea breeze on her face. She was tired and didn't want to awaken.

For a second she almost allowed herself to escape into oblivion. But then the nightmare of all that had happened hit her like cold sea water, and her eyes flew open with a start. She found herself flat on her back staring into the cloudless blue sky. She pushed herself to her elbows but immediately fell back as blackness threatened to return her to unconsciousness.

Her backside was soaked through from the thin layer of bilge water that covered the bottom of the boat. Somehow she'd lost her bonnet, and she wore only one glove. From what she could tell, she was alone in the boat. But why? And where was the coachman who'd kidnapped and drugged her?

Cautiously, she lifted her head and attempted to peek over the edge of the boat. Thankfully, the boat was still tied to the dock, and she hadn't been set adrift in the ocean.

At the squeal of a door opening in the nearby warehouse,

Victoria flattened herself against the hull. Was her captor coming out? If so, what was he planning to do to her?

She closed her eyes and swallowed a scream. *God help me.*

"Be calm, Victoria," she whispered. If she panicked, she wouldn't be able to think clearly. And right now she needed every bit of clarity she could find.

At the slap of footsteps on the wooden dock, she glanced around the boat for anything that might be of help. Her options included a fishing net, tin bucket, or rusty hooks. If she could get a hold of the hooks, she might be able to wield them like weapons. Or even the net. She could throw it over the man and trap him.

But the footsteps sounded close, and she didn't have enough time to reach those items. Instead, her fingers brushed the long handle of the oar lying by her side. She closed her eyes as the tall shadow of the coachman fell over the boat. He paused for a moment as though looking at her. Then the boat sank deeper into the water and wobbled as he climbed inside.

She tried to still the trembling in her limbs. She didn't know what this man was planning to do to her or where he was taking her. But she couldn't wait to find out. Especially because no one else knew where she was or what had become of her. Except, of course, Theresa.

Her friend's betrayal stabbed her anew. How could Theresa have done this? They'd been best friends for as far back as Victoria could remember. She didn't understand how a friend she'd trusted and loved could turn against her.

Did Theresa want to stop her wedding to Nathaniel? And why? Her friend had always seemed excited about it, had gone shopping with her for her trousseau, had helped her with so many of the plans. Why would Theresa do all those things if she didn't want the wedding to take place?

Victoria cracked open an eye and discovered that the coachman had begun to untie the rope that held the boat to the dock. His back was turned to her. If she acted quickly enough, perhaps she could take him by surprise.

Her hand shook as she gripped the oar. She wasn't a strong woman, and she didn't know how she would possibly be able to attack him. But she had to at least try. Before she could change her mind, she pushed up as nimbly and quietly as possible. The sway of the boat masked most of her movement. When she was standing, she tried to catch her balance and at the same time lifted the oar.

As if sensing a change in her presence, her captor glanced over his shoulder. His eyes rounded, and he swiveled. Before he could react any further, she swung the paddle as hard as she could toward his head.

The board connected with his cheek and temple with a resounding thwack. The momentum of the hit forced him backward. He stumbled over the middle bench, tripped over a tin bucket, and was unable to catch himself. Amidst a slew of curses, he fell into the small wedge of the stern, his feet sticking straight up in the air and his backside lodged against the hull. He struggled to rise from the tight spot, but could hardly move.

Victoria threw her oar overboard and pitched the other one into the water as well. She scrambled out of the boat. Then she unwound the last bit of rope holding the vessel to the dock and shoved it toward the deeper water.

"You won't be able to run from me. I'll track you down!" yelled the coachman, squirming in the tight spot. Victoria knew it was only a matter of time before he freed himself. She just prayed by that point the boat would have been swept out to sea. And that she could find a safe place to hide.

Without waiting for him to fulfill his threat, she kicked off her high heel shoes and raced down the dock back onto solid ground as fast as her fashionable skirt would allow. Her captor's vulgar calls trailed after her, making her run faster past the warehouse that reeked of fish. She dashed beyond the two weathered homes with their sagging front porches and broken windows.

They were clearly in disuse. Did she dare hide in one of them?

She circled around to the rear of one and tested the door. It was locked. She guessed the door on the other house was bolted too. With a growing sense of urgency, she eyed the road. If she ran, could she reach town before she was recaptured? She grabbed a fistful of her skirt into one hand and wished she could pull off the garment. As it was, she could hardly move in it. Fashion was apparently to be her undoing. If she escaped, never again would she place so much importance on keeping up appearances.

She examined the windows. Jagged glass remained in several frames and boards covered others. She couldn't enter the house that way. "Think like Tom," she told herself. "What would he do if he were here?"

Again, she studied the structure in front of her, trying to see it through Tom's keen eyes. Her sights came to rest on two wooden slabs that had been nailed across a section of siding. Why would someone nail boards to the siding if not to patch a hole?

She crossed to the spot. One of the boards hung by a single nail. She shifted it enough to see that indeed a gap existed. It was outlined with numerous spider webs that were filled with brittle insects. She couldn't see much of the interior of the house, except more dust and dirt.

She yanked at some of the rotten siding, and it fell away like crumbling toast. For a moment she worked on the hole, making it bigger, but then she realized she was leaving a trail of evidence on the ground. She scooped up the debris and tried not to think about the horrid things she might be touching. Instead, she peeled away the wood until finally she'd widened the gap enough so she could slip through.

The fit was tight, and halfway through she felt her skirt catch and heard a sharp rip. After sucking in her stomach and wiggling against the rot, she found herself face down on the floor of what appeared to be an old kitchen. Once she was fully through, she sat up and shuddered at her surroundings. In the dim light coming through cracks of the boarded windows, she could see that a portion of the ceiling had caved in and now lay in heaps among the remains of a table and two chairs. More cobwebs crowded each nook and corner, along with what appeared to be animal nests of some kind.

The stench of decay was overpowering, and the soft scamper of claws told her rats now made this place their home. She glanced with longing at the opening she'd made. She didn't relish the idea of spending even a few minutes in the hovel. But she braced her shoulders and again admonished herself to be brave and strong like Tom.

Knowing he would cover his tracks, she returned to the opening and attempted to force the board back into place as best she could, praying that from the outside her captor wouldn't notice the gap that she'd made bigger.

She tiptoed carefully through the wreckage, her silk stockings providing very little protection for her tender soles. As she moved out of the kitchen into a hallway, she knew if Tom were with her, he'd encourage her to find a good hiding place in case the coachman made it back to shore and decided to break into the house and look for her there.

The stairway was leaning dangerously to one side, and she decided not to attempt the second story. Instead, she peeked into the two remaining rooms—a front drawing room and a small bedroom near the kitchen. She didn't see any place she might hide except under what was left of the bed. She studied the kitchen again with growing despair and then saw a half door she'd missed in her first inspection because a ripped fishing net was hanging over it. Gingerly pulling aside the net, she pried the door open to reveal a dark pantry just big enough for her to sit in.

Except for a few tin cans and a broken plate, the closet appeared empty and somewhat clean—if something coated in layers of dust and cobwebs could truly be considered clean. She climbed inside and attempted to make herself comfortable, which was nearly impossible in her constricting skirt. Then she closed the door and prayed the fishing net had fallen back over the opening to conceal it.

Chapter 21

$\mathcal{T}$he pounding in Tom's temples matched the horse's hoofs beating against the road. The town of North Truro loomed ahead, but he veered his mount toward a fish warehouse with a lone dock and a dilapidated dinghy. From the saltwater corrosion in the hull bolts, he suspected the boat hadn't been used all summer.

Down shore he caught sight of a cutter, abandoned on the beach with its bow pulled up onto a rocky stretch to keep it from being washed out into the ocean. The water marks on the side indicated that it had recently returned from a trip.

Tom reined the horse and studied the area more carefully. He'd been tracking the carriage since Provincetown, and the tire marks ended at the warehouse, which made sense. If Butch planned to take Victoria out and dump her in the bay, he wouldn't risk being seen in North Truro. He would have brought her to a more secluded place. Like here.

Tom slid down from the mount and bent to study the horse prints. Some led to the building and others pointed back to the road.

Had Butch finished the job and already left? Tom glanced again to the cutter down the shore. His muscles tightened at the thought of being too late, of failing again to protect someone he loved.

He pried open the fish warehouse doors, his knife ready in case Butch sprang out of the shadows. But the only thing in the shed was a carriage. The horse was gone, which meant Butch was gone too.

Tom picked up a rag that lay discarded in a scattering of rotting hay. One sniff of the sickly sweet odor of chloroform in the scrap informed him that Butch had drugged Victoria. Probably so that he could take her down to a waiting boat.

Tom's pulse spurted with renewed dread. He tossed the rag back to the floor and raced out of the shack. He tried to tell himself that he wasn't too late, that the abandoned cutter down the shore didn't mean anything. But he stopped abruptly as he reached the edge of the dock.

There were Victoria's shoes. Fancy pointed shoes that he'd seen her wear back in Newport.

He stared at them for a moment, his chest hollow and his head light.

She was gone. And all that remained were her shoes.

His mind filled with images of her sinking beneath the waves, her layers of clothes dragging her down. Her lungs filling with water. Her body finally hitting the cold, dark bottom. He could picture her frantically trying to swim, to work her way to the surface against currents and waves that would only suck her back under. She would have been terrified.

The thought that she'd been frightened and in pain made him want to jump into the dinghy, row out, and try to rescue her—even though it was too late. He could only pray that she'd still been unconscious and had died peacefully.

He dropped to his knees on the edge of the dock, and a cry tore at his throat. For several long seconds he couldn't breathe, couldn't do anything but stare at the shoes. Then a moan worked its way loose. "Oh, God, I loved her."

Heat seared his eyes and burned his chest with the need to weep. He'd tried so hard not to fall in love with her, hadn't thought he deserved to have a woman's love after his past mistakes. Hadn't thought he was the right kind of man for Victoria. But somehow she'd broken through the walls he'd erected around himself. And after breaking through them, she'd worked her way into his heart so that she'd filled him thoroughly and completely.

And what had he done? He'd thrust her away. He'd let his fears of losing her, of failing her, and of disappointing her take control.

He lowered his face into his hands and groaned again. He had loved her. Still loved her. And always would.

If only he'd told her that, maybe she wouldn't have left Race Point. He'd nearly forced her back into Nathaniel's arms. And in doing so, he'd jeopardized her safety even more.

He fisted his hands and pounded his legs. "Why take her? Why not me instead?"

It was the same question he'd asked God after Ike had gotten shot. The same question he'd lived with for years. He'd failed to protect the people he loved. He was the one who deserved to die. Not them.

"*Some things are beyond our control.*" His brother's words whispered through his head again. "*You can't be perfect. No one is. That's why we need God.*"

He could admit he was far from perfect. But that hadn't

stopped him from aiming for perfection in his job. He supposed he'd thought that by protecting others he could make up for losing Ike. But he hadn't. He'd only failed all over again.

"That's why you need me." Instead of Ike's voice in his head, this time he had the distinct impression that God was reaching out to him. After the way he'd ignored, and yes, been angry with God over the years, the thought that the Almighty wanted him was too powerful to comprehend. If he'd been a more emotional man, he may have even wept at the realization that God still cared about him.

"I can't go on without you," Tom whispered, finally lifting his eyes to the ocean where Victoria had drowned. Only the soft echo of *"you need me"* kept him kneeling at the end of the dock instead of jumping into the water, swimming out as far as he could, and letting himself sink to the bottom so that he could die too.

He didn't want to live anymore, not without hope. And the only hope—perhaps the real hope he'd been missing all along—was found in God. At least that's what Mom had claimed. The fact that God still loved him in spite of imperfections and failures was all he had to cling to. If God still wanted him, then he couldn't let go of life yet.

"I don't know what my pathetic life is going to look like now, but I need you to help me survive."

For an endless moment he waited. He wasn't sure for what. But finally, even though his chest burned with grief, he stood. He walked to Victoria's shoes. Should he give them to her mother as a last remembrance?

He bent to retrieve them but halted. They were pointed back to the shore, as if she'd taken them off so that she could run away from the dock. One was flipped over, revealing a damp section at the heel.

Had she been in the boat and somehow escaped?

A large wave pushed against the dock, rocking it slightly. At a soft thump against the weathered boards, he got down onto his stomach and attempted to peer under the dock, dreading what he might find and praying it wasn't a body—her body.

At the sight of an oar—actually two oars—he breathed again. The swell of heavier waves and the rise in the water level was causing the oars to lightly bump the underside of the dock.

Tom hopped to his feet and stared with narrowed eyes at the cutter down shore. Had Victoria somehow freed herself from her captor, thrown the oars in the water, and then run away, leaving her shoes behind?

All of the evidence added up that way. Perhaps that's why the horse was gone. Butch had headed off in search of Victoria.

A thin beam of hope broke through the darkness inside Tom, but he tried not to let it shine too brightly. In his desperate state, he might be chasing a false lead. He had to stay calm and examine every detail. If Victoria was alive, she might be on the run from Butch. She might still be in danger. If he could track her before Butch found her, he might have a chance of saving her.

With the shoes in one hand, he examined the sand for her footprints. After probing closely, he finally found faint steps leading away, steps that appeared to be about the size of her feet. He followed them until he came to the weeded plot that led past the houses. He guessed she would have run to town to try to get help. But once on the road, he saw no evidence of her footprints either in the gravel or in the long grass on the side of the road.

He peered toward North Truro, hoping to see her bonnet, her parasol, anything that would alert him to her presence. But something in his gut told him she never went there. He turned and scrutinized the deserted houses that were falling in on themselves from disuse. They were both locked and boarded and had no port of entry.

He studied the warehouse and shook his head.

She wasn't here. But she hadn't gone to town. So where was she?

Maybe she'd attempted to run away from Butch, only to have him recapture her before she could reach the road. But even as that possibility crossed his mind, he didn't want to believe it.

He started toward the warehouse. He would inspect it further to see if he'd missed any clues the first time he'd been inside. He slowed as he passed the first of house. Nothing there had been touched in months, if not years, except by weather and wild animals.

When he reached the second house, he couldn't see a trace of anyone having been inside that house either. Until he reached the back of the house. A board had been adjusted near one corner. The movement was almost imperceptible, but the slight exposure of darker wood told him that someone had recently tampered with it.

He crossed to the area and dropped to one knee to inspect the suspicious area. He grazed his fingers along the ground and made contact with slivers of damp wood. When he shifted the board, it moved aside with surprising ease, revealing a gap, one that would be impossible for a man of his size to squeeze through. But not impossible for Victoria.

He trailed his fingers along the ridge. At the touch of something satiny, he stopped. He plucked the material loose and held it up to the sunlight. Blue silk.

He stood and almost felt faint at the prospect that Victoria had made it into the house. There could be no other explanation. She'd clearly crawled through the gap.

With a new urgency to his step, he approached the door, unsheathed his knife, and used it to pick the lock. He had it open within seconds and nearly ripped the door from its hinges in his haste to get inside. He ducked under a ceiling beam that hung down and stepped around a mound of debris.

His heart raced as he clomped from one room to the next searching for any sign of what had happened to her, for a scuffle of some kind, for evidence that Butch had somehow been there and already gotten to her.

But he found nothing. As he stood in the middle of what had once been a kitchen, he almost felt like weeping again. Where was she? What had become of her? Maybe she'd already left. If so, where would she have gone next?

A faint sound nearby silenced his internal rampage. He tried to identify what he'd heard. A breath? A sniff? Or maybe just a mouse in the wall?

He listened for at least thirty seconds but didn't hear anything again. However, he scrutinized the wall and was rewarded with the sight of the faint outline of a cupboard. In two swift strides, he shoved aside the fishing net and jerked open the half door.

A jagged piece of plate sliced through the air, aimed directly at his leg. He caught it just before the sharp edge reached his flesh. "Victoria. Thank God."

She was crouched on her knees, hardly able to fit into the space. Her hair hung in disarray, and tears trickled down her dirty cheeks. At the sight of him, she dropped her weapon, gave a soft cry, and buried her face into her hands and sobbed.

Tom dropped to his knees and gently pried her out of the tight space. Then he sat back on his heels and lifted her onto his lap. She didn't resist. In fact, she pressed her face against his chest, her broken sobs muted but desperate and heart-wrenching.

His own throat ached with the need to cry out his relief. He wrapped his arms around her and held her, his heart beating fiercely with all of the love he had for her. He laid his lips against her temple, and the strong beat of her pulse there reassured him she truly was alive, that she'd survived the horrific ordeal.

He tilted his head back and lifted a silent prayer heavenward. *Thank you.* God hadn't been obligated to save Victoria. God hadn't been obligated to do anything for him. But He hadn't let him go, had loved him, and promised him hope. Now, He'd done the one thing that mattered most to him in the world—He'd protected Victoria.

Her sobs began to lessen but her body continued to tremble.

He enveloped her more fully. "You're safe now," he whispered. "I'm here."

Her fists closed around the lapels of his suit coat, and she clung to him. "I thought you were the coachman, that he'd finally figured out where I was hiding."

"He's not here," Tom murmured, pressing a kiss against her forehead. "Don't worry anymore." He wanted to tell her that he'd never let anything bad happen to her ever again, but he couldn't. No one had the power to control everything, except God.

She finally pulled away far enough so that he could see her face. Tears still trailed down her cheeks. "Were you hurt? I realized they must have done something terrible to you for you to leave me all alone."

"I'm fine." He didn't want her to worry about him. Now that he had her in his arms, his pain had dimmed to a distant ache. She lifted her hand to his cheek and traced a streak of dried blood.

He drew her hand away from his cheek to his lips. He laid a tender kiss against her knuckles. "All that matters is that I found you."

Her eyes turned glassy. "I'm so sorry, Tom," she whispered. "I'm sorry for not believing you about the danger. I'm sorry for not staying at Race Point like you asked. I'm sorry for making light of your concerns—"

He cut off her rambling with a touch of his fingers against her lips. "It's not your fault."

"Yes, it is. I'm so spoiled and thoughtless and stupid."

"I pushed you away." The words were hard to say. But he couldn't hold back from her any longer. He had to tell her the truth about how he felt, even if it frightened him, even if she didn't want him anymore.

Her eyes widened, and her lips formed around a response, but he spoke again before she could. "If I hadn't pushed you away, you wouldn't have made plans to leave the lighthouse."

"You were just trying to do your job and protect me—"

"No. I've been a coward. Afraid to face the truth."

Her brow wrinkled. "Truth?"

"The truth is"—he swallowed hard—"I love you."

The lines in her forehead disappeared, and her honey-brown eyes rounded with wonder.

"When I thought I'd lost you..." His voice cracked. He cleared it and forced himself to go on. "When I thought you'd drowned, I wanted to drown too."

She lifted a hand to his cheek, her fingers cool and soothing against his skin.

"I don't want to live without you." There he'd said it. And now that the words were out, they felt right.

She smiled, and her smile was filled with all of the sweetness and forgiveness that she offered so freely—and that he didn't deserve. But maybe, as with God, it was time to finally stop condemning himself and accept the gift.

"Please don't leave me," he whispered, his voice turning thick, his need to wrap his arms back around her growing strong again.

"Okay," she replied, tilting her smiling face up. Her easy acceptance shook him down to his soul. She offered no protests, no conditions. She never had. She'd never seemed concerned about all she might be giving up or the censure she would get from her parents or the outcast she'd become among New York society if she claimed a common man like him.

Tom knew she was naive and that they'd need to have a thorough conversation about their future together at some point. But for now, he was content to know she still wanted him.

He started to pull her back into his embrace when the distant echo of hoofs made his muscles tense.

"What?" she whispered.

The horse was traveling north. When it slowed its pace, Tom guessed Butch was returning after failing to find Victoria in North Truro.

"Wait here." He slid her to the floor and stood. When she began to rise, he motioned her back. "Please, Victoria. Stay here and let me handle this."

She sat back down, and fear flitted through her pretty eyes. "Is he coming back for me?"

Tom nodded. "He'll look in here first." With the door torn away from the hinges, Butch would suspect that someone had come to help Victoria, especially if he saw the horse by the warehouse. If Tom could catch him by surprise and disarm him first...

He unsheathed his knife and made his way to the back door. He flattened himself against the moldy wall and tried to hide in the shadows.

Tom hardly dared to breathe. He would only get one chance to take out Butch. If he didn't, he'd risk losing Victoria all over again.

A darkening in the door frame and the huffs of heavy breathing alerted Tom to Butch's return. Tom's fingers tightened around the hilt of his knife. He was tempted to lunge now before Butch spotted him. But he fought against the urge and waited.

The tall, thin man entered with his knife outstretched, clearly expecting an attack. Thankfully, his gaze landed on the opposite side of the hallway from where Tom stood. The slight second gave Tom the advantage he needed.

He sprang out and plunged his knife into Butch's side, into the fleshy part of his back beneath his rib cage. A knife wound there would stun him, hopefully disable him. But wouldn't be mortal if he sought treatment.

Butch roared with pain but somehow managed to swing around and slash at Tom.

Tom was prepared for a counterattack. He jumped out of reach of the blade. But in the process, he tripped over a broken piece of floorboard.

Tom stumbled backward. His heel snagged on the door frame. He tried to catch his balance but fell to the ground outside the door.

In an instant, Butch jumped on him. Even though the man was wounded and a dark spot of blood was widening at his side, he slammed his knee into Tom's stomach.

Tom's breath whooshed from his lungs. Pain seared his ribs.

Before Tom could gather his wits, Butch's fingers wrapped around his neck. The man's thumb pressed hard against Tom's windpipe. The force cut off any ability to breathe.

At the same time, Butch raised his knife and brought it down toward Tom's heart.

Tom caught Butch's wrist. He held the blade at bay, but barely.

Butch's arm was thin and wiry, but his muscles rippled. His narrow face was sweaty and the veins in his long forehead protruded at the exertion. A swollen bruise at his temple and cheek told Tom that Butch had taken a recent blow across the head. From Victoria?

With Butch's thumb cutting off his air, and the knife only inches from his heart, Tom had the dizzying thought that he was about to fail again.

Butch's mouth was set into a tight line, and his eyes filled with cold determination. This man was a hired killer. And like Splash, Tom could tell Butch was good at what he did.

At the gasp and distressed, "No!" that came from the doorway, dismay rushed through Tom. Victoria had disobeyed his instructions and come out.

If he'd had his voice, he would have yelled at her. As it was, all he could think about was Butch getting his hands on Victoria again. If he did, this time the man would kill her first, then row her out and dump her into the ocean.

The mere picture of Butch touching her sent a jolt of energy through Tom. He brought his knee up to Butch's back and rammed it into the knife wound. Butch flinched but didn't loosen his grip. Tom kneed him again, this time more forcefully.

Butch's thumb slipped away from Tom's windpipe long enough for him to drag in a breath. But the knife angled dangerously close to Tom's shirt, close enough that he could feel the prick of the blade through the linen.

If he couldn't physically dislodge Butch, he'd have to roll over and throw him off. Before Tom could make his big move, a crack sounded against the back of Butch's head.

Butch's eyes widened. The pressure of his thumb ceased. The hand holding the knife wavered.

Tom didn't waste any time trying to figure out what had happened. Instead, he slammed Butch's arm and knocked the weapon into the air so that it landed a dozen feet away.

Butch wavered back and forth like a drunk man, and fell off Tom sideways, hitting the ground with a thump. Then he lay motionless in the sandy grass.

Victoria stood above them, a board in her hand. For a moment she stared at Butch, her face a mask of fury and determination. She toed him with her stocking foot, and when he didn't respond, she took a step away, her eyes registering worry. "Did I kill him?"

Tom sat up and sucked air into his starved lungs. A glance at the brute told Tom the man was still breathing. "No. You knocked him out."

"Let's tie him up before he revives." Victoria lifted the board as though preparing to strike Butch again if he so much as batted an eyelash.

Tom was already removing one of his suspenders. He rolled Butch to his stomach and made quick work of binding his hands with the sturdy strap. The blood from the knife wound Tom had inflicted had formed a wide spot on the man's coat. Tom slit a long bandage from the man's shirt and wrapped it around his torso to staunch the flow. All the while he worked, Victoria watched, pale and silent.

"Will he live?" she asked once Tom had used Butch's boot-laces to tie his feet together.

"Yes. I'll make sure of it." He didn't want Victoria to live with the guilt of this man's death on her conscience, even if he deserved to die. Besides, Tom wanted Butch alive to testify against Theresa.

Tom stood and took the board from Victoria's hands. She relinquished it, and he tossed it against the house. When he reached for her, she came to him willingly, almost eagerly. Her arms wound around his waist, and she rested her face against his chest.

"It's over," he whispered.

For a long moment he just held her, letting the sunshine warm them and the steady crash of the waves soothe their racing pulses. When he finally felt her breathing return to normal and her heartbeat grow steady, he brushed his fingers through her tangled hair.

"Did you mean what you said when we were inside?" she asked.

"What did I say?" Although he knew very well what he'd said.

"That you—" she hesitated. "That you don't want me to leave?"

He tilted back so that he could look into her face, which in spite of the dirt and tear streaks was still beautiful. Her eyes held expectancy but also reservation, as if she didn't quite know what to make of all he'd spoken in such earnestness.

"I'm not a perfect man," he started. "I'm flawed in many

ways."

"I'm far from perfect too."

He shook his head. "But that hasn't stopped me from falling in love with you."

"So I wasn't dreaming that you'd said the words?" She released an almost blissful sigh and smiled.

"The Lord knows how hard I've tried not to love you."

"And I know it too." Her words were light and her eyes warm. "But apparently I'm irresistible?"

"Yes."

"So I lured you in and snared you after all?" She cocked her head and gave him a playful look under her long lashes.

"I'm all yours." And he meant it. He wanted to spend the rest of his earthly days beside her, with her, loving, laughing, talking, teasing, and growing in faith.

"If you're all mine, does that mean I may do with you as I please?" Her voice dropped into a whisper that began to thaw his blood, which was still cold from the fear and anxiety of all they'd just experienced.

He thought back to one of the first times he'd accompanied her and how she'd attempted to wield her charms over him to get her way. She'd never be able wrap him around her finger, and he would never cater to her every whim like other men always had. But she certainly had more power over him than he'd ever believed any one could gain.

"What do you want to do with me?" He lowered his voice to the same flirtatious tone, unable to resist the play of a grin at his lips.

A rosy pink colored her cheeks, and he knew that even though she teased him, she was still innocent. He was much more informed about the ways between men and women than she was. "Do you know what I'd like to do with you?" he asked softly.

The pink rose into an even prettier flush. When she nibbled at her bottom lip, he realized that she thought he was going to kiss her or was at least contemplating it. Which, strangely, he wasn't, not at that moment. He had something more important on his mind.

He lowered himself to one knee before her, retrieved the ring from his pocket, and took her hand. "Victoria," he started, "I'm a simple man. And I can't give you much."

"I don't care—"

"But I can give you my promise to love you." He held up the simple wedding band that she'd worn the past month. He hadn't told her that the band had been the one Ike had been saving for his girl back home, Tabitha Lovell. After the war, when Tom had gone to give her the ring and a few of Ike's other personal items, he'd learned that she'd died around the same time as Ike, from consumption. Tom had taken some comfort in knowing that Ike wasn't alone in heaven, that at least he was happy with the woman he'd loved.

Victoria stared at the ring he held poised above her finger.

"No matter what the future brings, I'll never be able to stop loving you."

Something briefly flickered in her eyes. He might have missed it if he hadn't looked up into her face at that moment. It was fear. He'd recognize it anywhere. Yet just as quickly as the emotion appeared it vanished, replaced by excitement and thrill and wonder, which settled into every lovely curve and crevice of her face.

"Oh, Tom," she whispered. "I'll never be able to stop loving you either." The sincerity in her eyes told him she meant it.

"Then marry me." He slipped the band over her slender finger.

She splayed her fingers, making it easier for him to slide the ring all the way down to where it belonged. When it was in place, her eyes glistened. "Yes. With all my heart." She met his gaze with a radiance that made his chest swell to bursting.

He brought her hand to his lips and tenderly kissed her ring finger and then turned over her hand and pressed a kiss into her palm. Her breath hitched in that sensual way she had about her that told him she enjoyed his touch, that it never failed to move her.

One glance into her eyes, and he could see that not only did she enjoy his touch but that she wanted more. The temperature of his blood rose a degree. He readily obliged her with a feathery kiss on her wrist.

She closed her eyes as if to prevent him from seeing her pleasure, but it was written in the tightening lines in her face. "Tom?"

He kissed the skin directly above her wrist, this time lingering and caressing her wildly beating pulse. "Hmm?"

"How am I to marry you?" she asked breathlessly. "When we're already married?"

"We'll have a real wedding."

"At Race Point?"

"Wherever you want." He loved the texture of her silky skin against his lips.

"I want your parents to be there. And we'll invite mine to come too."

He nodded.

"But, Tom," she started and then ducked her head, "we're already legally married. What will be the point of the wedding?"

Heat spread into his gut at the remembrance of the few passionate kisses they'd shared, of how difficult it had grown to let go of her, of how close he'd been to picking her up and taking her to bed. Could he really wait for a wedding? And really, what was the point? She was right. They were married. He could take her home tonight and they could finally be together.

He shook his head, fighting away the temptation. "I want to do this right. With your father's permission. With my parents' full understanding. And with vows that we both mean this time."

Of course, it had been easy to agree to the judge's questions and to sign a document that night on the steamboat when they'd been leaving Newport. But that exchange had been a necessity, a business arrangement, not a real marriage ceremony.

He pushed himself up until he was standing before her. "I don't want our marriage to be by default. I want us to choose it and make it public."

A wrinkle formed between her eyebrows. "How will your parents feel when they learn the truth?"

"I suspect my mom knows more than she's let on." He couldn't say for sure or even how. "My dad might be harder to console. But I'll take care of him."

"I love them both. And I don't want them to be upset at us."

"They won't. They love you." He had no doubt he and Victoria would have obstacles to overcome, but it likely wouldn't be from his parents. It would be from hers. However, he didn't want to bring that up now. He tugged her close again and touched his lips against the tiny crease in her forehead, hoping to ease her worries.

She released another sigh that informed him she was happy again. He loved how quickly she could put aside her concerns and easily trust that everything would work out, even though he wasn't sure how.

Her fingers skimmed up his shirtsleeves, leaving a trail of heat on his arms. Suddenly, all he could think about was the fact that she'd survived and that she was his. *His*. Finally. He drew her body against his, which may have been a mistake because he was keenly aware of her nearness and how exquisite she was.

One hand glided up her back to her neck and the other to her cheek. He positioned her head so that he could bend in and claim her lips with all the desperateness that had overcome him earlier when he'd thought she was dead. His touch was neither gentle nor chaste. It was hungry and full of all the need for her that he'd denied for too long.

She rose on her toes to meet him, greeting his kiss with one as ardent as his. She didn't hold back.

Through the haze of his passion, he heard the clatter of carriage wheels coming from the direction of Provincetown. From the rapid speed, he guessed the newcomer was either Arch or Nathaniel. Or both. He knew he should stop kissing Victoria before anyone arrived. She'd be embarrassed to be caught kissing him so fervently. It was unladylike and even scandalous.

But he didn't want to stop. He wanted Nathaniel to see them together. He wanted Nathaniel to see Victoria kissing him in a way that she never had him.

He tipped her head back so that he had access to her neck. He broke away from her lips and moved to her lovely exposed throat. He kissed her jaw line and dipped to the spot below it, feeling the thud of her pulse and the heat of her skin.

From the corner of his eye, he could see that Arch was driving the wildly careening vehicle, which meant Nathaniel was riding as a passenger. As the carriage jerked to a stop, Tom captured Victoria's lips again. After his teasing kisses upon her neck, she was ready for him and responded with an ardor that would surely show Nathaniel who her choice was.

The horse's snorting and the banging open of the carriage door didn't seem to penetrate Victoria's passion. She was lost in their kiss. Tom waited until he heard Nathaniel's feet hit the gravel, and then he counted mentally to five before he released her.

She didn't immediately pull away and would have moved to kiss him again, except that he turned her slightly. "We have company," he whispered and nodded toward the new arrivals.

Her first glance was disinterested. But when she looked again and understanding lit her eyes, she broke away from him. He wrapped his arm around her waist, not intending to let her distance herself too much. She was his now. He hoped Nathaniel had gotten the message, but just in case he hadn't, Tom would make sure he understood.

Thankfully, Victoria didn't protest his need to stake his claim on her. Instead, she sidled into the curve of his arm.

Nathaniel's eyes were wide and bounced back and forth between him and Victoria. Confusion floundered across his face. His mouth was open as if he wanted to speak but didn't know what to say.

Arch didn't move from the high driver's seat of the carriage. But his broad shoulders visibly relaxed. Tom was sure Arch had assessed the situation as rapidly as he would have. The lone horse, the broken door, and Butch unconscious and tied up on the ground. Seeing that Victoria was standing and unharmed, Arch was content. In fact, Tom caught a glimpse of humor in Arch's eyes, as though he suspected what Tom was doing and why.

Nathaniel's eyes, however, had no humor in them, only hurt and surprise. "Victoria? I don't understand."

Tom felt the slight tremble in her arm as she wound it behind his back. "I love Tom."

"But you love me," Nathaniel stammered. "We're getting married."

Victoria shook her head slowly, almost sadly. "I'm sorry."

Nathaniel searched her face, and his shoulders sagged as though he realized he was defeated. Perhaps he'd suspected it all along but was finally admitting it.

A shard of guilt pricked Tom. He owed Nathaniel an apology for sending the telegram and allowing him to believe Victoria wanted to resume the wedding plans. Even though the deception had revealed Theresa as the culprit, Tom probably could have figured out a way to gain Nathaniel's participation in the process without setting him up for this kind of pain.

At the very least, Tom hoped Nathaniel would recover from his heartbreak quickly, and hopefully one day find another woman he could love as much as Victoria. He was a good man, but he had to realize by now that Victoria wasn't the right woman for him. Tom guessed that if she'd gone through with the plans to marry Nathaniel, she would have run away from the ceremony, like she had every other time she'd attempted marriage. In fact, if Tom hadn't intervened on her wedding day back in June, Victoria wouldn't have made it to the carriage.

She hadn't ever had the right man. And now she did. She had him. And this time, at their wedding, she'd have no reason to run.

Chapter 22

Victoria stood on the Provincetown dock and tried not to keep glancing with too much longing at the town behind her. The August morning was overcast and a brisk wind blew off the ocean. But even with the threat of rain and the gloomy gray of the low clouds, the view of the town with its neat rows of plain white houses, small shops, and austere hotel somehow seemed homey and welcoming. Even the salty fish odor emanating from the rows of drying cod didn't nauseate her the same way it had the first day she'd arrived.

She realized that her perception had changed a great deal during the past weeks. She'd thought this seaport town on the tip of Cape Cod was dingy, run-down, and with little to offer a woman like her.

How mistaken she'd been. Now she saw it as a place where she could live simply without focusing so much on herself and what she could get out of life. Away from the busyness and the glamor of society, she could take a look at herself and try to discover who she really was.

"You're absolutely sure I can't persuade you to come back to Newport?" Nathaniel asked again, standing in front of her near the gangplank. He was attired in an elegant green and brown promenade suit and a matching hat that highlighted his green eyes. His fly-away hair was shorter than usual and his mustache was neatly trimmed.

"As much as I truly adore you, Nathaniel," she said as she adjusted her parasol. "I'm simply not the woman you need."

"I think you are," he said in that same anguished tone he'd used before when trying to convince her to go through with the wedding.

She shook her head, once again feeling the weight of guilt for not having seen the incompatibility in their relationship much sooner. Even if she'd never met and fallen in love with Tom, she should have had enough sense to realize that she'd cared about Nathaniel for selfish reasons—for how he made her feel, what he gave her, the life he could provide, and how his status reflected so positively on her.

That wasn't to say that she hadn't cared about him, because she had. She'd enjoyed spending time with him. They'd had fun together. He'd been tender and sweet and considerate and giving. If she'd stayed with him, she might have had an easy life.

With Tom, she was sure to have more challenges. But she felt complete with him. He balanced her weaknesses. She didn't have to pretend to be anyone but herself. He saw the good and the bad in her and accepted her regardless.

"Oh, Nathaniel," she said, "you've been the perfect gentleman and lavished me with your gifts and love. But I haven't appreciated all of your attention the way a woman ought to."

"It doesn't matter—"

"I know God has someone better for you. Someone who

will need all you have to offer and will love you deeply in return." She'd already returned his engagement ring, for the second time. And she planned to return all of the other jewels he'd given her during their courtship. She didn't need them and prayed he'd find someone else to give them to soon.

She motioned to Arch, who was standing guard at the end of the dock. He had his arms crossed over his giant frame and scowled at any of the fishermen at the drying racks who stopped their work to stare at Victoria.

Even though her captors were in jail, Arch and Tom had both insisted that she have a bodyguard at all times. At least until they made sure Theresa and her family were brought to justice. Even now, Theresa was locked in a berth on the steamboat. Tom and Arch had already questioned her and learned that Theresa's father had conspired with his daughter to prevent Victoria from marrying Nathaniel so that Theresa could have the chance. She admitted to having been behind Arch's stabbing, that she'd purposefully dropped her glove and gone back to retrieve it so that Victoria would be by herself and more susceptible to an attack. It was the same tactic she used by leaving her grandmother's earring behind in the hotel.

Every time Victoria thought about her friend, she wanted to weep for not only the loss of a friendship but also for what would become of Theresa once her crimes were made public. Her striving to improve herself had brought about her downfall instead of the elevation she'd sought.

The sad situation was all the more reason Victoria wanted to break free of the constraints of the world she'd grown up in. If the desire to climb higher led people in her social circles to consider kidnapping and murder, then clearly that world had too much control over them.

Victoria had tried to speak to her friend earlier in the

morning when the sheriff had accompanied Theresa from the jail to the waiting steamer.

"I'm sorry for not being a better friend," she'd said as she walked with Theresa up the gangplank. "If I hadn't been so focused on myself, I would have seen that you cared for Nathaniel."

Arch had tried to tell her that Nathaniel wouldn't have cared for Theresa in return. Not even if Victoria had given him up much sooner. But Victoria still couldn't absolve herself of the guilt. If she'd been more sensitive and less selfish, she might have seen Theresa's hurt earlier and prevented all of the problems.

Arch's heavy steps approached her and his gaze told her that it was time to go. "Ready for this?" He held out the item she'd decided to bring along.

Victoria let her fingers linger over the grainy wood. As she'd prepared to see Nathaniel off, she'd asked Arch for a suggestion of something to give Nathaniel to ease his pain, to let him know that even if she couldn't marry him, she still cared about him.

Arch had nodded at her driftwood cross on the bedstead in her hotel room. Several years ago, she'd told Arch the story behind the cross, the same story her mother had written in a letter when she'd been separated from her father, not knowing what the future would bring, especially in relation to her blindness. During that time, her mother had learned not to place her hope in her circumstances or a man, both of which would change. But she'd learned instead to hope in the one Beacon that would always be there, no matter what darkness came her way.

It was finally time to pass the mementoes along to some-one else who needed hope more than she did.

She traced the pattern of the cross one last time. Then she held out the treasure to Nathaniel. "I want you to have this."

"Your cross of hope?" The surprise in his expression told her that he knew how much it meant to her.

"Read the letter that goes with it."

"But the cross is your mother's."

"I know she'd approve of me giving it to you."

Nathaniel studied the wood, which had cracked and lightened with age. The cross certainly wasn't anything spectacular. Most men in Nathaniel's position of wealth would have thought it a mere trifle.

When he looked at her again, his eyes were resigned but gentle. "I'll take good care of it."

"I know you will."

It was his turn to reverently finger the wood that had weathered many wrecks. Victoria prayed it would help him through this new wreck she'd made for him. "I'm sorry, Nathaniel," she said again, as she already had numerous times since he'd caught her kissing Tom yesterday. She wasn't sorry for kissing Tom, but she was sad she'd hurt Nathaniel.

He lifted a gloved hand to her cheek. "You're not entirely to blame, darling." He tenderly stroked her skin. "I think I always knew that you weren't mine, even though I tried hard to hold on to you and not let you get away."

A light drizzle had begun to fall. The breathy whistle of the steamboat rising amidst a cloud of white vapor alerted them that the captain was ready for departure. Around them, the shore was nearly deserted. Any passengers leaving on the *Blue Belle* had already boarded.

Nathaniel drew his finger down her cheek one last time before dropping his hand. "Good-bye, Victoria."

She rose on her toes and quickly kissed his cheek. Then she

strode away before she made a fool of herself and began to cry. She wasn't sure why she had the sudden surge of emotion at his departure. Perhaps because his leaving signified that she was cutting herself off from her old life. He had been her final link, and by turning him away, she was choosing a new course. That was more than a little scary, and she wished Tom were with her to assure her that she'd made the right decision.

Arch followed her silently to the waiting carriage. He squeezed her hand when he helped her inside. As the wheels rolled and took her away from the steamer, she prayed she hadn't made a mistake.

Yes, she loved Tom and wanted to be with him. But was she truly ready for this new life?

They'd only talked briefly yesterday after the wound in Tom's head had been stitched closed. He'd reassured her that they'd figure out a way to be together, a way that would work for both of them. She'd told him that she wanted to stay at Race Point, but from the reluctance of his response, she wasn't sure he was ready yet to face the demons of his past.

In the middle of their discussion, they'd received a telegram from her father in response to the one Arch had sent earlier in the day. Her father and mother were leaving Newport right away and coming to see her.

After getting the news, Tom had flinched. Although his reaction had been faint, it had still been there. No doubt he'd believed he'd let her father down, not only by failing to protect her from Theresa's schemes, but also by falling in love with one of his clients. Victoria had reassured him that her father would understand. But Tom had only shaken his head.

Once his wounds were tended, he'd gone back to Race Point for the night. He'd told her that they needed to sleep in entirely different places until their real wedding took place.

With heat lingering in every touch they shared, she'd agreed to his decision. He'd also planned to tell James and Zelma the truth about why he'd brought her to Race Point. She wanted to go with him, to stand by his side when he delivered the news. She didn't want him to face his parents' disappointment alone.

But Tom had claimed that the telling was his responsibility. He'd made the mess. Now it was his job to clean it up. She prayed James and Zelma had been quick to forgive him.

When she reached the hotel where Tom wanted her to stay until the wedding, she paced the length of her room. Restlessness plagued her and a swarm of doubts seemed to follow behind her, no matter how hard she tried to break free.

Finally, she heard strong, firm footsteps coming down the hallway. She paused and held her breath until a knock sounded on the door. When she opened it, there stood Tom. He was breathing hard, as though he'd been running. His coat and hat were damp. Dark half moons under his eyes attested to a lack of sleep.

Even so, he'd never looked more appealing than he did at that moment, especially as his murky blue eyes took her in. He'd dressed in his best and was clean shaven, accentuating his chiseled features. With his broad shoulders and thick muscles stretching the seams of his coat, he reminded her of how he'd looked the first day he'd started the job as her bodyguard, so handsome and yet so professional.

"Hi," she said with a tentative smile. Had he meant everything he'd said yesterday about loving her and wanting to be with her? Or had she only dreamed it all?

"Arch said you saw Nathaniel off." His brows slanted above anxious eyes.

Had Tom been worried that she'd change her mind and

return with Nathaniel after all? "I only wanted to say good-bye."

"How are you doing?"

"Better now that you're here," she admitted.

He started to reach for her but stopped and took off his hat instead, revealing his dark hair, which was longer and fuller than the close cropped cut he'd had when she'd first met him.

She longed to brush a strand back from his forehead, but she didn't want to appear too desperate for him. "How did your parents take the news?"

"Mom said she'd already figured it out."

Victoria nodded. Zelma was sharp. She suspected that's where Tom had gained his ability to assess situations so accurately.

"When you mentioned that you knew Arch, she suspected that I was your bodyguard."

"I'm sorry." She doubted that was the only thing she'd let slip over the weeks. She'd probably left a long trail for Zelma to piece together quite easily. "And your dad?"

"He wanted to take me out back and give me a whipping."

Her heart sank. "Then he hates me?"

"No," Tom replied quickly. "He loves you. He just thinks I took advantage of you."

"You didn't. You were completely honorable."

"He feels guilty and angry because of how much he pushed us together." He glanced at her mouth and then dropped his gaze to the wooden hallway floor, but not before Victoria caught sight of the desire in his eyes.

She couldn't stop from remembering the way James had goaded Tom into kissing her that time at the dining room table. Tom probably wouldn't have crossed the boundary he'd set for himself if not for all of James's pressure. "I'll have to let him know later how grateful I am for all of his pushing." Her voice came out softer and more seductive than she intended.

Tom's gaze snapped back to hers, and the anxious slant of his brows lifted. "Are you sure you don't feel coerced into this?"

"Not in the least. You should know by now I'm not easily persuaded." Her words were meant to comfort him, but somehow they made the worried crease return to his forehead. "Was your dad reassured when you told him of our plans to have a real wedding?"

"He said he'll believe it when he sees it."

"He'll see it all right," she said, trying to infuse confidence into her voice. "Let's have the ceremony as soon as my parents arrive."

He studied her face for a moment as if he were attempting to see deeper beneath the surface. "Are you sure?"

"I'm positive."

Chapter 23

$\mathcal{V}$ictoria loved the feel of Tom's fingers intertwined with hers as they strolled down the street, their shoulder's brushing, their footsteps slow. She breathed a contented breath.

Ahead, Arch exited the hotel and walked toward them. At the sight of his grim expression, Victoria's footsteps faltered.

"They're here," Arch said. When he exchanged a warning glance with Tom, anxiety wound through Victoria's stomach.

Tom's smile fell away. He let go of her arm and tugged on his lapels.

She tried to peer past Arch and through the glass doors to the lobby. She hadn't expected her parents so soon. Maybe this evening after supper. Maybe tomorrow. But certainly not midday. She'd only had a short time with Tom since he'd ridden out from Race Point, only time for lunch at a restaurant down the street.

"They're here much sooner than I'd anticipated," she said, brushing at her skirt, another of the fashionable creations that her mother had sent with Theresa.

Tom's face was pale and solemn. He squared his shoulders and opened the door.

Victoria had the urge to stop him, but she held herself in check. When Tom waved her to enter before him, she forced her feet forward.

Her father was standing in the middle of the lobby. His familiar face, tender eyes, and warm presence brought a lump to her throat. His expression was fatigued, almost beaten-down, but at the sight of her, his eyes lit and he rushed over to her. "Oh, Victoria." He drew her into his arms.

Within moments, her mother's arms were around her too, all three of them wrapped into one embrace. Victoria found her tears mingling with those of her mother.

"We were so worried about you." Her mother was wearing a new navy and cream striped traveling suit, and her dark hair was formed into a coiffure covered by an elegant bonnet with a veil of lace. She finally released Victoria and pulled back as though to study her.

Victoria knew her mother pretended to see so that onlookers wouldn't notice her blindness and pity her. Victoria smiled at her mother, also pretending that her mother could see it. She wanted to respect her mother's wishes for normalcy, but she couldn't help comparing her mother's way of handling her impairment to Zelma's. Zelma's acceptance of herself seemed freeing somehow.

"The *Lady Caroline* brought us here without any stops," her father explained, with his arm still about Victoria's waist. "Even though Arch's telegram said you were fine, I couldn't rest until I saw you for myself."

"As you can see, he was right. I am fine." She kissed her father's cheek, and he placed a kiss against her forehead in return. Over her father's head she caught Tom's gaze. She smiled at him, hoping to relieve him of his worry.

Seeing the direction of her attention, her father released her and turned to face Tom squarely. "Mr. Cushman," he started, his voice tight. "You saved my daughter's life. I'm in debt to you for your deed, and I shall reward you handsomely for it."

"No need, sir."

Her father took a step closer to Tom. "But before I give you that reward, I need to give you something else first." His voice was strained and his expression turned dark. Before Victoria could utter a word of protest, her father swung his fist and slammed it into Tom's jaw with such force that the smack echoed in the lobby, drawing the attention of a couple who was standing at the front desk speaking with the proprietor.

"Father!" Victoria cried, but her father's fist was swinging again and landed against Tom's stomach. Her father wasn't a particularly large man, but he was still strong enough to cause damage.

Tom gave a grunt at the impact but didn't move. He'd apparently decided to let her father beat him up without a word of protest. From the determined set of his lips, Victoria knew he thought he deserved the punishment.

Arch moved to Tom's side and reached out to block her father, but Tom only pushed the big man aside.

If he wouldn't let Arch come to his defense, then she would have to. "Father, stop!" She grabbed her father's arm before he could raise it for another blow. Her father didn't fight against her hold, but he glared at Tom as if he'd like to wrap his fingers around Tom's neck and strangle him.

When she'd told her parents in the telegram that she was marrying Tom instead of Nathaniel, she'd assumed her father would accept her decision because he'd always given her what her heart desired. Of course, she'd prepared herself for some resistance, at least initially. But she hadn't expected him to attack Tom.

Her father didn't move. Neither did Tom. He stared back, his open-legged stance giving the message that her father could continue to hit him as long and as hard as he wanted.

"Let me explain everything," Victoria started, but her father shook his head and signaled her to silence.

"I'd prefer to hear from Mr. Cushman why he broke his promise to me."

"I have no excuse, sir," Tom replied.

"Give me one reason why I shouldn't have you arrested and hauled off to jail." Father took a menacing step closer to Tom and held up the document Tom had signed saying that he would walk away from their marriage at the end of the month.

Mother's touch on his arm halted him. "Henry," she softly chided.

Victoria was grateful for her mother's presence and level-headedness. Although Victoria had always been closer to Father, who'd doted on her whims, she could count on her mother for influencing her father when needed.

"I'm partly to blame too," Arch said standing next to Tom, his large face chagrined. "I cajoled Tom into taking the position even when I knew his policy—"

"No. It's not your fault, Arch," Tom said. "I made my own decisions. Now I deserve any punishment Mr. Cole gives me. And I'll willingly accept it. But it won't change the fact that I love Victoria." Only then did he look at her, his steady gaze beckoning her.

Her heart quavered at what he was asking. He wanted her to break free of her parents and come to him. He wanted her to be willing to give up everything to be with him if that's what was necessary—all of her past, her wealth, even her connection to her family. He was asking her to show him that she was strong enough to make the sacrifice.

But was she?

She'd known Tom wouldn't pamper her or try to make life easy, that he'd challenge her to do hard things, as he already had. But could she do this?

As if hearing her question, he nodded at her, a faint light in his dark blue eyes encouraging her to be brave. She swallowed the words of uncertainty and left her father's side. She slipped her hand into the crook of Tom's arm and smiled up at him, even if it felt faint.

"Tom didn't break his promise to you, Father," she said. "He kept a boundary between us until I asked him to stop being my bodyguard. I knew he wouldn't consider me as a wife otherwise."

Her father cradled his knuckles, red from the impact of hitting Tom. "It wasn't your decision to terminate his employment."

"I fell in love with Tom even before we came here. I think I've loved him all along."

"Perhaps you're simply infatuated," her mother interjected. "After all, you've claimed to love others."

"Tom is different."

"That's what you said about Nathaniel," her mother said gently.

"This time it's true." She was passionate about Tom in a way she hadn't been about anyone else. She could feel her cheeks heating. Could her parents sense her meaning?

Apparently her father could, because he turned a fierce scowl upon Tom. "You better not have taken advantage of my daughter."

Tom didn't respond. He was a man of so much honor that he probably considered a few stolen kisses a crime. He wouldn't rise to his own defense. He'd likely allow her father to think the worst of him.

Sure enough, the silence incited her father, and he lunged at Tom again.

"No!" Victoria shouted, moving in front of Tom and coming face to face with her father's anger. Tom attempted to slide around her, but she fought him. "Tom's been honorable. He's a good man. Just like you, Father."

Her father stilled. He glared at Tom but allowed Mother to pull him back.

"Even though we're married," Victoria continued, "Tom has kept our relationship chaste." She wanted to hide her face at the awkwardness of their conversation. But she must defend him, since he wouldn't do it for himself.

Again silence fell around them. Thankfully, the couple at the counter had taken their leave and the proprietor had discreetly disappeared, leaving them alone in the lobby. Her mother tucked her arm around her father. At the embrace, her father seemed to shrink into her. His shoulders deflated, and the stiffness in his features gave way to grooves that showed his age.

Victoria's heart twisted with remorse that she'd caused her father so much worry and pain.

Behind her, Tom reached for her hand and wrapped his strong fingers around hers. The pressure soothed her and reminded her that he loved her. He would stand beside her, and together they would build a new life.

Her father finally released a sigh that was laced with weariness and defeat. "You understand that if you go through with your plans, you'll alienate yourself from your friends. Very few will understand or accept your decision."

She squeezed Tom's hand, hoping to ease the bluntness of her father's words. "I don't care. If friends reject me because of the man I love, then they weren't worth having as friends."

"Victoria," Tom started to protest.

She shook her head at him. "I mean it. I don't care."

"Your father's right," Tom said. "You'll likely become an outcast if you marry me."

Her father glanced at Tom again, and this time he seemed to study him more carefully, as though finding an ally instead of an enemy. The thought of the two of them joining forces made Victoria's heart quaver.

"You married Mother," she said quickly. "She wasn't from among your elite circle of friends. In the long run, it didn't matter. Did it?"

Her father opened his mouth as if to retort but closed it. He drew his mother closer and turned and kissed her cheek.

The tautness in Tom's hold began to loosen. Was he feeling the same relief that she was? She was tempted to pull him into a hug. But her father swung his attention back on them, on her.

"If Tom is really the man you want, then I'll do everything I can to help you both—"

"With all due respect, sir," Tom interrupted, "I can't accept your charity. I won't be beholden to—"

"If you want my daughter," Father's voice rose, "then you'll accept my *charity*, whether you want it or not."

Tom pursed his lips and narrowed his eyes on Father. Victoria could sense that he wanted to object but was holding himself back.

Her father rose to his full height and cocked his head first at Tom and then toward the door. "I think it's time we head down to the tavern and have a good long talk about the future and how you plan to take care of my daughter."

Victoria didn't relish the thought of her father and Tom planning her future without her input. But when Tom squeezed her hand and she looked up into his eyes, something there asked her to trust him.

She nodded and let go.

"In the meantime," her father said with a tender glance toward her. "I think you and your mother have a busy day ahead."

"We do?"

He smiled. "Yes. You need to plan a wedding."

She nodded, her throat constricting.

"Make it beautiful and spare no expense," he said, his eyes filling with love.

She threw herself into his arms and hugged him tightly. "I love you, Daddy."

Chapter 24

Victoria pressed a hand against her stomach to stop the wild crashing, but no matter how many times she attempted to calm the churning, her nerves wouldn't stop acting like a stormy sea. She retraced her steps to the second story window of the keeper's cottage, the same room she'd shared with Tom during her stay at Race Point.

She peeked past the curtains fluttering in the breeze to the large canopy that had been erected on the beach in front of the lighthouse. A royal blue carpet had been laid on the sand for the convenience of the guests, and the blue matched the large stunning bouquets of hydrangeas interspersed with lilies of the valley that surrounded the tent. Under the canopy, rows of chairs had been arranged facing the ocean, and most of them were already full. White lacy ribbons hugged each of the chairs and were also wound around the poles that held up the open tent. An orchestra was nearby underneath another smaller canopy. Placed slightly away from the orchestra was a tent filled with servants who were busy preparing the lobster and clam bake that would take place after the wedding ceremony.

Victoria had wanted to keep the wedding simple. But she hadn't been able to say no to her mother's plans. Victoria was, after all, an only child. And her mother had been anticipating a wedding for years.

Somehow her mother had been able to work miracles over the past three days of planning, having supplies shipped in from Boston and from other small towns around the Cape. She'd insisted on inviting a few of their closest family friends and had even arranged for Tom's sister, Ruth, and her family to be there.

Victoria could see them sitting in the front row next to Zelma and James, who thankfully had welcomed her with tight hugs when she'd arrived this morning. She'd appreciated Tom's parents' ready forgiveness for her part in deceiving them. Zelma had reassured her of her love and God's hand at work in everything.

Victoria smoothed her damp palms down the front of her wedding gown. Although lovely, it was plainer and more practical, something she could wear again. She lifted the train and turned away from the window. The creamy silk was studded with pearls at the waist, but otherwise had an unadorned V-neckline and just a little lace at the sleeves. A maid had fixed her hair into elaborate curls at the top of her head and decorated them with lace interwoven with seed pearls.

With everyone already assembled, her father would likely fetch her in a matter of minutes, especially when Tom took his place next to the rector, who had traveled with them from Provincetown.

As if the thought had summoned Tom, the tower door opened, and he stepped out in his black wedding suit with a crisp white shirt set off by a black bow tie. The dark color brought out the sharpness of his hair and eyes, but the white of the shirt showed the tan he'd gained in working outside over the month. There was no doubt that he was a swoon-worthy man. And not just in how handsome he was. But all of his qualities were admirable. Even her father was beginning to come around. Just that morning as their steamboat had docked, her father had finally admitted that he liked Tom. He'd called him humble and hardworking, but also tough, shrewd, and levelheaded.

"He's just the sort of man I want to run my business some day," her father had said.

His words had soothed Victoria's guilty conscience at depriving her father of the social status he'd lost when she'd walked away from Nathaniel.

Her father had monopolized Tom since the first day he'd arrived on the Cape. They'd shut themselves away in one dark room after another in private conversations until Victoria had no idea what the two men had left to talk about.

When she'd questioned Tom, he reassured her that they'd come to an understanding about the future, about Victoria's assets and Cole Enterprises. "I won't take your father's money or touch your assets," Tom had said. "But I told him that eventually, when we're ready to return to New York, I'll work for him and he can pay me a fair wage."

Victoria had smiled at Tom's declaration, knowing full well that her father's idea of a fair wage would likely supersede Tom's, and that the two men would fight another battle at some point. At the very least, she knew they both loved her and had her best interests in mind.

She watched Tom stride in his confident way down the beach. He walked about a dozen paces before stopping abruptly and glancing back at the house, at her window. With a quick intake of breath, she shifted out of sight. She should have known he'd realize she was watching him.

They hadn't had much time together since her parents had arrived, and she missed him. When she'd greeted him earlier in the morning, she'd wanted to throw her arms around him and feel his solid strength against her. Her mother had hurried her along, but not before she'd seen the burning ember in his eyes telling her that he wanted to hold her too, and that he would tonight and every night hereafter and forevermore.

Hereafter. Forevermore.

Her chest tightened at an incoming, all-too-familiar sensation. One she'd felt only a few other times in her life. The last was in June. On her wedding day. In the front hallway of the Newport cottage. As she'd walked outside to get into the carriage.

The swell was like a rising tide, drawing nearer, threatening to drag her under. She flattened herself against the wall and closed her eyes. "Calm down, Victoria. Calm down. You can do this." She took several deep breaths, exhaling and inhaling slowly.

She hadn't expected to feel this again. Not with Tom. He was different from her other fiancés. He wasn't a passing fancy or mere infatuation. She wanted to be with him. Longed for him. Had dreamt about when they could finally be together as a true husband and wife.

But to be together *forevermore?*

"Oh, Lord," she whispered through trembling lips. The haunting images of a bleak, black, sightless future rushed in to taunt her. She pinched her eyes closed to block them out. "No!" she almost shouted. Her heartbeat slapped hard against her chest, propelling her across the room to the door.

She had to leave. She had to get away before she was sucked under and drowned by her fears of the future. With a sob building in her chest, she clattered in her satin wedding shoes through the hall, down the stairs, and out the back door of the house.

A rush of sea breeze laden with the scent of baking lobster swirled around her. For a frantic moment, she huddled against the back of the house, panicked that Tom might see her and try to stop her. Ahead of her lay mile after mile of sand dunes and beach grass. She had to get as far away as possible before he noticed she was gone.

A sob slipped out, but she cupped her gloved hand over her mouth and started running.

Tom stood at the front of the gathering under the canopy and twisted the wedding band in his pocket that he'd reluctantly taken from her that morning. The longer the ring was off Victoria's finger, the greater his urgency to put it back on. He shouldn't worry about her precedence for running away at her weddings, but the thought nagged him nevertheless.

A trickle of sweat slid down his back between his shoulder blades underneath his shirt. He resisted the urge to scratch it. Instead, he reminded himself why Victoria wouldn't flee from their wedding. She hadn't loved any of the other men the way she did him. This time she had no reason to run, not when their love was so real and powerful.

Even though many of the guests were still quietly chattering among themselves, they were studying him too. He had no doubt they were wondering how he felt to be marrying Victoria Cole, the incredibly wealthy heiress to Cole Enterprises.

He hoped he looked more composed than he felt. He'd

known she was rich. He'd seen listings of Cole Enterprise's assets when he'd researched Henry Cole before taking the bodyguard position. But he'd miscalculated exactly how wealthy Victoria really was.

Thankfully, he hadn't known or he would have worked even harder to push her back to Nathaniel. To ease his conscience, he'd told Henry he didn't want any financial support. He wanted to take care of Victoria on his own.

Henry hadn't wanted any part of that plan and had insisted Victoria have access to her money and all of the luxuries she wanted. After a great deal of arguing, they'd finally compromised. Tom would provide for his and Victoria's everyday needs. But Victoria would have access to her account to use at her discretion.

Tom glanced at the front row, where Victoria's mother was already seated and talking pleasantly with Henry's sister and her children. In looking at her now in the latest fashion with the regality of a queen in her fancy gown, he'd never guess she'd once been a simple light keeper's daughter.

He doubted he'd ever make such a sweeping transformation. But he was willing to try to be a part of Victoria's world, if that would make her happy.

A movement by the house caught his attention. Arch, who'd been waiting by the door, was finally opening it. Tom held his breath. He needed more than the brief glimpse he'd gotten when he'd caught Victoria looking out the bedroom window. He needed to see her walking toward him on her father's arm. He needed to see her smile to know she was okay. He needed to put the ring back on her finger and make her his for good.

As the door widened, Henry stepped out. Tom waited for Victoria to make her appearance. But the door closed behind

Henry without Victoria anywhere in sight. The muscles in Tom's chest constricted. He willed Arch to open the door again and for Victoria to float out in her wedding gown. But the slight stoop of Henry's shoulders was all the evidence Tom needed to piece together what had happened.

Victoria was gone. She'd run.

Even though panic slammed him with the force of regular nor-easter, he forced his face to remain expressionless. "I'll be right back," he said to the rector, praying it was true. Then, as calmly as he could so that he wouldn't worry either his parents or Victoria's mother, he whispered, "Give me a minute."

At his words, Mrs. Cole's sightless eyes found him. The elegant lines in her face drooped with dismay. And Tom had the feeling she'd guessed what had happened too.

He tried to keep his stride smooth and unhurried as he crossed to Henry. But a fist was closing about his throat, choking off his air. The escalating panic made him want to tear off his bow tie and suit coat and sprint as fast as he could.

Henry shook his head gravely, answering Tom's worst fears. She was gone.

"I'm sorry, Tom," Henry said in a low voice, as they met halfway between the house and beach. "I really thought things would be different this time, that she'd finally make it down the aisle. I thought you were the right man. And I thought she loved you enough to make herself do it." His eyes held genuine remorse.

"She does love me." Tom hadn't imagined it. Had he? At times he'd feared her powers over him were turning him into a lovesick sap, that he wasn't thinking clearly anymore, that he was losing his edge. But even if he was growing a little soft, he couldn't have misread all of the clues.

Something else was holding her back.

Fear. He'd seen it in her eyes before. Especially the day she'd almost married Nathaniel.

She was afraid. He still didn't know of what. But he planned to find out.

"Do you know where she went?" he asked.

Henry shrugged. The motion was filled with resignation and defeat. Maybe a father could make excuses for his daughter running from a couple of weddings. But now? There were no excuses left. Clearly Victoria had problems that even true love couldn't conquer.

Tom narrowed his eyes on the house, on the window, and then returned to the door. "I'll find Victoria."

"But even if you find her—"

"*When* I find her."

"When you find her, she still won't go through with the wedding." Henry obviously spoke from experience, had likely tried to convince Victoria in the past, to no avail.

Tom moved away from Henry. "Tell everyone the wedding will start soon."

Henry shook his head. "Most of them will guess what's happened."

"We're getting married," Tom insisted. "Just tell them to wait." He didn't stand around to listen to any more of Henry's protests or nay-saying. Instead, he finished walking calmly to the house. He turned down Arch's offer to help look for Victoria. This was something he had to do for himself. He had to be the one to find her and talk with her.

Once he entered the house and the door closed behind him blocking him from the sight of curious guests, he jolted into high speed. He raced up the stairs, taking them two and three at a time. When he reached the bedroom, a rapid sweep of the room left him no clues.

He bolted back down the stairs and scanned the rest of the rooms before barging out the back door. One glance was all it took to see her footsteps in the sand, leading away from the house.

She had at the most a five-minute lead. From the deep indentations and wide spacing of her footsteps, he could tell that she was running. But as he sprinted after her, he surmised that she was getting tired, a fact that was confirmed when the spacing of her footprints showed that she'd finally started walking.

Within a minute, he saw her in the distance, struggling to reach the top of a dune. He didn't say anything, didn't want to alert her yet that he was close on her heels. Once she disappeared over the other side behind a tall clump of yellowing grass, he picked up his pace.

By the time he reached the dune, his lungs burned from his effort. When he crested the hill, he stopped short at the sight of her crumpled in a heap at the bottom. His heart skidded up into his throat. Had she fallen?

"Victoria!" He slid down the sandy embankment and fell to his knees next to her, attempting to assess her condition. "Are you hurt?"

Her face was buried in her hands, and soft sobs echoed in the hollow.

He lifted his hand to her shoulder but hesitated to touch her. He didn't want to frighten her any more than she already was. But the shuddering of her body and the brokenness of her sobs reached inside and ripped at him. He lowered his fingers to her back tentatively. At his touch, she leaned toward him.

He released his breath and gathered her into his arms. She came willingly, and he lifted his eyes heavenward with a grateful whisper of a prayer. She was afraid. But not of him.

"I'm sorry," she said against his coat. "I'm so sorry."

He hugged her closer and kissed the top of her head, which was covered with a sheer veil. For a moment, he held her, attempting to catch his breath and steady the frantic pace of his heartbeat.

When her shaking diminished to an occasional quaver, he finally spoke. "What are you afraid of, Victoria?"

"I don't know." Her voice was sad and muffled against him.

He brushed a hand gently down her arm. She sighed and snuggled into him. She might not know what she was running from, but he knew what he'd been avoiding all these years. How could he expect her to stop and face her fears if he wasn't willing to do the same?

"You asked me to tell you about Ike," he said quietly.

She sat up and looked at him, her long lashes wet with tears.

His jaw clenched, but he forced the words out anyway. "It's my fault he died."

She didn't say anything. She reached for his fingers that he hadn't realized he'd bunched into a fist. She gently pried them open and laced her fingers with his.

He didn't want to talk about this. But he swallowed the resistance that formed in his throat, and then he plunged back in the pit of hell where he hadn't wanted to return. To the frosty dark night with the mist falling and the stench of death all around. "The night Mom came after Ike and me, she cut me free from my bindings and started to work on Ike's. But he stopped her and told her to take me out of the camp before it was too late."

From their spot in the back of the wagon with all of the corpses awaiting burial, he'd been able to see the guard who'd been assigned to the night watch squatting two dozen feet away in the woods relieving himself. He supposed the guard had assumed that since Tom and Ike were bound and weakened, they wouldn't be able to go anywhere, and so the guard had taken his time.

"I told Ike I wouldn't leave without him. But he pushed me away. Told Mom to take me." Tom shuddered and felt Victoria stroke his arm.

"You don't have to tell me any more if you don't want to," she said.

Now that he'd started, he couldn't stop. "I told Ike that I'd carry him. But when I slid out of the wagon, I couldn't hold myself up without Mom's help. That didn't stop me from turning back to Ike and trying to free him." He closed his eyes as the nightmare repeated itself. "Ike told me to go. Mom tried to pull me away. But I was stubborn, and I kept sawing away at the rope around his hands. When those were free, I started trying to free his legs."

Thankfully, the wind and the rattling branches overhead had muted their whispered conversation and kept the guard from hearing them. Even so, Tom had sensed that time was running short and had sawed faster. "Ike warned me, said he'd kill himself first before letting me try to drag him away." He could picture Ike's gaunt face, and he could still hear the hiss of anger in his brother's voice. "I didn't believe him. I wouldn't leave him. And he knew it. So before I could stop him, he yanked the knife from my hands and plunged it into his heart."

Tom tried to block out the picture of Ike slipping lifelessly out of his grip and falling back against a corpse. The knife had stuck deep into his chest, the blood pooling against his thin shirt, and his arm falling away from the weapon.

His mom hadn't stopped to retrieve the knife, hadn't waited to even check Ike's pulse. Instead, she'd dragged Tom away, wrapped her arm around his waist, and hoisted his arm over her shoulder. Then she set out, having to half-carry and half-drag him most of the way.

"So you see," Tom finished. "I killed Ike. Maybe not with my own two hands. But if I'd listened to him and left when he told me to, maybe I could have figured out a way to return and save him."

"Your mom told me you both would have been hung for being spies."

Tom nodded. Deep down he realized Ike wouldn't have lasted another day, not with the amount of blood he'd lost from his wound. And deep down he also knew that if he'd tried to carry Ike away, they wouldn't have made it. His mom had hardly been able to manage him, much less attempt to haul Ike too.

"It sounds like Ike was a stubborn man," Victoria said. "Maybe even more stubborn than you, if that's possible."

Tom nodded. "Ike always did like to get his own way."

"But he was loyal, and he loved you deeply," she said "He sacrificed his life so that you could have yours. Don't you think he'd want to know that you're happy now, that his sacrifice wasn't in vain?"

Tom pulled Ike's ring from his pocket. "This was his. The one he was planning to give his girl."

Victoria's eyes rounded, and the wetness on her lashes sparkled in the morning sunlight.

"I think he'd be happy to know I'm giving it to you," Tom said, lifting her hand and kissing her ring finger gently. "He'd be happy to know all the joy and love we've found together."

"Oh, Tom," she said breathlessly, her eyes filling with tears again.

"Will you marry me?"

"I want to."

"But what?" he asked softly. "Why are you afraid?"

She took the ring and turned it, studying it as though seeing it for the first time. "I think maybe I'm afraid of the future, of *my* future."

When she lifted her gaze to his, her light brown eyes reminded him of her mother's. So pretty, clear, delicate, and…

His pulse halted. "Are you afraid of going blind like your mother?"

She started to shake her head, denial forming in her expression. But then she stopped. She caressed the ring and finally nodded. "I'm terrified of it. I try not to think about it, try to pretend that it's not a possibility, try to act like I'll have a normal future. But the truth always seems to catch up to me on my wedding day. It's the one time I can't keep from thinking about my future and the fact that I'm dragging someone else into my problems."

He hadn't considered that she might have inherited the disease. But if her grandmother and mother had both gone blind, there was the real possibility that she might someday as well. He released a breath of relief. At last he understood why she was running from commitment. "We'll handle whatever comes our way."

"But I don't want to burden anyone I love with such an uncertain future."

She started to pull away from him, but he held her fast. "Do you think my mom is a burden on my dad?"

Victoria shook her head. "Of course not. They adore each other."

"He loves helping her. He even loves being able to carry her around and hold her more."

A smile tugged at Victoria's lips. "I think you're right."

Tom traced his finger down her cheek. "I won't complain if someday I get to carry you around and hold you more."

Her smile turned tremulous and then her bottom lip wobbled. "I could go blind, Tom. Blind. Don't you understand that?"

He nodded. "And I could go deaf. Or lose my arm. Or die tomorrow." He rubbed his thumb across her lip to still the trembling. "None of us know what our futures will bring. But that can't stop us from living. Or getting married."

She was silent for so long that his pulse gave a thud. Then without warning, she slipped the ring onto her finger, back where it belonged. And she bestowed a smile upon him that made his limbs turn as weak as the sand. "Thank you for telling me about Ike."

He nodded and had to swallow before he trusted his voice to speak. "I think it's time we both stopped running from our fears, don't you?"

Without waiting for his assistance, she stood and held out a hand to him. "Does that mean you'll think about staying here at Race Point as the assistant keeper?"

He clasped her hand and rose, so that he was standing next to her. Victoria had wanted to stay with his parents, especially to be there for his mom. While he was glad to see her maturity since the first day they'd arrived, he hadn't planned on living at the lighthouse, at least not long term. But maybe it was time for him to put the past to rest once and for all. Maybe by remaining instead of running, he could finally find forgiveness and peace with not only all that had happened to Ike, but also what had happened to his mom.

Victoria squeezed his hand. "She wants you to stay. They both do."

"Only if you promise to stay here with me."

"Are you sure you want me? I have no doubt that I'll still have to battle my fears many more times in the years to come."

"I still have demons to fight too, Victoria," he said. "But we'll help each other do battle. There's strength in numbers, and we'll be stronger together."

She tugged him toward the dune, back the direction they'd come. "I guess we better not keep our guests waiting any longer. We wouldn't want them thinking that I ran away again, would we?"

He grinned. "No we wouldn't."

Chapter 25

"And now you may kiss your bride," the rector said as he closed his Bible and smiled at Tom.

Victoria tried to still the quavering in her chest. She'd done it. She'd finally walked down the aisle, spoken her vows, and promised that for better or worse she'd love and cherish her husband for as long as they both lived.

Of course, she and Tom had already been legally married. But somehow standing in front of their family and friends and pledging their lives to each other made their marriage truly real.

Tom's hold on her hand hadn't slackened during the walk back to the beach or during the brief ceremony under the canopy. She'd felt the curious gazes of the guests upon her and sensed the relief from her parents, but she'd kept her focus on Tom. Every time she'd begun to feel a sense of panic rising, he'd squeezed her hands and pulled her gaze to his. The steadiness and love in his eyes had reminded her that they'd get through any difficulties together.

Now a warm sea breeze teased a strand of Tom's hair. "Mrs. Cushman," he whispered, his blue eyes dark and filled with thrilling promises. As he bent his head toward hers, she sucked in a breath of anticipation. It didn't matter that everyone was watching them. She loved his kisses and had been waiting days for another one.

He tilted and brushed her lips with feathery lightness. The warmth and tingle against her mouth teased her and the spark in his eyes told her that he had more to give her. Later.

As he pulled away, she smiled at him, and together they turned to face the guests.

In the front row, James gave a loud snort, and his eyebrows were furrowed together in a glower. "That wasn't a kiss."

Tom tossed his dad a scowl in return before holding out his arm to Victoria. "Ready?" he whispered.

"Give her a real kiss," James demanded.

"Dad," Tom said through clenched teeth. "Don't do this now."

Next to James, Zelma's smile could have lit the tower lantern. Her eyes danced with delight. Suddenly Victoria knew that she'd done the right thing. If Zelma could find hope and joy despite the dire circumstances of her life, losing one son to death and another to grief, and also losing her feet, surely she could find acceptance and joy, too, in whatever would come. Zelma's secret was relying upon God's strength for her joy, which was another thing Victoria would have to ask Zelma to teach her to do.

"Show yourself to be a real man," James's voice rang with challenge, "and kiss your bride like you mean it."

Tom locked eyes with his dad. From the tensing of Tom's arm, Victoria sensed he was taking the bait.

Inwardly, she smiled. Later she'd thank James.

As Tom pivoted so that he faced her again, his features tightened, and all his desire for her pooled in his eyes.

A series of wild flips bounded across her middle. She lifted her face to him, giving him complete access to her mouth.

With the strength she'd grown to love about him, he made his move. His hand found the small of her back, and he drew her against him at the same moment his lips crashed against hers. Like the powerful waves breaking against the shore only a dozen paces away, his mouth moved with an all-consuming passion, unrelenting, drawing her away from reality.

She wanted it to be a place where it was just the two of them, but the clapping of the guests reminded her that they weren't alone. Not in the least.

The loudest clap and a shrill whistle of appreciation came from the front row, from James. "That's my boy! I taught him everything he knows."

Tom broke away from the kiss, but not before she felt his lips curving into a grin. "Think you'll be able to put up with all of his pressure?" he whispered against her ear.

"As long as he pressures us to kiss like that at least once a day," she whispered back.

Tom chuckled. "Around my parents, I guarantee that our marriage won't be dull."

"All the more reason to stay here, don't you think?" She could feel herself flush at her boldness.

His lips found the hollow of her ear. "I love you. Forever." The words and his breathy kiss held the promise of so much more to come. Whatever the future held. Whatever difficulties they might face. They would face it together. Forever.

Author's Note

Dear Reader, I pray that you enjoyed the continuation of the Beacons of Hope with Victoria Cole's story. While the previous books in the series are located at lighthouses in Michigan, with this particular book I decided to move to a lighthouse along the East coast. I decided upon Race Point Lighthouse on Cape Cod, Massachusetts, for several reasons. First, I love Cape Cod. My husband's family has lived there for many years. We took our first trip their together as a couple for our honeymoon and have vacationed there ever since.

Another reason I chose Race Point Lighthouse is because of the history. During the years of 1870 to 1885 the head keeper was James Cushman. His assistant keeper was a man by the name of Thomas. While not a father-son team, I decided to make them so for the sake of the story. Race Point Lighthouse needed both a keeper and assistant largely due to the steam-driven fog signal that required a great deal of effort to keep running.

I also decided to have my characters live at Race Point Lighthouse because the setting is isolated and made a perfect hiding place for Victoria. Today, if you were to visit the lighthouse, you would have to hike two miles over sand dunes to reach it (although volunteers do provide transportation to and from the light). Even though the lighthouse is alone on the tip of the Cape, it's surrounded by untold beauty and wildlife that made it ideal for this story.

As with all of the books in the Beacons of Hope series, I pray that you've been both encouraged and inspired to trust in the Giver of Hope. If, like Victoria and Tom, you're running away from past hurts or future fears, I pray that you'll learn to run to the One who promises to walk beside us through our darkest valleys and fiercest storms. He may not take us out of the valley or storm, but He will hold our hand and stay by our side. With Him, we will be forever safe.

Jody Hedlund is the bestselling author of multiple novels, including *Love Unexpected*, *Captured by Love*, *Rebellious Heart*, and *The Preacher's Bride*. She holds a bachelor's degree from Taylor University and a master's degree from the University of Wisconsin, both in social work. Jody lives in Michigan with her husband and five children. Learn more at JodyHedlund.com.

More From Jody Hedlund

Visit jodyhedlund.com for a full list of her books.

Shipwrecked and stranded, Emma Chambers is in need of a home. Could the widowed local lighthouse keeper and his young son be an answer to her prayer?

Love Unexpected
BEACONS OF HOPE #1

Caroline has tended the lighthouse since her father's death. But where will she go when a wounded Civil War veteran arrives to take her place?

Hearts Made Whole
BEACONS OF HOPE #2

Vowing not to have anything to do with lighthouses, Tessa Taylor is the new teacher to the children of miners. Can the light keeper's assistant break through her fears and win her heart?

Hope Undaunted
BEACONS OF HOPE #3

Would you like to know when my next book is available? You can sign up for my newsletter, become my friend on Goodreads, like me on Facebook or follow me on Twitter.

Newsletter: jodyhedlund.com
Goodreads: goodreads.com/author/show/3358829.Jody_Hedlund
Facebook: facebook.com/AuthorJodyHedlund
Twitter: @JodyHedlund

The more reviews a book has, the more likely other readers are to find it. If you have a minute, please leave a rating or review. I appreciate all reviews, whether positive or negative.

CPSIA information can be obtained at www.ICGtesting.com
Printed in the USA
LVOW08s0144240616

493837LV00008BA/648/P